ENDGAME

OLA TUNDUN

Storm

ALSO BY OLA TUNDUN

The Roommates Series

Roommates

Complicated

To anyone facing the impossible. It can be done.

ONE

ARIELLA

'We're here.'

I look out of the helicopter window as we circle the sprawling estate. From the sky, a spectacular white hotel situated in the middle of the property is gleaming in the sun, surrounded by picturesque cottages scattered through lush greenery, woodland, meadows and lakes. The journey from Boston has been short but the views from the air, as we made our way to Kennebunkport, were indescribably beautiful.

'Is that a vineyard?' I ask into my headset microphone, pointing.

'Yes,' Dominic says with a laugh as he leans over to look outside my window. 'It's small but still very much working. We've got about six acres and yield about twelve tonnes of grapes a year; so about nine thousand bottles. There's also an orchard, so we make cider too. Farmers' market stuff. We should go and play in the tasting barn a little later.'

'Definitely!' I accept enthusiastically as we start to descend.

When we disembark, we are led across the helipad and through an immaculately trimmed hedged path to the main building. We are then met at the hotel's imposing wooden doors by an older gentleman in a sharp, dark grey suit, and taken to meet a radiant lady of roughly the same age.

'Dominic. You made it! I am so pleased.' She reaches out to him for an emotional hug.

'Mrs Thompson.' He greets her affectionately as he steps into her arms. It's nice to see him like this, especially as he almost didn't make it here for his parents' ruby anniversary. It's a long, loving embrace, making it obvious that it has been a while since they have shared one. When they step away from each other, I see Mrs Thompson give him a warm smile before she straightens up, waiting to be introduced. I find myself straightening too. I know it's silly, but I want her to like me. When Dominic does nothing, she sighs, steps forward and extends her hand.

'Hello, Miss. I am Mrs Thompson, the house manager, and have been since Dominic was an ankle-biter. It seems he's forgotten his manners and how to introduce people to each other.'

'Of course, I'm sorry. Mrs Thompson, this is Ariella, she'll be staying with us for a couple of days.'

'Welcome, Ariella. Your bags will be delivered to Dominic's suite shortly. Let me just check where...' Mrs Thompson happily assures me as she reaches for the walkie-talkie clipped on to her waist.

'I was hoping we could find a cottage for her? It's only for a couple of days before she heads to Louisiana,' Dominic asks politely, interrupting a surprised-looking Mrs Thompson. This is news to her. I'm obviously not the first guest Dominic has hosted here, but clearly I'm the first who has required her own space.

'Dominic, an email or even a text would have been nice,' she scolds like a mother speaking to her adored, mischievous child.

'I'd be more than happy to stay in town and rent a car. It

looks impossibly picturesque in this part of the world and I'd quite like to take the opportunity to explore,' I offer.

'Oooh, you're British. Delightful. You will do no such thing, Ariella. It will be my pleasure to find you a cottage.' Mrs Thompson looks conspiratorially at Dominic, prompting him to lean into her.

'The Grahams were supposed to arrive yesterday and haven't showed up, as usual. *They* can stay in town. Silly me, something must have happened with the room allocation system. I'll have to get the technical team to take a look at it.' She winks at him.

'I really don't mind—' I start.

'Aari, you're staying. The Grahams are my mother's cousins. They do this all the time. They insist on staying the week before and after whatever they are invited to, but then just appear for a couple of days; or sometimes don't turn up at all. They can stay in town.'

'Also...' Mrs Thompson whispers theatrically as she moves closer, 'the staff are not fans.'

I can't help laughing. She makes it easy to imagine some of the trouble she and Dominic must have caused and covered up over the years.

'Thank you.'

'You are welcome, Ariella. If you'll excuse me, I'm just going to move a few guests around so that you're in one of the cottages closest to the house. Something I would have done if *someone* had sent a message in advance.' She tugs the jacket lapel of an apologetic-looking Dominic.

'I'll make it up to you,' he promises.

'You better. I want dinner in town and a detailed catch-up on the last five years.'

'Done.'

'I've missed you. Come here.' Mrs Thompson pulls

Dominic into another indulgent hug and it's clear from his submission that he has missed her too.

'Right. Would you like to wait for your cottage allocation first or would you like to join the family now?'

I can tell her question is loaded. 'Is Max with everyone?' Dominic asks.

'Yes, Maximilian and that trollop are here with the twins,' she confirms cautiously.

'Is everyone else here?' Dominic asks carefully.

'Yes, the powder keg is present and complete.' Mrs Thompson raises an eyebrow.

'We'll wait for the allocation please,' Dominic confirms, laughing.

Mrs Thompson nods, then shows us into a large drawing room and disappears.

'Is the trollop...' I start.

'Yeah...' His thoughts obviously drift away before he snaps back. 'Are you sure you don't mind staying close when everyone is around?'

'Dom, that's the only reason I'm here. I promised to stand beside you the whole time and that's exactly what I plan to do; but I am going to need you to explain what the powder keg is.' I smile.

'That's the name Mrs Thompson and I have for the whole family when we are together. It can be a little volatile. My mother is my father's second wife, so I have three siblings from his first marriage and a couple from the many affairs he had during it. He has never played it safe.'

'Wow. I thought Maximilian was your only sibling.'

'Nope. There are seven of us. My mother had Max and me but there are other families, and my father insists that all his children come together whenever there is a celebration. As you can probably imagine, that comes with its own unique set of challenges. Believe it or not, Maximilian isn't my biggest problem.'

'Uh-oh.'

'Yeah. There's a whole family issue about me being called Dominic.'

'Why?'

'Well, my father is obviously Dominic the Fifth. Someone got drunk at my christening and made a joke that he'd clearly had six inadequate kids before he found his heir. Since then, I've been a bit of a target, and being the youngest doesn't help.'

'And everyone is here right now?'

'Yup. With husbands, wives, kids – all with their own grievances and stories to tell. My mother is probably right in the thick of it too, being entertained and teasing my father for being promiscuous before he met her.'

We both chuckle.

'I'm really glad you're here, Aari,' Dominic says, smiling sadly, changing the mood.

'I'm so sorry that I can't stay a little longer. I wish I could.' I can tell being here is going to be hard for him.

Dominic carries himself with a gravitas that is intimidating to most people. My first impression of him as CEO of DMVI, and later, potential client, was exactly what he intentionally projects to the world. Dominant. Unrelenting. Focused. Entitled. His transition to friend evolved over an evening of smooth, jagged and barrier-setting conversation, revealing a warmer Dominic beneath his immovable solid exterior. Kind. Hilarious. Generous. Trustworthy. Cheeky. Wounded. Lonely. That's the Dominic I am here to support. The Dominic who made being away from home less cold and barren; especially when I needed it. The Dominic I said yes to, when he asked me to stay in Singapore, even though I desperately wanted to return home. I want to show up for him, the way he did for me in Singapore, but I'm going to have to walk a fine line. More than friendly feelings occasionally surface when we are alone and, while I'm sure Dominic would be an incredible partner to tackle life with, my heart is held captive elsewhere.

'Me too, but I refuse to cut into your granny Grace's time. You're here for the worst days anyway, so you'll have earned that time off. Maybe we can come back next year? It's beautiful here in the summer. We can fly the other way around and stop in London on the way next time, if you like?'

'If I don't get to hit that tasting barn, I might beg for us to do that.'

'Oh, we're hitting the barn. It's just a matter of how many times you'd like to. We have a lot of wine!'

'Do not go into that tasting barn with Dominic unsupervised. I have almost been fired on more than one occasion because I made that choice!' Mrs Thompson happily approaches us with what looks like a large wooden leaf with a key dangling from it.

'Thank you for the tip.' I laugh.

'My pleasure. You're in Maple. Your bags are in your cottage. Hit nine on your phone if there is anything you'd like and grab your walkie when you leave your room just in case you need some assistance. Cell phone service is intentionally non-existent on the property, but the Wi-Fi is strong and fast in all the bedrooms. Dominic, do you want to show Ariella to the cottage or shall I?'

'I can show her where Maple is.' Dominic gets up. 'Thank you.'

'No problem.' She beams. 'Next time, please remember two words. Need Cottage.'

'Yes, Mrs Thompson.' Dominic laughs as he walks me down the huge corridor that runs through the entire building and out of the other side. We disappear into a covered wooded path and stop at the first building we encounter, with the word Maple carved in bronze on the white door.

. . .

The chatty hubbub suddenly dies to almost silence as Dom and I walk through a groomed hedge into the pristinely manicured gardens. His walk slows to a stop as all eyes settle on us, so I reach out for his hand and lace my fingers through his to remind him that I am here. We stand still for a couple of beats, and then I see a strong, tanned, beautiful woman with fire-red hair in a loose white dress, running at full speed on bare feet towards us.

'DOM!!!!' she screams as she throws herself at him, pulling him down to her petite height and kissing his face, mouth, forehead and eyelids fervently.

'Hello, Mother.' He laughs as he lets her do what she needs to. I can't help how happy I feel for him. Thankfully, slowly, the hubbub of chat returns to normal as people turn their attention away.

'Selene, don't scare him away, he just got here.' The resemblance between Dominic and his father is striking. He is basically just an older version of Dominic and looks nowhere near eighty. 'Hello, young lady, I'm the original Dominic. You're an impossibly beautiful creature, aren't you? Who might you be?' He shares a charming smile and I can't help but smile along.

'There were four Dominics before you, darling, making you not the original at least four times,' Dominic's mom interrupts before I can answer.

'But in this context, I am.'

'No, your father is over there on the oxygen tank, trying to keep up with the names of all the kids, grandkids and great-grandkids you have running around here.'

'Hello, Father.' Dominic steps forward to hug his father.

'Hello, son.'

'Mother, Father. This is Ariella Mason. She's my friend from Singapore. She's staying for a couple of days.'

'I hope that's all right, Mr and Mrs Miller?' I ask.

'Of course it is! You know, you remind me of a girl I was in love with back when I was a student. Back then we had to keep it a secret, but she had the softest, iridescent skin and beautiful —' Dom's father starts.

'Don't fall for it. He has enough kids.' Dominic's mother tuts at her husband. 'Hello, Ariella, lovely to meet you, I'm Selene. Welcome to our home.'

'Thank you. It's gorgeous here.'

'It is. Sadly, we don't spend enough time here.' Dominic's mother laces her arm through mine and begins taking me on what looks like an impromptu tour.

'Mother, do you think I could have Ariella back?' Dominic calls after us.

'You can for now, darling, but I'd like to spend some time getting to know her later.' His mother seems like a formidable woman; I'd definitely like to spend some time with her later too.

I walk beside Dominic as we move through the party. He keeps his hellos to family and friends swift. After a few minutes the party atmosphere returns to normal, with the guests enjoying the copious amounts of food and wine provided by sharply dressed waiters.

'How are you feeling?' I check in with Dominic.

'It's not as bad as I remember. Things have mellowed. The last time we were all together, everyone was at each other's throats. But I'm still not taking any chances. Let's grab a buggy and I'll show you around.'

'Is it okay if we walk for a little while? I could use a leg-stretch.'

'The whole property is just over nine hundred acres,' Dominic says proudly. 'We can walk for as long as you want.'

Dominic grabs my hand as we navigate our way past some

guests and through another hole in a hedge, to be confronted by a huge equestrian centre. I am dazzled by the immaculate turf racetrack, riding trails, round pens, paddocks and pastures with run-in sheds. The Millers are obviously riders. We make our way through more barns, the orchard, vineyard, outbuildings, several garages, and the property's own independent water system. Out of nowhere, we come across what looks like a quaint little village cluster of twelve detached homes, and two three-storey apartment buildings with driveways filled with buggies as well as carefully tended gardens. There is a small bakery, butcher and convenience store onsite.

'This is our staff residence,' Dominic explains.

'I want to live here! It's very pretty.'

'Yeah, I spent a lot of time here when I was much younger and hadn't learned to defend myself yet. Besides, we could hardly live in that monster of a house and make the team that looks after us day by day sleep in barns.' He smiles.

'Wow.'

'Not quite. Wait till you see the pools.'

'You have more than one?' I tease.

'Oh yes, but it's a bit of a trek. Are you sure you're up for it?'

'Are you tired of walking?' I make fun of him.

'Nope, just checking you're still good.' He laughs and we head to the main house. After a hard walk back, we sneak past the garden party on the other side of the hedge, childishly running past the openings to avoid detection. We make our way past my cottage, sticking closely to the rear of the house. On the other side, we are confronted with a humongous pavilion-style pool house and venture inside.

'That fireplace is amazing! I'd easily come in here to read and fall asleep. This is not a pool, it's...'

'I know. It's a bit much, right?'

'How big is it?'

'About a thousand square feet? Next door there is a gym, sauna, steam room, ice room, changing rooms, and it has its own kitchen. You'll be pleased to hear that there are hot yoga and dance studios, so you can practise in the morning if you want.'

'And this just sits here while the family isn't here?'

'Oh, no. It's a fully functioning private country club and resort when we aren't here. There are lots of weddings held here too. We get thirty days of private use every year so we don't piss the members off.'

'Is this where you got married?' I recognised some bits from the picture he showed me at our first dinner.

'Yeah. It was—'

'Six?'

'You lost the privilege of calling me that five years ago, Mackenzie Miller,' Dominic answers as if on cue.

We both turn around and there she is. The woman he was holding affectionately in the wedding picture, now his brother's wife. I can feel her assessing us with her big, green, kind eyes. In real life, she is even more beautiful and fairy-like with her pixie-cut. All her short green fitted dress needs is a pair of wings and she could give Tinker Bell a run for her money.

They stand, seemingly spellbound, staring at each other and saying nothing for a few seconds. Actually, I think they're saying plenty to each other, I just can't hear it. She finally musters the courage to speak again.

'Yes. I'm sorry. Please do you think I could have a few minutes?' she asks, her voice shaking.

'Sure.' Dominic reaches for my hand and pulls me towards him. 'What do you want?' I can feel how tense he is.

'Alone?' she pleads.

I can see why Dominic fell in love with her. She looks so vulnerable, I want to give her anything she wants too. Dominic is silent for a moment. He sighs deeply before turning to me.

'Aari, please can I meet you back at the party?'

Poor Dominic. She clearly still has a hold on him. Witnessing this interaction, I can see why he wanted me here to attend his parents' celebrations with him, but this is a battle he will need to fight alone.

'Absolutely,' I respond quickly, relieved. I untangle my fingers from his and walk, as quickly as I can without breaking into a sprint, out of the pool house. He's still in love with her, that much is clear. I really want to go back to my cottage, shower and get some sleep, but I find the strength to return to the party and face a bunch of people I don't know. I eventually find the right hedge to pop through after a couple of errors and, as soon as I walk through, I am approached by a woman who could easily be Dominic's sister.

'Hello, Ariella. I'm Beatrice.' I assume everyone knows my name now. 'Where's my brother hiding?'

'He asked me to meet him here. I'm sure he'll arrive soon.' I try to evade her real question.

'I saw you two sneak off earlier. No doubt he was showing off the size of his acreage.' She winks at me. Oh no. Please don't let it be one of *those* conversations.

'The grounds here are beautiful. Are you all equestrians?'

'No, not really but you'd be forgiven for thinking so. Only Max and Dom managed to take full advantage of this property. Father didn't acquire it until after he and my mother separated.'

'How old were you when that happened?' I try to keep the conversation on her so that she doesn't ask what she really wants to.

'I was ten.'

'That must have been rough.'

'It was, but then I got to know Selene. It took a while to realise that she was just a beautiful, harmless, crystal-wielding hippie and enthusiastic nudist. I think my father needed that. He's always had a lot on his shoulders, as will Dominic. I think she lightens his load.'

Beatrice nods at a laughing Selene as she playfully chases some of the little children around under the night sky.

'So how did you and Dom meet?'

I'd been so caught up in admiring Dominic's mom that I'd left an opening for Beatrice.

'I work for a company that delivers DMVI's engagement programmes across Asia. We met at the end of the tendering stage and became friends.'

'You look good together. It'll be nice to inject a bit of colour into the bloodline. We are all a bit white, aren't we?'

I don't know how to respond to that, so offer a tight smile.

'Just so you know, I'm an ally. The way black people have been treated and continue to be treated by our oppressive systems is appalling. You know, last year I was at a Black Lives Matter protest and got tear-gassed and everything—'

'Where's Dom?' Someone who could only be Maximilian stomps up to us, saving me from Beatrice's proof of allyship.

'He asked me to meet him here. I'm sure he'll be here soon,' I say, delivering my line again.

'I can't find Mack either,' Maximillian says.

'Oh...' Beatrice responds. They don't know that I know; and I am not about to tell them either.

'I'm sure Dominic will be here soon,' I offer. They both look at me with varying degrees of sympathy in their eyes.

It doesn't take long for the news of Dominic and Mackenzie's disappearance to spread through the guests. Unfortunately, Dominic doesn't make it back to the party, and neither does Mackenzie. When the evening starts to wind down, I say goodnight to the group I am standing with and I can't help but notice the looks of pity I'm being given as I head for my cottage.

I feel instant relief as I step under the shower and take my time, allowing the water to wash the day away. I climb into bed, reach for my phone and connect to the cottage Wi-Fi for the first time since I landed in Boston. A message from Caleb pops up and I feel warm with affection, simply at the sight of his name. I'm smiling before I realise it.

> Wanted to make sure you got there safely, little Mason.

I respond quickly, trying to calm the butterflies in my tummy that he still controls.

> Yes, I did. Thank you for checking in.

A text comes back immediately.

> So, has he put the moves on you yet?

> Please, Caleb. I'm just here as his friend.

> I know we aren't together and I promised that I'd give you space, so I won't say what I'm thinking right now.

> Thank you.

> When do you catch your flight to New Orleans?

> The day after tomorrow.

> So I just need to not be paranoid for one more day.

> Trust me, I'm the last thing on Dominic's mind at the moment.

> We said we'd be honest with each other and we both know that isn't true.

> I am being honest. He's dealing with some stuff out here.

> Ok. Text tomorrow?

> Yes. Goodnight Caleb.

Goodnight Aari.

I read his final text with a deep longing, wishing I'd never taken the job in Singapore.

The move to Asia was meant to be a fresh start for both of us, but our new life turned out to be a carefully constructed lie that he'd kept hidden from me. While I can understand why he made the decisions he did, I'm still hurt because of how much devastating effort he put into keeping the truth about our lives from me, and how long it took for him to come clean. I want to move on. I want nothing more than to trust him again. However, the anguish that has kept me awake for the last few months makes me petrified to open myself up to him again.

None of that, however, stops me from wanting his body curled round mine right now, as I tune in to his heartbeat. With over nine thousand miles between us, this is the furthest we have been away from each other, but it doesn't make a bit of difference. My heart is determined to love that boy until the pain is gone.

'Ariella!'

I'm wandering through the gorgeous-smelling orchard the next afternoon, about to help myself to a carefully selected apple with the biggest stick I can find, when I see Dominic again.

'Hi!' I smile, drop my stick and wave at him as he jogs towards me.

'Hey. Did you like breakfast?'

'I thought that was you!' I laugh. I was surprised to get a grapefruit, yoghurt and hibiscus tea breakfast that morning.

'Me and Ms Pat via Lydia.' He smiles. 'I wish my house-keeper and personal assistant cared half as much about me as yours do. So, I wanted to apologise for last night.'

'Please, don't worry about it. You two obviously had a lot to talk about. How did it go?'

'Not very well.'

'You're still in love with her, aren't you?' I ask, feeling sorry for him.

'I don't know.' He is. He just doesn't want to admit it.

'Where did you leave it?'

'In pieces. Same as before.'

'Do you mind telling me what happened? Maybe I can help?'

'After our honeymoon, she had to work in New York for a few weeks while I was stuck in Chicago. The story they are sticking to is that they met up for drinks, both got wasted and ended up in bed together. The twins arrived nine months later.'

'So she made a mistake.'

'With my brother. That unravelled at our first baby scan, when the numbers she was feeding me didn't check out.'

'Do you think you can forgive them?'

'I'm trying.'

I pull my friend into a deep, long hug.

'Sooooo, want an apple?' I ask to lighten the mood. 'I've found the one I want and it has a good one next to it.'

Dominic nods, smiling at me. I pick up my earlier stick and start jumping to knock them out of the tree.

'What are you doing?' He starts laughing.

'Getting our apples!' I jump again, missing them. 'Okay, watch your head.' I throw the stick into the tree, then run to safety, but no apples. At this point Dominic is doubled over laughing as he pulls out his phone.

'That's it. I'm only getting my apple. You can fend for yourself.' I continue to jump and throw.

'I'll just lie here, watch you and record this for posterity then.' Dominic leans against a nearby tree, happily recording my many attempts until I give up.

'Stupid apple.' I kick the leaves at the base of the tree.

'You're adorable when you're frustrated. Here, I'll get your apple.' He smiles. As soon as he walks behind the tree, I know what he is going to do.

'There's a ladder, isn't there?' I start to laugh.

'Yes, there's a ladder.' He scurries up, grabs both our apples and climbs down again.

'Thank you.' I wipe and bite my apple. It's delicious.

'Want to check out the tasting barn?' Dominic asks, playfully bumping into me as he takes a bite out of his.

'Unsupervised?' I reference Mrs Thompson.

'Yeah.' He wears a naughty grin that makes it difficult to say no.

We make our way over to reception to get the keys, and navigate through some hedges to arrive on a large patio at the back of the house. I am so busy being amazed that anyone would know what hedge to come through, that I don't spot Maximilian before he shoves Dominic.

'Stay the fuck away from my wife!' Maximilian shouts at Dom as he rushes to push him again.

'Hey!' I protest and step between them. People suddenly start to emerge from the house onto the patio.

My eyes travel to Mackenzie, who is watching the altercation. She is concerned, but also seems to be enjoying the spectacle.

'I'm nowhere near your wife,' Dominic shouts back.

'Bullshit. She didn't turn up until ten this morning.'

'Then you'd better ask her where she was. Keeping track of time has never been Mackenzie's forte. You of all people should know that.'

'Dominic!' I reprimand him as I put my hand on his chest to try to get him to back away. Maximilian reaches round me to clip Dominic on the side of the head.

'Hey, stop it!' I turn round to face him.

'Oh fuck off, you're not fooling anyone,' he dismisses me angrily. 'You didn't give a shit where he was last night. You just stood in the corner of the party, sizing us all up, you gold-digging house Negro!'

The last thing I see before I feel something really hard smash into me, is Dominic going red and charging. After that, everything goes black.

I wake up in an unfamiliar bed with a violent headache.

'Ariella, it's Selene.' A soft and soothing voice pulls me into the room. 'You're in our medical cottage. Don't move. I have some clear and rose quartz crystals on your tummy, head and chest.' She rubs the back of my hand. 'Would you like some water?'

I produce a croak, then try again. 'Yes please.'

Selene pops a straw leading to a bottle of water in my mouth. I try not to disturb the crystals.

'Can you handle a painkiller?'

I nod carefully. She removes her crystals and presses a button that folds me up into a seating position. I pop the pills in my mouth as soon as she hands them to me.

'Is Dominic okay? What happened?'

Her face softens. 'Dominic is fine. Your little accident put an end to things pretty quickly. I am so sorry you got caught between my two monstrous children. I heard what Max said. I am deeply horrified and ashamed.'

I fight the tears I feel pricking my eyes.

'Dominic asked me to call him when you are awake. Can I?'

I shake my head. I'd really like some silence.

'I think I'd just like to be alone in my cottage, if that's okay?' I get up. I'm a little sore and my head is pounding, but I'm fine.

Selene helps me outside into a buggy with a driver, which

whizzes both of us back to my cottage. When she starts to follow me in I stop her.

'Thank you for being so kind to me, Selene. I'll be fine from here.'

She nods and jumps back into the buggy.

My father's voice kicks in as I lock the door behind me, and I do what he always taught me to do should a situation like this arise. I locate my bag and slowly start to pack away my clothes and toiletries. When I have finished, I dial nine.

'Hello, reception? Please may I arrange for the next available car to take me to Boston Logan?'

'My apologies, Miss Mason, we don't have you leaving until tomorrow and the chopper is already arranged for your transfer,' the gentleman at the end of the phone stutters.

'My itinerary has changed. May I have a car to Boston Logan as soon as possible, please?'

'I can try. Are you not happy with your stay—'

I feel my throat closing with panic, so I push my next words out quickly. 'If you could arrange a taxi for me as soon as possible, I'd be very grateful.'

'No problem. I will be in touch as soon as I have arranged something.'

Shortly after, the phone rings. That was fast.

'Hello, Ariella. It's Mrs Thompson. We don't have you leaving until tomorrow.'

'I understand, but I would like to leave now, please.' I hear my voice crack.

'Oh, sweetheart. Do you think I could come to visit you?' The compassion in her voice breaks me and the tears start to fall. I just want to leave.

'I'm fine, thank you, Mrs Thompson. I'd just like a car, please.'

'All right.'

There is a knock on my door five minutes later. When I

open it, a sorry-looking Dominic is standing there. I stand aside to let him in before I shut the door wearily behind him.

'I'm really sorry about earlier, but you can't leave. You promised.'

'I can leave, because I don't feel safe, Dominic,' I whisper quietly, shaking.

'Is it because of what Max said? He wants to apologise.'

'An apology means nothing. He could have called me anything, but he made that choice. Those words came from his gut, Dominic, and they were filled with venom. That's what he thinks and feels. I'm not safe here.' I start to sob and there is nothing I can do to stop. I have to sit to catch my breath.

'Fuck! What can I do?' Dominic pleads.

'I just want to leave so I can feel safe again.'

'I'm coming with you.'

'Please don't. I fly to my gigi tomorrow anyway, so it's only one night.'

There is another knock on the door and Dominic goes to open it. Selene walks in.

'Mrs Thompson said you're leaving us.'

I nod. 'Thank you so much for having me and looking after me, Selene.'

'Why?' she asks.

'Because she rightly doesn't feel safe with a violent, racist, narcissistic bigot on the loose when she is staying in a cottage in the middle of the woods by herself,' Dominic snaps.

'Can we move you into the main house?' Selene offers.

'No thank you, I'd rather just go.'

'And I'm going with her,' Dominic states.

'Nooo, Dom! You just got here!' Selene protests with a trembling lip.

'Dominic, please stay. I'll be all right, I fly out tomorrow—'

There's another knock on the door. Dominic goes to answer

it as a distressed Selene sits beside me on the bed. To my surprise, his father walks in.

'Ariella, how are you feeling?' he asks.

'I'm much better, thank you.' I can't wait till my car arrives. It's getting a little crowded in the cottage.

'She's leaving and Dominic is going with her!' Selene tearfully tells Dominic's father.

'Why are you leaving us so soon, dear?' he asks.

I can't bring myself to tell him about his son's horrific words.

'Maximilian crossed a line and she doesn't feel safe with him around,' Dominic explains. 'He said—'

'Please, Dominic... I can't hear it again,' I beg as I try to hold back a sniffle. When Dominic's father leans his ear in, Dominic whispers it and I watch his father's eyes bulge in horror.

Without another word, Dominic's father grabs the walkie on his hip. 'You, my dear, are not going anywhere. Mrs Thompson!' he barks into his handset.

'Yes, sir,' she immediately responds.

'Have you ordered Miss Mason's taxi?'

'Yes, sir. It will be here in under fifteen minutes.'

'Good. I want you to clear out Maximilian's family's cottage. Put him, his family and their belongings into it, and send them into town.'

'Yes, sir.'

'They are not to set foot on the premises, for any reason, until Miss Mason has left tomorrow.'

'Yes, sir.'

'And they are no longer to reside on this property until further notice.'

'Yes, sir.'

Dominic's father clips his walkie back on his hip. 'I will not stand for such obscene behaviour. You are our guest, and please know that you have my sincere apologies.'

'What shall we do about the anniversary dinner tonight?' Selene asks.

'Selene, Maximilian and his family will not set foot on this property until Ariella has left, so they will be excluded from dinner. When he is allowed to return, we will have to have a serious conversation about his future as a member of this family.'

Dominic's father turns to his son.

'Stay with her until Maximilian is off the property.'

Then his wife.

'Come on, Selene. Let the staff deal with Maximilian. He cannot pull on your heartstrings if you're not there.'

As soon as they leave, Dominic locks and bolts the door behind them, then sits beside me on the bed. It dawns on me that this is the second time in so many months that I have allowed someone to prevent me from going home.

'You look exhausted,' he states softly.

'I am a little,' I agree.

'I shouldn't have let you jump so many times for those frikkin' apples.' His light laugh makes me smile. 'I'm so sorry, Aari,' he continues. 'I shouldn't have asked you to leave Mack and me, or requested that you go to the party by yourself. I forgot how much you hate crowds.'

I turn to face him. 'You needed closure and you may not want to admit it, but you're still in love with her.'

'Maybe, but I made a ton of wrong decisions last night. I shouldn't have kept her all night. I knew it would piss him off.'

'Did anything happen between you and her?'

'No. She wanted to talk, so I let her. I kept us in the drawing room though, because she has a way of getting whatever she wants when we are alone. We were there all night putting each other through one emotional wringer after another. I'd had enough by four a.m., so I went to bed. I don't know where she was the rest of the night.'

'I'm sorry that it happened and you're having to deal with this.'

'I'm not. If I was still married to her then I wouldn't have met you.' He strokes my face.

When our eyes meet, I know what's coming. I watch as Dominic closes in but, just before his lips meet mine, I find the strength to stop it. It comes out as a whisper.

'Dom, I can't.'

He stops silently, frozen in space with his lips millimetres from mine. He is so close; his breath warms my Cupid's bow. When his eyes flick up from my lips to meet mine, I watch him struggle to restrain himself. I recognise the feeling. I am charmed by Dominic and my attraction to him only seems to be intensifying, but I don't trust my feelings for him. Dominic's friendship is important to me, but we often seem to be caught in tight spaces that force me to navigate around him. What I do know for sure is, no matter how annoyed I am with Caleb, I'm still in love with him.

'It's still him, isn't it?' Dominic asks quietly, keeping his eyes on mine as frustration radiates from him. 'But you haven't been together in a while.'

He's too close and feeling his breath on my mouth as he speaks is eroding my ability to resist him. I break eye contact to give his hand a squeeze, create some space between us and escape from the intensity of his gaze. He may be my friend, but he's also now my boss, which makes this a little bit more perilous to navigate.

'No, we haven't.'

'But you're still in love with him?' he presses.

'I am. I'm sorry, Dom.' I can't find the courage to look at him again.

'Then what's happening between us?'

'I don't know but it's...' I try to find the words.

'Painful.'

I nod in agreement.

'You feel it too?' he asks.

'I do,' I admit.

'I really wish our hearts weren't being held hostage by other people, Aari – because I am so ready to fall in love with you.'

I don't have a response for Dominic, so I reach for him and pour all my feelings into a hug, more grateful than ever for the plane I have to catch tomorrow. That'll put the distance I need between us.

TWO

CALEB

To say that I am sick and tired of Ariella's shit is a colossal fucking understatement. I accept the fact that I messed up and that I'm mostly responsible for the way things went down. But she messed up too. Yes, I told her she could do whatever she liked and I'd still be here – but happily hopping on Dominic's private jet to leave the country, knowing that he's going to have at least twenty uninterrupted hours to execute whatever he has planned to seduce her, is just bang out of order.

It's been six weeks and I'm still dealing with the emotional hiatus I asked her to put us in. It doesn't help that moments that inspire real annoyance keep popping up. The latest is a video captioned 'Throw-by fruiting in progress' posted on social media by none other than Dominic. He's not even original. Ariella is laughing while jumping with a big stick to get an apple from a tree. When she doesn't succeed after a few tries, she throws the stick at the apple in frustration and runs for cover. Still no apple. I have to remind myself not to laugh when I catch myself doing exactly that. Fuck Dominic. I don't care that he is now going to be our boss's boss.

I am under no illusions. Ariella may not have said it, but the reason he decided to invest, trapping us all here in our Singaporean purgatory, is because he has hopes with her. I would have laughed it off and labelled him deluded if I hadn't seen the way she responded when he kissed her.

The forty-eight hours after Ariella found out that everything in Singapore wasn't as it seemed, was hell. It shattered everything we'd worked and hoped for. I knew that rebuilding the love and trust we lost was going to be a battle, but what I didn't expect was for Dominic to make his perfectly timed move in an attempt to blow up the tiny chance we had left. All I can remember is her not pushing him away. If Lara hadn't held on tightly to my hand while she took the piss out of both of them, I don't know what I would have done. Ariella may have sent him home immediately afterwards, but the damage had already been done. After witnessing their kiss, I spent the rest of the night with a bottle of rum until a comforting, hazy blur settled in. I vaguely remember Jasper helping me to bed after that.

Things moved quickly from that point on. The day after, Ariella in her capacity as COO told us that Dominic was going to buy Ivory Bow, the company that we both work for. She then filled us in on what our options were as employees. I was ready to quit there and then, until Ariella then told us of her self-imposed demotion. She'd basically shackled herself to Ivory Bow and Singapore for the next two years in order to save our jobs. With that, the dream of returning home to London disappeared. I wasn't leaving without her, so I found a way to get comfortable, doing her time with her. She also announced that Melissa, our previous owner, had agreed to be removed from her role. The week after that, we found out we were getting a new CEO. They'd be responsible for taking on a lot of the processes that Ariella was working on, putting new systems in place and ultimately finding a COO to replace Ariella. Within two weeks, the landscape of Ivory Bow had completely changed.

Melissa cut all ties to the business, although the team's presence was still required at her wedding to 'save face'. It also turned out that Ariella's flat was owned by Melissa, which effectively forced her out of my building and into one of those impossible to secure, colonial black-and-white houses in the same residential community as, you guessed it, Dominic Miller. She didn't even tell me she was moving. That same week, she cleared out her office to make way for the new CEO. My little Mason, creature of habit that she is, picked the furthest desk from everyone, wedged tightly in a corner. Lydia promptly followed, and set up her desk protectively in front of Ariella's.

Interviews are still ongoing for the right CEO candidate, so Ariella, Bryce and I are now steering the company. Since the launch, we've received an overwhelming amount of interest, and the three of us agreed that it was too much for one person to handle. With Dominic's approval, I now have the arduous task of hiring two sales managers. One will be for Ariella's more traditional industries and the other will focus on interest from new sectors – which is why I am sitting here on a Saturday afternoon looking at completed job applications to distract myself from the video that Dominic posted.

'Pubic lice! Get me ice! Wait. Ooooh... I should be a poet!'

Ugh. Lara.

'Why are you still here?' I complain.

'I'm homeless, you unsympathetic ogre,' she moans from the sunlounger by my pool.

'You're not homeless. You have a perfectly good home in London and a business class ticket ready to deliver you to it.'

'What? Go back to that prison? No thank you. I like it here.'

'Prison?'

'Ivory Bow UK was too restrictive and they underappreciated my efforts, so I have decided that my future lies elsewhere.'

'Lara. The whole company knows you got sacked. It was the last thing Harrison did, quite ceremoniously, I might add, before Christopher bought him out.'

'Exactly. Harrison fired me. Now that Christopher has taken over Ivory Bow, we don't know what his position is, do we?'

'I'm pretty sure you're still unemployed.'

'Well, if that's your conclusion, that would make me homeless.'

'You are not home— You know what, it doesn't matter. Can't you find a coven to take you in? Or maybe stay at Aari's? I'm sure Ms Pat will let you in.'

'No she won't. I've tried. Besides, Ariella doesn't have a pool any more. It's much more fun here and someone has to keep an eye out for when you revert to type and drag some poor unsuspecting thing home. I want to be the first to tell Ariella.' She pulls down her sunglasses and looks at me suspiciously. Lara Scott knows exactly how to push my buttons.

'So what's the plan? Lounge around until you're booted out of the country? You're going to have to return eventually.'

'I am returning. Temporarily. I'm not missing Zachary's wedding for anything. Speaking of which, are you still Aari's plus one or did she get rid of you?' Lara sniggers loudly.

I'd completely forgotten about Zachary's wedding. We RSVPd a long time ago, when life was perfect.

'I'm not sure I'm still invited.'

'Doesn't matter anyway. Dominic will just go with her if you're not around.'

'There is no way Ariella's taking Dominic to the wedding,' I state forcefully.

'Bloody hell. Calm down. She's in town for the wedding, he'll be in town to meet Christopher, you'll be six thousand miles away...' Lara takes a long sip from her drink as she watches me from over the top of her sunglasses.

'How on earth do you know all this?' It can't be true.

'I still have access to my emails and Christopher's diary – I guess no one told IT about my change in circumstances.' She chortles. 'There is a lot of Dominic activity that week. There are dinners, strategy meetings, golf... all pretty boring. There isn't a strip club down in the diary as "community outreach" in sight. Harrison's diary was much juicier.'

'Dominic is not going to that wedding,' I say to myself as I open a browser tab and start pulling up return flights to London.

'He might. I'd take him. He's hot in that classic alpha way. He's steady, mature, loaded and he's always there, ready to solve her problems. All you seem to do is create them.'

That hurts, only because Lara is right. 'And it has absolutely nothing to do with the fact that you want a job?' I retort weakly.

'It has everything to do with that. I was going to stick around to get a job with Ivory Bow Asia, but Ariella has destroyed both our futures by falling on her own bloody "demotion" sword. Now, I'm going to have to go back home to charm Christopher, before I bribe or blackmail Dominic into giving me a job out here. And not just any job, I want a house and a car and a housekeeper and all that fancy shit.'

'You honestly think that you're going to rock up for a job you're unqualified for, demand a massive pay packet from Dominic and he is just going to give it to you?'

'Why not? You men have been doing it since the beginning of time. There are presidents of whole countries that give me good reason to question whether they ever finished primary school. This is just a job. No nuclear codes, international incidents or deaths.'

'That's not going to happen, Lara. You have more of a chance of staying in London and getting your old job back.'

'You know what I have a 100 per cent chance of getting?'

'What?'

'Front-row seats to Honey beating the living daylight out of you tomorrow morning. It really sets me up for the day.'

'Is that what you're really looking forward to when Honey is around, Lara?' I tease her.

'What's that supposed to mean?' She sits up. I've hit a nerve. I'm going to enjoy this.

'I think someone has a little crush...' I sing, and I see Lara go beet red all the way from here.

'I do not!'

'Yeah, you do...' I relax.

'Shut up, Caleb.' She's getting angry and I'm the happiest I have been in a while.

'If you write a note, can I pass it to her in class?'

'You're a dickhead, do you know that?' She narrows her eyes at me. 'I categorically do not fancy Honey.'

I'm laughing too hard to care what Lara's defence is.

'I don't!' she protests. 'And even if I did, I'm not going to go there. That whole Bamidele thing scared me off straight girls looking to experiment for ever.'

'Wait, what?' Lara still doesn't know about Honey? They have spent so much time together recently that I assumed Honey would have told her by now.

'Ariella didn't tell you about Bamidele? Nice. Get me drunk on the expensive stuff one day and I might spill. Your disgusting little mind will enjoy it. There's a *lot* of lesbian sex.' Lara pushes her sunglasses back up and reclines again.

As annoying as Lara is, I'm secretly pleased she's here. In her own acerbic, insulting way, she has been largely responsible for holding me together since that night of the kiss, especially after Jasper went back to London. She forced me to keep training with Honey even when I didn't want to, and was always a willing participant when I wanted to drink, moan and be petty. She currently is very much in the anti-Dominic camp, although she repeatedly warns me that her allegiances might switch, based on whether or not he hands her a truckload of cash. The one thing she has never wavered on is Ariella. No matter how broken I have felt, she stands firmly in her best friend's corner. However, little acts of kindness that show the empathy she clearly feels keep slipping through the hardened armour she defends herself with. Armour that magically disappears when Honey is around. Lara isn't fooling anyone. She is crushing hard on Honey. She is always up to watch my training and gets Honey's hot-water bottle ready for her every morning. This is going to be interesting.

Forgetting that things aren't great between us, I grab my phone and send a text to Aari. By the time I remember, it's too late to delete it. Argh! Why is everything so hard at the moment?

THREE

ARIELLA

> Lara still doesn't know that Honey is gay?

Is the first message that comes through as I touch down at Louis Armstrong New Orleans. I love it when Caleb gets gossipy and I'm ready to dive into the juicy details with him until I stop myself and craft a more restrained response.

> No. Why?

A message comes straight back.

> They've been spending A LOT of time together.

> Really? Still?

> Yup and I think our Lara might have a crush.
> This is going to be hard to watch.

> ...and challenging to keep our lips sealed! 😬

I chuckle as I finish it with a stressed-looking emoji. As

always, Caleb has managed to pull me in. The 'our' Lara did it. She belongs to both of us. I really want to share what happened with Maximilian with Caleb, but I know nothing good will come of it.

> I know! How is your gigi?

> > Just getting into arrivals so I haven't seen her yet. She'll be great though.

> Ok. Have fun. I'll leave you to it.

I instinctively type 'I love you' and catch myself before I send it. I delete it quickly. I do love him still, but it would be unfair to send mixed signals.

When Dominic asked if I could join him to help get through his parents' anniversary, I was ecstatic to discover that it almost coincided with my gigi's flight to the UK for Zachary's wedding. Getting precious alone time with her before the wedding was a gift.

When I see my gigi's silver hair neatly parted into the two French braids she always wears, my feelings can only be described as joy. Her tiny frame is comically dwarfed by the huge suited gentleman she is standing beside and laughing with – she always makes new friends wherever she goes. I smile to myself as I notice that she is wearing the Converse I sent her for Christmas with high-waisted jeans, a billowy blouse and a sun hat. I quickly deduce that she was in her garden before she came to the airport.

'Gigi!' I smile. Her love hits me before she even looks at me.

'Ariella!' she calls fondly. I am now much taller than my gigi, but when she wraps her arms round me I feel like a child again. Her warmth envelops me with such an intense shroud that I feel like I could burst into a thousand tiny lights.

My gigi was my very first best friend. For as long as I can remember, we shared just as many hours with me on her lap as we traded secrets and got up to mischief. I especially loved that she was usually the instigator of enacting vengeful acts against Mommy. She actively encouraged me to keep a list of Mommy's transgressions and, as soon as she arrived for a visit, I would hand my list over. She'd inspect it carefully, always adding a couple of her own grievances, before we'd spend the whole of her visit hiding one thing or another that belonged to Mommy. It used to drive her crazy. My gigi especially got a kick out of when we were enlisted to help find the missing item we'd hidden. Even at this age, with our thirst for vengeance gone, she is still the only person that I feel that I can trust unreservedly with the contents of my mind.

After our embrace she holds me at arm's length to appraise me, stopping at my head. I know what she is going to say before she says it.

'What have you been doing to your hair? A bird is going to make its home there soon if I don't sort that out! Come on!'

We walk hand in hand out of the airport and make our way into the car park. I spot Grandpa Spence's Shelby Cobra. It's going to be a frightening ride back to hers. Grandpa Spence loved cars and treated his Shelby Cobra like a particularly delicate child. After he died, my gigi treated it with a level of disrespect that would make my grandfather consider haunting her. If he isn't already. Mommy and Daddy insisted on buying my gigi a more practical car a few years ago to keep her from casually cruising around New Orleans in a car worth so much, but she won't be told.

'Gigi, why aren't you in your new car?' I ask, worried.

'Your grandpa Spence kept this tin can in the garage and only used it for special occasions. Look where that got him. I'm going to enjoy it,' she says with a laugh, taking a sharp corner. I know exactly where Mommy gets everything from. Her. My gigi has a heavy foot that she happily uses to speed out of the airport, and we make it to her Garden District home in no time.

'Meet me in the conservatory, let's sort out whatever is happening on your head.'

I know the routine, so I drop my bags, and grab a towel and an old T-shirt from the drying cupboard. Then I make my way to the large glass conservatory that overlooks the huge, colourful garden. My gigi is already sitting in her chair, with towels draped everywhere. She has an array of combs and hair products sharing a coffee table with a jug of ice-cold lemonade and glasses. A comfortable cushion waits for my bum in the space between her feet on the floor and I happily find my way over to sit on it. She carefully and lovingly unfurls my hair and starts to section it.

'Your hair is really dry, Ariella,' she admonishes softly as she tenderly applies her home-made treatment to a section she has isolated and starts working it through. The familiar smell of the coconut from the treatment fills my memory with warm highlights of all the times we have sat like this, laughing and chatting. I look across to an empty leather recliner and Grandpa Spence's absence hits me hard. I want him back in his chair, reading bits of the newspaper out to us while my gigi and I debate, gossip and agree over its contents. I try to wipe a tear as subtly as I can.

'I miss him too, sweetheart,' she whispers into my ear. 'So, what are you trying to find on the other side of the world that can't be found at home?' She finishes masking and combing the first section of my hair, puts it in a loose twist and lays it over my shoulder carefully before she starts to work on the next.

'I don't know, Gigi. I think I am trying to find out if I can stand alone.'

'Well, I'm glad you got away from that Jasper boy.'

'Gigi!' I laugh. 'I thought you liked Jasper.'

'I seem to remember telling you to dump him.'

'Yes, at Grandpa Spence's funeral. I just thought you were being emotional and slightly racist.'

'I wasn't being racist!'

'You said I should dump that white boy,' I remind her.

'Was I wrong? I'll admit he was a good boy, I just didn't like the way you followed him around. It held you back. You are meant to destroy barriers and conquer new worlds.'

'I'm not doing either of those at the moment, Gigi. I'm actually struggling a little in Singapore.'

'Struggle and hardship is in our DNA. It runs through our blood; but so do perseverance, drive and victory. You don't need me to remind you that you're here because the enslaved that make up our bloodline survived capture, crossing the Atlantic, and enduring the dehumanising slave markets and treatment that animals must never be subjected to. We made it because of them. Even when we managed to buy our freedom, it wasn't over because we had to help those who couldn't achieve freedom in other ways. And it still isn't over. I was twenty when that King boy had a dream, and we're still getting choked and shot in the streets. We were victims of their hate, then we were victims of their violence – and now we're victims of their guilt.'

I hear the anger rising in her and feel it as she completes the twist of the section she is working on in half the time the other took. Whenever my gigi talks about our ancestors, it always invokes a deep need and responsibility within me to be better, work harder and push further to make my existence worthy and meaningful. She makes me feel like I'm not here just for me, I'm here for them too. I love the part of me that comes from Gigi, but, whenever we have talks like this, it's hard not to remember that the blood of the perpetrators flows through me too. The challenges Mommy and Daddy faced by choosing each other is no secret in our family.

'Gigi?' I call quietly.

'Yes, baby?'

'Is that why you're angry with Daddy?'

I love my gigi but her coolness towards Daddy has always been an obstruction that we all have to navigate around. I've wanted to talk to her about it for years but have only now found the courage. She is silent for a few seconds, then she sighs.

'I'm not angry with your daddy. I'm still angry with Dee Dee though,' she admits quietly, using my mother's childhood name.

'Why? I know they didn't tell you when they got married...'

'No, Ariella. That's not why I'm angry. Your mother knew better than to abandon her family to follow some man across the ocean to a country she had never been before. It was the worst thing she could have done to us.'

'She said she felt she had no choice.'

'She was engaged to a very nice boy. We had a date picked out already. Then out of nowhere she brings your daddy home and your grandpa Spence didn't take it very well.'

'What happened?'

'Grandpa Spence pointed a shotgun at his temple. He explained that he had a twitchy finger, acres of land that could use some fertiliser, no neighbours to intervene and the stain of war. He gave him five minutes to get off our property and told him he never wanted to see him again. Dee Dee was pretty upset, but we didn't expect her to go to college after her break was over and never come back home.'

'She didn't tell you she was leaving?'

'No. Dee Dee was naughty right from when she was born. Cried like she didn't want to be here. From the minute she could speak, she was always running that little mouth of hers and getting into trouble for talking in church. Questions. Always questions. She would regularly disappear, get into the communion wafers and stuff her little cheeks so full she couldn't even chew on them. She wasn't even cute-naughty, she was naughty-naughty, so I knew she was going to be trouble.'

Despite the words, affectionate laughter escapes from my gigi, then she continues. 'I was just hoping it was trouble she would use to help others – but what she did was heart-wrenching. For a very long time, we didn't know how to deal with the pain that our daughter was gone.'

I want to bring Gigi back from the memory, so I try to focus on the positive.

'What brought you back together?'

'Your daddy wrote, and wrote and wrote. We got a letter about once a week, with news, where they were living, what they were doing. We never wrote back once, but the letters kept coming. Finally, when she became pregnant, he started to phone. The first call was difficult. He admitted what they did was wrong and asked that, even though we may hate him and he may never be forgiven, we find some space to love our grandchild. After that, he phoned us every day, we would have little talks with both of them. It ended with your daddy begging us to come. So when Zachary was born, we did.'

'Oh, Gigi.'

'I know it's been decades and I really should get over it, especially as it has brought you to me, but it's hard to unsee and unfeel.'

I hear Gigi exhale deeply to let her feelings go before she changes her mood.

'I'm excited to get on the plane for Zachary's wedding. I was so pleased to hear that he is marrying a nice West African girl. Are you still messing with white boys?'

'Gigi...'

'What's his name?' I feel her roll her eyes behind me.

'Caleb.'

'How is this one different from the other one?'

I catch myself smiling and a little giggle escapes.

'Jesus, take the wheel,' I hear her murmur.

'Anyway, Mr Ramon isn't black.'

My gigi flicks the comb on to my shoulder.

'Ow!'

'What do you know about Mr Ramon?'

'I know he's invited to the wedding and he isn't coming. Why don't you bring him, Gigi?'

'He changes my light bulbs and is handy around the house. There's nothing more to know about Mr Ramon.'

'I know he's been around changing the light bulbs quite regularly, since two years after Grandpa Spence died. I also know that those are LEDs and they don't need to be changed for a very, very long time— Ow!'

I get another flick of the comb.

'Mr Ramon is Puerto Rican, he's mixed – and besides, he's just a friend.'

'Okay, Gigi,' I chuckle.

'You want hair left on your head after this?'

I say nothing else as I smile silently to myself. We all know Mr Ramon is her boyfriend. Gigi is beautiful and deserves someone who makes her feel that way. Over the years, we've observed the six foot plus, handsome, distinguished, kind, quiet gentleman support, spoil and be there for Gigi. We are all happy for her, Mommy included; but, for whatever reason, Gigi refuses to admit it. I bet he turns up tomorrow to fix something and say goodbye before we head to the airport.

I decide to focus on romances that do not involve her and Mr Ramon, and home in on the gossip from her circle of friends.

'How was the church trip to Vegas?'

'Great. The girls and I gambled the whole trip and only made it to the brunch at the House of Blues. Oooh! Miss Margot got herself into a situation-ship with Deacon Corrigan from the Baptist church across the way.'

'No!'

Miss Margot was the sweetest little old lady with iconic church hats and a blond wig that made her look like an older

Mary J. Blige. She was quiet and frail and always had candy in her purse at church – not someone you'd readily associate with a 'situation-ship'.

'Uh-huh. He apparently just *happened* to be there. We think they planned it. At least it's an improvement – she met the last guy at a funeral and had to go on antibiotics.'

I settle down to enjoy the news from the surprisingly promiscuous elderly community my gigi belongs to as she finishes masking my hair. It's always much more scandalous than I could imagine. When my hair is fully masked, she places a shower cap over my head to steam the products into my hair before we go through her closet together, picking outfits for the wedding. Isszy's family insisted on having African print couture made for Gigi, so she was asked to send her measurements. We have a lot of fun as she tries the outfits on. Each fits perfectly. The fabrics are heavy and colourful and I feel myself radiating admiration as she exudes regal beauty in them.

Besides gossip, what I love most doing with Gigi is cooking, so, when packing is over, she suggests we head to the kitchen to cook before I wash the products out of my hair. Delighted, I happily skip after her. Frustratingly, she never measures anything, so it's impossible to record her recipes, but it all ends up tasting consistently and reliably incredible. Like magic, it's a bit of this and a bit of that, some of this and just a pour a load of that in, and it's always perfect. I'd never dared to replicate any of her recipes until Dominic came over one evening a couple of weeks ago. It was a 'welcome to the neighbourhood' and 'thank you for my island birthday' dinner when I moved into my new home in his community.

The memory of that night is now tainted by Maximilian's words. My gigi catches my eyes filling before I get the opportunity to blink the tears away.

'What's wrong, baby?' she asks, concerned.

'Someone said something terrible to me when I was in Maine and I'm not sure how to process it.'

'What did they say?'

'They called me a gold-digging house Negro.' I let my head drop.

'Oh, baby.'

Gigi walks round her cooking counter to give me a hug in her warm and love-filled kitchen. I stay in her safe arms for as long as I can and allow myself to break down and cry, letting the hurt release itself freely.

'The fact that you are here, now, hopping over the world, sharing spaces that were never intended for you, being free in this home right now, holding on to me without fear or restriction, is a victory, sweetheart. We have the privilege of being able to choose what our lives look like without interference from others. You are the manifestation of your ancestors' brightest dreams. He just sounds like the manifestation of his ancestors' darkest. There's only one way to beat a guy like that, and that is to thrive; and that is exactly what you are doing. So, keep doing it.'

It was exactly what I needed to hear, and it makes me hold on tighter to her.

'Okay. That's enough now.' Gigi rubs my back lovingly. 'If you make that fiery lamb of yours, I'll teach you my jambalaya. If we don't eat too late, I'll put cornrows in your hair and tell you all about when your mother brought her first boyfriend home.' She finishes with that naughty titter that fills me with excitement.

The rest of the evening goes by in a peaceful blur, and, by the time I wake up the next morning, the wound Maximillian left – while still present – now feels more bearable.

After breakfast, as we make preparations to leave for the airport, the doorbell rings. I open the door to a smiling Mr Ramon.

'Ariella, you look more and more like Grace every time I see you.'

'Lovely to see you, Mr Ramon. Please come in.'

He takes off his fedora before stepping into the house – he is so elegantly old-school. 'She says you've been running a company all by yourself in Singapore. You've grown into such a confident young woman. Grace is very proud.'

His words make me feel warm inside.

'We're leaving for the airport soon, so you've just caught us.'

'Yes, I'm taking you. My car is outside.' He points to the front door with his hat so sweetly, I hope Gigi isn't playing with his feelings.

'Can I get you a drink, Mr Ramon?'

'No, thank you. Is this your bag?'

'Yes, it's a little heavy—' I start reaching for the handle.

'I've got it. It can't be any heavier than Grace's bag when we got back from Vegas.'

I stand there in shock for the entire time it takes for Mr Ramon to load the first suitcase into his shiny black vintage Chevrolet. I decide to say nothing about Mr Ramon's little revelation as we put the rest of the bags in the car, and commit to my silence for the quiet ride to the airport, even when I catch him throwing affectionate glances Gigi's way. My resolve to say nothing is broken when he has helped us to check in and he gives Gigi a light, tender kiss on her temple to say goodbye. Embarrassed, she shoos him away and walks quickly through the first flight checkpoint. It's not until we've taken off and are settled in, champagne in hand, next to each other, that I tell her what I know.

'Gigi, you didn't mention that Mr Ramon came to Vegas too?' I ask, cheekily, wiggling my bum in my seat in anticipation.

I see her suppress a smile successfully. It's very cute.

'Ariella Hope...' she starts.

'Yes, Gigi?' I ask, leaning towards her, ready for her admission.

'Keep your little nose out of grown folks' business.' She winks at me, before reclining and shutting her eyes. She's happy. That's all I need to know.

'Yes, ma'am,' I reply, grateful for every second that I get to spend with her.

FOUR

CALEB

'You've improved,' Honey says as she casually steps past where I am lying on the floor by the pool, completely spent.

'You still destroyed him though!' Lara claps happily, before shimmying after Honey to help with her hot-water bottle.

I use all the strength I have left to get myself up, have a quick rinse under the shower, pull on some swim shorts and dive into my pool. The water feels nice. I close my eyes to enjoy the peace as I float, before my day starts. Lara, unsurprisingly, interrupts it.

'Oi! Nutter magnet!' she whispers hastily. I open one eye to see her on one knee by the pool, looking back and forth from my living room to me. 'Invite Honey to London when she comes back from the loo.'

'Invite her yourself,' I respond, lazily, shutting my open eye. I try to return to the few seconds of serenity I have left. Lara puts a stop to it by repeatedly splashing my face with pool water. I keep ignoring her. Frustrated, she grunts.

'You can ask me for one favour and I'll do it. No questions asked,' she offers quickly.

'Four,' I negotiate casually. I actually don't need anything but I'm enjoying Lara's discomfort.

'Two. That's all you're getting.'

I pretend to think about it as I feel her getting more agitated.

'Come on, Caleb.'

'Two favours, no questions asked and two thirty-minute-silence requests.' I can tell she's annoyed. 'Promise, Lara.'

'Fine. She's coming,' Lara whispers before scurrying away to a nearby sunlounger. I haul myself out of the pool and wrap myself in the white towel Lara throws at me from where she is sitting, then walk into my living room.

'Thank you for my bottle, Lara,' Honey calls, then turns to me. 'Have a good one, Caleb. See you tomorrow.'

I stop her as she starts to walk towards the door.

'Before you go, Lara and I are going back to the UK next week. I'll be gone for a couple of weeks.'

The expression that comes over her face is adorable. Honey Kohli is the toughest person I know, but right now she looks helpless. She walks past me, towards Lara.

'Lara, you're going home?' Honey sounds so devastated, I feel it.

'Yeah. I have to. I'm not sure if I have a job and I've been dodging my landlord's calls.' She shrugs sadly.

The silence between them is heartbreaking. They are obviously very fond of each other, but Lara is still in the dark about Honey, and Honey isn't ready to share.

'Honey, I was thinking,' I start as I walk between them. 'Fancy taking a break from safety, sunshine and celebrity? I'd love to introduce you to the teens, keep training, and you could come out with us and be a tourist for a bit? I'm sure Ivory Bow has some relationships with hotel managers in the city who could do us a good deal?'

She brightens immediately.

'Are you sure?' she asks, a smile making its way across her face.

'Yeah. I'll even split the accommodation cost with you.'

'What do you think?' she asks Lara cautiously.

'I think it'll be amazing. I can show you around while Caleb is pretending to work remotely, if you like?' Lara beams.

'I'm going to London,' she says to herself, then looks at me. 'I'm going to London with you!' She turns to laugh in Lara's direction.

Lara leaps up, runs towards Honey and gives her a big hug. The next thing I know, they are squealing and jumping up and down in each other's arms.

I leave them to it and head to my bedroom. My work here is done.

I'd forgotten how cold the flat can get when the temperature drops. I leave my suitcase by the front door in the living room and rush to put the boiler on. It's not only the temperature that makes the flat feel unwelcoming. It's the first time I've been back since I, with painful determination, scrubbed the flat of Ariella's presence. Unfortunately, I may have done too good a job. I couldn't reintroduce her into the flat even if I wanted to. I locked everything related to her behind her bedroom door and distributed all the keys. What was I thinking? I was such a dickhead. I need to get out of here. It doesn't feel like home, at all.

I unlock my phone to text Jack and Tim, to confirm that I'll be over for the 'welcome home' meal Em has planned for me. Before I head over, I have to deal with the admin that is associated with an empty house. I sit at the kitchen counter to sort through the post Em has stacked neatly during her weekly visits to check on the place. I reach straight for the forest-green envelope in the middle of the pile. I recognise it from when Ariella was helping Isszy to choose her wedding stationery. It is addressed to both of us. I open it carefully, to reconfirm what I already know.

Isszy and Zachary's wedding is a week-long affair, with a series of smaller social events happening almost every day before the traditional church wedding on Saturday. The first event is an 'intimate night of cocktails and casual chops' hosted by Isszy's father. Looking at this itinerary, I realise I'm not going to see Ariella unless I attend these events, so I go to the online link provided and RSVP yes to everything. I then send her a text, unsure of how she will react to my presence. I try to keep it as casual as I can.

> Just got back to London for the wedding. Flat is freezing!

I get a response back immediately.

> Welcome home! I got in a few days ago with my gigi. I'm sorry, I didn't realise you and Lara were landing today. I would have turned the heating on for you.

Of course Lara would have told her I was coming back for the wedding. I've been worrying for nothing. I take the risk and try to find out if she's coming home.

> Want me to get your key from Jasper and get your room cleaned?

> I'll be staying at home for this trip. There is so much to do!

I thought that might be the case, but it doesn't make it any less annoying.

> Okay. Let me know if I can help?

> Will do. I'm happy you're here.

That last text was all I needed to feel good.

'Caleb!' An older-looking Alfie runs into my arms as the front door to Tim's home opens.

'Big man,' I respond, matching his enthusiasm, then I catch him, lift him, toss him up and dangle him upside down. I walk from the front door into the living room gripping his feet securely.

'He's missed you, and so have we,' Em says affectionately as she approaches with her arms open wide. I let Alfie down gently and hug her back.

'I've missed him too. Thank you for keeping an eye on the place, Em.'

'Good to see you back in one piece, mate.' Tim pats my back. 'Jack's on his way. Seb! Leo!'

Tim's two older sons appear after a thunderous descent from upstairs.

'Welcome back, Caleb,' Seb says quickly, followed by Leo's 'Good to see you back.'

'Great to see you, boys.'

They both stand there looking impatient.

'Fine, go back to whatever computer game you were playing. Take Alfie with you,' Tim instructs.

'Tim!' Em protests, just as the doorbell goes.

'What? Alfie could learn a thing or two. They're minting it on YouTube. Far be it from me to stop them,' he says as he gets up to answer it.

Em tuts at her husband as he leaves. When we're alone, she asks me quietly, 'How are you?'

'I'm okay. I told her everything and she lost her shit. We're not together any more but trying to work it out.' I'll leave the details until we have more time.

Em looks suspicious. 'You told her *everything*?'

'Well—'

'As I live and breathe. If it isn't hashtag-bad-boy-Black.' Jack appears before Tim, already taking the piss. I groan as Tim and Em burst out laughing. I can't help joining in.

'I'm hot, broody and dangerous – girls better watch out,' Jack continues in a terrible Liverpudlian accent, pulling me into a rough hug.

'I'm half naked and so sweaty, I've been working out,' Em joins in from behind me in a smarmy nasal voice.

'Et tu, Em?' I give her a dirty look.

'Mate, your Instagram is a bit much.' Tim laughs.

'Bloody hell, I hate you lot. Is there going to be food at some point? I'm bloody starving.'

'Come on then,' Em says. We follow her to the dining table in the kitchen and take a seat. 'Boys! Dinner!' she calls. Seb, Leo and Alfie appear noisily, grab plates, load them up with food and disappear back up the stairs. I wait until the coast is clear.

'Where's Lou?' I ask Jack.

'We're taking a breather.'

'Yes!' I rejoice, pulling my balled-up fist to my chest. 'How likely is it that this breather will be permanent?'

'We're still trying to save it. Don't be a dick, mate. You've only been back five seconds.' Jack is clearly struggling, so I leave it – but only because I don't see any fresh bruises.

'Fair enough. I suppose she's keeping London's international heiress community safe for now. We can thank her for that.' I back off.

'Not quite as safe as the global "anything female that moves" community. Ariella deserves a humanitarian award for that one.' Tim and Jack laugh. Em gives me a private sympathetic look, but it's not needed. The mere mention of her name makes me happy. When Em encourages us to tuck in, we do just that. It feels good to be back with Jack, Em and Tim – my chosen family. I've missed them so much.

FIVE

ARIELLA

'Mason family?' A tall woman with a sharp bob under her headset, holding a tablet and dressed head to toe in black, opens our car door as we pull up to London's affectionately nick-named Walkie-Talkie building. We get out of the chauffeur-driven car Isszy's father sent for Daddy, Mommy, Gigi and me.

'Yes?' Daddy says, unsure about what's going on.

'This way please.'

The lady quickly leads us past the long queue outside, straight to some private lifts at the side of the building. As soon as one arrives, she holds the door open for us to step inside.

'Platinum VIP in Indigo lift,' she says into her headset, then she hits a button and exits the cabin.

'Have a lovely evening,' she says to us.

When we arrive and the doors open at the top floor, it is clear that this 'intimate evening' didn't refer to the guestlist. There are already hundreds of people here. The host who meets us when we step out of the lift whisks us quickly to one of the restaurants that has been reserved exclusively for family members. We can see most of the venue from the restaurant and it is very clear that the entire roof garden, thirty-five floors above

London's streets, has been hired for the event. Looking through the glass walls of the restaurant, I count fifteen beautifully constructed, rustic and colourful food stations, evenly spaced out over the floor. From here, I can see that each station is dedicated to a specific type of Nigerian, British or American dish, with a chef cooking live or assembling the final plates at each one. The two hosts assigned to each station are explaining the dishes to interested guests, as an order manager from the side of the station sends food out on waiters' trays to the rest of the guests in the space. There are also six large cocktail bars, two representing each country. The busy mixologists are speedily fulfilling drink orders for the patient waiting staff, while the flair bartenders chat with guests and keep them entertained. The live, upbeat music ties the party together, making it feel more like a carnival than a casual dinner.

'Wow. A good number of MPs are here.' Daddy points through the glass wall to a cluster of gentlemen talking in the main space.

'...and senators from Washington DC too,' Gigi says, adding her finger to the glass.

All Isszy has ever told us about her family is that her father owns his own business. We've moved on to spotting members of the House of Lords and congressional appointees we recognise, when a bubbly waitress joins us.

'Good evening, I'm Angela and I'll be looking after you tonight,' she says, beaming. 'This space will be your sanctuary for the evening and here are your menus.' She hands one to each of us. 'You can order any food or drink you would like through me or from the tablet on your table. If you'd like to explore, detailed maps of all the food and drink stations tonight are on the other side of your menus. The suya, jollof rice, chapman and palm wine cocktail stations are extremely popular. If you need me, please hit "Call" on the tablet and I will be right with you. In the meantime, can I get you anything?'

'Yes! We'll take a selection of everything from the popular stations please?' Gigi immediately requests.

'And a couple of bottles of water, please,' Mommy says, giving Gigi a pointed look.

'Dahlia!' we hear from behind us.

'Aderonke!' Mummy responds, getting up to give Isszy's mother a hug. She is a beautifully curvy, elegant woman with a big smile and a warm energy. Her dress is loose but perfectly tailored, with a bold African print. She looks bright and glorious in comparison to the solid and nude colours Mommy, Gigi and I are wearing.

'Good evening, Ma.' Isszy's mother curtseys deferentially as she greets Gigi. Her arms are outstretched with her palms open, inviting Gigi to place her palms on hers. She does. There is something so beautiful and humbling about this exchange that it makes me feel like this is less about Isszy and Zachary's marriage, and more about our families merging.

'Hugh, Olawale is somewhere down there. I will ask someone to get him for you. He has been looking forward to your arrival with some enthusiasm.'

'Oh no, there is no need,' Daddy protests. He's not a big fan of attention and I can already tell that all of this is a little too much for him.

'Please. He will be very upset if he isn't told that you have arrived.' She gives him a smile that is difficult to resist.

'Thank you for your generosity, Aderonke, I will go down there and find him.' Daddy gets up to leave the restaurant before Isszy's mother insists again.

'You must be Ariella.' She comes for me next, and envelops me in her loving arms.

'Good evening, Aunty,' I respond, as Isszy suggested I do as a sign of respect. I bend my knees into a small curtsey and bow my head slightly. Nigerians are open, warm and loving people. Formality, politeness and a deep respect for age and life experience runs through their veins. While some cultures may chase youth, according to Isszy the wisdom one acquires as one gets older is what is truly cherished in Nigerian culture.

'Good evening, my dear. Now please, Dahlia, Grandma...'

I see Gigi's face fill with shock and devastation at being called Grandma. I do everything I can to stop the laughter from erupting. Mommy isn't so successful and Gigi throws her a dirty look.

'Aderonke, we refer to her as Gigi. You are our family now, we'd be delighted if you would do the same.'

'Thank you, Dahlia. Please, if you don't mind coming with me, I would love to introduce you to my mother. She arrived last night.'

The three of us go over to meet Isszy's grandmother. She is a quiet woman who exudes an indescribable calm and knowing from where she is sitting, between other female relatives. When I see that Mommy and Gigi are enjoying themselves with Isszy's family, I excuse myself to find a quiet space, but it proves impossible. Everyone is happy, chatty and unafraid to introduce themselves. After I've had a third person ask me why I'm sitting alone and if I'm enjoying the evening, I decide that it will be better to find a different kind of quiet space.

> Hey Jas, are you here yet?

Yes, where are you?

> In the restaurant reserved for family. Where are you?

In the brasserie next door for the bride and groom's friends. It's like a nightclub here and it's PACKED. You're not going to like it.

Right now I feel a little exposed. I'd be happier hiding in a crowd.

I'll be over there shortly.

Jasper is not wrong. As I approach the entrance, the Afrobeat music gets increasingly louder. I look inside to see everyone talking excitedly, laughing, drinking, and quite a few people are dancing. I give my name to the list holder at the door, and spot Jasper waiting inside the entrance for me.

'There you are!' He gives me a hug, laces his fingers through mine and pulls me close to him. He helps to guide me through the jubilant crowd singing at the tops of their voices to the music. The atmosphere makes it impossible not to feel happy. We weave through until we reach a circle of couches around a large table with 'VIP' branded in the middle. Sophia and some of our old friends are sitting there, chatting away.

'Hello,' I say, and Jasper asks everyone to move up to create a space for me.

'Aari,' almost everyone responds cheerfully as they quickly shift up.

'What are you drinking?' Jasper asks me, grabbing the tablet.

'I'll have a clementine martini,' Sophia requests loudly.

Jasper pauses to give her a look I don't quite understand.

'Are you sure?' he asks.

'Yes,' Sophia responds defiantly.

'Okay,' Jasper agrees quietly. 'Ariella?'

'That sounds delicious, Sophia.' I smile at her. She doesn't smile back. 'Please can I have one too?'

'Okay, anybody else?' Jasper places a few more orders for our friends on the couch.

'How are you, Sophia?' I ask, trying to break the odd tension that seems to have developed between us in the last few seconds.

'Fine,' is all I get. She doesn't even look at me. Instead she stares at Jasper.

Just when I am about to try again, she speaks, keeping her eyes on Jasper.

'Ariella, where is Caleb?'

'Oh yes. He told me that you got along at the engagement party. I'm not sure if he is coming tonight. I can check?'

I pull my phone out and text Caleb to see if he is coming.

'You don't know whether or not your boyfriend is coming?' She finally looks at me.

'Fi—' Jasper starts.

'I'm not speaking with you, Jasper,' she responds coldly. Uh-oh.

'Come on, Sophia.' Franco, our childhood friend, puts his hand on her arm. 'How is Singapore, Aari?' he asks me, trying to release some tension. Sophia turns to face him.

'Why ask her when you can ask Jasper? He's been there often enough.'

'I—' Just then the drinks arrive and Jasper distributes them, safely starting with Sophia's.

'Clementine martini for you, Fi—'

'Excuse me!'

Sophia stands abruptly and pushes past me.

Jasper sighs and gets up to follow her.

'Jas, please can I?' I ask.

I've clearly caused some discomfort and I need to make it okay for Jasper. I wait for his nod before I follow Sophia through the crowd and into a private dining room that has been converted into a storage space.

'Sophia?' I call as the door shuts behind me.

'Go away!' I hear her choke as she cries.

'I'm sorry that I've upset you. Please can you tell me what's wrong?'

'What's wrong? You! You're what's wrong.'

'I'm sorry, I—'

'Why is he so scared of you?'

'Jasper? He's not scared of me.'

'He's scared of you because he's still in love with you!'

'Sophia, we grew up together and we both got confused – that's all. He loves you.'

'No, he doesn't.'

'Yes, I promise you he does.'

'He ordered me a martini!' she screams at me, before bursting into fresh tears. Oh. The realisation hits me.

'You're pregnant,' I whisper.

Sophia looks at me, frightened, like I'm scaring her. Before I know what I'm doing, my arms are around her, holding her, as she sobs loudly. This is my fault. Jasper and I may have ended things but we still orbit tightly around each other. I asked him to make amends with Caleb but I didn't think about doing the same with Sophia. When he came out for my birthday and he didn't bring her, I didn't reprimand him for leaving her home alone. I definitely wasn't thinking about Sophia when I asked him to come out to Singapore to help when things got bad. Tonight, when I was uncomfortable being by myself, I reached for him first because I knew he would come. All the while, I was hurting the person he loved.

'Jasper loves you, Sophia. He's not scared of me or in love with me. He's in love with you. However, I have been asking him for things that I maybe should have cleared with you first. I'm sorry.'

'I really don't like you. You're such a horrible person,' she cries, still in my arms.

'I'm not sure I like me right now because of how I have made you feel, but I want you to know that, regardless of what you think of me, I never meant to hurt you.'

'Well, you do. It's torture having you around.'

'How can I make things better?'

Sophia tearfully extracts herself from my embrace.

'Please leave him alone. Stop contacting him and please stay away from us,' she begs from a place of such deep despair that it hurts. I also don't have a choice.

'If that's what you need, I will.'

'That's what I need,' she confirms, forcefully.

'Consider it done.'

'Thank you,' she whispers as she tries to pull herself together.

'Can I help you clean up in the—'

'No. I'm fine.' She sniffs as she runs her fingers under her eyes. Without another word, she straightens her posture and walks out of the room. I wipe tears that fall when she leaves. I need to get out of here.

I leave the room, disappear into the dancing crowd and make my way carefully towards the brasserie door, away from Jasper and our friends. Once outside the brasserie, I do everything I can to pull myself together before I descend the stairs and navigate my way through the main party space, where everyone is having a wonderful time.

'Aari!' I hear, just before I turn left to the bank of lifts that will take me down to the building's exit. It's Caleb. The sound and safety of his voice alone cuts through all the strength I've managed to gather in order to hold myself together.

'This party is insane! So much for intimate! Ivory Bow is going to make a killing by the time I'm done tonight. I've just been doing ogogoro shots with the Nigerian Minister of... Mason, what's wrong?'

I finally fall apart. Caleb steps forward to hold me close and shield me from anyone around us who might see.

'Come on,' he says softly as he walks us to the lifts.

I bury my face in his jacket as he hands both our cloakroom tickets to the attendant.

'Allow me to escort you to the Platinum VIP lifts, sir,' one of the attendants offers.

'Platinum VIP? Very snazzy. I had to fight like a wild

animal to get into the sardine tin that brought us up here an hour ago,' Caleb whispers as we follow the attendant, making me smile and reminding me of how much I love him.

We step into the lift and descend in silence. All he does is hold me, and I inhale his familiar, safe smell. My phone dings. I look at the notification. It's a text from Jasper asking where I am. When I turn my phone off, Caleb doesn't say anything, he just holds me tighter.

'What would you like to do?' he asks when we finally make it outside.

'I want to go home.'

'Ours or your parents'?'

'My parents', please.'

We climb into the first black cab we see. The driver groans when we tell him that he is going to Surrey.

'I'll text Dahlia to let her know that I'm taking you home and that she has nothing to worry about.'

I nod and lean against him.

'Aari, we're here.' Caleb gently strokes my cheek awake.

'Thank you,' I croak, and get ready to step out of the cab as he pays.

I let us in and we head straight for the kitchen.

'If you get into the shower, I'll make you a cup of tea and bring it up,' he says quietly, before gently holding the back of my neck to kiss my forehead.

I do just that. I go up to my bedroom, strip, enter the shower and release all the emotions I am feeling. I stand patiently as I let the water wash the edges of my exchange with Sophia away. When I emerge, Caleb is sitting on my bed, the tea he's made me is on my bedside table. He diverts his gaze as I pull on a long shirt and put my hair up, then sit next to him and sip my tea.

'Do you want to talk about what happened?' he asks quietly.

'Sophia is pregnant. She asked me to stay away from her and Jasper. She said I was a horrible person and it was torture for her to have me around.' I feel myself welling up.

'I'm sorry, Aari.'

'No, she's right.'

Caleb doesn't argue. He just sighs, and eventually admits, 'She is, to a certain extent. You're definitely not a horrible person, but to someone that doesn't understand your history it could look like you and Jasper are in love. You're so inextricably linked, it's difficult to explain it any other way.'

'You don't think that, do you?'

'No, I don't. He's your best friend and I know that moving through life without him would devastate you.'

'That's what I'm going to have to do. I don't want his relationship with Sophia to fail. I want him to have a sublimely happy life with her.'

'All she needs is some time. She's only going through what I had to. It's a nightmare to navigate but it will all work out in the end. When she gets it, she'll see that she has nothing to worry about.' Caleb leans in to kiss my temple lightly.

'When did you get it?'

'It took a while, but I think it was when I realised that Jasper actually wasn't terrible in bed. It was just that both of you *really* didn't want to sleep with each other.'

'How did you know that?'

'For you it was obvious.' He raises an eyebrow with a smirk and it makes me giggle. 'For him though, when we met up in the name of civility after you left for Singapore he asked me when we first slept together. He didn't want to know anything else apart from when. He didn't care who initiated it, if you'd enjoyed it, or if I'd been attempting to seduce you. He just wanted to know when he lost you because he genuinely thought he had... plus the disgusting things he does to Sophia in bed on a regular basis should put him on at least a couple of watch lists.'

'Ugh, yuck, Caleb!' I smack his arm.

Caleb erupts with laughter and I join in.

'I'm messing with you, I have no idea what he gets up to with Sophia, but your reaction to that proves my point. You love and look out for each other. You're just not meant to be lovers.'

'I'm going to miss him.'

'Give it time. You have Lara to fill in. Speaking of which, are you going to that Zombie Apocalypse escape night she's planning for after the wedding?'

'Yeah. She wouldn't take no for an answer. It'll be a nice opportunity to see Honey while she's out here, though.'

'It'll be a nice opportunity for me to see Honey too. We were supposed to be training every day but Lara told her I'd given her the time off. Thankfully she remembered that I asked her to join on Wednesdays for the boys' training. Your best friend is a liability,' he complains.

I can't help smiling. I do love Lara, even if she is planning what will possibly be the most dysfunctional double date, by making four of us fight fake zombies during a dramatised apocalypse.

'Anyway, I'd better head out.' Caleb stands.

I don't want him to go. 'Please will you stay with me?'

I climb into my bed and move over to leave as much space as I can for him. Caleb stops to look at me. He's thinking about it. He exhales deeply, before taking off his jacket, tie, belt and shoes. He keeps everything else on but undoes the top button of his shirt, exposing the white T-shirt beneath.

'Okay, but only because you need a friend tonight. Things between us are still a little problematic, Aari,' he says, sliding in next to me.

'I know. Thank you, Caleb,' I say, then kiss him lightly on the cheek. He holds me as I put my head on his shoulder, my hand on his heart, and fall fast asleep.

SIX

CALEB

When I open my eyes, I'm reminded of just how peaceful long dark winter mornings are under the covers with Ariella. There's no sun chasing us out of bed and it feels even cosier knowing the cold that awaits the second you leave the comfort of her body under the duvet. There is something almost sacred about waking up in the bed Ariella grew up sleeping in, with her body wrapped around mine. I really don't want to get out of bed when I look at her face as she sleeps peacefully.

With intense regret, I plant a long, soft kiss on her head, then carefully untangle myself while trying not to wake her. I look at the time and it's almost seven. I quickly check my emails to see if I need to respond to anything urgent, because I was supposed to have started my day at four in the morning. Thankfully there is nothing pressing I need to attend to, but it's time I disappeared. I'm meeting Jasper just before lunch and training the boys with Honey later, but the main reason I need to leave is Hugh Mason. The last thing I want is for Ariella's father to find out that I spent the night. The house is quiet, so I might be able to sneak out before everyone gets up. I pick up my shoes and make my way down the stairs slowly to nothing but silence. Yes. The front door. I've made it.

'If you're going to stay over, you could at least have the decency to thank us for our hospitality, Caleb.'

Fuck. Hugh Mason. He may not be actively hostile towards me any more, but he isn't exactly friendly either. Thankfully, Hugh and Dahlia aren't aware of what's going on between Ariella and me. When I offered to come clean to them about how much I'd hurt her, she insisted that we keep our issues between us while we worked it out, which relieved me no end. She also made Jasper promise not to say anything. I turn round to see him sitting at the dining table with his nose in the paper.

'Good mor—'

'Hugh, don't be so antagonistic. Just because Jasper never stayed over doesn't mean Caleb can't. Besides, Isszy was here all the time.' I see Dahlia's radiant, smiling face pop into view from the other side of the kitchen door frame. 'Come. Join us for breakfast,' she says, beckoning, before disappearing again. I see Hugh Mason's effort to keep his face neutral and decide that I've missed Dahlia too much to decline.

'Wait,' a tiny caramel-skinned older lady with wavy grey hair shouts at me from beside him as I approach. Her mouth is turned down at the edges as she gives me a scathing look. She must be Ariella's gigi – I've heard so much about her. 'Are you the American whose brother called her a gold-digging house Negro?'

'What?!' Hugh Mason, Dahlia and I ask, shocked, at the same time.

'Clearly not. Forget I said anything. I promised I'd keep my mouth shut.'

'Momma, how was that keeping your mouth shut? Tell us, now.'

'No I won't. And don't ask her because you'll get me into trouble. She'll tell you when she's ready.'

'I'm going to ask her,' Dahlia says defiantly.

'Don't you dare, or I'll tell everyone about that time we caught you in the barn with that boy from church.' Gigi smiles.

'Go ahead. I'm more than happy to share what happened in Vegas on your last church trip. Especially with Mr Ramon. I follow Ms Maribelle on Instagram, you know.'

'Dee Dee!' Gigi threatens. 'Stop your nonsense. You will, under no circumstances, tell Ariella anything.'

'It was Dominic's brother…' I seethe, putting the pieces together as I feel the fury rise.

Ariella's father puts his paper down and rises, his knuckles pressing hard against the tabletop.

'The "Dominic" from her birthday?!' he asks. I mentally prepare to fall in line with whatever vengeance Hugh Mason is planning.

'The same,' I confirm angrily.

'Caleb, Hugh. Behave. She said it was his brother, not him,' Dahlia interrupts.

'It just goes to show, Dahlia—' Hugh starts, but doesn't get to finish.

'Goes to show what? Your family called me much worse in the beginning and you told us about your family's hobbies, Caleb,' Dahlia says casually, and then takes a tray of warm croissants out of the oven. Damn. I love how understanding Dahlia is, but this is the one time I need her not to be fair.

'What did your family say to my child, Hugh?' Gigi asks.

I see Hugh Mason immediately shrink back before he sits down. I already know he's not going to answer the question, so I deflect.

'Gigi, I'm Caleb. I've heard so much about you. Is it all right if I give you a hug?'

I get an accepting smile and a single nod, so I walk round the table, bend to her height and give her a quick hug. I give

Dahlia hers next, then help her move the warm croissants to the centre of the table.

'I'm really grateful for the breakfast invitation, but sadly I can't stay. I'll nick a croissant though. It's a full day today and I'm already three hours behind,' I explain.

'Thank you for the text last night, Caleb. Did something happen?' Dahlia asks as she hands me a platter of sliced fruit to take to the table.

'Sophia asked Ariella to stay away from Jasper and not contact him again. Ariella promised that she would.'

Hugh Mason's forehead creases in frustration at the news. 'That seems rather unfair,' he grumbles.

'Perhaps, but Sophia is pregnant and it seems that Jasper chose to honour her request for an alcoholic drink rather than tell Ariella.'

'Oh,' Dahlia and Hugh acknowledge at the same time.

'I suspect she has been asking him to tell her for a while,' I add.

'How is she?' Hugh asks.

'Fine. I wasn't there when it happened. I caught her as she was leaving. She was crushed, so I brought her home.'

'Maybe it's for the best. I didn't like the way they followed each other around,' Gigi says.

'It can't be easy for Sophia. Ariella casts a long shadow with Jasper,' Dahlia adds.

'But to ask her to stay away from him? It's a bit extreme.' Hugh isn't taking the news well.

'They are going to start a family, Daddy. Her needs come first,' Ariella says quietly as she enters the kitchen. She goes straight to Hugh, who is already standing with his arms open. She disappears into his hug and stays there.

'Ariella...' Dahlia starts and I watch Gigi scowl at her daughter. 'Are you okay?'

She nods against her father's chest. 'It's my fault. I should have done more to embrace her. There was just so much going on. When Jas told me that she wanted to start a family... I just thought I'd have more time, I suppose,' she says, resigned.

'I'd better head out,' I announce, making my way round the dining table back into the hallway.

'Thank you for staying, Caleb.' Ariella extracts herself from her father to give me a quick hug.

'Chin up. Everything is going to be okay.' I smile as I lift her chin with my index finger to comfort her. After I move away, I say a quick goodbye to everyone and let myself out.

'Not bad, Goldsmith,' I say, impressed, as I am escorted into Jasper's massive office by one of the receptionists. It is located on the twentieth floor in one of Canary Wharf's huge glass buildings.

'Thanks.' He rises to his feet and adjusts his sharp suit, then extends his hand. I take it.

'Who did you have to kill to land this?' I look out of his floor-to-ceiling window to watch a descending plane aim for City Airport.

'My boss.' We both laugh. 'Coffee?' he offers, pointing to the chair opposite his desk.

'Nah, mate. Thanks, by the way. For all of this.'

'No need for thanks. I offered to help. Besides, you're going to need to resolve your finances quickly now that Melissa is out of the picture and we know her financial dealings are less than pristine.'

'Yeah. I'm happy to give the flat back, to be honest.'

'You don't need to do that. Besides, you can't. It's yours. With the financial power of attorney you granted me, I went digging and it all seems above board.'

'That's a relief.'

'I do suggest we cut all ties though, sell it now and get all your money out of Singapore. You could, of course, decide to keep it, because the Ivory Bow rent is great passive income.'

'I don't want any of it.'

'For goodness' sake, use this to get off your bicycle and get into a car, Caleb.' Jasper's rather hackneyed financial analogy can't help but make me smile.

'How do you propose I do that?'

'Do you still want to start your Thai boxing business?'

'Eventually. Right now, it's a burden more than anything else. I'm paying a trainer to chase a bunch of young boys around their council estate to get them to their free class, in addition to paying for the actual class itself. I'm due to run a session that will include a bollocking tonight.'

'I took the liberty of looking up the boxing gym you use.'

'And?'

'The owner has two. The one in the north-west, near you, and another in the south-west. His business is not in great financial shape. If you decide to sell the Singapore flat, and with the rent you've already accrued, you could make the owner a reasonable offer and buy the business and both buildings.'

'What am I going to do with two gyms in London while I'm living in Singapore?'

'Rent it? Keep the owner on a salary and get him to run it? I can look after the finances for you. It won't take very long. You need a plan for when you leave Singapore, and this could be it.'

'If the owner that's here, doing the graft, can't make a success of it, what makes you think I stand a chance from Singapore?'

'You've got me.' Jasper shrugs. 'Let's start a conversation and see where it gets us. You don't want cash lying around. Let's put it into something that aligns with your goals.'

'I'll give him a call. See if he's willing to talk.'

'It's better if I make the approach. I'll also arrange for us to see both gyms before you head back to Singapore.'

'What's in it for you, Goldsmith? You better not be secretly plotting to take the deal over and turn it into flats with your property bros.'

Jaspers laughs loudly. 'No, I promised to help you get rid of your Melissa problem. This is the last thing tying you to her. Once this is done, that's it.'

'Thanks, mate.'

'No problem. Besides, the day might come when you may beg me to reach out to my "property bros" to turn it into flats. But we're not there yet.'

'Now that's done, where's a good pub around here? Fancy some lunch? I'm buying.'

'I could have lunch,' he says, grabbing his phone and leading the way to his office door.

We exit his building and cross a couple of squares and bridges to find a quiet pub away from the hustle and bustle. Jasper secures us a table as I grab us some drinks from the traditional wooden bar.

'I hear congratulations are in order, Daddy Goldsmith.' I put Jasper's pint down in front of him.

'That sounded a little mistressy but yeah, thanks,' he says solemnly.

'You don't sound like you want to be congratulated.'

'I do, but things with Sophia are moving extremely quickly and it's posing... well, a unique set of challenges.'

'What do you mean?'

'We're getting married the week after Zachary and Isszy.'

Wow. Extremely quickly sounds about right, but I keep my opinions to myself. 'That's great news, mate!' I pat him on the back.

'We're keeping it tiny and quiet, surrounded by the people we love.'

'Sounds brilliant. What's wrong with that?'

'Sophia doesn't want Ariella there. Dahlia and Hugh are

holding the date, but they have no idea what's going on. I can't invite them and exclude Ariella, even if I want to. But I don't. She's my best friend. I want her there.'

'Jasper, you're about to marry Sophia. She's automatically your best friend now. To her, Ariella is your ever-present ex-girlfriend who won't go away. Besides, after last night, if you invite Ariella she'll most likely decline anyway.'

'She's not going to decline because Sophia is pregnant. She'd never do that.'

'Hold on, what do you think happened last night?'

'Ariella guessed Sophia was pregnant right before she got a call and had to leave.'

Normally, I'd keep my mouth shut, but I've grown to like Jasper and he needs all the help he can get because evidently this is an area that he isn't very good at.

'Caleb! What happened last night?' Jasper insists.

'Sophia told Ariella to stay away from both of you and not to contact you again. Ariella promised she would.'

Jasper's phone is in his hand, he has hit a name and is holding it to his ear before I can blink.

'Who are you calling?'

'Ariella.'

'Stop,' I say. I grab the phone from him and cut the call off.

'Caleb, give that back right now!'

'No. You're about to be a father. You've asked Sophia to be your wife. You're trying to mend the wrong relationship right now. You need to call your soon-to-be wife.'

'But—'

'Ariella is always going to be there. Your bond will survive whatever nuclear blast life hits it with. It always will. It used to piss me off, but now I get it. However, you and Sophia, who happens to be carrying your child right now, may not survive this. That's where your energy needs to go. You have a terrible habit of focusing on having what you want, Jasper, rather than wanting what you have. That's what landed you here in the first place. Maybe it's time you change that. It's caused you enough problems, mate.'

I slowly place his phone back on the table in front of him and nod to it. 'You know what to do.'

I wait quietly as he sighs heavily, looks at his phone, then unlocks it. The screen shows that he is calling 'Fi' before he slowly picks it up, puts it to his ear and stands.

'Fi, I'm sorry...' is all I hear as he walks away. I never imagined the day that I would feel sorry for Jasper would come. He has had almost everything he wants handed to him on a plate of privilege and power, but he has still managed to build a cage around himself that he struggles to see – let alone escape from.

I suppose we all have our battles to fight.

SEVEN

ARIELLA

I relish the nostalgia of walking into Ivory Bow's office building. I stop at the café on the ground floor for what used to be my daily hibiscus tea, before making my way to the bank of elevators to take me to Ivory Bow's floor. As I step into the company's UK space, everything feels different. It takes me a few seconds to realise what it is. The normally busy, loud office, filled with laughter and people hanging around each other's desks being distracting, is quiet. All I can see are the staff at their desks, with their eyes ahead, focused on their computer screens, immersed in work.

'Ariella,' Christopher says, beaming, as he walks towards me. As soon as he breaks the silence with my name, it feels like all the people on the floor lift their heads from their computers and look in my direction at the same time. It makes me shrink back.

'You haven't changed,' he says with a laugh as he leads me to one of the glass meeting rooms. Dominic is already in there waiting. He stands when Christopher opens the door.

'Aari.' He gives me a big smile as he pulls the chair opposite him out for me.

'Dom.' I can't help returning it.

'Hi,' he says quietly, planting a light kiss on my temple. It feels unnecessarily intimate, especially in front of Christopher.

'Hi,' I return, embarrassed.

Christopher takes a seat and quietly observes Dominic and me with a curious look on his face. When we are both finally sitting at the boardroom table, he pauses.

'Is there anything either of you would like to share about your relationship that we might need to consider before having discussions about the future of Ivory Bow?' he asks, looking very uncomfortable to be doing so.

'Nothing of relevance,' Dominic says with a cheeky grin and a brow twitch that suggests there might be plenty of relevance.

I'm mortified and shake my head quickly, which only makes Dominic chuckle.

'Okay. As you know, Harrison is out and, consequently, sales have slowed. Clients aren't dropping us yet but project enquiries coming through have dipped considerably. We've removed all the questionable clients and, while the company will be fine, it isn't the roaring success it once was. We will be able to keep the team on their salaries, but bonuses will be a fraction of what they used to be and I suspect we will start losing people. Clearly, the vibrant energy of the office has disappeared.'

'Sounds like you need a sales lead,' Dominic offers.

'I do.'

'Can you promote from within?'

'I could, but I need a specific personality type and no one currently fits the bill. Besides, Harrison had total autonomy in that area, so I'm concerned about promoting someone only for them to jump ship a few weeks later because of their loyalty to him.'

'Are there any challenges you anticipate if you hire someone from the outside?'

'Ivory Bow works in a very specific way. That could be the solution to our problem, but I'd need someone loyal with a proven track record, who knows the company inside out, to show them the way the sales side of the business works.'

'You want Caleb,' I conclude, when I realise where Christopher is going.

'I need Caleb,' Christopher confirms.

'Caleb? Didn't he significantly contribute to this current situation?' Dominic asks.

'Maybe, but even without the questionable clients he was still, by far, the most successful member of the sales team. I don't see him replacing Harrison – I'd be jumping over two good people to do that – but he'd be useful when it comes to guiding the person we do bring in to replace Harrison.'

I'm relieved. If Caleb was asked to replace Harrison, he'd have to move back to the UK. Things may not be as they should between us, but I'd be destroyed if he had to leave Singapore.

'What is Caleb currently focusing on in Singapore? Do you think he could take three months out to help Chris?' Dominic asks me.

'He's currently recruiting for the Singapore sales team, so he'll need to be around, but I'm sure he'd like to support Christopher in order to make amends for any problems he has caused. You'd have to ask him though.'

'If you're happy with that, Dominic, I'll arrange for him to come in for a chat,' Christopher confirms.

'It's still Aari's call until the new CEO starts.' Dominic shrugs. 'I'm just the money guy.'

'I'm going to need a little more than a money guy for a thirty-three-per cent stake in the business,' Christopher stresses. 'I've lost my sounding board, I don't have a finance department because they all had to go and Ivory Bow has lost its frontman. Cash isn't the entire solution. You've built and acquired businesses; I need your experience and expertise to weather this.'

'You now own a third of Ivory Bow?' I ask Dominic, confused.

'Sort of.' Dominic looks like he has just been caught doing something extremely naughty. He clears his throat. That bit of news was obviously meant to stay a secret. 'So, what does the hiring timeline look like?' he says, changing the subject.

'I've started on a job description; the team has been helpful with that. Once we've had a chat with Caleb and he's had a look through, we'll go live with it. I'll set a week aside for the first interviews. I'll need him here then. Once they go through the interview process and we've selected someone, I'll need Caleb for another week to help with their induction.'

'Aari?' Dom asks.

'That isn't a huge ask at all. I'm sure he'll be happy to help.'

'Great,' Dominic says as he stands. 'I have to be in White-hall in thirty minutes. Is there anything that we can't discuss on the golf course tomorrow?' he asks Christopher.

'No, see you there.' He stands to shake Dominic's hand.

'Okay. And see you at dinner tonight.' I nod. Dominic walks over and strokes my shoulder affectionately. I let him, but make a note to set some boundaries with him at dinner.

Christopher waits for Dominic to leave before he turns to me. He looks very worried.

'Ariella, Dominic may have started off as a client and become a friend, but he now owns Ivory Bow Asia in its entirety and is largely responsible for funding Harrison's buy-out. I've never had anyone hand so much money over so easily. I'm not sure what's going on, but be careful.'

'Nothing is going on, Christopher. We're just friends.'

'I've known you for two and a half years longer than he has and we're still at "Christopher" and "Ariella". Dominic comes across as someone who is used to getting what he wants. That's usually fine if the person at the other end of his demands wants the same things too. If they don't, I suspect that he will make it almost impossible to say no. In your case, it will be especially difficult now that he is your boss. Your relationship is no longer a level playing field, Ariella. Friend or not, the power balance has shifted. He's now in charge.'

Dominic is already sitting in a private corner booth right at the back of the restaurant when I arrive.

'Hey.' He gets up when he sees me, and only takes his seat again when I have taken mine. 'I don't come to London often enough. I've forgotten how much I love the city. It's so walkable.' He's light and upbeat, like he always is. That's something I've always admired about Dominic. His energy always has a sparkling playfulness to it. It's not something that comes easily to me, so I welcome it. Usually.

'Welcome to my home. Sounds like you've been busy.' I may be glad to see him, but I'm not letting him off the hook.

'I have, but we can talk about that later. I picked this restaurant because I know it's one of your favourites, so I'm going to need some menu guidance.' He shakes the menu at me and opens it in front of him.

'Can we talk about it now?'

'I knew you weren't going to let me get away with that,' he says with a laugh, shutting the menu and putting it to the side, then interlocking his fingers in front of him. 'There isn't much to tell. Chris wanted Harrison out. He called and asked me to help. I said yes, mostly because of you. I told him I'd take fifty per cent, he said that he didn't want to hand over half of the control. So I told him to raise what he could and I'd mop up the rest when he felt he'd done all he could. That's it.'

'Dom, you can't bankroll Ivory Bow "mostly" because of me.'

'We did our due diligence. It's a solid business that was about to crumble because a few people got greedy. That's fixable. But also, yes I can. You love this job. You're incredible at it. I'm not going to stand by and watch something you love die. I knew that I could do something about it, so I did.'

'It's a lot, Dom.'

'This is my challenge, Aari. What isn't a lot? Right now, on my list of things that make you happy, Korean zombies and your job are all I've got. We've spent quite a bit of time together and, aside from those two things, I have no idea what puts a smile on your face.'

'This dinner is nice,' I offer.

'It is, but it's a cheap shot. Everyone likes to eat *something* and Lydia arranged it. Even tonight, I'm willing to bet that we'll sit here and spend a couple of unforgettable hours together, but I still won't know any more about you than I did before we sat down.'

'I'm sorry.'

'How do I get in here?' Dom asks, tapping his forehead.

'As my boss or as my friend?'

Dominic looks so hurt, I feel terrible.

'Really? Of course as your friend, Aari.'

'I don't know. Can't we just let things unfold naturally, the way they have done up to this point?'

'Here's a question. If we had twenty-four hours together and no commitments, how would you spend it?'

I understand his frustration. I like Dominic, I really do. He has been nothing but kind, supportive and sweet to me, but the energy that continues to develop between us seems to be forcing me into my shell rather than coaxing me out of it. Christopher's warning hasn't helped. The harder he tries, the more I *want* to open up to him, but I just seem incapable of doing so. I go against my natural feelings and force myself to share something meaningful.

'I might walk around whatever city we're in to discover

something new, and perhaps figure out how to cook something local that we've never tried before?'

'That's it?'

'That's it.'

'Maybe we can do that one day when we get back? We could skip to Borneo for the day.' Dominic raises an eyebrow.

'Can we just clarify—'

'It's not a date. I know. We're just hanging out as friends, right?' Dominic smirks.

'Dom—'

'I hear you loud and clear. I have my own baggage to deal with too, but I need to check. You're not holding me at a distance because of what Maximilian said, are you? Because—'

'No, of course not. I know who you are, Dom.' I instinctively reach out and cover his hands with mine. 'I'm not sure you're over Mackenzie yet – I saw the way you looked at her. And I'm still in love with Caleb.'

'But you're attracted to me.' It's not a question and there is no point denying it.

'I am, which I know makes things awkward, but I really want to work things out with him. I'm still hurt and angry with him, but I want to try.'

'I think you're making a mistake. He's with Honey, Aari, and he's kinda cheating on her with you.'

'They are genuinely just friends.'

'I'll back off. But I'll be here if you need me,' Dominic acquiesces.

'Thank you for understanding.'

'Oh, no, I don't understand at all, but if working things out with Caleb is what you feel you have to do then I won't interfere. My parents adore you, so they'll definitely give me a hard time, and Mrs Thompson will be positively heartbroken. She may have started knitting little booties for our babies with the number seven on them.' He laughs that laugh that makes me want to join in.

'I was going to ask – what did you mean when you said Mackenzie had lost the privilege to call you Six?'

'It's a weird tradition. As a "Dominic Miller" in my family, from the moment you're born you're representing all the Dominics that came before you, all the time. The only time you get to be an individual is when you're married, and only with your partner. They get the sole privilege to individualise you and call you by your actual name, which just happens to be a number.'

'So calling you by your number...'

'Was a massive overstep by Mackenzie, because it's the same as saying we still belong to each other. Which we certainly do not.'

'How does your family decide who gets called Dominic?'

'It's usually the first male child from the previous Dominic that doesn't cry when they're born.'

'That's a lot of pressure to carry, Dom. For you and the woman who merely gets the privilege to call you Six.'

'I like the way you say Six,' Dominic says, smiling, then continues, 'It is a lot, especially from a bunch of dead Dominics, but there are perks.' He laughs softly. 'Like having the ability to make your friends happy no matter how difficult they make it.'

'It's a good thing I'm one of those.' I smile at him, removing my hand from his.

'Let's hope it stays that way, because we've found your new CEO. He starts in two weeks.'

'Is there anything I can do to make things easier for him?'

'No.' Dominic snorts at a private joke. 'Samir relishes a challenge.'

'We're certainly that,' I say as I smile.

'He has his way of doing things. Expect some chaos.'

'We can handle chaos.'

'You continue to intrigue me, Ariella Mason.' He looks at me with a little smirk, then picks up the menu again and hands it to me. 'Feed me? Please?'

I take the menu and do as he asks. Dinner is easy and laughter-filled, like all the dinners we have had before. Dominic may have committed to backing off, but I know that his mere presence is going to make my reconciliation with Caleb difficult. Also, the one thing I have observed and that I admire about Dominic, working with him over the last few months, is his tenacity. He seems incapable of backing off anything. It worries me because we've had the friendship conversation before, but the last time Dominic showed up expecting me to feed him, it ended with both of us crossing a huge line.

A few weeks ago, Dominic reminded me that I'd promised to make him mac and cheese to say thank you for my birthday party, so after I moved into his community he came over with an empty belly and some champagne as a house-warming present.

'Hey!' He happily shook the two bottles of Bollinger at me as I opened the door.

'Hi. Come on in,' I said as I gladly let him in.

'I came armed with my streaming username and password – I'm determined to set your TV up so we can watch something good!'

'Brilliant! I'll put the champagne in the fridge.'

'Let's pop one right away. I know it's your favourite.'

'I have colder bottles in the fridge.' I relieved him of both bottles to put them away.

'I feel like celebrating the fact that we are finally hanging out alone in your home. I actually managed to make it over without being interrupted by Lara.' He laughed loudly, reminding me that it was the first time we'd been alone since the kiss in front of my apartment building.

He followed me to the kitchen, where I handed him a much colder bottle of Bollinger and grabbed a couple of glasses. Dom made a show of popping it loudly, then filled them.

'Cheers!' we said in unison and took our sips.

'Your home is much nicer than mine,' he quipped, walking through the kitchen. 'You'd know if you ever actually took up any one of the many invitations I've extended. Are we eating out here?' he asked, pointing at the laid dining table in the garden.

'I thought it would be nice to sit outside?'

'Hell no. We're having a movie night and you've made us American classics. Tradition dictates we eat in front of the TV. I'll move this stuff over while you finish up.'

I watched Dominic pick up the cutlery, crockery and linen, then turned back to the stove. Cooking before he turned up had been fun. It was wonderful to have a stab at Gigi's recipes tonight. Ms Pat had gone on the ingredients hunt for me, so I had to improvise when she couldn't find what I was looking for. It was exciting to come home to make sense of it all. The smoky lardon macaroni cheese was easy. I'd made it plenty of times before with Gigi but never alone. I grilled some salted chicken wings that were to be served with buffalo sauce that Ms Pat had found, and blackened some shrimp before adding it to the potato salad to make it a little more interesting. The first batch of almost everything was such a disaster that I was worried that the night's meal was destined for the bin. Thankfully, I ended up with final results that were passable. It wasn't perfect – and certainly not up to Gigi's standards – but each dish had a good amount of flavour and no one was going to die of food poisoning.

'What do you want to watch? I'm looking at a bunch of chick flicks and hoping you'll go easy on me and pick *Brides-maids*,' Dominic shouted from the living room.

I laughed to myself as I brought the platter of food in. Dom cleared the coffee table and set places for us there, with cushions on the floor for us to sit.

'I'm in the mood for something scary...'

'How do you feel about foreign-language films?'

'I love them!'

'*Train to Busan* it is!'

I grabbed the ice bucket, poured us both more champagne and set out the rest of the condiments. Dominic hit the lights.

'You want to see this one in the dark, Aari,' he suggested, then sat next to me and tapped the play button on the screen.

The next two hours flew by. My eyes were glued to the screen. The film was phenomenal, with absolutely no let-up.

'You barely touched your food!' Dominic said with a laugh. The plate beside him had a roughly piled pyramid of chicken wing bones. Most of the mac and cheese was gone, but he had had the decency to leave me with two prawns and a tiny bit of salad.

'That was amazing! Do you have any more recommendations?'

'No, THAT was amazing. Do you have any more?' Dominic pointed to the food on the table. 'You can cook for me any time. Especially if you continue not to eat so I don't have to share.'

'Thanks. What are we watching next?'

'Nothing, yet. Let's tidy and take a bathroom break? I need to flip through the movie database in my head for a minute to find you something. What's for dessert?' Dominic asked, starting to clear up.

'Chocolate brownie ice cream. Ben and Jerry's. I thought you might like a bit of home,' I explained as I followed him to the kitchen with the rest of the dishes.

'Yummy. Let's get two spoons and eat it straight from the tub. First, bathroom.'

I pointed him in the direction of the bathroom and finished

clearing up. When he returned, the dishes were in the machine and the macaroni cheese bake dish was soaking.

'So, it's not as "everything" as *Train to Busan* but *Parasite*'s fantastic and won a bunch of Oscars?' he offered.

'Let's do it.' I returned to the living room with the tub of ice cream and two spoons.

'I've never seen you this relaxed. I like it. A lot. You've kept this part of you carefully hidden, Ariella.' He moved the coffee table away and rearranged the cushions closer together so we could share the ice cream tub.

He was right. *Parasite* was no *Train to Busan* but I was still gripped by the funny, then devastatingly violent, social satire. By the time it ended, I was emotionally exhausted.

'Wow,' was all I could manage.

'I'm demanding from now on that we have more movie nights.'

'Done,' I agreed enthusiastically as I stretched through a yawn.

'I better head out, it's one thirty.'

'It's a miracle I'm still awake.' I got up with Dominic to walk him to the door.

'See you soon?' he called back as he walked out of the door.

'For sure. I had a fantastic time tonight, thank you, Dom!'

'Can we keep this girl please?' he teased.

'I'll try. See you soon.' I waved him goodbye.

It had been a great night – it was nice to have someone else to just hang out at home with. I've been missing that. Just as I put the spoons away, the doorbell went again. I saw Dominic through the peephole and opened the door.

'What did you forget?' I chuckled, rolling my eyes. Dom's lips were suddenly on mine and, before I could make sense of what was going on, I was kissing him back and pulling him inside. Dominic Miller is an intoxicating kisser and, for a moment there, I forgot everything. He slammed my front door shut before pinning me against the adjacent wall with his body.

His kiss was unrelenting, with my lips matching his every motion. I'd felt the tension between us slowly build all night, and knew exactly when his energy shifted during the second film.

'You were so different tonight,' he whispered, before re-engaging our kiss. I felt his hands travel up my body and undo my shirt's top button. Just as he started with the next button down, I gasped and clutched my shirt together. Dominic disengaged immediately to lean his forehead against mine. His eyes may have been closed, but I could feel his frustration in the silence that descended between us. A heavy sigh followed after a little while as he pulled away.

'I can't begin to tell you the hatred I have right now for Caleb Black.'

Dominic refused to look at me, so I adjusted my head so that my eyes would meet his. 'I'm sorry, I really am.'

'You need more time,' he whispered, bringing his forehead back to mine. 'Until you deal with your Caleb problem, you're going to be stuck, Aari.'

'He's not a problem, he's...'

'He's a consideration, you've said – but he's not, or shouldn't be. He's a problem. He hurts and embarrasses you. He's the reason you're here, in a country you don't want to be in, and, as much as I hate to say it, dealing with me. You're letting him hold you captive, Aari. When are you going to decide you've had enough?'

'When I've had enough. I'm still in love with him, Dom. It's complicated with Caleb.'

'I'm not sure there's a simple answer when it comes to him.' Dominic took it too far with that last statement.

I manoeuvred myself out of the space between him and the wall to open the door. Things may be messy, confusing and difficult to wade through at the moment, but I refuse to let Dominic think he can take shots at Caleb and I'll be okay with it.

'It's getting late, Dominic,' I said curtly, refusing to meet his eyes.

He groaned, walked to my door and looked at me like he felt sorry for me.

'I don't know what it is with this guy, but I'm around if you need me.'

It was the last thing he said to me until amnesia roses and an apology note arrived the next day.

Friends really shouldn't kiss friends without their permission, no matter how enchanting they may have been. I should have kept my hands and thoughts to myself last night. Dom.

I responded with a phone call and, by the time I'd hung up, we'd agreed to keep our friendship as it was.

EIGHT

CALEB

I remind myself that Ariella is happy that I am in the UK for Zachary's wedding as I check my white shirt, navy tie and petrol-blue suit and straighten my pocket square in my bedroom's mirror one last time. Eden, Ivory Bow's resident stylist, called in some favours to get the Brunello Cucinelli suit fitted at the last minute. I fix my cuffs and tuck a stray hair back into my side-sweep. I want to look good for her.

'Come on, Caleb! There will be drunk bridesmaids and a whole load of women from a country that has never heard of you, so at least someone, at some point, will want to talk to you.' Lara calls loudly from the living room.

I adjust my tie and walk out.

'Why couldn't you just go straight there, again?'

'Because I'm not invited until the party later, so I need to hang on and pretend to be your plus one.' She waves the invitation she stole from the kitchen top at me, then pops it in her bag. 'Also, Honey is on some random bus trip to Ireland for the next few days and I bought a dress and everything.'

'Speaking of Honey, that was a dirty move you pulled, telling her that I gave her two weeks off.'

'What? When she called you to check if you were sure, you said yes, so what's the problem?'

'She was so excited, I was hardly going to say no, was I?'

'Stop complaining. She came to the Wednesday class with your hoodlums, didn't she? Besides, she deserves the time off. I'll call us a cab.' Lara whips out her phone and opens up her taxi app. 'It'll be here in two minutes. Too late to cancel now. Come on.'

She grabs my hand and drags me out of the apartment. As we hit the pavement, she adjusts my tie. 'There. It's straight now.'

We hop into the taxi and make our way through London towards Kensington Palace. The car drops us off and we take a stroll through the grounds. Lara lets out a low wolf whistle as the Orangery comes into view.

'Scottish meatballs, how fucking minted are they?'

The glass building overlooking the palace looks like a clearing in the woods, surrounded by perfect rose-filled hedges. It is covered with vines and an intricate network of perfectly placed leaves. We notice that guests are walking through myste-rious white-flower-framed gaps in the hedges and disappearing, so we follow.

Lara and I round the corner to discover that the walkway has been created with flower-covered arches, that lead to a softly lit white room filled with roses. It smells like berries, citrus and woodland. As we walk in, two ladies in wispy green dresses hand us each an order of service and float their hands towards the seats.

'It's so stunning, I'm not sure I'd want to fart in here,' Lara whispers.

The laughter that escapes from me is sharp and loud, prompting everyone listening to the elegant cellist to look round. Zachary laughs when he spots us, and gives us a little wave; while Jasper quickly approaches and places us on the same row as Sophia.

'Lara,' he says curtly.

'Jasper,' Lara responds, matching his frostiness. There is clearly no love lost between those two.

'What's up with you two?' I whisper to Lara.

'Personality clash. Nothing to worry about. He thinks I'm dangerous and I think he's a personality-less do-gooder.'

'He's all right, you know.'

'Oh God, not you too. Is there anyone's arse you're not kissing at the moment?'

'Behave. Anyway, he's with Sophia now,' I say, pointing to her.

'What? Barbie? Hilarious – I'm pretty sure she knows exactly where she stands when it comes to Ariella. Look, she's already scowling and nothing has happened yet. It's only going to get worse when she gets the whole maid of honour and best man implied romance.'

I look down the row. Sophia is holding her hands in her lap so tightly that the whites of her knuckles are spreading.

'We should sit next to her,' I suggest, feeling sorry for her.

'Why? No. I want to be at the end.' Lara pouts.

'Stop whining. You're less likely to get kicked out in the middle of the row.'

'Oh! When you put it like that...'

Lara and I get up and scoot down.

'Hey, Sophia. Remember me – Caleb?'

Relief washes over her face. 'Hi! Of course! Caleb!' she says chirpily.

'Sophia, this is Lara, Ariella's best friend.'

'Hi.' She smiles cautiously at Lara. 'How are things in Singapore?'

'Great. Busy.'

'It must be wonderful for you and Aari, moving somewhere and starting a new life away from everyone and everything.' She looks wistful.

'Well, Ariella and I aren't really together any more.' It's hard to say out loud but, truthfully, I'm soothed by the night we spent together recently. I know, deep down, that we've not quite truly finished with each other yet.

'That's a shame, you seemed perfect for each other.'

'Yeah. I think so too.'

'Whatever, Caleb,' Lara says. 'What he's not telling you is that Ariella dumped him because he failed to recognise and disclose that his psycho ex-"frenemy-with-dodgy-benefits" needed a sanatorium and a straitjacket.'

Sophia tries to contain her laughter.

'Thanks, Lara,' I sigh.

'They'll get back together eventually, but things are especially tense at the moment because there is a hot, loaded guy circling.'

Sophia's face fills with fear. I act quickly.

'Dominic Miller. He's very American,' I add and she relaxes.

'American or not, he's hot, has loads of dosh, treats her like a queen and takes her and her friends on yachts to expensive islands for her birthday,' Lara adds.

'I'd like to cash in my first thirty minutes of silence now please.'

Lara opens her mouth and I hold my finger up.

'Nope. You promised,' I remind her.

Lara folds her arms with a face like thunder and stares ahead. Peace. At last. I lean towards Sophia.

'I heard about the baby. Congratulations. He's going to be a fantastic father.'

I nod at Jasper as he steps up to stand beside Zachary.

'He is.' The absolute devotion that Sophia has on her face

when she looks at Jasper and strokes her tummy makes me hope that Jasper is making it up to her.

The bridal march starts to play and we stand with the rest of the congregation. It's only then that I notice the space has filled up with guests.

Isszy walks in looking like a beautiful woodland goddess in white, and is escorted by her father in richly coloured green and gold African robes that make him look like royalty; but Ariella is the one that takes my breath away. She's wearing a simple, long, soft, green sleeveless dress as she walks behind Isszy and her father, straightening Isszy's train and ensuring that she keeps up.

The whole ceremony has a beautiful serenity to it, and with every smile and laugh that escapes from Ariella I'm pulled in deeper. She's happy. For the first time, I realise, in a very long time, Ariella is happy.

'Thirty minutes are up. You have one silence left. Sophia is preggers?' Lara whispers mid ceremony.

Without hesitation, I reward Lara's commitment to her promise and whisper back, 'Yes. And there's a wedding next week. Aari isn't invited.'

Lara's eyes widen and her mouth opens in shock. 'Shut the front door!'

A lady behind us shushes us.

We stay silent, but when Zachary and Isszy are pronounced man and wife, the whole venue erupts to the point that the pastor and registrar have to instruct Zachary to kiss his bride during a standing ovation. I see Ariella do a couple of cute little hops between the standing congregation as she laughs and claps for her brother and his new wife. Even Lara is beaming.

'I want her back, Lara. I need your help.'

'Here's my help. Don't tell me. Tell her. And get out of your own way, Caleb.'

We follow the couple out into a private garden within the

palace grounds where champagne, canapés and photographers are waiting.

The atmosphere is vibrant and colourful, with guests wearing an equal mix of Western and Nigerian clothing. Everyone is talking, introducing themselves, making fast friends and finding out about each other. I join in, meeting new people and catching up with some of the guests I recognise from the engagement party. When I suddenly spot Dahlia, I go straight to her.

'Congratulations, Dahlia. You look absolutely breathtaking.'

'Caleb!' She pulls me into a hug so warm only a mother could give it. 'I must say you look very handsome.' She puts me at arm's length to look at me from head to toe. Before I can respond, Ariella's gigi appears from behind her daughter.

'Come here, young man, and keep an old widow company. If you call me "Grandma" like everyone else, you're toast.'

'You had a plus one. You should have brought Mr Ramon. I'm sure he's hurt.' Dahlia looks tickled.

'Dee Dee, for the last time, Mr Ramon just helps around the house.' Gigi laughs and winks at me in front of her daughter. 'Dee Dee is very sensitive – she loved her father very much, but light bulbs don't change themselves.'

I raise my palm and happily offer an invitation. She places her hand in mine and starts leading me away.

I mouth, 'I LOVE HER' to Dahlia and point at Gigi.

Dahlia laughs, shoos me away and walks into the crowd. I spend the rest of the wedding reception by Gigi's side trading stories. I give her a sanitised version of my past and present and she reciprocates by telling me about her life, the challenges growing up in the South, a stubborn and flighty Dahlia, her own initial reservations about Dahlia and Hugh's relationship and her worry for the quiet and shy Ariella. By the time I sit down to dinner with Lara, I feel the need to spend even more time with Gigi.

· · ·

The Orangery has been converted into a dining space with lowlights and candelabra. I end up next to Sophia on a table of nine because Lara has created a problem for the catering staff and they've had to make an extra spot for her. We sit with friends of both Ariella and Jasper and are accepted quickly into the fold. The meal is sumptuous – until Lara finishes her dessert and steals mine. The speeches are brilliant. Isszy's father gives the best one, reducing my table to tears. Jasper's is a moving tribute to his brother and Zachary's is drily hilarious. Isszy participates by throwing a bread roll at his head – which he successfully ducks – because he seems keen for us to know that her right little toe is so tiny, it looks like just a nail that he lovingly calls 'the claw'. Isszy definitely has her hands full.

When the first and parent dances are over and the party starts, everyone rushes onto the dance floor. I excuse myself to dance with Gigi, only to see that she is already dancing with an older, distinguished-looking gentleman from Isszy's family. He is very obviously flirting and she is giving him a run for his money. I'm enjoying their dance when I spot Dahlia leaving the dance floor and practically run over.

'Nope. Not so fast, "Dee Dee",' I tease, grabbing her hand.

'Call me that again and I'll have Hugh break both your knees,' she joyfully threatens, then follows me.

'Understood.'

Dahlia has always been a great dance partner and doesn't disappoint. She matches me step for step, bump for bump.

'What is up with the women in your family?' I ask above the girl group singing. 'You're all so...'

'Lovely?' She chuckles.

'Naughty.'

Dahlia lets her head fall back as she laughs. Before she speaks, Hugh Mason interrupts us.

'Dahlia?' He reaches out his hand.

She smiles apologetically at me, then takes his. 'That was a lovely dance, thank you, Caleb.'

I look around to find Ariella and spot her at a table having a deep conversation with someone from Isszy's family. He is dressed immaculately and is apparently being very charming because Ariella is laughing and having too good a time. I approach them, Hugh Mason style, with my palm outstretched.

'I'm sorry to interrupt,' I say to both of them, not sorry at all, then turn to her. 'Aari?' I ask.

She smiles apologetically with a 'Lovely to meet you, Babatunde,' before she takes my hand. It makes my heart soar. I give her a soft kiss on the cheek as she stands, and I walk her to the dance floor.

'Hi,' I say quietly when we come to a stop.

'Hi,' she responds, smiling that slow shy smile of hers. Bloody hell, she's beautiful.

I pull her tightly into me by the hand, hold her close and let her head rest against my chest, and we start to sway to the music. Everything else disappears as I watch Ariella close her eyes. I do the same – after I bend my head to kiss her neck. She pulls me closer. I have no idea how long we are like that, holding on to each other, swaying to the music, but we are soon interrupted by Lara poking my shoulder.

'We've been watching you two sway out of sync to the last four songs. It's not your wedding and we're bored. Do something else or get off the dance floor.'

I look up and see that a few people are watching us, including Hugh Mason, wearing a neutral expression as he listens to Jasper chatting away.

'Can I find you later?' I ask.

'I'm sorry, maid of honour duties, but maybe we can have lunch this week?' she offers and I nod.

'I think about you all the time,' I whisper in her ear before I release her.

'Me too.' She cups my face and plants a small kiss on my cheek, then walks away.

'She's in loooow-oh-oh-OVE! With a monster!' Lara sings along loudly as she shimmies against me to the song the DJ is playing. Ugh. She knows how to kill a mood. Before she can do anything more ridiculous, I grab her by the hand and waist, then spin her round twice and bring her to a stop. She gasps.

'Caleb Black. You have skills. More!' she demands, and we dance the night away.

When I walk into Ivory Bow the following Monday, it's hard to believe it's the same company. Everyone is silent. They all look like they are slowly being killed by administration. It's so bad, I even wonder where that creep Piers is.

'What happened, Chris?' I ask as I see him approaching.

'Hello, Caleb. In here.' He guides me to one of our meeting rooms, then tells me everything that has happened since Melissa-gate. Harrison was a big personality, but I did not expect such severe cultural devastation. I immediately commit mentally to helping Christopher revive Ivory Bow as much as I can. It's not until he fills me in on the new financial structure that one of my nightmares is realised.

'Are you really saying Dominic Miller will own a third of Ivory Bow?' I try to keep my voice steady.

'Caleb, Ivory Bow could not continue with me and Harrison in charge. One of us had to go because we agreed that it should not fail. He volunteered. Whatever his errors in judgement, he built this company. We needed investment to carry on and I wasn't interested in faceless venture capitalists. So I approached Dominic.'

'Ariella isn't going to be happy about this,' I state.

'She knows.'

I feel the anger rise. I'm supposed to be meeting her for lunch after this and I already know that it's not going to go well.

'He's only doing this because he's got a thing for her. You can't hand thirty-three per cent over to him!'

'They did have a chemistry that made me pause when I met them last week.'

'They were here together?'

'Yes. We had a few Ivory Bow items that needed reconciliation.'

'Like what?'

'I'm recruiting a replacement for Harrison. I'd like you to be part of the process.'

'No. I'm not leaving Singapore. Promote someone else.' There is no way I am leaving Ariella alone with Dominic Miller.

'I wasn't offering you the job, but I could use your help. Your questionable sales aside, you brought in the most revenue while you were here and you're the closest cultural fit to Harrison.'

I'm not sure if I should take that as a compliment or an insult.

'I'd like you to interview some candidates with me and, once we've hired them, I'd like time with you to be built into their induction.'

'How long are we talking about?'

'I think a week in London for when we interview and then another week once the selection has been made and the paperwork is complete?'

That doesn't sound too painful.

'As long as Ariella clears it, I don't have any problems with that.'

'Both Ariella and Dominic are happy with the plan.'

'I bet they are,' I growl.

She's at the table with a glass of water in front of her. She looks thrilled to see me when I arrive. Initially.

'Caleb, what's wrong?' she asks, reading my expression.

'I just got told that Dominic owns a third of Ivory Bow and that you knew.'

I watch her sigh heavily, but I hold my tongue. I want to hear what she has to say.

'I found out last week. I had no idea until my meeting with Christopher. It turns out that they had been talking to each other for a while.'

'You know he's doing this for you, right?'

'I know.'

'Are you going to do anything about it? And when were you going to tell me all of this?'

'When we found some time to spend together. It's been really busy with the wedding,' she explains gently.

'Ariella, he's obsessed with you. It's unhealthy.'

'He's not obsessed with me, Caleb. He's my friend.'

'That man is not your friend. Does he think he has a chance?'

'No, he doesn't. He knows that I'm still in love with you and he's happy to be just friends.'

To hear her declare it after all these months makes me feel like I can finally breathe with some ease again, but then, for the first time, Ariella looks away and doesn't meet my eyes. Fuck. I know exactly what that means.

'Aari. Are you attracted to Dominic?'

'Yes,' she whispers.

All the anger in my body leaves and is replaced with choking desolation.

'Caleb, I don't want to be with him. I want to try to work things out with us. It may take us a while but I want to try.'

I can't even look at her.

'I really didn't want to hear that you're attracted to Dominic, Ariella.'

'You asked and I want you to know the truth.'

'I wish you'd lied.'

Before I can say anything, the same kind of hurt that she had on her face, when she found out about Melissa, resurfaces.

'You have learned nothing,' she starts quietly. 'This is the exact reason why we are here. Secrets and lies. Do you realise the damage you've caused?'

'Hold on, you said you'd forgiven me.'

'And I have, but forgiving you doesn't free us of the consequences of your actions. Those don't just go away, Caleb. We're going to deal with them for a very long time and I'm prepared to do that; but to hear that you're still open to accepting dishonesty to make life easy is... disappointing.'

She starts gathering her things up.

'Where are you going?'

'I need more time, Caleb. I can't have lunch with you,' she says, her eyes filling with tears. Shit. 'I'm sorry,' she says as she walks out of the restaurant. I call the waiter over and order a double whisky, then pull my phone out of my pocket and start my text.

> Em, are you around?

Sure. Want to come over for dinner?

I look at the time. I can make it to Hampstead and have a chat for about an hour before she has to leave for the school run at three.

> Actually, are you free in forty-five minutes?

Sure. Have you had lunch?

No.

Come round. I'll put chicken nuggets and chips
in the oven for you.

I neck the whisky when it arrives, pay the bill and head
straight out.

NINE

ARIELLA

'Lara, I'm not sure I want to go into the zombie apocalypse house.'

I've missed my lunches with Lara. We haven't had the chance to chat since I came home for the wedding, so we decided to meet a little earlier to grab a bite to eat before the experience. I can't wait to catch up on her news properly and indulge in her unique brand of hostile but useful advice.

'Come on, it'll be fun. It's only an hour and a half. Honey is going back next week and I haven't spent much time with her. She's been up and down the country on bloody coach trips.'

'Why don't you just take her to dinner rather than have us all fighting pretend zombies for an hour and a half?'

'I plan to, afterwards. I already have a table for two booked at a fine dining Sri Lankan place.'

'When is she flying back?'

'She's on the same flight as Caleb while I'm stuck here trying to look for a job.' She frowns.

'How is that going?'

'It's not. I was going to start looking properly when you all leave. CrimeSpree asked me to come and work for him but I'd rather poke my eyes out. At least it's there should I get desperate though.'

'I'm not sure you can take it anyway, Lara. Our contract says you can't touch Ivory Bow clients for two years.'

'Great. I don't even have a soul-destroying backup now. Are you still okay to write me a reference?'

'It's already written. I just need to press send when I get the email addresses.'

'Thank you, babe.'

'Have you given up on finding something in Singapore?'

'Nope. Just waiting for the dust to settle at Ivory Bow. I plan to send an application to the new CEO, seeing as you destroyed my chances with your self-demotion. Who does that?'

'It was a lot of pressure. I feel like I have spent every single moment in Singapore trying to be someone else. I'm starting to worry that I won't know who I am when this is over. I just need things to be normal for a while.'

'Are they normal now?'

'Nowhere near it.'

'What's going on?'

'Dominic now owns a third of Ivory Bow and the entire Singapore franchise. I trust and respect him, but I'm worried because we're attracted to each other—'

'That lip-lock in front of your building; I've never been prouder!' Lara makes loud, childish kissing noises.

'And he is now technically my boss. I wasn't going to act on it before, but I definitely am not getting involved with my boss.'

'Caleb will be thrilled to hear that.'

'I'm not sure Caleb and I are going to work out, Lara.'

'Why?'

'He asked me if I was attracted to Dominic.'

'Please tell me you lied.'

'No, Lara! That's why everything is a mess at the moment.'

'Okay, listen, goodie-two-shoes – you have a lot going on, but hear me out.'

I'm already suspicious of what she's going to say.

'Men are disgusting creatures. They just are. No shade. They want to screw everything all the time. That is one of the many reasons why for me they are just – ew. If every man was completely honest with their thoughts all the time, it would be the end of humanity as we know it. I love you, Aari, but you're dealing with this all wrong. I get that you're pissed off with him and hurt, but telling the man you want to work things out with that you're attracted to another man is kind of mean.'

'I just want to be honest.'

'Okay, but did he *need* to know that? Being caught snogging Dominic may have been unfortunate and, while you know I'm firmly in your corner, that would have been excruciating for him to watch. All you've done by answering that question is confirm to him that you liked it. Stop it. It's cruel.'

Lara is right and I feel guilty and ashamed. I want to go to Caleb to make things right as soon as he arrives tonight.

'And no, you're not going to do that either,' Lara says, narrowing her eyes at me.

'Do what?'

'Go running back to him and overcompensate for mistakes you made because it makes you uncomfortable. He fucked up with Melissa, big time. You need to take the time to learn to live with what he did and truly forgive him. You also fucked up – maybe not as much, but you need to forgive yourself, apologise to him and just not do it again. You're both dealing with several shit shows all at the same time, and you need to clean it up before you move forward. Together, or not.'

I look at my best friend. She's changed.

'Lara, when did you start giving me practical, sensible advice that doesn't involve choosing violence or arson?'

She reaches over and pokes me with a chopstick.

'Ow!' I laugh. There she is. But I'm not done.

'So, are you going to admit that you more-than-like Honey with all your Sri Lankan fine dining plans or am I going to have to drag it out of you?' I ask, winking at her.

Lara gives me a dirty look. She doesn't want to share, which is a first, but I know she's going to.

'I like her,' she whispers, then groans. 'Like really, *really* like her.'

I squeal, leap up and give my best friend a hug in the middle of the restaurant.

'Aaaarrgghh! Get off me!' Lara shouts and tries to squirm out of my grasp, but eventually gives up and lets me hug her. Other diners are watching us but I don't care. I eventually return to my seat.

'You haven't said anything to her?'

'Of course not! She obviously knows I'm gay and she's fine with that, but it's another thing entirely when you know your gay friend is trying to sleep with you. It's kind of gross.'

'But you don't just want to sleep with her, right?'

'No. I don't,' she admits painfully. I reach out for my friend's hand and she takes it.

'Tell her. She might surprise you.'

'No chance of that. She's leaving soon.'

I've never seen her like this and I have to do something.

'Come back to Singapore. You can stay with me. You need to wait another two weeks for the revisit time to elapse after we leave, but you should come back out. I can put a good word in with the new CEO, and your track record speaks for itself. The project team could benefit from your experience.'

'Are you serious?' She brightens.

I nod and this might be the first time that I have ever seen a tear form in Lara's eyes.

'If that doesn't work, we can explore other avenues,' I reassure her.

'We both know there is only one other avenue that is almost guaranteed to work and, as long as I have your blessing, I plan to exploit every angle.'

'You're going to target DMVI, aren't you?'

'He has a ready-made soft spot I can poke. I have access and influence around something he desperately wants.' She smiles.

'Lara!'

'What? I'm just saying that he has plenty of reasons to want to be nice to me...'

I can see a plan forming already. 'Lara...' I warn.

'Don't worry. No promises, just letting him know I can be an ally. He'll just be unaware that he's not immune to betrayal.'

'You are so toxic.' I shake my head.

'I know!' She cackles loudly, then does a little happy shimmy as she places some lobster in her mouth. I know I'm going to regret this at some point, but I love her more than the repercussions.

'Oh. Caleb and Honey are here.' I point as I spot both of them walking through the entrance and straight to the bar.

'I'll pay, you go get them,' Lara offers.

'You are currently unemployed, I'll get this,' I counter. 'I'll join you in a second.'

'Okay.' Lara has a last swig of her wine, then gets up to head to the bar.

I take my time. I didn't want to lie to Caleb but she is right. He didn't need to know and I didn't need to answer. I was hurtful, and I hate myself for it. I take a deep breath, then walk over and hug Honey before turning to Caleb.

'Hi,' I say quietly.

'Hi,' he responds with a small smile, and he digs his hands into the pockets of the wool coat he is wearing over his thick navy hoodie.

'Can I have a minute outside please?'

'Sure.'

Caleb walks ahead and opens the door for us. I find a patio heater for us to stand under, and turn to him.

'I'm sorry. I didn't mean to be cruel yesterday. I—'

I don't get to finish before Caleb steps forward and pulls me into him.

'I know,' he whispers into my hair. 'But we're about to fight fake zombies and I want us to have a good time tonight. Can we talk about this another time?'

'It's busy tonight. I'll come with you to make sure you catch your train at Waterloo.'

Caleb snakes his hand round my belly protectively from behind and pulls me closer to him on the crowded platform as we wait for the tube. Lara and Honey rushed off to dinner immediately after the zombie house, leaving Caleb and me to make our separate ways home.

I like how safe I feel, being so close to him. I take in the laughter, noise and music filtering through from the busker we walked past as we made our way through the station. I've missed the raw, unique energy of London.

'Did you have a good time?' Caleb exhales into my hair from behind.

'Are you kidding?! It was amazing! Terrible food, sickly cocktails, murder, puzzles and zombies? What's not to love? The actors were so scary. Maybe a little too scary for you, Caleb?' I tease.

'No, I was trying to clear a way for us all.'

'You ran, screaming.'

'I was luring them away.'

'We were meant to be silent so we didn't attract them.'

'I was sacrificing myself.' He laughs.

'Oh I believe you, the group didn't though.' I join in with his laughter as he holds me tighter still.

'You were impressive. How come you were so calm?'

'I spotted a scare pattern early. Plus, I only volunteered for the puzzles because I didn't want to have to stand guard against whatever they were going to throw at us.'

'I'm picking you as my apocalypse partner.' Caleb spins me round to face him.

'I'm picking Honey. And that Rowan guy.' When I exclude Caleb from my imaginary apocalypse plans, he appears to be shocked.

'He was infuriating. How many times do you think he's done stuff like that?'

'He said a lot. He really got into it, so when it comes to the real thing I know he's going to keep me alive.'

'I can keep you alive too!'

'Not when teenage cheerleading zombies are involved.'

'She jumped out from nowhere!'

I can't help my laughter.

'Oh look, there's Rowan! Let's go and say hi!' Caleb says loudly.

'No!' I immediately start searching the platform, panicked.

'Ha! I thought he was your apocalypse partner!'

'He is, but all's not lost yet!'

'That's good because— Ah, tube's here.'

We inch forward and Caleb holds on to me as we attempt to squeeze into the carriage. I step into a space made for someone a quarter of the size as the Londoners around me shift and adjust.

'I'll get the next door. There's a gap there.' He makes sure I'm in safely, then disappears. I watch to make sure he gets on, and prepare to step off just in case he doesn't. I can just about see his navy-blue hood and jacket combo make it on, in between a sea of bodies smashed together as the tube doors close. I am pushed against the poor gentleman in front of me.

'Sorry,' we say at the same time, half smiling with apology. I keep my eyes trained on that hood, ignoring just how close

everyone around me is. As the train gets less busy at every
station, more of Caleb becomes visible, until I see his beautiful
eyes and cautious smile. He starts to move towards me while I
am still pinned by my neighbour. After a few stops, Caleb is
much closer and we are nearly at a massive interchange that
will almost empty the carriage. I'm relieved that we will be able
to get off the tube for a few minutes as we change lines to get to
Waterloo. I take a look at Caleb and mouth, 'one more stop'. He
laughs and mouths my words back to me and that's when it hits
me. It's a tiny gesture but it sparks a realisation. He's still here
with me and I am most definitely still here with him. Through
Jasper, the move to Singapore, disappointing ourselves, disappointing each other, our insecurities, external interference and
confusing emotions. We're still here. Together. Refusing to let
go. I gently push against the gentleman beside me and duck
under the arm of my other neighbour, moving closer to him.

'Sorry,' I whisper repeatedly as I manoeuvre past moaning
Londoners to get to him.

'What are you doing?' Caleb mouths at me, perplexed. All I
do is smile at him. We hit the interchange before I get to him.
As the carriage empties, we reach each other, and he takes my
hand to step off the tube. I don't follow, instead forcing him to
stop and face me.

'Can we stay out a little longer?' I ask. It's still early and I
don't want to leave him yet.

'Sure. I'm supposed to be going over to Em and Tim's
tonight. We're going to the pub – do you want to come? I don't
want you to feel uncomfortable or—'

'I'd love to.'

Caleb keeps our hands interlocked as we step off the tube to
change lines and head for Hampstead station.

. . .

'Ariella! What a lovely surprise.' Em shrieks, then pulls me towards her. I like Em a lot and I reciprocate the lovely welcoming hug she gives me.

'Em!' I laugh.

'You have been a busy young lady! I've been stalking you on Instagram and you're a fashion icon, an industry leader...'

'It's cold out here. Can you fangirl inside?' Caleb pleads.

'Sure, Bad Boy Black,' Em says and guffaws, making Caleb groan. She leads us into their cosy living room, where Jack and Tim are relaxing on the couch with a couple of drinks.

'Ariella!' they say at the same time before getting up to hug me, making me feel like I belong.

'What would you like to drink?' Tim asks as he lets go.

'Please may I have some water?'

'There's champagne? We're celebrating Caleb's imminent return to Singapore and being free of his nuisance,' Jack teases Caleb as he hugs and holds on to me.

'That's enough hugging for you,' Caleb says, shooing Jack away.

I settle into the comfort of Em and Tim's home. They may be Caleb's friends but I feel like they are mine too.

'Is Lou joining us?' I ask as I sit next to Caleb on the couch.

'We're taking a break,' Jack says, nonchalantly.

'Are you okay?'

'I'm fine, she isn't though.'

'Is she still calling? She promised me she'd give you some space,' Em says.

'No, but we've been texting. She thinks I'm seeing someone else, though, which I'm not.'

'She must miss being with you all.'

'I still see her away from the boys, but yeah. It's not the same without her,' Em says. 'It's also nowhere near the same without you and Caleb. How is Singapore?' she asks me, quickly changing the subject.

'Good. Busy. Lots of changes, but nothing insurmountable.'

'What changes?' Em asks.

'We have a new owner.'

'That can't have gone down well?'

'It's okay. I'm locked into a two-year contract, which gives me enough time to do the best I can with the transition before I leave.'

'Are you going to stay in Singapore?'

'No. I want to come home.'

'You do?' Caleb asks, looking at me intently.

'Yes. I have no intention of staying any longer than I have to.'

'Will you come back to your old role?' Em asks.

'I don't think so. I want to do something completely different. I'm just not sure what that will be.'

'You should open a restaurant,' Jack exclaims, his eyes shining.

'Yes!' Tim and Caleb say at the same time.

'Jasper tried to buy me a restaurant years ago. I've looked into it, and I know a lot of chefs. But the probability of financial failure is extremely high and I think I might need something a little quieter. Work is noisy and I could really use a break.'

I feel Caleb lace his fingers through mine and give them a squeeze.

'I'm gutted I won't be able to have any of your cooking before you leave,' Jack muses.

'Are you that good?' Em asks with a supportive smile on her face.

'Yes!' The three boys all nod enthusiastically.

'These two I get, but you can calm down, Tim. It's not like you're suffering!' Em humorously reprimands her husband.

'She is that good, Em,' Tim affirms happily.

'I was going to make you ingrates some dinner, but now—'

'Ariella, you can make it!' Jack says too quickly, making us all laugh.

'Cheers, Jack,' Em says.

'Please? Em, you have to try her cooking!' he reinforces.

'Do you mind?' Caleb whispers and I shake my head. He squeezes my hand.

'So now I'm curious.' Em chuckles. 'You don't mind, do you?'

'It's been a while, but I'd love to.'

Em and I spend the next fifteen minutes going through her fridge, freezer and pantry. I settle on some simple salted garlic, thyme and toasted bay leaf lamb steaks, served with minted peas and honey-glazed carrots.

'It's so good to see you, Ariella,' Em says as she grabs a bag of frozen peas from the freezer and tosses it on the counter.

'It's lovely to see you too. How have things been?'

'Mixed. Prosecco?' she asks. I nod and two glasses appear. 'Tim is working a lot, the boys are growing up too quickly and, while Alfie still needs me, I'm beginning to realise that unless I want to have another baby I need to start thinking about who I am when I'm not a wife or mother.'

'That sounds brave. Redefining the person you have been for so long takes a lot of courage. How long have you been feeling like this?'

'I think the feeling has always been there for the last sixteen years, partly because we got married when Tim was twenty-one and I was nineteen. I was in my first year at uni when we found out that Seb was coming. Leo followed shortly after. Then Alfie much later. I suppose I slipped into a Wife and Mum identity and stayed there.'

'What were you studying at university?'

'Fine art,' Em says with a frown on her face.

'Would you consider going back to it?'

'Not sure. Things are very different now.'

'That's true, but you'd be surrounded by people who are also trying to learn the same things as you. My suggestion would be to maybe start with something you know you love and navigate from there, but only if you want to.'

'I could start a course from home? You and Caleb literally moved country and your worlds didn't shatter. I can sit at a computer for a couple of hours a day.'

'You could, and your world most certainly won't shatter.' I try to sound upbeat but I hear the break in my voice at the end. I really like Em and I feel privileged that she is trusting me with her inner thoughts. I really don't want to make the conversation about me.

'Ariella, are you okay?' Em walks over and puts her hand on my shoulder.

The ball of fear, uncertainty and hurt I'm holding on to rises to the top and a tear falls. And then another. After that they are unstoppable.

'Ariella, tell me what's wrong,' Em soothes gently, rubbing my back the way my mother would. It's out before I can stop it.

'Our world did shatter, Em.'

'Oh, that. Yes. He told Tim and me.'

'He did?'

'Yes. I can't imagine how you must be feeling, but he needs you to get through it. You're so good for him, Ariella.'

'I don't know if I can get through it.'

'You have to. For him. If you love him.'

'I do, but I need to be able to trust him. He kept it a secret for so long, Em, and because he did... She's going to get away with it.'

'It makes my blood boil too, but it's not his fault, Ariella.'

'He was complicit, Em. He should have said something sooner.'

Em steps back from me and crosses her arms against her chest. She has always been protective over Caleb and I can understand why she may be defensive, but the last thing I expected is the rage I can feel emanating from her.

'I'm sorry that I've upset you, Em,' I say quietly, stepping towards her. She steps back, disgusted.

'He was raped. How could you possibly think that it was his fault?'

The words hit me like a blow to the stomach and I start to feel a cold, familiar, calm numbness settle over me.

'What did you just say?'

I see the anger drain from Em's face. It is replaced with horror. She thought I knew.

'Ariella...'

'Caleb was raped? By who? Melissa?'

Em's hands are shaking as she nods nervously. I finally let comforting nothingness infiltrate my emotions, and welcome it. It's too much to process, think about and understand all at once.

'I'm going to finish making this meal and deliver my polite excuses and leave.'

'Ariella, please—'

'Em, that's the only way this evening is going to end without me falling to pieces. I'd appreciate it if you keep our conversation to yourself. I need to think.'

Em sits at the kitchen island and silently watches me as I quietly prep, cook and plate their meals.

I call a car before Em tells them dinner is ready.

'I'm sorry, I need to head home,' is all I say, before I walk through the house to stand outside. Caleb follows.

'Stay a little while longer?' he asks.

I look at the man I love and kiss him deeper and longer than I have ever kissed anyone. This is all I have. There are no words to describe what is going on in my head. When we break away, he has the wrong idea.

'Let's go home together. I don't need to stay.'

'No. Stay. I love you so much, Caleb.' A tear escapes, signalling the departure of my inner armour.

'Aari?' he says as my car pulls up.

'I'll see you soon,' I say, and quickly walk away.

The anger at Melissa, frustration with Caleb, helplessness and powerlessness that I'd kept at bay as I diverted all my focus to cooking catches up with me and erupts in the back of that car as it whisks me back to Surrey. I sob until I have no more tears left to cry.

TEN

CALEB

'Ariella!' Tristan, the youngest boy, shouts, and runs up to her as she walks into the gym.

Yup, I've lost the class. There will be no more training after this. When we got together, Ariella came to a few training sessions with me as my assistant. I eventually had to ban her because she was a hugely disruptive influence on my mostly hormone-riddled students.

'Hi, Tristan.' She smiles, squats and opens her arms to hug him.

'Tristan! Get back here!' I instruct but he ignores me.

'I want a hug too, Ariella,' one of the older boys says, making the other boys around him snigger.

'Then come and get one, Shekhar,' she agrees, and stands. She beckons him over as Tristan runs back. The look I give him makes him freeze on the spot. Good.

'Actually, nah. Fuck it,' he says as he chooses to ignore my threat, decides he's fine with the consequences and bounces towards her.

Really?

'You got so tall,' she says as she hugs him.

'I've grown, Ariella. Everywhere,' he says, raising his eyebrows at her. What the fuck?

'Shekhar. Honey. Mat. Now!' I instruct. Honey has been kicking their butts all evening even though she is shorter than most of them.

Shekhar groans.

'Show Ariella what you've learned.' I smile.

'That's not fair. You know Honey's going to win.'

'Maybe, maybe not.'

'Come on, Shekhar, I'll be gentle,' Honey says, then chuckles and waves to Ariella as she steps on the mat from the side. This UK trip has lightened and opened Honey up. It's been wonderful to witness when we've seen each other.

My daily training sessions may have gone out of the window but it has been nice to have Honey join me and Phillip, the trainer I hired to look after the boys while I'm in Singapore. She has helped out with both of the Wednesday sessions in the UK. When she first turned up, the boys thought it was a joke. It took two and a half minutes of them watching her demolish me for the laughter to die.

I ignore Shekhar complaining very loudly about how unfair I am being as I walk towards Ariella.

'Hey. What are you doing here?' It has been a couple of days since she made us dinner at Em's and left.

'I wanted to talk to you. I also missed the boys, and wanted to see how they are doing.'

'They're the same. Annoying. Hard work,' I moan, and she laughs.

'Can I watch the rest of training and maybe come back home with you?'

'Of course. We'll have to cab it back because I'm going to drop Honey off at her hotel first, but yeah.'

Aari sits in a chair I get for her, present but also far away.

She cheers the boys on, even against me. I was wrong about training. This is the hardest I have ever seen them work.

'I'll order us some food while you're in the shower. What would you like?' she asks, following me into our flat. It's an hour later.

'Burger. Big. Dirty. Everything on it,' I plead. I kiss her temple, then retreat into the shower. I stay under the warm spray for a little longer than I need to because a substantial part of me is hoping that she'll come in and join me, especially after the way she kissed me a couple of days ago. When I realise it's not going to happen, I get out and quickly pull on some soft jogging bottoms and a T-shirt. She's sitting silently still on the sofa so I sneak up behind her and make her jump.

'Caleb!' she reprimands as she places a hand on her heart. I snigger. It's been a nice night. I'd like for it to stay that way.

'Did I not tell you very politely that you weren't welcome at training any more?' I remind her as I hop on the couch next to her.

'It was a visit. I haven't seen the boys in a while. They are so big! They've really shot up!'

'They have. Phillip has been good for them. He actually likes teaching.'

'I can tell they've missed you though.'

'Not sure. Phillip is kind and patient with them. I usually spend half the time swearing silently and wishing it was over.'

'That's not true. You love them.' Ariella pokes me softly.

'I do,' I admit. 'So, you want to talk. Tell me. What's up?'

'I want to apologise for lunch the other day. I didn't do that properly before the zombie house. What I said was cruel and it wasn't helpful.' She means it.

'It's okay. You were just being honest. It's one of the things I admire most about you, even if it can be heartbreaking.'

Unexpectedly, Ariella's lips find mine as I finish the sentence. I live for this girl's kisses. Whether it's a quick one on her way out, one of the longer ones we have that welcomes the other home, her tentatively suggestive ones when she'd like me to take her clothes off or the shy ones she returns when she responds to me suggesting exactly the same. This one feels different. It's loaded. Heavy. I feel the need to pull away, and do so slowly.

'Tell me what you really want to talk about, Aari,' I ask, fearing the worst.

'Caleb, why didn't you tell me what Melissa did?' she asks quietly as her eyes start to fill. Fuck. Em must have told her. I did think she looked shifty the other night after Aari left. That's why she disappeared so quickly.

'Aari...'

'I'm sorry I've been so furious with you. We're going to be navigating the consequences of what happened for a while and it's hard not to be reminded. I wish you'd told me that you were dealing with the consequences of her actions too.' Ariella strokes my arm so tenderly, I have to move it away. 'There is no way we are going to her wedding. I'm going to do whatever it takes to minimise contact—'

'Aari. I didn't tell you because of this,' I say, wiping a falling tear from her cheek with my thumb. 'What Melissa did is a completely separate issue to what we are trying to get past. I really need you to forgive me, Aari.' I look into her eyes for a moment before I continue. 'I will do almost anything for things to go back to the way they were, Mason. I'll run through the fire of your anger. I'll even continue to take the suffocating disappointment from you that frequently resurfaces; but I don't think can I carry the weight of your pity.'

'This isn't pity, Caleb. She did something horrific to you. The Ivory Bow agreement with her includes some extended contact with us; the biggest being attendance at her wedding. I can't let you go through with that, and I never want to see her again after what she did to you.'

'You have to. Don't worry about me. We'll do it for the team. If her crimes and our cover-up somehow become exposed, she'll get five minutes with an ankle bracelet; and that's only if she isn't quick enough to pick the jet she wants to disappear with. And she has a fleet on standby. We won't be so lucky.'

'Caleb, she hurt you.' Ariella is losing her fight to be strong for me as little sobs start to emerge.

'I know,' I say, pulling her into me. 'Sue went out of her way to make sure that I understood what she did. It was tough.'

'Sue? The counsellor from the shelter?'

'Yeah. I spent a lot of Saturday nights there, volunteering on your behalf, when you were gone. We had some hard but good chats.'

'Tell me what I can do to make it better,' Ariella pleads.

'Nothing. I've battled through a lot, but I'm never going to truly get over it. Working things out with you will help, because I feel lost and alone without you, Aari. However, that means we have to deal with what's actually going on between us, and we're not going to resolve it by making an unrelated side issue the scapegoat.'

'Can I stay?' she asks quietly.

'No. You can't. Not for the reasons you want to – but we can cuddle, keep talking and watch a couple of *Walking Dead* episodes. I'll put you in a car when you start making snoring noises.' I smile at her.

'I love you, Caleb.'

I don't doubt for a second that she means it.

'I love you too, my little Mason.' I kiss her forehead and pull her into me.

She falls asleep just over halfway through the episode we are watching and I pull her closer because I miss this. Just before I call her a taxi, I shoot Em a text.

> That was bang out of order, Em. But thank you.

> It was an accident. That girl loves you, Caleb.
> Don't fuck it up by keeping the things she
> needs to know to yourself.

I text it before I think it.

> I want to marry her Em.

I get nothing for a few minutes, then, just as I close the app, a vibrating alert comes through.

> You're going to have to stop being a dick first.
> Or at least pause long enough for her to forget
> you're a bloody liability. Stop texting my wife
> and getting her excited. It's late. She just
> screamed so loudly, the idiot that just moved in
> next door might call the police. – Tim.

I open the taxi app and, after almost a minute of staring at it, I shut it again. I turn the living room lights down from my phone, use the remote to switch off the TV and gently place Ariella's hand over my heart. Then I hold it there, close my eyes, and fall asleep right next to her.

When I open my eyes the next morning, her little familiar morning wriggles tell me that she's already awake.

'Morning,' I say softly, kissing the top of her head.

'Good morning, Caleb.'

'What are you thinking about?'

'I'm trying to figure out what happens now.'

'We need to find a way to forgive each other. You've hurt me too. I need to find a way to move past some of that and forgive you.'

She nods.

'Do you want to talk about it?'

'No, not yet, but I promise I will as soon as I'm ready.'

'When do you head back?'

'Honey and I fly on Saturday so that we can sleep off the jet lag on Sunday. You?'

'I'm going to be here until Tuesday, so I'll see you at work on Thursday.'

I nod and stop myself from asking if Dominic is staying for three additional days as well.

She plants a long, loving kiss on my forearm before she extracts herself from my embrace and stands. She silently gets her coat from the hook behind the door and wraps her scarf loosely round her neck.

'I love you,' she says sadly as she opens the front door quietly. She doesn't wait for a response, she just steps out of the flat and shuts the door behind her.

Things move quickly when we get back to Singapore. The very day Ariella returns to the office, the identity of our new CEO is revealed and everyone is on edge because we don't know what to expect. Ariella, in response, suggests we give him a chance and invites us all to dinner at her new home in three weeks for a Friday night review. She also takes the opportunity to remind us that we will always be a team, whatever happens.

No matter how much we attempted to anticipate what was coming, we were severely underprepared for the changes about to hit us.

When Samir Hussein steps on to our floor the following week in his sharp, expensive suit, bank-breaking watch and shiny shoes, I immediately know that everything is going to change. He spends most of his first week silently observing, quietly asking questions and getting to know the business. He keeps his cards so close to his chest that we have no idea what to expect when he calls a staff meeting the following Monday. The fact that he called it a 'staff meeting' rather than a 'catch-up', 'kick-off' or just a random time like 'the 2 p.m.' should have been enough warning. It doesn't help that he is ten minutes early, and pacing the room as he watches us all file in.

'This company is run like a day-care centre,' is his opening line. I try not to laugh as I watch everyone's faces drop. Ariella is silent at the back of the room as she fixes her expressionless eyes on him.

'There is more focus on employees having fun than actually doing your jobs. There is no project structure, effective tracking, efficient collaborative software and no disaster recovery plan. There's too much independence here, and individual account-ability is easily handed off to your COO – who has indulged that, perilously.'

He walks up and down like a predator, with everyone's eyes trained on him. I'm warming to him.

'There is no discipline. This meeting started late. You are all meant to be here ready to start at the allocated time. You do not waltz in chatting and laughing at the time it was meant to commence. We lost eight minutes this morning. That is hardly surprising because, as there are no time sheets, you all come in and leave whenever you like—'

'Excuse me. We work hard and we work late, often attending events,' Sian interrupts abrasively.

'We must be much busier than I thought. So, these projects you often work hard and late at – we're being paid to deliver all these, are we?'

'Not always, we go out to raise awareness and network for the company,' she argues.

'Oh really? And how much in sales have these so-called projects dragged in? Is there a business case for these evening events you attend? Is there a return-on-investment projection drawn up?'

'No, but the PR value is immeasurable,' she counters.

'Everything is measurable. Only the laziest PR companies sell you immeasurable PR. While we are on the subject, I'll be terminating the agreement with our PR company. We are engagement specialists, not college students running around Singapore having romances and getting drunk with celebrities. I've seen your expenses. We are not a hospitality charity for our clients to feed on freely and the dry-cleaning bills stop now. The only person who has a permanent solid reason for being out on the town is Caleb. If you are not Caleb or supporting him, I want to see a business case and pitch for every single after-hours event you decide is worth attending.'

Let's face it, Ivory Bow as we know it is fucked – but I like this guy. I love the team but we need this. Ariella has done an exceptional job getting us to this point, but he's right. We do work our butts off, because we have fun while we are at it, but we should be more focused. It's our job and we are being paid to do it. Loving it is a bonus.

'I am introducing digital time sheets. I want you all clocking in and out. Project team, your diaries are a mess. I want to see all your appointments scheduled and diarised. No more time blocks with "Popping to the venue for a cheeky lunchtime drink with the client". That is not an appropriate reason for a meeting.'

'Well, there goes my calendar,' Jess says and the project team all titter between themselves.

Samir silently folds his arms until they have finished. The laughter stops as quickly as it starts.

'I will be reviewing the structure and job descriptions of all the staff this week and in all cases you will be reinterviewing for your jobs—'

'No, they won't.' Ariella lifts her head from scribbling in her notepad and speaks calmly, for the first time, before the room gets a chance to react.

'This company will be restructured and—'

'I understand that. I can see why you would like to make the changes you've listed thus far. I am willing to accept that I was severely underqualified for the job and have made some significant errors, but you're not touching the team,' she says quietly and respectfully. Without giving him a chance to respond, she turns to Bryce and Lydia. 'Bryce, please could you send Samir all of our updated employment contracts, and Lydia, can you please send our HR consultant's details over too?'

Lydia and Bryce both nod and Ariella goes back into silent mode at the other end of the table. Her calm but firm interruption makes two things clear. Firstly, that Samir's power is not absolute. Secondly, not that it would ever be her intention, but Ariella has made Samir understand that she could stage a coup if she wanted to, and she'd win. She has never been sexier to me.

After Samir finishes scaring the shit out of all of us by laying down the law, he dismisses everyone else but holds Ariella and me back.

'Caleb, your performance since you joined has been exceptional. I'd like us to look at building a team to sit under you. There is a lot of work out there and we need more "you" to get it through the door. Ariella, is there a reason why you haven't done this already?'

I was ready to throw her a supportive smile at this confirmation that our decision to recruit weeks ago was the right one, but the harshness of his last sentence has stopped me.

'We've talked about it and Caleb is currently—'

'Who is "we"? Weren't decisions like that yours? Didn't Caleb report to you?'

'Well, yes, but we also got a lot of steerage from—'

'It looks to me like you've been coasting. The way this business has been set up is weak, at best. Your job was to establish, solidify and grow the business. Instead, you seem to have been lazily taking instructions and direction from someone who has no experience whatsoever in the industry and focused on dangling your private life in front of anyone who cares on social media in an effort to gain some kind of popularity. Your staff are out there partying indiscriminately, as if they don't care about the projects clients are paying us a fortune to manage. You have failed on almost every possible count in your role as COO.'

It looks like I'm not going to like this guy after all.

'Samir—' I start, ready to defend her.

'You're not wrong. What happens now?' Ariella interrupts, subtly putting her hand on mine.

'I see the decision to demote and replace you as COO has already been made. You will stay on and babysit the role until a new COO is found. Caleb, you will now sit on the same seniority level as Ariella does, and report directly to me. Ariella, I see that in your last role you managed event operations in London. Let's make a home for you leading the project team while you stand in as COO. Once that person is hired, they can work closely with you to straighten out your team and get this company going in the right direction. You will report directly to the COO. I also expect...' Samir trails off as his attention is caught by Dominic Miller walking in with lunch for the team. Prick.

'Excuse me.' Samir clears his throat and walks out of the meeting room. Ugh. Of course he is going to suck up to Dominic. Just when I was beginning to think he was different. No surprises there then.

'How can we help you, Mr Miller?' He stops in front of Dominic with his hands clasped behind him. We can hear every word of the conversation through the door he's left open.

'I was just dropping some lunch off for the team.' Dominic grins.

'As generous as that may be, this needs to stop. It is a significant distraction. Everyone employed here is paid more than enough to get their own lunches. If by some miracle they are struggling, then we would have to put together a consistent staff lunch programme to supplement their generous remuneration. You are a client and an investor, Mr Miller. This makes an already murky relationship more difficult to wade through. There will also be no more extended visits to Miss Mason during office hours. You cannot date my employee on my time. You have weeknights, if she is free, and the whole weekend at your disposal. Although, I would strongly suggest you reconsider your intentions as she is now also, indirectly, your employee.'

I try to hear what Dominic says in response, but I don't catch it. He follows it with a relaxed nod and extends his hand. Samir immediately shakes it. Dominic drops lunch on one of the tables and leaves.

'He's a bit hard isn't he?' I comment to Ariella, trying to disguise my glee that Dominic has just been kicked out of the office for good.

'No, he's not. He's just doing what needs to be done.' She sighs.

It doesn't take long for Samir to return to the room.

'Mr Miller has dropped lunch off for the team. He has been asked not to return. We are going to change the landscape of this business and turn it round completely to a fully function-ing, thriving investment. I know I need your help to do that, but you must understand that we will no longer function this way. Trusting everyone to do their job to the best of their ability is not enough. We need effective internal processes and our external messaging must be clear. I am going to need support. Are you both on board?'

'Absolutely,' Ariella responds without missing a beat. I agree.

'Thank you, both,' Samir concludes, and leaves us both standing there.

· · ·

Things at work after that are turbulent and sometimes explosive. Lydia is moved into a team manager role for the project team, and often inputs their diary entries for Samir's approval; while Ariella helps the staff acclimate to the new Ivory Bow by keeping the peace and quietly setting up systems that meet Samir's demands.

By the end of his third week in the role, Ivory Bow is running smoothly with all the new changes – and Samir is operating under the assumption that it was all his doing. The only people Ariella couldn't save were Eden and Ruby. They have been dismissed with three months' pay and an open freelance contract giving them first consideration should their skills be required. Getting Samir to sign off on that was like pulling teeth, but Ariella just kept on at him.

I, on the other hand, am doing great. Samir has got me out with him almost every night at functions aimed at senior leaders in influential companies. The opportunities are fantastic because not only does Samir know everyone, the 'everyone' he knows are the cheque signers, and they all trust and respect him. We've settled into a perfect working relationship. He gets me in the room and leaves me alone to build lucrative relationships and haul money into the company. It's time to revisit the list of applicants I abandoned to follow Ariella to London, and fast. I am going to need a team more urgently than we thought.

ELEVEN

ARIELLA

I knew that the introduction of the CEO would change things drastically at Ivory Bow. Samir has shaken so many things up that everyone seems to be threatening to walk out. We need this dinner. I also see it as an opportunity to share a little more of myself with the team.

Months ago, I was surprised to find that Dominic was able to secure a black-and-white house for me in his community. I'd fallen in love instantly with the quaint two-bedroom, its beautiful garden, the open-plan living space and humongous kitchen that opened fully out to a gorgeous dining patio. I moved in within forty-eight hours. Thankfully, with the help of Ms Pat, Eden and Ruby, I unpacked quickly and the space felt like home within a day.

The team were just as enamoured with my new home when they arrived for the dinner, and went exploring as soon as they grabbed their bubbles on arrival. I'd played it safe and gone Italian, putting my two large double ovens, vast kitchen islands and extensive hob space to use. I felt extremely lucky to have such an amazing kitchen; even Ms Pat commented on the state-of-the art appliances. I made little antipasti canapés and freshly baked focaccia for starters, large platters of beef braciole, olive and tomato baked baccalà, a simple pasta, pesto, pine nut and Parmesan dish and lots of Mediterranean salad. For dessert, I thought I might attempt a tiramisu, but I ran out of time and cheated with some shop-bought gelato.

Spending the whole day in the kitchen with Ms Pat made me happy and reignited my plans to discover local produce, recipes and the best food suppliers. She made me even happier when she finally agreed, after much convincing, to join us for dinner as a guest. She had one caveat: that she sit next to Caleb, because they apparently have news to catch up on. It makes my heart warm that Caleb has grown to love Ms Pat just as I have.

When we sit to eat, I'm expecting an evening of complaints, placating, negotiating and maybe even some begging because of the frustration the team has been feeling. Instead the evening feels like a celebration. The team is lively, full of laughter, stories, gossip and gratitude that we've managed to stay together in spite of everything the last few months have thrown at us.

'Devin asked me out on a date after he left, and I told him to suck it!' small, sweet, quiet, exceptionally polite Akiko announces out of nowhere, making the entire table erupt with laughter.

'He asked me out to lunch,' Sian adds. 'I was much ruder than telling him to suck it, and he hasn't reached out since.'

'While we're on the topic of office romances,' Jess says, raising one hand in the air while pouring more red wine into her glass with the other, 'I heard a rumour that you and Caleb used to date when you were both in London. Is it true?' she finishes, looking at me for answers, with a cheeky grin and a raised eyebrow.

Eden, Ruby, Akiko, Bree and Sian follow her gaze to land on me. They all seem to lean forward with enthusiastic interest at the same time, and I shrink back.

'I'll answer that,' Caleb says, thankfully, lifting a glass of champagne to his lips to hide his smirk. Oh no. Wait. I know that look.

'The question here is' – he shrugs lazily before fixing me with his glinting eyes – 'who says we're done?'

The 'oooooohhhh' that erupts from the table is so loud, I have to remind them that I have neighbours. Even Ms Pat, who has been a close witness to everything, is looking at me with wide, happy eyes, and her mouth is shaped into a tiny 'o'. Bryce and Lydia, who also knew, both have their faces in their hands and are smiling.

'I told you something was going on, the morning we busted him leaving with breakfast!' Eden pokes Ruby.

'What?' the four project girls ask at the same time.

'We got to Ariella's apartment early one morning and Caleb was leaving in his pyjamas. Ms Pat tried to cover like he hadn't been there all night!'

Ms Pat throws her head back and laughs so deeply it makes my love for her bubble up.

'Mr Caleb want breakfast that morning, that is all I know.' She looks naughty.

'But did he arrive that morning?' Ruby presses, enjoying herself.

'Noooo. I love you, Caleb, but I like Dominic better for Ariella. He treats her like a princess.' Akiko, forever the sweet romantic, frowns sadly. I react quickly.

'Akiko,' I address her lovingly. 'Dominic is our very dear friend and our boss. It's better to keep it that way.' I placate the most delicate member of my team and resist the urge to give her a hug. I decide to put a stop to the circus Caleb has created at the table.

'Caleb is a troublemaker, and none of you should pay attention to him.' I can't help the joy I feel though. 'But yes, we were more than colleagues in London for a while.'

The table erupts again and I decide to let them have as much fun with that bit of information as they want.

Everyone is full, drunk and happy by midnight, under the soft, twinkling fairy lights that hang above the humongous hand-carved wooden table and chairs in my outdoor dining space.

When Lydia makes her excuses and offers to drop Ms Pat at home, everyone helps to clear the table and put a full load in the dishwasher. Eden then suggests that the night is young and orchestrates a mass exodus to a private rooftop party.

'I'll help to tidy up. You guys head out,' Caleb volunteers when they ask if he is coming.

'It's okay, you go,' I offer as there isn't much left to do tonight. He shakes his head quietly and we tidy in silence until I am rinsing and stacking the last few dishes ready to go in the dishwasher when the first load is done. It's not until I turn the tap off and the house is silent that I can feel him watching me. I decide that the sink isn't quite clean enough and turn the water on again to break the silence.

'Clearly, Akiko thinks I'm a scumbag.' I hear him chuckle. His mood is light. I relax immediately.

'Akiko's screen saver is Donkey and Dragon from *Shrek*, staring lovingly at each other. The bar is high.' I chuckle too.

'I think the sink is clean, Aari,' Caleb says, suddenly, from behind me as he reaches past slowly to turn off the tap. 'You didn't tell me you were moving,' he almost whispers. Light mood over.

'It happened a lot quicker than I expected,' I answer, lacking the courage to turn round.

'I had to hear it from the doorman.'

I feel the heat from his body warm mine.

'I'm sorry...' I start to explain, but then I feel his breath on my neck. My body's Pavlovian response has me weak at the knees. I'm a disgrace. I can't see him and he hasn't even touched me.

'I miss you,' he exhales as he places his mouth at the base of my neck. Oh Caleb.

'I miss you too,' I admit involuntarily. I start to turn to face him but Caleb holds me in place by covering my hands with his, leaving me facing the sink. He heightens the intensity on my neck as he presses against me from behind. I grip the sink to steady myself.

'Tell me to stop.'

The gasp I produce is sharp but quickly disappears into the silence surrounding us. He knows I am not going to do that. I've missed his closeness, his smell, his hands, his mouth, his infectious happiness. He laughed a lot tonight as he sat in the furthest chair from me, chatting with Bryce and Ms Pat.

We haven't had much to laugh about in the last few weeks and I desperately want to return to that. I watch Caleb's hand release mine, find the bow of my wrap dress and slowly pull the ribbon's edge until it falls open. The feeling when his fingers touch my tummy and trail up my ribs is sensational. I immediately reach behind me to bury my free hand into his hair. He exhales deeply when his fingers reach their destination and I instinctively arch my back, pushing my chest forward into his hands. When he slowly circles his middle finger over my bra, around my nipple, I almost crumple with yearning. He presses gently against me and I can feel every part of his wanting. I can barely breathe with the desire coursing through to possess my body. It's not long before Caleb releases my other hand, takes his fingers once again to my belly and heads in the opposite direction. They disappear smoothly behind my underwear and, when he touches me, I feel like I am about to combust. The feeling of him pressed against and wrapped around me is indescribable. I push myself into his hands, wanting more. Caleb obliges, settling his fingers into a sensational rhythm between my legs as the plea-sure begins to tighten in my stomach. He easily takes me to the top of my desire, with nothing else to do but fall apart in his arms.

'Stop. Please.' I quietly break the silence as I return my hands to grip the sink. He steps away instantly. I wait until I have my breathing under control before I turn to face him. He eventually meets my eyes.

'Aari...'

At that point nothing else matters. I launch myself at him, with a kiss so urgent and demanding that it takes him a couple of seconds to respond. I detach quickly to hop onto my kitchen island. As soon as I do, I grab the collar of his shirt and pull his lips towards mine. We make quick work of the buttons on his shirt and Caleb has me hovering above the island for a second to lift me closer to him before he puts me back down again.

I'm straight on to his belt, unbuckling it quickly and savouring the noise it makes before I unzip his trousers. I've always loved that sound. It's Caleb's turn to gasp when I slide my hand behind his boxers. With our kiss still engaged, Caleb grabs his wallet from his back pocket and uses one hand retrieve a condom from it. He puts it on quickly, spreads my legs, pushes my underwear to the side and sinks deeply into me. The sounds we produce at the same time dance around each other before disappearing into the night. I feel whole, holding Caleb so close with him inside me. Caleb is not perfect but neither am I. I feel safe with him. I feel wanted. I feel in control. He makes me feel that I can go anywhere I want, do anything I want and he will still be there. He makes me feel powerful, I love him and he is mine.

But something is wrong. We fall out of sync, then Caleb slows and stops altogether. The feeling evaporates. I let my head fall to rest in the crook of his neck.

'Tell me what's on your mind,' I coax gently.

'I'd rather not,' he responds and pulls me closer.

'Come on, Caleb.' I bury my hand in his hair, knowing that usually ends all resistance.

'I can't stop seeing you kiss him. I know it's unfair and you don't owe me anything but I can't stop seeing it.'

'He kissed me,' I defend myself quietly. I know it's weak.

'Yes. But you didn't pull away. He ended that kiss. Not you, because you're attracted to him.'

'I'm sorry.'

'I'm sorry too, Aari. I really am. I don't think we can do this until we've truly forgiven each other.'

Caleb and I straighten to look at each other. His lips meet mine so softly I well up. I could kiss this boy for ever. When he slowly reintroduces his fingers between my legs, I stop him with my hand.

'I'm not going to leave you hanging, Aari,' he says, leaning his forehead against mine.

'I don't want to orgasm without you tonight.' And I mean it. I don't want to do any of this without him.

'Aari, is your heart still mine?' he asks earnestly.

'Yes. Entirely.' I don't even need to think about it.

'It hurts to see how happy you are without me.'

'I'm not, Caleb,' I admit.

'Then we need to resolve our bullshit, and fast.' He gives me a small smile.

'We do. Want to stay?'

'It might be best if I leave.'

I understand. We both need the space.

I hear Akiko scream Dominic's name before I see him. She runs towards him with her arms wide open, prompting the rest of the team to do the same. I've missed my friend too. He did so much to galvanise the team and keep the office motivated with his regular visits, impromptu team trips and sporadic lunch deliveries. We've all felt the change since Samir put a stop to all of that. We're more organised and effective, but we don't enjoy being here anywhere as much.

'Hey, girls.' I hear his deep laugh. He's enjoying the attention.

'Can you fire Samir? He sucks,' Jess asks with an earnest urgency. She has taken the change the hardest, and she requests his termination so loudly, it's almost like she wants Samir to hear her.

'I wish I could. I've missed our lost lunchtime trips,' Dominic admits.

'She's not joking,' Bree confirms.

'And that signals the end of the work day,' Caleb grunts disapprovingly next to me, packing up the job applications I've been helping him work through.

'We have more time, he's got a meeting with Samir,' I respond.

'To be fair, all the candidates are beginning to look the same to me. I can take this home and work on it while he tries to put the moves on you.'

'Caleb, stop it. You know I'm working with him and Christopher to stabilise Ivory Bow UK.'

'Uh-huh,' Caleb whispers, his narrowed eyes following Dominic as he strides into Samir's office.

'Aari, before you go, do you think you could look through Sian's business cases for next week?' Lydia swivels round from her desk to face us.

'Absolutely.' I nod quickly.

'And that's my invitation to get lost.' Caleb finishes packing up, but before he stands I reach out and cover one of his hands with mine.

'It's just work, Caleb,' I whisper to reassure him.

'Maybe for you,' he replies, and gets up to return to his desk.

By the time Dominic emerges I've cleared my tasks for the day, leaving my mind free to let the anxiety in.

'Ready?' he invites me warmly as he stands there confidently with his hands in his pockets. I try to put myself at ease.

'Yes.' He was my friend before he became my boss. I'll be fine.

We exit the tower and get into his waiting car.

'Are we going to your office?'

'Nah. I thought we'd take the boat out. Chris is set to dial in. After that, we could have some food and just get away from it all for a little while?'

'Sure.' I swallow nervously.

'This isn't a date, Aari, don't worry.' His mouth tilts up at the corner. 'You're trying to work things out with Caleb and I don't need another judgy "stop trying to date your employee" conversation with Samir; so I thought it might be a good idea for us to completely stay out of sight— Sorry, one sec.'

I relax as Dominic takes his call. His logic makes sense. He stays on the line, calmly thinking through an investment problem and sometimes laughs through parts of the conversation. It reminds me of why we became friends. He's always steady, clever, considered, unafraid to take calculated risks, and makes you feel that you'll never have to face your challenges alone. He's the perfect investor for Ivory Bow. If he can find a way to give Christopher more than just money, there'll be no limits to where the company can go.

'We've arrived, Dom,' his driver announces before getting out to open my door. I know what to expect but the quiet evening makes the craft even more beautiful. When Dominic finishes his call, he helps me on board and guides me to the dining area, where a screen and a conference table for two have been set up.

'Please could we get some water?' Dominic asks a member of his crew before we sit. Soon, Christopher is on the screen.

'Hello, Ariella. Unusual conference room, Dom,' Christopher observes happily. I see he is now in 'Dom' territory too.

'You should come out and use it some time. Okay. So you wanted me, Chris, you got me. What do you need?'

I listen as I remove my laptop from my bag.

'There's a heavy operations weighting that Ivory Bow can't sustain. There aren't enough new sales to maintain that volume of staff. We're going to need to move some of the current staff roles into account management or pure sales to keep everyone.'

'Makes sense.' Dominic nods.

'And maybe consider people we may have dismissed in the past?' I offer.

'Ariella, Lara was sacked and it's going to stay that way,' Christopher interrupts. Dominic guffaws so loudly he has to apologise.

'Not just Lara,' I mumble. 'A great example is Nicole. The clients adored her. We could tempt her back after maternity with flexible work hours and a generous bonus structure.'

We spend the next two hours working through departments, people and restructuring reporting for the new 'Harrison' when he is selected. We then spend an additional thirty minutes passing and accepting some applications for Harrison's role. By the time we have finished and ended the call with Christopher, I'm tired and hungry.

'Right. It's my turn to feed you,' Dominic says, mirroring his London request.

'Yes. Please.'

Some dim sum and seafood canapés appear, with a cold bottle of Bollinger.

'Thank you.'

'My pleasure,' he says, tapping his nose twice.

After we've scoffed the lot and as we wait for dinner, Dominic invites me to sit on the bow.

'You should know that your crazy, violent and uncontrollable best friend with a propensity to disappear when she is meant to be working is sniffing around DMVI for a job. I've evaded her so far, but I agree with you. Her persistence is evidence that she'd be unrivalled in a sales role. She's kinda scary!' Dominic's eyes widen comically with feigned fright.

I try not to laugh. Oh, Lara. 'She'd be an asset to any organisation that will have her,' I confirm.

'And that assessment has nothing to do with the fact that you love her, as you have told me countless times?'

'It has plenty to do with it,' I admit unashamedly. 'Besides, she'll be here soon and will be able to frighten you in person. She's my date to Melissa's wedding.'

'Ah. Your final dreaded duty. You're not going with Caleb?'

'No. He's taking Honey.'

'I see,' is all Dominic says.

We sit on the bow chatting leisurely until we've drained the Bollinger bottle which luckily coincides with dinner being ready. When we return, the dining area has been turned into an outdoor kitchen with a side table full of raw meats, fishes, seafood and vegetables. At the top of the table is a collection of sauces, powders, oils and thinly sliced marinade ingredients.

'So, rather than just dinner, I thought we could have some fun. Are you allergic to anything?'

I'm too shocked to speak, so I shake my head.

'Well, if you are, we're about to find out. We have EpiPens ready. Chef, tell us what we've got.'

'We've deconstructed a tasting menu of popular local dishes. For example, with chilli crab, we've isolated the white meat and pulled the ingredients apart. Same with the nasi lemak, and so on. The idea tonight is for us to experiment with lots of tiny dishes. We can construct traditional dishes, enhance them, isolate ingredients or ignore the rule book. We can create new types of dim sum, so we have our steamer here, or we can use the grill. There is also a hotplate if we want to play with some stir-fry or put something on the hob to cook.'

I'm squealing and clapping with excitement before I catch myself.

'I think she's happy, Chef,' Dominic says, then places his hand on the base of my spine to guide me to the table.

'Thank you, Dom!' I say, reaching over to give him a tight hug. 'And thank you, Chef.'

'Your initial reaction was all the thanks I needed, Miss Ariella. I won't forget that in a hurry. Now let me tell you what you have in front of you.'

We spend the next few hours playing with the food laid in front of us. Dom and I try lots of combinations, with eye-opening results. His combinations are interesting but safe. I listen to the chef and throw the rule book out. The chef's assistant is incredible at making notes of the combinations that work, ingredients we like, recipes never to be attempted ever again and the winning dishes of the night, which the chef play-fully promises to steal for his own use. When Dom and I can't fit any more food in, we realise that we've barely made our way through half the choices presented before us. The second bottle of champagne certainly hasn't helped. I can barely move when we have to change location so the crew can clear up. We make our way slowly to sit by the stern, with blankets to keep us warm.

'You know, if I had the choice, I would have been an astronomer,' Dominic says, breaking the silent joy I was indulging in and moving closer.

'See that?' My eyes follow his middle and index finger pressed together into the sky.

'There's the Crab – the Cancer constellation – it has a particularly unusual star cluster. And right next to it is Leo. The Lion.' I follow his fingers, entranced. 'Above that is the celestial star – you know, the one that guided Mary and Joseph? Whenever that's above Leo, like it is tonight, it's called the Ariella cluster, which, as you should know, means the Lion of God.'

'Wow. That's incredible, Dom. And it's up there tonight?'

'Yes,' he whispers in my ear, so gently it makes me shiver. 'There's more. There's a line that you may not be able to see in this light, that links the Ariella cluster to the Crab. That line is known as the Bollinger, scallop and chilli dumpling tummy.'

'Wait. What?'

Dominic bursts out laughing so loudly that a member of the crew appears to check that everything is okay. I wait for them to leave before I smack his arm.

'Ow!'

'You had me! I actually believed all that nonsense! Do you know anything about astronomy?'

'There's a sky, there are a whole bunch of things burning in it that we call stars... that's about it.'

'You were so convincing!' I laugh, turning to face him.

'I can be.'

Dominic's palm comes up to cup my face and he runs his thumb lightly across my lips. He moves even closer. I'm partly to blame for this. I'm here because I didn't want to lose him as my friend. Part of me knew backing off was going to be a challenge for him.

'Dom, please, stop. I really want to work things out with Caleb. I'm sorry.'

Dominic sighs, resigned, as he drops his hand. 'Let's get you home. Stay here. I'll be on the bow. It's better for both of us that way.'

It's not until I watch him disappear from view that I let myself cry.

We're silent in the back of his car all the way home. Just before we turn in to my driveway, he strokes the back of my hand with his finger.

'I can be aggressively competitive, Aari, and I know that

isn't easy to handle. I felt it tonight. I'm going to stick around and I will always be there when you need me, but I don't think it's a good idea for us to spend time alone any more.'

'At least Samir will be pleased.' Even I hear the sadness in my voice. I hate that being attracted to each other has engulfed our friendship. Dominic is an awesome person to spend time with. I have also valued his guidance and mentorship at work, because he is such an inspiring collaborator. But then there's—

'And Caleb,' he adds.

I nod. There's nothing more to say. I exit the car relieved. Dominic can no longer occupy the role of friend. He can now only ever be my boss. I will miss him but I just have to get comfortable with the sacrifices that come with keeping my heart where it belongs.

TWELVE

CALEB

I'm not looking forward to this wedding at all, but thankfully it's the last uncomfortable thing Ariella and I have to do before we can leave Melissa in the past for good. We haven't talked much since she went out with Dominic and unusually, absolutely no evidence that it happened showed up online. It made me yearn for the days they were plastered together everywhere, because then at least I knew what was going on.

It doesn't help that Samir has me in front of clients most nights, setting up the deals for me to close. Between that, mentoring the two new sales guys I hired and pinching Bree from the project team to join sales, work has been relentless. Ariella has spent most of the time buried in the back corner of the office, working hard and late to deliver the new projects we have coming in. She has been so busy, she hasn't managed to spend much time with—

'What are you roaming around with a face like a slapped arse for?' Lara asks, lifting her head from my laptop. She has been staying here since she arrived a couple of weeks ago. She refuses to move in with Ariella because of one obvious reason called Honey. Not that she's admitting it. 'You've got the afternoon off from your paying job, Ariella can't escape you for the next few days and you somehow haven't been arrested for Melissa's crimes. Not yet anyway.'

'Have you packed? Honey and Aari will be here soon.'

'Yup, and I have my elevator pitch ready. I can't wait. Someone at the wedding is bound to give me a job.'

'Feel free to unleash your full "Lara" on Dominic while you're at it.'

'Ah, you're still stewing over the no-more-kissy-but-these-two-are-desperate-to-jump-each-other's-bones vibes. You've got to admit, they do have an insane chemistry.'

'Thanks for rubbing it in, Lara.'

'It's true though. Frankly, you're getting off much more lightly than you deserve. If I was Ariella, I'd be snogging him up and down Marina Bay just to stick it to you.'

'You really think I deserve that?'

'I know Aari deserved the truth but all you did was lie. And then when she tried to do you both a favour and end it—'

Thankfully the doorbell cuts Lara short. I dash to get it.

'Bloody hell, Caleb, you're so fucking desperate,' she calls after me.

'Hi! Am I too early?' Honey asks, dragging her suitcase behind her.

'No, not at all.' I take her suitcase from her and wheel it in.

'Hi, Honey.' Lara smiles warmly towards her.

'Hi! What are you doing?' Honey asks, bouncing over to Lara to see what she's working on. She's soft and playful around Lara. You wouldn't think she was kicking my butt for a full hour every morning without breaking a sweat. It's cute.

'Just giving Caleb some home truths. Like I was saying, she tried to do you both a favour and end it, to put a stop to both your miseries, but you wouldn't let her. Instead you dragged her into limbo with you. Now neither of you can move forward, and we both know you sure as hell can't go back.'

'What was I supposed to do? Get dumped and not fight it?'

'Yes. What's that saying everyone knows about freeing the bird you love and it flying away...'

'"If you love someone, set them free. If they come back they're yours; if they don't they never were." Richard Bach,' Honey fills in.

'See? Not only can Honey kick your ass, she's smarter than you too! Thanks, Hunbun.' Lara reaches her arm out and pulls a happy-looking Honey into a quick side hug.

'Hunbun?' I ask, fighting a smile.

'What? She likes pork buns. So? You know what? Honey? Kick his arse.' Lara points at me.

'Caleb, please can I grab a drink?' Honey asks, laughing, as she walks to my kitchen. She doesn't even acknowledge Lara. It seems Honey Kohli is the one person on the face of the planet who actually doesn't react viscerally to Lara. Interesting.

'I'm not letting her go, Lara.'

'Is there someone paying you a shit-ton of money to invent new kinds of stupid? That's exactly what you should do.'

'I'm not letting Dominic Miller win.'

'Not that she's a prize or some object to be owned, but, newsflash, carry on like this and Dominic Miller will win. You think that she's going to choose him over you because he's rich and hot and whisks her off to private islands on his bloody cruise ship. She already lived that urban myth with Jasper and, as we both agree, he's the budget version. Maybe normal human beings, like me, will quite happily turn off our natural revulsion for the penis and sleep with him for a job at this point, but not Ariella.'

'I know that.'

'Do you? Because you being threatened by his existence is him winning. Every time you act a fool because social media isn't letting you spy on them like you normally would, you let her know that he is winning too. Want to know what winning looks like? Release Aari from this ridiculous pact, watch her dance around Dominic Miller and eventually fly her lovable but stupid Stockholm Syndromed arse back to you.'

'That, you don't know.'

'Fucking hell. Everyone knows that. Even Dominic Miller! That's why I don't have a job. If he thought for one second that I could influence Aari his way, I'd be Chief Something Officer of Something by now. The guy felt he had to buy her a whole bloody company just so he could have her around for two years. He's struggling,' Lara exclaims, raising her hands in the air.

'What's going on between you two does feel intensely deep, Caleb,' Honey chimes in.

'Exactly! And Honey has only known you for five minutes. No offence, Hunbun.'

Honey waves Lara's comment away light-heartedly.

'Let's lay off Caleb for a little bit, Lara,' Honey says softly, returning to her side. Lara is not going to like that. No one tells Lara what to do. I brace myself for what's coming.

She turns to Honey. 'Fine. Oooh, want to hear my elevator pitch? It's very good.'

'Sure!' Honey pulls up a bar stool.

'So, after I'm all nice and interested in whatever crap they are telling me about themselves and their jobs, I thought I'd start with...'

The bell goes again, I open the door and there she is.

'Hi.' She smiles that smile that makes my heart stop. I instinctively pull her into a hug and she in turn wraps herself around me. The images in my head of her and Dominic disappear instantly. Maybe Lara is right, but it's not a theory I want to test.

'No one should be hugging their ex-boyfriend like that,' Lara complains from behind me. 'I'm your date. I should be the one getting the borderline inappropriate hugs.'

'You and Honey are already here?' Aari asks as she drops me and heads, arms wide open, to Lara.

'I live here,' Lara clarifies, and she pulls her best friend in for a hug.

'No, you do not live here, you freeload here.'

'Same difference.'

'Hi, Honey.' Aari offers a friendly wave. 'Are you all ready? The car is waiting.'

We pile into the car, chatting excitedly as we fill Honey in on the wedding and why we are bound to go. Lara kindly leaves out any implicating details. When we arrive at the airstrip to join a horde of other guests, we are all in a great mood and looking forward to the long weekend away. As we make our way slowly through check-in, Lara starts identifying potential employers while I am stuck beating off people who want to say hello to or take a picture with Honey.

'I knew you were a big deal, but not this big a deal,' Lara comments.

'Yes, you can use my popularity to secure employment, Lara, if you must.' Honey anticipates Lara's next question.

'Nah, I only save that for people I don't like. Like Caleb. And sometimes Ariella when she's being naughty.'

'Wait. What?' Ariella turns round to give Lara a shocked look, making us all laugh.

If things stay like this, it's going to be a great weekend, as long as we stick together. It'll be even more fun when Ruby, Eden, Bryce, Lydia, Bree, Jess, Sian and Akiko join us tomorrow.

Finally we get called to our private jet, and as we board the very first person we see is Dominic. Of all the eight-seater jets in all the world. I try to get ahead of it.

'Hey, Dominic. Good to see you slumming it like the rest of us, eh? I bet your pilots are pleased they got the day off.' I extend my hand. If he doesn't take it, he'll be the dick, not me. Unfortunately, he does.

'Actually, this is my plane. I donated it because I figured you guys might want to fly with someone you know rather than a whole bunch of people you don't.'

Bastard.

'Thank you, Dominic, that's very kind.' Aari steps forward for him to give her a kiss on the cheek.

'Dominic,' Lara squeals, and his smarmy look disappears and is instantly replaced with utter fright. I fucking love Lara Scott.

'Lara?'

'Yes! Good to finally meet you properly. I've been trying to get your attention.' Lara immediately takes the seat opposite him.

'Hi, Dominic, thanks.' Honey quietly acknowledges him before walking to her seat. Ariella and I take seats opposite each other, much to my delight, but as soon as she is settled she pulls out her laptop and starts to type away.

Dominic doesn't get to move the entire ninety-minute flight. Lara keeps him occupied, finding out about his business, asking questions, making him laugh, selling herself and being the most charming I've ever seen anyone be. By the time we land, she has not one, but two interviews lined up with DMVI. Dominic helps with her bags, walking right alongside her through immigration, customs and arrivals, deeply engrossed in their conversation.

It's a short car journey through beautifully colourful tropical vegetation to Melissa's wedding resort, where she has taken over the property for the weekend. I enjoy the warm, breezy air from our open-top jeep as I admire the breathtaking sea views that are the omnipresent backdrop as we travel to our destination. When we arrive, we are separated from Dominic after we check in and a white buggy whizzes us to our two-bedroom villa.

'I'm switching allegiances. Dominic is far more useful.' Lara sighs and flops on the large soft couch in our villa's living area.

'I'm not surprised, Lara,' I say, giving her a dirty look. All she does is snigger and stretch on the couch.

'Right. Sleeping arrangements. I refuse to be complicit in any shenanigans, so, Honey, want to share the twin upstairs with me?'

'Sure.' She shrugs.

'I'll take the couch,' I volunteer.

'None of us were born yesterday. Unless you do something incredibly stupid, which I won't put past you, Caleb, there'll probably be some drunken sneaking around later. I saw the way you two hugged each other. I want to be far away from that,' she says, pointing at Aari and me.

'There will be no sneaking around, Lara,' I confirm, and make my point by calling the front desk to request that the couch be converted into a bed while we're at the pre-wedding cocktail evening.

'And my creepy uncle is a priest. Come on, Honey, let's settle in!' Lara drags Honey behind her as they make their way up the stairs.

'Do you think they are...' I whisper to Aari.

'No. Lara would have told me. But they like each other. That much is obvious,' Aari whispers back conspiratorially.

'She made Lara back off me earlier by just asking her to.'

We both laugh.

'Come on, let's put your stuff in my room,' Aari offers. 'If you need to shower, it might be best to do that now. I have some work to do before Ruby and Eden get here to make me magazine and social media ready.'

'I thought we got rid of them?'

'We did, but Melissa wants everyone looking beautiful for

her wedding and I can't be trusted to deliver on the homework. They're here in the morning too.' Aari rolls her eyes.

I take her up on her offer and indulge in the massive cut-out spa shower. When I emerge, I hear her declining pre-drinks in Dominic Miller's villa, citing Eden and Ruby's anticipated assault, and I've never been more grateful for those two.

When Ariella and Lara step into the garden cocktail reception, it feels like the whole party stops for a few seconds. Ariella is draped in a long, light and wispy flowing orange dress that moves and shifts with the wind, exposing large but safe parts of her glowing skin while reflecting the colours of the sunset.

'You're in trouble tonight,' Honey whispers to me as we watch them both approach us.

Lara has been put in a daringly low-cut, long, green leaf-patterned dress cut right up to the top of her thigh and cinched at the waist to expose her killer legs and accentuate her unbelievable curves.

'Not as much trouble as you're going to be in when Lara starts casing the party for a job,' I whisper back. 'Ariella is stunning tonight, but if I was any of these guys I'd want to take Lara anywhere she'd like, and give her anything she wants, regardless of the consequences. I'd risk it all.'

Honey takes a possessive step forward.

'Careful,' I warn under my breath. She steps back to wait patiently for them to get to us.

'I swear, if someone doesn't hire me tonight on the slight suggestion that there is a minuscule chance that I might sleep with them, I'm going to be pissed off. These fucking control knickers are killing me. You're all on employment duty. I want the ones that will hire me and forget that they created a role for me. I'm thinking, old and healthy,' Lara declares quietly, grabbing a glass of champagne as it glides past.

'I'm not sure I'll make it to "later" to sneak around, Mason,' I whisper in her ear.

'You may not be the one doing the sneaking. You look sexy tonight.' She arches an eyebrow at me. Holy fuck.

'Ariella! You look phenomenal.' Dominic approaches. 'If you'll excuse us, there's someone from a charity that the Conscious Experience app supports here. She'd like to meet you.' With that, Dominic whisks her off, and it's the last I see of Ariella all night.

By eleven, I've met all the contacts I had on my hit list. When Dominic asks if I've seen Ariella because there's yet another person he wants to introduce her to, I know exactly where she'll be. I slip some Singaporean dollars to a waitress I've been exchanging nods with all evening, and ask for a favour before I head back to the villa. I find her exactly where I expected to; sitting on the couch in the living room, laptop in lap, fresh from a shower with wet hair, a bare face, in some loose shorts and a vest. Braless. Shit.

'Had enough?' I ask, plopping down beside her.

'Yeah. It's going to be a long day tomorrow.'

'Where are Lara and Honey?'

'No idea.' She sniggers and her breasts jiggle. Bloody hell. Hold it together, Caleb.

'I hope those two get it together. How they haven't already is beyond me.'

'Honey has a lot to lose and Lara doesn't. I can see why Honey is being particularly cautious, especially in her... cultural climate.'

'She could at the very least tell her.'

'Have you met my best friend, Lara? She'll have Honey convinced that it's fine to sing it from the rooftops. Singing it, however, could cost her more than her livelihood, belts and

endorsements. Honey needs time and space to adjust – if she
wants to...'

'I'm not sure I can take much more of the fake-boyfriend
thing, Aari. I'm getting to a place where—'

The villa bell chimes.

'I'll get it.'

I open the door to my tittering waitress, who is carrying a
platter of food enough to feed ten. She has also recruited a
friend to bring over some cutlery, crockery, water, sake and red
wine. I let them set up on the coffee table and, when they are
done, I tip them heavily. The look of surprise and gratitude on
Ariella's face makes me feel like I've done a good job. Yes. That
look is exactly what I was hoping for.

'You can never eat at these things and it wouldn't surprise
me if room service has been shut down for the night, so...'

'Thank you, Caleb, I'm starving.'

She lifts two plates from the stack and pairs each of them
with chopsticks and a napkin before she invites me to dip in first.

'Nah, I might have a nibble but I stuffed my face tonight.
Especially with those.' I point to a mini platter of smoked beet-
root tarts and she dives in immediately.

'Sake or red?' I ask, pouring us both some water.

'I'm a little warm, so water is great, but if you pick I'll join
you?'

I put the sake in the fridge to cool for tomorrow and open
the red. When she is comfortable and eating, I dive in.

'So how are you surviving Samir?'

'Well, he keeps me busy. I'm learning a lot from him and it's
all useful, but I can't wait to leave Singapore.'

'I'm on the same page, Aari. I'm doing my time and then I'm
out too.'

'Really?'

'Yes. Really,' I confirm.

'What are you going to do afterwards?'

'I haven't really thought about that. I suppose I might be stuck too. I miss teaching the boys but Phillip does a much better job. Maybe I could go back to supporting him in some capacity?'

'You could, and you'd love it.'

'We should have more conversations like this. It's nice to know what you're thinking.' I poke her in the ribs, making her jump.

'We should. You're doing so well, Caleb. I thought you'd want to stay.'

'I can't wait to leave, but I'm not going without you, Aari. Whenever and wherever you're going, I'm coming too. It's that simple for m—'

Ariella's mouth is on mine and she is climbing on top of me before I finish. She just fits. My mouth opens up to receive her while my tongue searches hungrily for hers. I inhale her exhales as she does mine, and nothing else matters.

'I forgive you, Caleb,' she whispers. 'Do you forgive me?'

She places her open mouth on mine once again as she grinds down on me. How could I not? This is not going to end with me being decent. I'm past that point.

'Ariella Mason, I am going to take your clothes off and—'

'Disgusting! I knew it! Both of you are— Ooh, food, I'm ravenous.' Lara and Honey walk through the door. 'Shift!' Lara demands as she pulls at the control shorts underneath her dress with a few yanks, followed by lots of wiggles to get them off, then discards them behind her, before plonking herself beside us on the couch.

'Aaaaaahhhh...' She exhales with relief, then loads up a plate and impatiently pops some confit cod into her mouth. 'This is sooo good. Honey, want some?'

'I'm okay.' Honey approaches with an embarrassed smile.

'How are your job prospects, Lara?' Ariella asks curiously, climbing off me. No. Please, don't go, I silently plead.

'Great! I have a load of business cards and job openings that I've been told I could easily fill coming out of my ears. That Eden is a magician, the dress totally worked. I have so much respect for girls who use their bodies to get what they want. People who judge them are complete idiots and need to be slapped. They have no idea. It's bloody hard work,' she declares with her mouth full.

'That's fantastic. Tell me more tomorrow? I'm going to head to bed. Goodnight, guys. Caleb, thank you for the food and the talk.' Aari kisses my forehead, then Lara's, and, with a little wave to Honey, disappears into her room.

'Bloody hell, slow down, Lara,' I advise, pouring her a glass of water.

'Shut up. Stop pretending you're not dying to follow her. What are you waiting for? Skywriting? Just keep it down, you two, some of us will actually be sleeping.'

Lara is right. I don't even argue. I jump up and follow Ariella.

She's in her bathroom doing her teeth when I enter. Our eyes meet in the mirror and she knows I'm not here to talk. Lara and Honey be damned. I'm going to make her scream my name until she's hoarse; but if I jump on her now, I'm going to last about two seconds, so I slow us down.

'Mind if I take a shower?'

'Nope. All yours.' I hear her disappointment as she leaves me to it.

The cold shower serves me well and, when I emerge, I'm much calmer.

She looks up just as I enter the bedroom wrapped in a towel, and I register her surprise.

'What?'

'Nothing.' She smiles and goes back to the resort map she is studying. Oh, it's definitely something.

'Tell me. What?!' I laugh as I walk round to her side and sit on the bed.

'It's silly. I forgot how beautiful you are, that's all.' That's all I need.

'How beautiful am I, Ariella?' I tease.

'Put some clothes on and come to sleep.' She waves dismissively, trying to control the smile pulling at the corners of her lips.

'In a minute. How beautiful am I?' I inch closer.

'I am ignoring you, Caleb.' She tries not to laugh. I move closer still and our bodies touch slightly.

'Go on. Tell me.'

She sighs loudly.

'You're such a nuisance. Very. Happy? Go.' She tries to shift away, so I put my hand gently on her knee. She stays.

'Well, now that I'm here.' I bring my face close to hers. I hear her swallow.

'Now you're here, what?'

The first kiss lands on her neck. Her shiver confirms her delight. I plant another light kiss next to it. She doesn't move. I've missed her smell. I run my tongue along her collarbone and hear her take another sharp breath. I make my way back to her neck and start to make my mark with my mouth. She used to love being temporarily branded by me. I love it too. It's my way of sending 'get lost' signals to anyone who might get ideas.

Aari unfolds and parts her legs, with her knees bent and pointing to the ceiling. I move her knees wider, ease between them and lie on top of her. I hold my face a breath away from hers for a couple of seconds to study hers and make sure she doesn't want me to stop before I kiss her. I expect it to be frenzied and urgent but it isn't. It's soft, gentle and seems binding somehow.

'I love you, Aari, and it's time to put my pride away.' I hear her little sniff before she gently puts her fingers through my hair and brings my face back down to hers again.

I move her hands away slowly and help her out of her vest to bare her beautiful body.

'Goodness, I've missed your body.' I rest back on my knees, taking in her beautiful, smooth café-latte skin against the white cotton sheets. I trace my fingers along the base of her neck, down the middle of her chest and slowly around each nipple, thanking them for coming alive for me.

'I've missed these too.' I smile to myself.

'They've missed you,' she confirms softly. I explore her body with my mouth as she goes on her own little tour, leaving little sparks when she touches my skin. The sound of Aari's laboured breathing is threatening to undo me, so I take a break to silence her with a kiss and feel between her thighs. Her underwear is soaked, so I place my fingers where I know it matters and slowly edge her towards her tipping point.

'Caleb, I need you inside me.' She strokes my arm.

'We have a supply issue. We have one condom and no backup. The way this is going, we're going to blow through it if we're not careful.' I look up apologetically.

'Please, Caleb,' she pleads with her eyes closed, and wriggles uncomfortably.

That's all it takes. I rip open the packet, pull off her drenched underwear, place her ankles on my shoulders and enter her. She welcomes me in. The feeling is still unbelievable. I start slow because this is a new position for us and I'm going deep. Her gasp is a warning, so I ease off.

'Are you okay?' The last thing I want is to hurt her.

'Yes.'

We develop a rhythm with our gazes locked on each other and everything between us seems bigger than the act itself. I'm particularly relieved that we have made it past last time, when our fears and anxieties got the better of us.

Ariella, without warning, slides her legs from my shoulders and plants both feet, trapping my hips between her knees.

She reaches for me and, as I bend forward, she places her hands on my shoulders, pulls herself upright and manoeuvres us into a loving kiss. She then uses her body to move me back onto my knees, forcing me to sit on my heels. Chest to chest, face to face, still linked, she wraps her legs round my hips, with her arms anchored round my neck and shoulders like she is holding on for dear life. As she settles on top, our foreheads meet and stay together.

'Fuck, Aari,' I exhale, millimetres from her mouth, as she begins to move.

'I need you close, Caleb.'

Ariella keeps us moving as I steady her hips with my hands, controlling our pace. Then something transcendent happens. Being with her here, now, stops being about getting us to a climax. Instead, holding her close, moving as one, everything slows, our breathing syncs, my mind empties and my eyes shut. A magnetic force I have never experienced before holds us in place and I feel her. All of her. Her breath on my face, her hands clutching my back tightly and where we are joined feels inde-scribably intense considering how slowly we are moving. It almost feels out-of-body. I have no idea how long we stay like that but, when Ariella starts to move with a familiar urgency that breaks our trance, I don't have to think about matching. I just do.

I hold my girlfriend steady as she grinds down hard against me, pushing harder, deeper, further. Aari suddenly stops, takes in a sharp breath and, for lack of a better word, detonates in my arms. It's silent, contained, but forceful. She contracts around me so tightly and rapidly that what starts as a tremble amplifies through her body and she takes me with her. I instinctively pull her off me, flip her round so that she's on her knees and plunge into her. Again, again and again. The explosion that starts at the base of my brain shoots down my spine and rips through me so hard, I hold on to her tightly, until it subsides. My body feels heavy but my head is light.

What. THE FUCK.

Neither one of us moves for a while.

'Please will you shower with me?' I eventually ask quietly. She nods.

She hugs me from behind, with her head resting on my back, as we quietly make our way to the shower.

We slip into our old routine, washing each other. Ariella has washed my hair countless times before but when she does it this time I struggle to keep my emotions in check. I'm not sure what's going on, but it's all too much. I step out first as always, wrap a towel round me and, before I return with the usual two for her hair and body, I quickly grab a third and lay it on the huge wet patch we created in bed.

That night, we fall asleep facing each other, legs intertwined, with not just me holding her hand against my heart as usual, but Ariella also holding mine against hers.

'It's you, Caleb. It will always be you. It will never not be you,' she says quietly.

I'm asleep before I can think of how to respond to the gravity of her words.

THIRTEEN

ARIELLA

It's especially bright when I open my eyes the next morning. Caleb is awake with his palms crossed behind his head, looking up at the ceiling in deep thought.

'Good morning, Black.' I reach my palm across and place it on his warm chest.

'I need to start behaving like an adult, Aari.' He sighs deeply. 'You may be my first actual relationship, but that excuse isn't going to hold up for much longer with my bullshit.' He drops his head to the side so his eyes can meet mine. 'I know that you love me. I need to trust that you're not interested in running away with... someone else. For us to survive, I need to share everything, no matter how frightening, because holding on to you dictates every single move I make. No one has ever really truly cared about me the way you do, and you deserve more than I give everyone else. I'm sorry it's taken me so long to get here. I know you'll disagree, but it's time that I publicly break up with Honey. I'm done playing games. If I don't change the way I handle things and grow the fuck up, I'm going to destroy us.'

'How long have you been awake, beating yourself up?'

'Not long enough. We're in this mess because of me. So much of this could have been avoided if only—'

'I need to grow up too. I sway to your heartbeat, Caleb, and I must stop being scared of that. Also, please stop being hard on yourself. I know that you always try to do the right thing, even when your decisions are a little murky.' I laugh a little.

'A little? That's generous.' Caleb snorts and it makes me smile.

'My decisions can be murky too. You fought so hard for us. You have never made me feel like I had to conform to any expectations with you and I've maybe taken advantage of that. I'm so sorry.'

Caleb leans forward slowly to kiss me softly and my mind empties. This is where I belong. When he pulls away, I open my eyes and see my favourite smirk in the world.

'Before we both grow up and start behaving like sensible human beings, I've got to ask.'

'We're imperfect, but we try. That's the main thing. Carry on.'

'What the hell was that last night?' His eyes are wide with excitement. I can't help being sucked in and a huge part of me is delighted that we don't have to act like grown-ups just yet.

'I'm just as perplexed as you are. I really just had this deep longing to be close to you. Then we started breathing together and there was all this tingling in my body and I think I was meditating at one point and then I felt like I exploded.' I giggle from behind my palm, embarrassed.

'That has never happened to you before?'

'You've got the orgasm monopoly here, Caleb.'

'Nice.' He grins, before attacking me with tickles.

'I thought we were meant to be grown-ups now,' I complain happily.

'Maybe only when it counts?'

I pull my boyfriend's face to mine and kiss him deeply.

The way Caleb and I connect is indescribable. This morning everything seems slower and deliberate, with a sense of permanence enveloping us as we carefully claim each other. We don't bother to untangle ourselves as we indulge in a short nap.

We are woken by loud knocking on the bedroom door.

'I demand you stop whatever nastiness is going on now. I'm coming in!' After a generous pause, Lara opens the door to point at Caleb.

'You. Honey is ready and waiting in the garden to beat your arse in training. And you.' She moves her finger across to me. 'Eden called to say Ruby will be here in an hour,' she instructs.

'I'll jump in quickly before Honey.' Caleb tosses the white sheets off him without a care in the world, forcing Lara to turn quickly.

'My eyes, Caleb. I'm so young and I still have so much more to see,' she complains. I don't have the same issues. I could look at Caleb's cute bum all day.

As soon as Caleb is safely in the shower, Lara demands I move over to his side before she lies on the bed next to me.

'You whored yourself last night and you're his again, aren't you?' she asks, giving me one of her judgemental looks.

'I did and I am.' I hide my face under the blankets, embarrassed.

'What is it about that boy? Cats must look upon him with envy. He's on his ninety-ninth life.'

'I don't know – but enough about me. How are things with Honey?'

Lara casts a glance towards the bathroom, then moves closer.

'She gave me a little kiss on the lips before she got into her bed last night. It wasn't a tongue-y one, just a quick goodnight one. It was nice.'

The happiness radiates out of her and I can't help the joy that is bubbling inside me.

'You're a lot in love with her, aren't you?'

'No I'm not! Take that back.' Lara pokes me in the ribs through the blanket.

'Ow! I take it back.'

'Thank you,' she responds forcefully, staring at the ceiling silently. Lara is in love. I struggle to keep my face neutral in order to hide the pure delight I feel. 'And even if I was, it would only be a tiny, TINY bit,' she admits, giving me the same dirty look I got earlier.

'It's some sort of admission at least,' Caleb says, walking in wet, wrapped in a towel.

'God, please, if you can hear me, I really hope today is the day Honey accidentally breaks something...' Lara prays loudly, looking up to the sky with her palms together.

'God, please, if you can hear me, I really hope today is the day Lara gets hit with so many feels for Honey that she writhes in excruciating—'

The pillow hits Caleb squarely in the face. How it managed to land between his praying hands and face is a mystery.

'What's this?' a sweaty, post-Honey Caleb asks, pointing at the thin, lacy underwear Eden delivered for me to wear today.

'Lingerie.' I start laughing because I know Caleb is going to make fun of me.

'Why is it all orange, tiny and pretty? I quite like the passive-aggressive resistance of your usual. This one poses no challenge whatsoever.'

'My dress is cut strangely, so if it slips a little bit and something shows, I'll be all right.'

'I suppose the silver lining is it'll be easy extracting you from it later.' He leans in to kiss me before heading into the shower.

I take my time getting into the asymmetrical fishtail dress

Eden sent. She went for a bold, blue and burnt orange African print with large leaf details with holes everywhere. It's so confusing, I'm on my fifth attempt getting it on when Caleb emerges.

'Eden stitch you up again?' He raises an amused eyebrow.

'At this point, I'm comfortable with Eden doing whatever she wants – but she could at least send me instructions on how to get into the clothing she selects.'

'Hold on. We can sort this out between us.' Caleb approaches and takes it from me gently. It turns out I've been putting my foot into the armhole. When I get it on, it's beautiful, but a little exposed because of the massive gaps between the leaves.

'You don't like it?' Caleb asks, a laugh playing on his lips.

'It's pretty, but I asked her to make me blend in, not stand out!'

'Well, I like it. It's tempting.' Caleb slips his hand up my dress so quickly he is halfway to his destination before I smack it away.

'Stop it. You're naughty. No.' Thankfully, my phone dings. It's a text from Lara letting me know that Ruby has arrived, enabling me to leave the room quickly.

'Eden asked me to pop by quickly to see if the dress needs adjusting and to put a little bit of make-up on you,' she explains. She's wearing what looks like a huge bum bag and dragging a trolley case.

'How is it going over there?'

'It's busy but we're there. Melissa looks unbelievable and I'm not even done yet. Look at you. Eden will be pleased. It's perfect. It's the colour of the sea and flowers along the beach. Are you happy for me to do a deep-orange shadow on you and smoke it out softly with a dark blue? We can leave the rest of your face bare and just put some gloss on your lips?'

'Mason! Get your beautiful behind in here, I need your

bowtie-tying skills,' Caleb calls from the bedroom, then pokes his head out.

The shock on Ruby's face settles into confusion, then realisation, as she looks back and forth at us.

'Hi, Ruby,' Caleb calls happily. 'Make-up time? I'll leave you ladies to it.'

'Is this what I think it is?' Ruby whispers excitedly.

'It's exactly what you think it is.' Caleb appears again. 'And maybe quite a bit more.' He raises his eyebrows twice before he disappears.

'Ignore him,' I plead, as I fail to control how joyful I feel.

'Yes, ignore him,' Lara announces, coming down the stairs in a short, delicate peach dress with a long tail, followed by Honey in an elegant, feminine, cobalt-blue fitted suit.

'Ruby, think you could shove some make-up on us when you're done with Aari? We've done our bases; we just need colour!' Lara asks, plonking herself on the couch and shooting Ruby a charming look that makes it impossible for her to say no.

'Sure!'

Today is going to draw similar reactions from a lot of people. Caleb's interview with *The Singaporean* is still making the rounds on the internet. Samir has done everything he can to stamp it out, but social media is keeping it very much alive.

My worry disappears when Caleb emerges in his suit. Ruby has just finished putting a delicate and pretty arrangement of flowers on the side of my loosely pulled up hair.

'You look very handsome, Caleb.'

'I've obviously got to come through, as the hot one in the Ivory Bow delegation.' That smirk. Still.

'Obviously,' Ruby agrees, chuckling, as she starts on Lara's face.

'Want to go ahead and meet the guys? They should be here by now.' Caleb stretches out an open hand and nods to the front door.

'Yes, please.' I take his hand and follow him to where the guests are already gathering for Melissa and Kevin's wedding.

'This is weird, Ariella,' Akiko mutters to me as we find our seats for the ceremony. She's right. There are no flowers, no theme and no live music. There is nothing soft or romantic about it. The location in front of the water is stunning and everything is set up with absolute precision; but as someone who has worked with Melissa for the past few months, it still feels unusually cold to me.

'She doesn't care about this,' Caleb responds to Akiko as he gently guides her to sit in front of him. Kevin is already at the altar, chatting with someone who is presumably his best man. He looks unbothered and relaxed.

'Maybe Kevin planned it.' Akiko frowns.

'I think it's chic,' Bree comments as she takes her allocated seat behind Akiko.

'I love how it's all about hard angles and sharp edges,' Sian contributes.

'It's probably a nod to her surgical life and Kevin's IT company. Weddings. Brought to you by precision and efficiency. Dull,' Jess responds with deep disapproval.

'I don't like it. It's cold,' Akiko protests. 'We should have done this. It would have been so pretty.'

'I wish we organised weddings. This is terrible,' Jess agrees. 'Ariella, can we do weddings?' she calls out so loudly that a few guests around us hear her. I love Jess. Her incredibly creative bones always seem to be tingling with new ideas.

'Ladies, can we talk about it at work?' Lydia diplomatically shuts the conversation down, throwing a wink at Jess to soften her response.

The first bars of Tina Arena's 'Chains' song start up. As the lyrics begin, Melissa appears alone on the white carpet leading directly to the altar, prompting everyone to stand. She looks stunning in the casual-looking strapless white top and shorts she has picked for her dress, with a simple long train attached at the back. She starts to slowly dance and sing down the aisle by herself. When the chorus hits, she extends her arms above her head, sings it at the loudest volume she can and encourages everyone to sing along.

'I'M IN CHAINS!' The guests, seemingly unsure at first, start to sing along as requested, hesitantly clapping along to the chorus. None of us from Ivory Bow are in a singing mood. Melissa takes the full four and a half minutes to make her way to the altar. The crowd bursts into applause, probably with some relief, when she gets there and stands next to Kevin.

'There is more truth in that song than everyone realises. She's clearly working those emotions out,' Caleb whispers to me. I'm struggling to empathise.

'She's something.' I'm not sharing Caleb's need to analyse the situation. Not gonna happen. Caleb and I haven't spoken about Melissa since our chat in the flat after Em accidentally told me what happened. My heart can't take it. I know avoiding it is unhealthy but the alternative is to let the anger at Melissa rise to the top, and today isn't the day for it.

'Okay. Let's get this over with,' Melissa instructs the registrar, causing everyone to laugh.

The weirdness that no one else seems to pick up on doesn't end there. The vows are short, and, while poor Kevin is the doting groom in love, Melissa seems bizarrely disconnected. During the vows, her 'You finally dragged me here after all these years, so I suppose I'm stuck with you' draws more tears from the audience than Kevin's sincere and emotional 'I do.' When Kevin is finally asked to kiss the bride, Melissa jokingly ducks, before allowing him a quick peck on the cheek. As soon as they are presented as a married couple, Melissa turns round to the crowd and shouts, 'Right, who wants to get really REALLY drunk with me?'

The guests cheer. 'Chains' plays again as they walk down the aisle, a dejected-looking Kevin following behind a dancing and singing Melissa. There are no speeches, we all get individual cake slices, so there is no cutting ceremony, and the first dance is Kevin and Melissa dragging everyone but each other onto the dance floor.

I decide to slip away from the main party in the glass pavilion to the garden outside. I spot Caleb in the thick of the dancing, taking turns with different guests. When our eyes meet, he gestures for me to come over. There is no way I am getting on the dance floor. My fury at what Melissa did to him has been intensifying all day.

I blow him a subtle kiss, shake my head, mouth, 'I'm okay' and continue my journey. The further I get from the noise, the calmer I feel, so I walk through the surrounding garden and end up alone on the beach. I make my way to the deserted water's edge.

'Had enough of our circus?'

The voice startles me and I turn round quickly. It's the groom. He nods respectfully before introducing himself and stepping forward. I feel a little ambushed.

'Kevin Wong.'

'Ariella Mason.' I nod back.

'I know. You're impossible to miss.'

I'm not sure if he's trying to be charming but he is making me uncomfortable. I take a deep breath to calm myself down, and step back.

'Congratulations,' I say, as a way of ending the conversation.

'I'm not sure that's the word I'd use. My wife is beautiful, but she's mean.'

'You've been married for less than four hours and I've only just met you, Mr Wong. Congratulations are all I have to offer.'

'Mr Wong?' He laughs. 'Dominic did tell me that you were... painfully polite.'

'I can live with that.'

'Are you not enjoying the party?'

I don't know where the conversation is going and why he is so far away from his own wedding reception, so I tread carefully.

'It's noisier than I am used to.'

'Go to a lot of quiet weddings?'

I have no intention of indulging Kevin Wong. 'No, just different. The groom disappearing mid-celebration is new.'

'My wife litters the entire wedding ceremony and breakfast with indications that she's a prisoner in my dungeon and that's the bit that's new?'

'Mr Wong, I don't mean to be abrupt; but—'

'Melissa and Caleb aren't done with each other. You should know that.'

'Haven't you just exchanged vows with one of them?'

'She's Melissa Chang. I know what I'm getting into. I'm not sure you do.'

'Thank you for your thoughts, Mr Wong.'

'I can see how you've driven Dom nuts.'

'It was enlightening to meet you, Mr Wong.' I shut down the conversation immediately and turn to make my way back to the glass pavilion. I'd rather deal with the noise and the people than be alone with Kevin Wong.

'Enlightening? Ouch!' Kevin calls as he speeds up to catch up with me. Just before we reach the pavilion, he reaches out to stop me, with what seems like concern. 'I think you're going to be okay, Ariella Mason; but, just in case you aren't, please stay close to Dominic. Ah, speak of the devil.' He looks towards the pavilion. I turn to see Dominic emerging from the glass dome.

'Look who I found wandering out on the beach by herself!' he shouts to a surprised-looking Dominic.

'Don't believe a word he says.' Dominic calmly makes his way towards us. I muster a smile for him as I walk up to meet him.

'Dom.' I give him a hug, genuinely relieved to see him. Kevin was beginning to scare me.

'Dom, eh?' Kevin teases as he slaps Dominic's shoulder. 'All I got was Mr Wong.'

'People get what they deserve, Kevin,' Dominic lightly teases Kevin before he steps in front of me slowly and uses a hand to secure me safely behind him. Kevin gives me a final smile, then walks back into his sham wedding.

'Are you okay?' Dominic asks. 'You looked a little shaken.'

'Yes, thank you. He just came out of nowhere, that's all.'

'Okay. Good. Lara's having a great time, by the way. She has most of the men at the edge of the dance floor right now, salivating at her dancing with Honey. If only they knew. I might hire her after all.' He winks at me conspiratorially.

'Knew what?' I panic. I trust Dominic but the fewer people know about Honey, the better.

'Christopher told me about her affair with a client's girlfriend and a few other offences when I hinted that I might hire her. Not that it changed my mind.'

'You're going to give Lara a job?'

'I'm thinking about it. And no, I'm not doing it for you, although making her happy makes you happy, which makes me happy. She's difficult to ignore and very convincing.'

'Thank you, Dom.'

'You're welcome. Come on, let's get back to the party.'

FOURTEEN

CALEB

For a wedding none of us wanted to attend, it's bloody good fun. They've turned the reception into a nightclub and everyone is on the dance floor. The DJ is on fire and we are all quarter-to-drunk because we are never too far from a glass of something delicious. I've even managed to generate a few leads, because everyone who's anyone is here.

Apart from Ariella. I watched her wander out a while ago. I would have followed, but she looked like she needed the alone time away from the noise and I decided to stay to keep my eye on Honey and Lara. It seems Lara made a few 'friends' the night before. Every time one of her victims would try to cut in to grab Lara's attention, she'd expertly dance away to find Honey again, crushing one ego after the other. It's not until Honey throws me a worried look that I grab Bryce and we both cut in. I get it – the last thing Honey wants is the attention.

Bryce is a fucking rock star. He steps up, grabs Lara by the waist, pulls her right into him and holds her still before letting her sway along with him. The attention Lara has drawn is so intensely focused on Bryce making her submit to him on the dance floor that it gives Honey and me the distraction we need to casually dance away to one of the hidden tables to take a break. Not that anyone cares – we've supposedly been a couple for so long, we're old news.

'I don't think I can do this.' Honey is panicking by the time we sit down. I understand. Lara can be a little too sparkly and Honey has found hiding peaceful and a source of comfort.

'Breathe, Honey. Embarrassingly, it was only a few weeks ago that I realised that most things can be solved by talking. Have you told her?'

'No, how can I? She's a lot, Caleb. I know she's loud and amazing and funny – and look at her, she's beautiful. But she lives her life out in the open. I can't do that. She could jeopardise everything.'

'Trust me, I'm never more than ten minutes away from wanting to strangle Lara, and yes, she is a force of nature, but she is kind, loyal, trustworthy and absolutely dependable. She will fight for you and keep your secrets. She will tell you the truth but protect you from the consequences. She will bend the rules for you, including hers. And if you let her love you, the day that you regret that choice will never arrive – because I may want to kill her most of the time, but I fucking love that woman and, whether or not she admits it, she loves me too. And I don't think we'd want to have it any other way.'

'I don't know, Caleb. I don't think I'm ready and I'm not even sure if she realises how serious this is.'

'Honey, you really have no idea what's going on here, do you? Watch this.'

I whip out my phone and send a text to Lara.

> Get your exhibitionist arse off the fucking dance floor and stop causing a scene. It's making H uncomfortable. We're on the back tables by the gifts.

We both observe Lara look at her watch and tap it.

K

Lara stops, hugs Bryce very suggestively and leads him off the dance floor in the opposite direction to exit the pavilion. The broken hearts she leaves behind slowly disperse.

'She cares about you, Honey. Probably more than you know. Go back to the villa. Tell her.'

It doesn't take long for Lara to appear.

'Sorry we took so long, we had to lose the lechy eyes. Hunbun, are you all right? I'm sorry.'

'Yeah. I think I've had enough. I'm going to head back to the villa.'

'I'll come with you. Make sure you're okay. This dress is killing me and, besides, I'm sure I'll be employed by the end of next week, so my work here is done. Shall I nick a bottle of wine? We can go back and watch a film.'

The smile Honey rewards Lara with as she stands makes my heart melt. I think these two might make it.

'Nicely done, Bryce.'

'Meh, I owe Lara several favours. We look out for each other,' he says, then pats me on the back and walks away.

Honey and Lara have left me all warm and fuzzy, so I find my happy place.

> Mason, you beautiful creature, where are you?

> Having a chat with Dominic and a couple of others outside away from the noise. Come and get me when you've had enough?

Just as I start to cross the dance floor to retrieve my girl-friend, a very tipsy Melissa stumbles up, drinking champagne straight from the bottle even though she is holding a perfectly useable flute. I've been sticking close to the team and avoiding her all day. I was just starting to feel like I could get through her circus without any contact.

'Wanna dance with the bride?' She isn't quite fully drunk yet, and all eyes are on her, so I can't exactly decline. I wrestle the champagne bottle and glass from her and put them down on the closest table.

'Of course.' I force a smile. Thankfully it's a fast track and we can dance at a distance. The good thing about weddings is that people tend to follow the bride and dance around her. It won't take long before we end up in a dancing group. I plan to slip away as soon as a Whitney Houston or Beyoncé track comes on and sends all the women in the vicinity into a frenzy. Thankfully, the DJ is being generous with those tonight. It's just a matter of time.

'Are you having a good time?' she asks over the music.

'For an event that required our mandatory attendance, it hasn't been terrible. Are you and your "chains" having a good time?' I already know the answer.

'The drink was helping me come to terms with it.' She points to the bottle I confiscated, then grabs my hand and clumsily makes me twirl her.

'You really don't want to be doing this, do you?'

'I had no choice.' She shimmies away and shimmies back again.

'You're Melissa Chang. All you have is choice.' I bring her back to me and twirl her properly.

'That's where I messed up.'

'How did you mess up?'

'Ask me if I come back from my honeymoon.' She dances around me suggestively.

'If?'

'Did I say if?' She feigns a shocked face. 'I meant when.'

I leave it because, at this point, I don't care. It's her day and, as much as she doesn't want to be here, she is making the best of it. Thankfully, after an unusually long hiatus, the DJ finally hits us with 'I Wanna Dance with Somebody'. There is joyful screaming, and the women on the dance floor immediately gravitate towards Melissa. Perfect. Time to find Ariella and take her home.

The pavilion has several doors, so it takes me a few tries to find the right one. I spot Ariella standing with Dominic Miller, Kevin Wong and a couple of other people I don't recognise. I join them. I don't particularly want to stay, but she is talking passionately about expanding our Conscious Experience app and I love watching her when she's like this. Dominic Miller's jacket is draped over her shoulders as he listens, standing protectively next to her in his white shirt, black bow tie and cummerbund. It's not a visual I like, at all.

'Hey, congratulations, Kevin.' I approach. Aari's face lights up as soon as she sees me and I'm not the only one who notices. In fact, it's so obvious it doesn't bother me any more that Dominic's coat is over her shoulders.

'The infamous Caleb. Thanks.' Kevin reaches out his hand and Dominic stifles a chuckle as I shake it.

'The infamous Caleb indeed. How are you doing? Getting ready to head to London next week?' Dominic asks, extending his own hand. I take it.

'Yes. Should be a good trip.'

I promised Ariella I would grow up and, to be honest, it's not very difficult after last night. Whatever that was between us created such a deep tie to her that I don't feel the usual need to draw big, fat, red lines around her. Her heart is mine, we belong to each other and nothing is going to touch that.

I am introduced to the other two guys, who work in the same industry space as Kevin and Dominic.

'Are you ready to go?' Aari asks, hinting that she is.

'Noooo, stay.' The guys turn to Ariella together.

'Yes, Caleb. Stay,' Kevin directs at me instead. 'I've got to tell you guys, Caleb is a big reason why I'm getting married today.' He puts his hand on my shoulder. Shit, he knows. No, he can't know. He simply can't.

'Why?' one of the other guys asks.

'Mel is absolutely obsessed with him.' Present tense. What the fuck is going on?

Ariella slowly reaches for my hand and I see Dominic notice it. My palms start to sweat because this is not supposed to be in the public domain. I need to stop this but I don't know how.

'Oh yeah!' Kevin continues. 'She's had him on her mind for so many years, it left space for nothing else. He's had a massive impact on her and all he had to do was meet her once. She even went to London to find him. Thankfully, she also came back with you, Ariella, and you are absolutely delightful.' He takes Ariella's hand and kisses it. Ariella puts that polite smile on her face that, if you knew her, you'd easily decode as 'get the fuck away from me, now'.

'It was a while ago, I'm hardly responsible...' I try to break his story, but he's committed and mid-flow.

'Oh, come on! Me, you, Dominic and Melissa sat at the same table at the Tech Awards, about three, four years back, remember? I think she told me you shared a car home.'

Dominic was there? Kevin looks like he's telling a happy-go-lucky story, but he's making it clear that he definitely knows. 'Or maybe you put her in a car to take her home. It's hard to recall. Either way, there was a car and she got home. Eventually.'

Okay. I relax. He's not going to say anything. I know that because Zheng has been driving Melissa since she was six. Even when she went to Stanford, he moved to California with her and drove her around there too. I don't believe she has ever been put in a car that isn't hers, ever, in her life. He just wants me to know that he knows. I play along.

'Possibly.' I exaggerate my nonchalance.

'Anyway, I'm glad she got you here. You've been her little project and kept her busy for the last couple of years. Now you're in Singapore, she can mark it as complete and move on to other things.'

'I'm glad it worked out. He's an incredible director of sales,' Dominic adds to end the conversation, even though his expression tells me that he is enjoying this.

'Oh, he definitely worked out. The very next day after he moved to Singapore to start this role, Melissa finally committed to our wedding date. Isn't that nuts?' Kevin confirms to Ariella.

Right now, all I can think about is going to find Melissa. I need to know what Kevin knows and if it's going to be a problem for me going forward. I just need to get away without it looking like I am beating a retreat after the exchange with Kevin. Dominic gives me the break I need. He's been unusually helpful this evening, albeit unintentionally.

'Ariella, can we go for a twirl on the dance floor? I promise to be gentle with your boss, Caleb.'

'Please return her in one piece,' I say as I shake his hand again.

'Well?' Dominic asks Ariella.

'Sure,' she responds, not sounding sure at all, but she lets him lead her away anyway.

I nod my goodbyes to the others and walk in the other direction. When I am a safe distance away, I whip out my phone and text Melissa that we need to talk. We agree to meet at the altar in five. It's as good a location as any, given the mockery she made of her vows earlier.

I quickly make my way over and find her waiting for me in the dark.

'Kevin knows?' I don't waste any time.

'Yes,' she confirms, obviously irritated that she has to.

'What the fuck, Mel. He's telling everyone you're marrying him because of me.'

'What did he say?'

'That you're obsessed with me and—'

'Asshole,' she spits.

'Did you tell him?'

'Of course not!'

'Then how?'

'It doesn't matter.'

'Of course it fucking matters!'

'Caleb, I don't want to—'

'Melissa! Tell me right now.'

'Fine. He has pictures, texts and recordings. From Singapore and London. He knows everything. Even about our last night together. He said he'd release them if we didn't come to an agreement with the prenup.'

'He threatened you?'

'No, dumb-dumb! I can take care of myself. He threatened *you*. Kevin and his felonious relatives can't even consider that I might be engaging in pillow talk. Not that it would even cross their minds if I was a man. Thankfully I'm valuable. You, however, are dispensable.'

'You married him because of me? Why?' I soften.

'Because I loved you, you fucking liability! I'd rather have you alive, running around rubbing Ariella in my face all over Singapore where I can keep an eye on you, than have you found dead, naked and alone, with some cryptic threat shoved up your anus, on Hampstead Heath.'

'Kevin could do that?'

'Kevin is an idiot. It's the people Kevin might inadvertently inform, connected to his evil father, that might be a problem. Argh. I'm surrounded by so many stupid people.'

She paces back and forth. It's out before I realise it.

'Thank you.'

'Shut up, you moron,' she responds quietly. For the first time since I've known her, I feel her emanate a sorrow so deep that, if I don't hold her, she will fall apart. I step forward, reach for Mel and pull her into my arms.

'I miss my dad, Caleb. I feel so lonely without him and, contrary to what you may believe, he didn't put me through medical school, residencies, years of no sleep, abuse and navigating egotistical God complexes only for me to become a common criminal. This is not what he wanted for me and it sure as fuck isn't what I wanted for myself.' And her admission is all it takes for Melissa Chang to burst into hard, heartbreaking sobs in my arms.

I hold her for as long as it takes for her to calm down and, when does, she steps away quietly.

'Not a word about this to anyone, Caleb,' she says angrily, wiping her tears.

'Trust me, my legacy at this wedding isn't going to be the guy that you cheated on Kevin with.'

'I didn't.'

'You didn't what?'

'I didn't cheat on Kevin. Today was our first kiss. That was revolting enough. Kevin and I have never slept together and we never will.'

'I don't understand. Then why...'

'You'll understand soon enough. I'd better get back to my wedding and my plan to make Kevin's life the definition of misery.'

She straightens her body, hardens her face and gives me one last look.

'Goodbye, Caleb. Look after yourself. And whatever happens, trust me, I'm going to be fine.'

FIFTEEN

ARIELLA

Dominic is a conservative dancer and, the moment we take the dance floor, he puts me in a hold. He clutches one of my hands with one of his and places the other loosely round my waist. It takes about a minute but, surprisingly, we find our rhythm and eventually start to move to the music together. It's endearing.

'You dance like someone professional taught you,' I observe.

'They did. A lot,' he admits, unashamed. 'But you're a natural.' He twirls me away and brings me back again. 'Why am I your only dance today?'

'I'm not a big public dancer and this is more work than fun for me.'

'That's something I didn't know. I suppose being forced to attend a wedding takes all the romance out of it.'

'Especially one like this.'

'My bet is that it's a wealth-preservation move. Two families, consolidating.'

'But Melissa has no family. It's just her, and she wasn't jumping for joy the last time I checked.'

'Maybe protection? Kevin's father is... not a nice guy. I think Kevin spends a lot of his life doing as he is told.'

'You think he was told to marry Melissa?'

'The whole Kevin and Melissa thing is weird. They both always seem to want to be elsewhere.'

'Maybe that's where they should be.'

Dominic launches me away from him in time with the music, then pulls me back in so he's behind me, holding me close as we dance. This in no way feels like I am dancing with my boss and it makes me a little uneasy. I feel him lower his head to speak into my ear.

'Would you rather be elsewhere?'

'Yes.'

'Where?'

'Anywhere but here.'

Dominic releases my waist but keeps hold of my hand as we leave the dance floor. He leads me past the people milling around outside and through the gardens surrounding the pavilion until we find a quiet bench.

'You've been sad all day. Would you like me to see if I can get you back home to Singapore tonight?'

'No, thank you, Dom. We made a commitment and I'd like to see it through.'

'But you look like you're aching, Aari. You may have been charming and excited when you were talking about the app, but you're clearly hurting. What's going on?'

'Melissa is a monster. She has hurt so many people that I care about and I'm finding it really hard to be relaxed at what is clearly a sham wedding. But the people she has truly hurt seem to be okay, so who am I not to be?'

'The pain of the observer is often greater than the sufferer; as it is bolstered by the limitless power of imagination.'

'Who said that?'

'No idea. How can I help? I can call Lara, take you back to mine for a little while, walk you back to yours? This thing is pretty much over.'

'I think I need a walk to clear my head. I really hope this is the end of Melissa and everything that comes with her, Dom.'

'I hope so too, and, if it's not, we'll figure it out. You're not alone any more, Aari, you've got Samir and me now. What you went through to get Ivory Bow to the other side of that disaster wasn't lost on me. Just because you're tough and strong and you can carry this company through alone doesn't mean you should. You were smart to demote yourself, but you don't need a CEO because you can't do the job, Ariella Mason, you're more than competent. You need a CEO because someone needs to teach, support and look after you until you decide you want it, if you ever do; and that person can't be me because I have conflicting interests.'

'Dom, I need to tell you—'

'I know you're back together with him, Aari. I genuinely hope it works out because, above everything else, I want you to be happy. It's just that I see you doing a lot of fighting for this guy. I just hope he fights for you too.'

'He does. The way Caleb shows up may not be visible to anyone else, but it matters to me.'

'Just know, you can come to me for anything, Aari. Anything at all.' Dominic extends his hand. 'Let me walk you back to your villa.'

Lara and Honey are sitting together sweetly on the couch, watching a film, when I get back.

'Hey!' they say at the same time, their eyes glued to the screen.

'Looks like you both had a lovely evening. What are you watching?'

'Some French film about a guy in a wheelchair that hires a male nurse from the wrong side of the tracks,' Lara says, waving me away.

'Want to join us, Aari?' Honey asks, moving to the edge of the couch. She pulls Lara towards her so that Lara will be sandwiched between us. It's cute.

'No, she doesn't,' Caleb says, coming through the door, before hugging me from behind. He plants a kiss on my shoulder and I smell the whisky on his breath. He's been hanging out with Lydia. I don't know why, but it makes me smile.

'Hi,' I say, enjoying his closeness.

'Did you have fun today, considering the circumstances?'

'It wasn't horrible. Before I forget, we may have two potential new clients. The two guys outside? I've emailed you their details.'

'Thank you.'

'Shhhhhh!' Lara scolds us.

'It's in French!' Caleb complains. 'You're reading the subtitles.'

'Come on,' I interrupt before they start attacking each other. I lead Caleb into our room and he leans in to kiss my lips as soon as he shuts the door behind us.

'You're still in your dress. Nice.'

'You did promise to help me out of it earlier,' I suggest.

'I did, didn't I?'

Standing behind me, he slowly unzips my dress, his fingers leaving little sparks down my back. 'I forgot about your little lingerie surprise.' He strokes my bum as the dress drops to the floor. I turn round to help him out of his suit.

Everything with Caleb feels final since we reunited. Like we can take our time with each other because we know that neither one of us is going anywhere. I want him to feel safe with me, like I have always done with him, no matter what external forces may be at play.

After he fulfils his promise, we shower, locate bathrobes and sit in bed to catch on how bizarre today has been.

'So, I've got three weeks on Melissa and Kevin,' he bets casually.

'They'll go the distance. This wedding was a contract. As long as they stay away from each other, keep their affairs discreet and don't attempt to have a loving home, they'll stay together.'

'Ariella Mason, you romantic.' Caleb tickles me and I yelp. 'I have something to tell you but before I do I'm going to need you to tell Icy Ariella to back off. I want to share everything with you and I need you to try to understand.'

Oh no. I close my eyes, take a deep breath and let it out slowly. This is Caleb. It could be anything. When I'm ready I open my eyes to his worried face.

'Okay. I'm listening.'

'I met Melissa tonight. Privately.'

I feel the familiar numbness start to creep over me. 'Wait, please.' I take a few more breaths before I feel it dissipate. 'Okay, continue.'

'I needed to find out how much Kevin knew and if it was going to cause any further problems. Do you want the details or the highlights?'

Normally, Caleb telling a good juicy story is my happy place, but this isn't a good or juicy story and the thought of him being alone with Melissa makes me deeply uncomfortable. Especially after what she did.

'Highlights, please.'

'Kevin knows everything. He was going to go public unless Melissa married him. She's not coping well.'

'How does that have an impact on you, me or Ivory Bow?'

'It doesn't and it won't – it's baked into the prenup. They can't "embarrass" each other.'

'Anything else that directly or specifically affects us?'

'No, but Icy Ariella just showed up,' Caleb says, then strokes my face. It's true. I'm numb.

'I don't know how to deal with this, Caleb. You sound almost... sympathetic. Kevin Wong's extortion plot doesn't seem anywhere near as egregious as what she has been getting up to.'

'I do feel a little sorry for her. She burst into tears, Aari.'

'Caleb, please tell me that you did not spend part of your evening consoling the rapist who successfully orchestrated moving our lives across the world and then tried to get eight innocent people convicted for her financial crimes?'

'I didn't know what to do.'

I want to scream until my lungs give out, because that's the alternative to being numb. I'm angry and I'm hurt, but being able to share things like this with me is new for him and I promised I'd try to understand.

'I need to know if you'll keep running to her if she calls, Caleb. I'm trying to remove this person from our personal and professional lives, and I don't think I can cope with her reintro-duction – especially by you.'

'That's not what this is, Aari. She has been blocked this entire time. I genuinely just needed to know what Kevin knew.' He looks at me regretfully. 'Things just took a turn, that's all.'

It takes me about a minute to breathe through the conversa-tion we have just had. Eventually, I reach for his hand and lace my fingers through his. I didn't handle that well.

'I'm sorry. Thank you for telling me. The next time some-thing like this pops up, please can we maybe talk about it and find a way to get what we need without involving her?' I pull my boyfriend close and kiss him deeply.

'You're not pissed off?'

'I'm more thankful that we're using this to try to be kinder and more open with each other. It happened, we talked about it, you said it's not going to happen again and I believe you. I think that's kind of how the growing-up thing is going to work.'

'Ugh. I hate that we're out of supplies,' Caleb says, pulling me in even closer.

'Maybe if we're careful...' I raise my eyebrows twice at him.

'Good girls would shut me down and suggest we go to sleep.'

'True, but naughty girls tend to do whatever they want.'

It doesn't take long for Caleb to pounce.

Morning comes too quickly. I am up before him and feeling playful, so I straddle him to wake him up. Without opening his eyes, he reaches out, grabs me and pulls me into his chest before he shifts my hips to a place where I get a crystal-clear idea of what his morning plans are.

'Goodness, Caleb. You have such a one-track mind!' I laugh and he laughs right along with me.

'One-track mind? I'm not the one straddling a sleeping man.'

'You're not sleeping any more, are you?'

'No, I am not. I am very much awake, in every sense,' he says, placing his lips on mine.

After we shower, Caleb and I decide to skip the wedding brunch and explore the island. Lara's exploits over the last couple of days have left her more infamous than she would like, so she and Honey decide to join us.

As we make our way to the far end of the beach away from the party, we are quickly approached by an island resident who suggests that we go further afield for a mangrove lunch. After Caleb vehemently votes no because he doesn't want to get killed while protecting us from our poor choices, Honey volunteers to be our group muscle if anything goes wrong. With Caleb outvoted three to one, we get in the gentleman's car and are taken to a shuttle boat ten minutes away. The floating restaurant is peacefully empty when we arrive. We have a lazy brunch, navigating the items sent to us from the kitchen, and I wish we had more days like this. After we have had some food, we pick a hammock each from the many tied to the boat's structure and allow the motion to rock us to sleep. After what feels like seconds, Caleb wakes me. The restaurant is much busier. He looks concerned.

'Mason, we have to go.' He gives me a quick kiss, then goes off to find our waiter. By the time I get out of my hammock, our bill is paid and the shuttle boat to shore is waiting.

'What's wrong?'

'We're going to miss our transfer back home.'

Thankfully our car is waiting at the shore to take us back to the resort. We pack quickly and make it just in time to get through immigration and get on Dominic's plane. When we board, he's not there, so I shoot him a quick text.

> Hey Dom, we just made the plane. We're on board now.

Where were you this morning?

His response is a little sharp. It's expected; we were cutting it fine.

> Went to a floating mangrove restaurant.

Was Caleb with you?

This is weird.

> Yes, with Honey and Lara.

Ok. Good. Head home. I'll fly with Kevin.

> I'm sorry we were running late.

Don't worry about it. Mel didn't make it to brunch and Kevin is losing his mind because he can't find her.

> She couldn't have gone far. How was she this morning?

Our groom may have spent his wedding night with someone other than his wife. Delete this.

I swipe right, select the last message and hit delete immediately. Another message follows.

> Get home safely. I'll drop you a message when I'm back.

'What did he say? Is he coming?' Caleb asks.

'No, we're going home alone. Melissa is hiding from Kevin and they are trying to find her. Your three-week prediction might have been too generous.'

After we land, I head back with Caleb to spend some time with him before he goes to London for the week. He takes care of our supply issue with an overenthusiastic restock and the afternoon unfolds with a beautiful ease around us. We spend it swimming, stealing kisses, napping under the sun by the pool and picking at the spread of food he has ordered in for us. This lazy day with him is what I need before he prepares to fly to London for the Harrison-replacement interviews in the morning. When we get into bed that night, everything feels quiet and normal. It's a feeling I have craved since I arrived in Singapore, and for the first time I allow myself to see past our lives here.

'Caleb, when all this is over, what do you want to do?' I ask as I climb into his bed.

'I don't know, but I apparently now own two boxing gyms, which funnily enough will leave me homeless in Singapore.'

'What do you mean, homeless?'

'I've liquidated everything in Singapore and moved it back home. That includes this apartment, so I have to move out by the end of next month. Let's hope that's not a sign of things to come.' He laughs.

'Want to move in with me?'

'You don't think it's too soon?'

'It's not soon enough. This is what I wanted when I took the job, Caleb. I wanted us to live together and to have a big adventure.'

'I think we got the big adventure in spades.'

I laugh as I shake my head. My boyfriend plants a sweet little kiss on my lips. 'And it looks like there's more adventure to come with your gyms. It's wonderful but it's also a huge commitment.'

'We'll see. I'm not sure what to do with them, to be honest. The plan for now is to rent them. Obviously, whoever leases them needs to guarantee that Phillip and the boys will have a place to train, but that's it. Have you been thinking about what you want to do?'

'I don't know. I've been thinking about the shelter a lot and I might volunteer full time for a little while until I decide.'

'Would you consider working with food? Jack's idea wasn't bad.'

'I'm not good enough.'

'First of all, you are definitely good enough. And maybe there are other ways that we haven't thought of yet.'

'I'm not. I haven't cooked properly in months and things are only going to get busier at work as we grow.'

'We can find the time to get you cooking again. That's the easy part...' he says, closing in and tracing a finger up my leg.

'Caleb, we're not going to find the time at the top of my thigh.'

'We're not, but we have supplies again and time tonight is precious. Any requests, seeing as I'll be gone all week?'

'Yes. Please can you make your love bites last? You?'

'Dig your nails in. Your cute little short-nailed scratches on my back remind me of you.'

'I didn't know you had a kink!'

Caleb stops and then suddenly erupts with laughter, making me laugh too.

'Ariella Mason, what do you know about kinks?'

'Enough for me to recognise one and wonder what mine could be. It'd be exciting to find out.'

'What the hell do you think your absolute obsession with my love bites is? You, my little Mason, are very kinky.'

Caleb's hand travels above my vest, finds my nipple and brushes his palm lightly over it, making me gasp as my back arches instinctively.

My boyfriend then chuckles to himself, before he covers my mouth with his.

At the end of the next day, Ms Pat, for the very first time, turns up at the Ivory Bow office with a shopping bag, an invitation to Tekka Market in Little India and a message from Caleb.

Mason, I'll probably be about eight hours into my flight right now, but if Ms Pat is showing you this she's an angel. Block off this time in your diary every week and use it to explore. She'll be with you for as many weeks as you want the training wheels to stay on. I love you. Go. Have fun.

And that's where I am when the text comes through from Lydia. Following the recovery of her mobile phone and wallet, Melissa Chang has been officially declared missing.

SIXTEEN

CALEB

Melissa Chang is not missing. I don't know what she's playing at, but I'm sure that little psycho is fine. Thankfully, she's Kevin's problem now and none of my business. I send Lydia a reply to her message.

> I'm sure she'll pop up eventually. She always does. Wedding recap over whisky when I get back?

Our flat is chilly when I get in. Referring to it as ours again makes me smile. Thanks to the time difference, it's only noon on Monday, and I'm not due at Ivory Bow until tomorrow morning. I send a quick text to Ariella to let her know I'm home, to put her mind at ease. My tummy flips when I think about how sincerely she asked me to promise to let her know when I got home safely.

> Home safely Mason. How is my bite?

Which one?

> You know the one.

Tender. Stop it, I'm in public. Thank you for
what you did. Ms Pat is teaching me the art of
aggressive negotiation. I love you so much.

> I can't wait to come back home to you.

I'll be waiting. Impatiently.

I call an emergency locksmith and organise the same-day
cleaning service I used last time. I then shower, sort through my
post and catch up on some work before the locksmith turns up
to break into Ariella's room.

I spend the rest of the afternoon replacing our items around
the flat. I put back her clothes that I moved from my drawers,
and place some of my clothes back in hers. Her shampoo, conditioner and spare toothbrush are returned to the space I cleared
on my shower shelf for her. Then I carefully check the spices I
packed away, chuck the ones that have expired and diligently
place the good ones in the spaces she reserved for them. I rehang the print she loves and put our framed cheesy image back
on the shelf. I make sure it feels like home again before I text
Tim and Jack.

> Boys! Pub quiz tonight?

Tim replies first:

Why do they keep letting you back into the
country? I'm up for it.

Jack joins in:

Bloody hell. We were doing so well. I suppose
we were going to start coming last again,
sooner or later. See you there.

I have a quick shower but take my time washing my hair

with Ariella's shampoo and conditioner. Apart from the stuff actually working, it makes me feel close to her. Once the cleaning crew arrives, I leave our flat to them and make my way to the pub.

'Bad Boy Black!' Jack laughs out loud when I enter the warm pub, and his piss-taking puts me in an even better mood.

'I'll sign your arse if you like, mate.' I laugh as I pull him into a hug. I've missed this loser.

'Would you? Can you make it out to the Thirsty Girls and Boys With no Standards Club?'

'Absolutely, Mr President.'

'You both need to get a room,' Tim says, walking up behind us.

'Mate.' I turn to hug him.

'What's up with you?' Tim gives me a quizzical look.

'Ariella. That's what's up with him.' Jack raises an eyebrow. 'He's radiating happiness, smelling like her and everything.'

'Shut the fuck up, Jack. What are you two drinking?'

It takes the entire trip to the bar and back with our beers to wipe the grin from my face. They're right. It's her.

'What's been going on?' I ask as I sit.

'Want to tell him or shall I?' Tim asks Jack.

'Lou and I are over.'

'Champagne. Shots. We need to celebrate! When did this happen?'

'You're such a dick, Caleb.' Jack laughs. 'Last week.'

'How does it feel?'

'Freeing. Obviously, we were together for years and that comes with its issues, but it's all right.'

'Mate, the only thing I'd miss is that huge apartment.'

'Wait for it,' Tim says, holding his palm up.

'Well...' Jack starts.

'Oh, bloody hell, now what?'

'I'm still staying there at the moment. We agreed I could stay until I found somewhere.'

I put my face in my hands.

'Jack, for fuck's sake.'

'That's exactly what I said,' Tim says as he sips on his half pint.

'She's in Milan for the next few weeks. I'll be gone by the time she gets back.'

'Wait.' I stop him.

'Yup,' Tim says as he crosses his arms, looking exhausted. 'Ask him, Caleb.'

'Was Louisa in Milan when you broke up with her?'

'Yeah. I'd had enough and I needed to do it there and then.'

'Fine. How did she take it?'

'She said she understood and that I could keep the Tesla and stay as long as I needed to until I found somewhere else to live.'

'Lou is as sensitive as a toilet seat. Tim?' I get the nod and Tim drains his half pint.

'Van's outside,' he says, slamming down the glass. There is still some beer left in it.

'What?' Jack asks.

'We're going to Lou's and we're getting all your shit. You're moving in with me tonight.'

'Thanks, mate,' Tim says, standing, his keys already in hand. 'I've been on him for the last week. He wouldn't be told, and Em is not helping – she thinks Lou will be reasonable.'

I don't give Jack the opportunity to argue, I just follow Tim out of the pub. Jack eventually catches up. We get into the two front passenger seats of Tim's van and head to Knightsbridge. When we finally manage to get through the London traffic and arrive at Lou's building, our suspicions are confirmed before we set foot in the property. We are asked by the guard from the car park to go through the front.

'Good evening, Patrick,' Jack calls to the usually friendly doorman as we follow him in.

'I'm sorry, sir, but we have been told by Miss Gabrielli not to allow anyone into the apartment aside from you.'

'Patrick, I'm just getting some things.'

'We've also been instructed not to allow you to remove anything from the apartment, sir.'

'Come on, Patrick. I'm just getting some of my clothes.'

'I'm sorry, sir. You're welcome to go up, but you may not remove anything and your guests must stay here.'

'Guys, what the fuck?' Jack turns to us, distressed. 'She's not back for weeks!'

Something in Jack's voice has made Patrick's hard mask slip. He knows. Of course he knows. Doormen know everything.

'You know,' I confront him as I walk up to him. 'You know what's going on.'

'It is not my job to interfere. Sadly, I can only adhere to Miss Gabrielli's instructions, as the owner of the apartment. As I must adhere to the instructions of *any* other resident.' Patrick's inflection on the word any is all we need. I turn to Jack.

'Jack. Your neighbours. Please tell me you get along with at least one other person in this building that can invite us in.'

'I play squash with Ahmed sometimes.'

'Call him now. You're going to have to tell him what's going on. Can you do that?'

Jack unlocks his phone and dials. Within ten minutes, and after making us promise Jack will take just his clothes, shoes and laptop, Ahmed is downstairs vouching for us to get into the building. The second issue is posed by Louisa's front door camera. To avoid it, we camp at Ahmed's as Jack fits all he can into three suitcases and brings it to his neighbour's apartment.

That way, he is technically not leaving the building with all his belongings.

'Jack, have you got everything you need? You can't come back,' Tim reminds him, putting a comforting hand on Jack's shoulder.

He nods silently.

Jack exits the building through the front with his daily personal effects. Ahmed, Tim and I take the lift directly to the car park with the rest of his stuff. When we've loaded the cases into the back, Ahmed instructs the security guard to allow Tim's van to exit. As soon as Jack join us, Ahmed invites us to visit him in Dubai, before going back into the building.

Suddenly, we see the lights of the Tesla come on.

'Jack! What are you doing?'

'She said I could keep the Tesla.'

'Fucking hell, Jack!' Tim says, exasperated. 'We told Ahmed we'd only take your personal effects. What else did you take?'

'The engagement ring.'

'You have to return it.'

'No! It cost a fucking fortune!'

'Tough shit. If you want it back, you're going to have to fight her for it. If she comes back, sees it's missing and unravels what we've just done – because there are cameras everywhere – you will have put Ahmed in the shit. Give it back!' Tim is dangerously close to losing it.

'Come on, Jack.' I move him away from a stressed-looking Tim and return with him to the doorman. 'We'd like to leave a couple of high-value items for Miss Gabrielli. Please can you keep these in a safe until she returns?'

He finds us a small postage box, into which we place the ring and the key.

'Would you like to leave a note?' he asks and Jack nods.

I watch him scrawl *Stay THE FUCK away from me Lou. J.* with pride. I think I notice a small smile crossing Patrick the doorman's face. Once the box is sealed, security-stamped and photographed, Patrick reaches out his hand.

'Good luck, Jack. I hope I never see you here again.'

Jack takes it. 'Thanks, Patrick.'

By the time we step out, Tim has pulled up in front of the building. We turn the music up, laugh, sing and celebrate in the car. We stop at my local corner shop for some beers before parking up in front of my building.

When we get in, I remove my mattress topper, then move all my clothes and personal effects from my bedroom into Ariella's. I get clean sheets from the drying room and toss them on the bed before helping to wheel the cases in.

'Thanks, mate,' Jack says before pulling me and then Tim into a hug.

'You should thank me, you've got the bigger room, with the better bathroom,' I joke.

'What's the rent?' Jack asks nervously.

'Cover the bills, look after the place, fix whatever you break, buy your own sheets and invest in a new mattress topper tomorrow that you will take with you when you eventually move out. I'm not sleeping on the same bed as your swipey victims, now you're free to do what you like. We'll stay in Aari's room when we visit, so don't even think about subletting. Aari and I will be gone for a while. It's yours for at least a year and a half. We'll give you a six-month warning before we come back.'

'Are you sure? I want to pay something.'

'Ariella has refused to stop paying rent and the company pays for everything out there, so I'm good. If you feel the need to pay something, then just pay what you can afford. You should have my bank details from that twenty quid you still owe me,' I remind him jokily.

'Are you sure Ariella is going to be okay with this?' Jack asks.

'Not only will she be okay with it, if I'd done nothing she'd be fuming in that infuriatingly quiet, polite way she does when she gets annoyed.'

'Let me guess, when you ask her what's wrong, she says it's nothing. When it, very scarily, is something.' Tim laughs to himself.

'Yes!' I turn, surprised at him.

'Em's the same. Mate, stay away from anything that causes that. It's torture.'

'I know!' We both howl.

We help Jack unpack, then I order us a takeaway and we open the beers in the living room.

'So, were you serious about wanting to marry Ariella?' Tim asks casually, prompting Jack to inhale mid-drink and choke on his beer.

'When did this happen?' Jack splutters.

'Late one night, he texted Em. I think he was drunk. Em's been looking at floral arrangements, wedding presents, flights to Singapore, dresses for her and suits for me, since. You should see the ridiculous outfits she's considering putting Alfie in as a pageboy.'

'I can assure you, Alfie is not going to be my pageboy, ever,' I reassure Tim, and see the relief flood his face. 'Alfie's going to be my best man. I'm asking her parents at the end of the week, when work is done.'

'Shit!' Tim and Jack say at the same time.

'He's not joking,' Jack says to Tim.

'No, he's not.' Tim stands with pride in his eyes. 'Well done, mate. Come here.'

I stand and step into Tim's hug and double pat on my back.

'Dads, release your daughters,' Jack announces, doing the same. 'We've hugged a lot tonight.'

'A lot has happened,' Tim says.

'Can we all relax and go back to being boring now? I've only been in the country for ten hours.' I hold up my beer and toast. 'To a boring week!'

The boys cheer as they meet my bottle with theirs.

Jack is a good flatmate that week. He is quiet, tidy and buys our takeaways, even though he is insisting that he'll start cooking when I leave. He is exactly what I need, because the week is tough. All the candidates are qualified and any one of them could do the job, which is making it difficult to give Christopher my top three. Usually, the gym on Wednesdays is a great place to clear my head, but all I can think about during my training and the class with Phillip and the boys is how I, the worst possible choice in Hugh Mason's eyes, am going to break it to him that I want to marry – according to Dahlia – the love of his life.

'Caleb!' Dahlia opens her loving arms and I step into them. There was a time when hugging Dahlia was foreign and unfamiliar, but now her hugs feel safe and assuring.

'Thanks for making time for me.' The nerves I feel dissolve, but not completely.

'Of course! Have you eaten? Would you like something?' She leads the way to her kitchen.

'No, I'm okay.' Eat? I can barely swallow. I take a deep breath as I lean against the kitchen island and exhale. Dahlia studies me quietly for a couple of seconds.

'Caleb, relax. We think we know why you're here.'

Dahlia is not making things easier with her revelation. I don't even have the element of surprise on my side.

'You don't know if he keeps guns in the house, do you?'

'Don't be silly, it'll be fine.'

'It may not be. Hello, Caleb.' Hugh Mason enters the kitchen from behind me.

'Hello, Mr Mason.'

'Okay. We're here. What would you like?' He pulls a seat out for himself at the dining table.

'Hugh...' Dahlia warns behind me.

If he's going in hard, I might as well join him, so I stay standing where I am and spit it out.

'I already know I don't deserve to be here. It's not even luck. It's a miracle. If you'd told the seven- to twenty-seven-year-old me that I'd be here, the sheer impossibility of it would have made it difficult to imagine, because my physical, mental and emotional beatings started early.

'They started with my own father, continued with the people I didn't sell drugs fast enough for and was pure sporting fun for those that simply saw and heard that I was from Toxteth. Then there were the beatings I inflicted on myself and to a certain extent still do.

'I'm telling you this because you are the two people Ariella loves the most in the world and you need to know who I am, before I even think about us potentially making a commitment to each other. She loves and respects you both and she will ask for your opinion. So I'm not asking you for Ariella. I'm asking if you'll have me as part of this family. It is the only way we will work, because Ariella won't be who she is without you, and I most certainly won't be who I am today without your influence.

'I don't want to take another step or make another decision without you. Dahlia, you're the mother I never had, and Hugh, you're the example I didn't get the privilege to see. Ariella can make her own decisions. She will either choose to have me or not. But I want you, because we are going to need you. Will you have me if I ask her and she says yes? If your answer is no, then we won't take any further steps, because I would never do that to her. But if you'll have me as part of your family, then I will be asking her and seeking your blessing.'

There. Bloody hell. I feel like I've given them more reasons to change their locks and phone numbers than to accept me.

Dahlia silently approaches me where I stand, wraps her arms round me and holds on so tightly, I well up.

'You'll always be welcome in our home, Caleb.' Hugh Mason looks at me sincerely. 'But you're not ready. I can't give my blessing for you to ask Ariella.'

'Hugh Mason!' Dahlia turns, shocked at her husband.

'Dahlia.' Hugh says it so softly, his love wraps around her. 'Please can I have some time alone with Caleb?'

With that Hugh Mason walks to their sliding door, pulls it open and invites me outside. Dahlia just nods, rubs my back and encourages me to follow him.

When Hugh Mason plants his feet apart and digs his hands into his pockets, I mirror him, ready to hear what he has to say.

'Remember what happened to the last man that did this?'

'With all due respect, sir, I'm not the last man.'

'I know that, but I gave my blessing and look at how that turned out.' The regret oozes thickly from him. 'I don't think I can do that to her again.'

'Jasper wasn't a bad—'

'Jasper didn't know how to love her. He had the duty and responsibility perfected, but he didn't know how to make her shine. He provided anything she could possibly want, then protected her by hiding her from the world, but he only did that because that's what he saw me do all her life. My worry is that my daughter is so vibrant and bright around you that the pendulum may have swung too far the other way.'

Hugh Mason finally admitting that he sees how happy I make Ariella is such a shock that I forget that he's telling me that I can't marry his daughter.

'I didn't do that, Mr Mason. That's all her. I'm blinded by it too. I mostly stand back and watch.'

'And that's my point. You can't just spectate. Do you have any idea what it takes to love a black woman? There are fights you didn't even know existed that you will have to jump into. There will be conversations that you won't understand, but because you love her you will have to stand beside her, feeling absolutely useless, letting her just do her thing. Then you have to go, educate yourself and be ready for the next one. You will feel like you literally have to defend her from the entire world because so much is set up to accelerate her failure. That's why she has to be tougher than most – and she is. It's just not in the way people expect her to be.

'I've seen the social media. Both of yours. The micro- and macro-aggressions. People are falling over themselves when you post your half-naked and partying pictures. Meanwhile, she's out there actually doing good work with the business and this new charity app, but she mostly gets neutral comments or straight-up abuse. At least your company is good at cleaning those up. And that American boy's brother calling her a gold-digging house Negro. Did you see how silently she moved on from that? She didn't even complain. It's gut-wrenching to know that we live in a world where she chooses to deal with that level of disgust quietly, because society often demands that those harmed by this behaviour forgive their perpetrator.

'The one thing that helps your case is you've experienced it too, but from a financial and societal perspective. So you under-stand it a little. Hypocritically, that's the pressure I'm putting on you. You need to be stable, Caleb. It's easy to have a wedding but do you have what it takes to sustain a marriage? What is your future like? Do you have a plan? If Ariella decides she never wants to work again, to look after your kids, can you live with that? Can you help her raise children, keep them safe, love them even when they are behaving like little psychopaths? Can you give them a better life than you and Ariella had? Can you teach them integrity, honour, truth and kindness? Can you get over those battles that you say that you've spent your entire life fighting and show them softness?'

This is not the conversation that I expected to have with Hugh Mason. It's sobering because he's right. I haven't even thought of half of those things.

'You're not ready, Caleb, but that doesn't mean you won't be. I know I've held you at a distance and in some cases been positively hostile, but you're about to assume responsibility for the most important thing in my life. I made a big mistake once already, so you can understand my caution. And just in case you aren't aware, Dahlia and I want nothing more than for you to be ready. Ariella comes alive around you, and you most certainly have something to do with it.'

Hugh Mason steps forward, pats me on the back and pulls me into a rough side hug.

'Stay for dinner.'

With that we walk together back into Dahlia's kitchen, where she is waiting with open arms and a warm smile.

SEVENTEEN

ARIELLA

None of us really truly believed Melissa was missing until we heard that the police were conducting interviews and arranging to speak to everyone at the wedding. In order to sail through the interviews without implicating ourselves in Melissa's other crimes, Dominic sent over an advocate and a solicitor the very next Tuesday to prepare us for what questions may be asked and to help us frame our answers as tightly as possible.

Who we weren't prepared for was the private investigator Kevin hired. He camped at our office for the whole day on Thursday, calling us in one by one, asking us all accusatory questions, while expressing what seemed like worrying excitement to meet Caleb on his return. Samir eventually threw him out, when Lydia pulled a record of complaints about him off the internet. It has been a long hard week, so I am delighted to see Lara at mine when I return home.

'Thank goodness you're back. Ms Pat is refusing to feed me.'

'Because you eat everything in the house, Miss Lara,' Ms Pat responds, not bothering to hide the judgement in her voice.

'I'm a growing girl!'

'Yes, I see,' Ms Pat claps back.

'Did she just call me fat?'

Even if I knew how to respond to that, I really don't want to.

'You want something to eat, Miss Ariella?' Ms Pat asks lovingly.

'So I didn't eat everything in the house.' Lara narrows her eyes at Ms Pat.

'No. Vegetables survived and I hide the crab. Everything else, gone. You like too much cookies.' Ms Pat points to the empty packet of biscuits next to Lara.

'I—'

'Thank you, Ms Pat. Anything you have will be wonderful,' I interrupt to put an end to the exchange, then flop into the couch next to Lara.

'Long day?'

'Yeah.'

'Ugh. I might have to go back to London.'

'Why?'

'Samir responded to my CV with just "no thanks" in his email. Your competitors were much more polite but are all still telling me to sling my hook. Also, Dominic isn't responding to any of my threats to give me a job.'

'I'm literally counting down my two years.'

'I'd kill for two years.'

'So, how are things going with you and Honey?'

'You're just as bad as Caleb. We're just friends at the moment, which is more than I can say for you.'

'Why? What did I do?'

'You could have told me she was gay, babe.'

'I couldn't, Lara. I—'

'I know. She already defended you. I just wish you could have snuck me a little clue.'

'I'm sorry.' I reach over to hold her hand and she nods her

forgiveness. 'So, where have you been all week? I tried to reach you. Have the police been in touch?'

'Honey had an exhibition fight in Bangkok so I went along for the free flights, hotel, room service, VIP seats and parties. You know, hanger-on, entourage shit.'

'That's all?' I tease.

Lara immediately buries her face in a nearby pillow. When she pulls it away, she has the most adorable smile.

'I hate you so much,' she groans.

'I know. So what are you going to do?'

'Nothing.'

I've never seen Lara this unsure about anything. Honey has definitely got under her skin.

'You know, Caleb is moving out of his apartment at the end of next month. You're welcome to stay here with us or...'

'Or I can get my own apartment as soon as someone gives me a job. I'm definitely not moving in with Honey and there's too much drama going on with you two. I'm not quite ready to back up Ms Pat when she helps you dodge Dominic and I refuse to watch Caleb undressing you with his pervy eyes from across the living room.'

'You have a bit of time. I'm sure something will come up.'

'I just wish it'd hurry up.' She pouts.

'Crab salad, Miss Ariella?' Ms Pat announces, setting a place for one in front of me while eyeing Lara.

'Thank you, Ms Pat.'

'My pleasure. I will bake you fresh cookies for dessert,' she offers kindly.

'You BAKE cookies?!?' Lara whips round. 'Babe, I want your life,' she complains, picking up my fork and tucking into my crab salad.

She is on her third mouthful when her phone vibrates.

'NOOOOO!' she screams, almost knocking the crab salad and our drinks over.

'What?'

'I got a job! I just got an email from DMVI. I smashed the interview Dominic set up for me. They have offered me a job!'

'What is it?'

'I'm the experience director of your charity app thing.'

'What is that?'

'We talked about it on the plane. I'll be going to see the "loadeds" to make sure the offerings on the app are actually relevant and luxurious enough for them to use; then I'll be beating suppliers over the head to provide it. While trialling the experiences first, of course.' Lara leans back and kicks her legs in the air, laughing and relishing the excitement.

'Ooooh, let's see how much it's paying,' she goes on as she grabs her phone. 'Ugh.' She frowns and shows me.

'Lara! That's an incredible salary.'

'Yes, but no bonus, no housekeeper and driver. And I only get an apartment allowance. I want a fancy penthouse. This sucks. I'm going to negotiate.'

And that's what she does, the following day. By the time she is done, Lara has got her bonus, apartment – and a pay rise before she has even started. Lara Scott has finally found a home in Singapore, and I couldn't be more pleased for her.

EIGHTEEN

CALEB

The second the door to Ariella's home opens, she jumps on me, forcing me to drop my travel duffel where I stand. Her lips find mine as she anchors her thighs to my hips and crosses her ankles behind me.

As I support her bum in my hands, it occurs to me that this is the first time I've ever returned home to my girlfriend after a trip.

'Can I at least get inside the house?' I laugh into our kiss.

'No.' She shakes her head as she beams before re-engaging our lips.

With her attached to me, I awkwardly kick the bag into the house with my foot before using it to slam the front door shut.

'You've been cooking.'

'The results were terrible but it's a start.'

I somehow doubt that. 'Where am I taking you?'

'The shower. You just got off a thirteen-hour flight.'

'Risky. But I like it.'

For someone who didn't just get off a thirteen-hour flight, she is particularly keen to get in too.

We do our best to wash each other without getting too

carried away, which, with Aari's enthusiasm to stay close, is challenging.

I will never tire of tossing Ariella on a bed, spreading her legs and burying my head between them. It's not just the way she tastes – which is, quite frankly, delicious – it's the hands in my hair, the nails on my shoulders and back... It's her total submission and vulnerability. Until she realises that she is about to tip over and stops us to bring me along. She deftly brings my mouth to hers, flips us over, situates herself on top and lets me sink into her before interlocking our fingers. I love supporting her weight in my hands as I watch her use her body to edge me closer to her. From here, I get to appreciate her beautiful face, her parted perfect lips, her elegant neck, soft full breasts with her hard, beaded nipples, that shapely waist and the way she employs the muscles in her legs and stomach to create motion for both of us.

'Caleb...' she moans.

And that's the call. That I've lasted this long is beyond belief. I follow her lead to create the movements that she needs and, the second she collapses, I hug her close and finally release.

'Welcome home. I really missed you,' she says softly before she wraps her arms round my neck and places her head on my shoulder like she never wants to let go.

We spend Saturday moving me in. It's not difficult. I've been using the apartment like a hotel, so, apart from my washbag, my Mac and the mountain of clothes Eden filled my wardrobe with, there was nothing else. As I put my clothes away in her walk-in wardrobe, Ariella attempts a nasi lemak in the kitchen. It's delicious, despite her concerns that she hasn't got the sambal quite right. Knowing her, I'm willing to bet that there are at least six other sample-sized variations neatly labelled and stacked in the fridge.

After dinner, we drag the couch blanket from home onto her sofa and watch her new favourite character, Shane, threaten to empty bullets into the zombies that emerge from Hershel's barn in *The Walking Dead*. When I look at her to speculate about Carol's daughter, she's asleep, and I know that we have found our home with each other again.

'I'm not sure about this guy.' I'm lying on the couch looking at job applications with my head on Ariella's lap.

'Let me see?' She stops running her fingers through my hair and takes the sheet from me.

'Noooo...' I complain. 'Keep going. It's soothing.'

'I only have two hands, Caleb, and the other has a pencil in it. I'll be quick.'

'You better, or I'm going to start looking for places to tickle you.' I poke her ribs gently and she jumps. 'So, what do you think?'

She takes her time reading through. 'Give him a chance. His application may not be exactly what you're looking for, but he could be hungry for it, and that rarely shows up on paper.'

She hands the sheet over and bends to give me a quick kiss on my puckered lips before returning to playing with my hair.

'I'll keep him. That's me done. What are you working on?'

'Homework for Ms Pat. We're off to the market again tomorrow. I might try chilli crab next. I've found a recipe that breaks every single item down and it's a long list. Once I've learned how to cook the authentic recipe, I'm really tempted to get rid of some bits and swap in some scandalous ingredients for fun. I'm going to need to learn how to deshell crab in a way that keeps the jumbo pieces together so that it's easier to eat.'

Ariella glows when she is talking and thinking about food. I'm happy that she has started experimenting with it again. It's too soon to revisit the 'after Singapore' plan but, if she decides to leave Ivory Bow, the natural progression would be for her to work with food in some way.

'Nice. I might tag along tomorrow.'

'You can't. Dominic is sending an advocate over after work to walk you through questions you may be asked by the police about Melissa.'

'I saw that. Do I really need someone to prepare me?'

'Yes, it's good practice to ensure that you don't drop any hints about her previous shenanigans with us. You're with the police on Tuesday morning, so you need some preparation.'

'I don't need *his* help.'

'It isn't his help. The company is doing this to protect its employees. Please can you just sit through it and retain whatever you may find useful?'

She sounds a little exasperated, so I leave it, get up from the couch and try to make amends.

'Fine. I'll behave. So, fancy cheese on toast for dinner?'

Her eyes immediately light up. She loves my cheese on toast.

'Is that what's in the bag in the fridge marked "Caleb"?'

'You didn't look?'

'No. Ms Pat told me not to.'

This is one of the things I love about my girlfriend. She can be so sweet. I'd have found a way to open, take a peek and reseal the bag without leaving any evidence.

'Yes. And a couple of other things. Now that you're going to be cooking again, I know there will be some nights that you'll be knackered or won't feel like it and Ms Pat has gone home for the day, so I thought I'd get some basics in so that I can quickly rustle something up for you.'

I'm unprepared for the force with which Ariella hugs me. I know what you're thinking. Do I really deserve relationship-affirming hugs for doing the bare minimum like making sure she doesn't starve? Probably not, but I don't make the rules. I'm just a grateful beneficiary who got bloody lucky, and I feel like now is a good time to bring up the shift that's about to occur in our relationship.

'So, I spoke to Honey while I was away,' I start, tentatively. 'We've come up with a plan to break up publicly.'

'What about her blackmailer?'

'You're not going to believe it,' I tease, knowing that she'll get excited and beg for details. It's cute.

'Caleb. Spill, now.' She puts her pencil and paper down, then sits up, erect, to listen.

'It was her father. When she decided to take a break from her career, he wanted her to keep fighting. They had a huge falling-out.'

'How did she find out?'

'Lara. She texted the blackmailer, said she worked for Honey and had pictures that he may want. They met, Honey recognised him, all hell broke loose.'

'Her dad?' Ariella says, wide-eyed.

'Her dad. Not everybody is lucky enough to get Hugh Mason.' I give her a soft smile and she lights up at the mention of her father's name. 'Anyway, long story short, Honey and I are breaking up this week.'

'What are you going to say?'

'Nothing. We're going out the way we came in. Social media is going to tell the story for us.' I wink, then make my way to the kitchen to start our cheese on toast dinner.

We slip too easily back into our London routine out here and work that week is great. The DMVI lawyers don't show up on Monday, so I go in on Tuesday without Dominic's help, like I wanted. Honey and I also executed the perfect public break-up. All we did was attend the same high-profile charity event separately. I arrived first like we planned and, while I was standing to get my photo taken, she walked past me, texting on her mobile phone like I didn't exist. When the photographers called for her, she insisted on standing as far away from me as possible. Then, as we expected, a photographer asked her for a picture of us together. She simply replied with an incredulous 'I don't think so' and walked into the event. Lara caught it on video and sent it to *The Singaporean*. It was up within half a day and we all spent most of the week being entertained by all the speculation online.

Ariella and I decided to keep our relationship quiet until the drama died down at least, which allowed us to enjoy our quiet corner of the world in the only way that mattered to us. However, just when I thought Dominic Miller had cooled his heels, the very next week he popped up and pulled a stunt that you wouldn't believe.

'Ariella.' The doorbell ringing incessantly startles both of us. It's Friday evening, which is usually the quietest night of the week for Ariella. 'Ariella, it's me. Open up.' I recognise Dominic's voice.

Aari rushes to the door and I follow.

'Dom?'

'I've been calling you. Where's Caleb?' Dominic comes through, followed by a heavyset man.

'What's wrong?' Ariella asks, frightened.

'Caleb. We need to get you out of here now,' Dominic demands urgently. 'Ariella, put your shoes on. Victor will take you to mine. You've been there all night.'

'What's going on?' I ask, confused.

'Singapore police will be at your home soon. Formally, they are going to pick you up as a suspect in Mel's disappearance. Informally, they are picking you up for her murder.'

'What? That's ridiculous...'

'They've found her bloody clothes and you were the last to see her. You need to leave now.'

'We can go to them and—' Ariella starts.

'Do you have any idea what they will do to him? Caleb needs to come with me now. We need to get him away while they figure it out.'

'Oh my God, Caleb!' Ariella starts crying.

'Hey, hey.' I hold my girlfriend's face. 'It'll be okay.'

'Where are you taking him?' Ariella asks, shaking.

'I'm not sure yet. He's going to need to disappear, and fast. I can get him on a plane tonight but we have to go now,' Dominic explains.

'I'm coming!' Ariella runs into her living room to grab her wallet, phone and keys.

Dominic looks at me and shakes his head.

'No, you're not,' I say to stop her, resigned.

'Caleb?' she questions, confused.

'If I have to disappear, you can't come,' I explain calmly to her.

I watch Ariella's face crumple.

'For how long?' She turns to Dominic, desperate for answers.

'I don't know, until this blows over.' Dominic sounds unconvinced.

'That could take months.'

'He has to come now, Ariella,' Dominic repeats.

Ariella throws herself at me and pulls me into a kiss. 'Don't go too far, please,' she begs. 'Will you let me know when you're safe?'

'He can't. He has to stay moving and stay gone,' Dominic explains sadly.

'I *will* find you,' she cries, and she pulls me in to kiss and hold me. I inhale the centre of my universe and try to bury this feeling deep in my memory.

'Come on, Caleb,' Dominic urges for the last time before I walk out of the door. Ariella starts to follow us, but the hefty man Dominic turned up with blocks her way. 'I'll look after him,' Dominic says to Ariella, then follows me out of the front door.

All I can think about as I sit immobile next to Dominic in the back of his car is Ariella's fear and panic-stricken face. 'I *will* find you.' Her last words to me replay in my mind as I try to hold on to our last kiss, mixed with both our tears. I try to keep my emotions buried.

'Hopefully, this will blow over soon,' Dominic says quietly, looking out of the window at the night lights as we speed to the east of the city.

'Do you honestly think taking off is the best option here? Surely this will make me look more guilty?'

'Have you ever been in a Singaporean prison?' he asks, incredulously. 'And that's if you're lucky. The maximum penalty for murder here is death. You were the last to see her and the bloody clothes don't help.'

'Fuck.'

'Good job you were at Ariella's and not yours. You'd be in custody by now.'

'How did you know?'

'Kevin. I was with him when he got the call.'

'Why are you helping me?'

'You know why.' He has the decency not to meet my eyes. After a pause, I accept my fate and decide to help him out.

'You can't make her choose you,' I tell him.

'That's not what this is.'

'It doesn't hurt you though, does it?'

'No, it doesn't,' he admits.

It kills me to let Ariella go. She has become the sun my existence revolves around and living without her seems impossible to fathom. Dominic moves his gaze back out of the window. We are silent for the rest of the journey, until we pull into an airfield, where another car and a plane are waiting. Two men move towards the car as we come to a stop.

'We're here.' Dominic opens the door and steps out into the night. I do the same.

'Is it ready?' Dominic asks briskly.

'Yes, sir.' One of the men hands him a black rucksack.

'What's going on?' I ask.

'We're getting you out of here. There's a hundred thousand US cash in this rucksack, a burner and an address. Here, take it.'

I do as I am told.

'My plane is going to fly you just outside Cà Mau in Vietnam tonight. Nothing will be waiting for you. The first thing you need to do, when you land, is to get a new identity. Find your way to the address in the bag. He has already been paid. Lie low. It will take a couple of days. Once you have your new ID, call Ariella on your burner, let her know you're okay, then toss it. I think that should be the last she hears from you until all this is sorted. Once you've tossed the burner, you will be given the details of another plane arranged for the same night, to fly you out of Vietnam.'

'Where will that plane be going?'

'I don't know yet, but somewhere Caleb Black didn't land and doesn't exist. You'll need to use the cash to keep moving.'

I take the bag.

'Good luck, Caleb. I'll look after her.'

'She doesn't need looking after.' I turn round and walk towards the plane.

'Anything you want me to tell her?' Dominic shouts after me as I take the first step to ascend.

'No.'

I actually don't give a shit about what happens to me. This

is just another beating life is dishing out, one that I will have to fight through. Then it occurs to me. I *could* choose to dodge immigration, customs and police in a bunch of foreign countries so I don't end up facing the death penalty for someone who, I am sure, is pulling all our strings and will resurface eventually.

But things have changed, and more importantly I am trying to change. While I still don't give a shit what happens to me, leaving means driving Ariella mad with worry, because I believe her. She will stop at nothing until she finds me again. I'm not going to put her through that. I can't and I won't. I'm going to hand myself in and call the British High Commission in the morning, if Ariella hasn't left them a dozen messages already. I stop at the top of the stairs, turn round, make my way back down and walk directly towards a perplexed Dominic. I throw the rucksack at his feet.

We are exactly the same height, so I step up to him, nose to nose.

'I'm not going anywhere. I'm pretty certain that you know more than you're letting on, Mr Nice Guy. I'm going to do whatever it takes to find out just how involved you are in this mess, because I don't think this is just about Ariella. I think you have a lot more to hide.'

I look at him dead in the eyes and smile.

'Almost, Budget Jasper. Almost.' I pat him on the shoulder, walk off the airfield, find my car app and drop a pin to be picked up before I send a text to Ariella.

> I'm not going anywhere. Sit tight. I'm coming to get you.

NINETEEN
ARIELLA

The text from Dominic comes through before Caleb's.

> Caleb is staying. He needs to go the police
> rather than wait to be picked up. I tried.

It turns out someone saw Caleb and Melissa having a heated argument the night before she went missing. The police didn't have much to go on aside from the information Caleb had told them already at his interview so, much to my relief, they let him go after a few hours. I'm waiting for him at the station reception when he is released.

'I've been in touch with the British High Commission and they are going to help,' I say, hugging him.

'I'm not worried. Melissa is fine.'

'How do you know?'

'She told me that night. She knew something was going to happen.'

'But they can't prove that.'

'No, and I suspect it won't be my last visit to the police. They told me not to go far.'

'I'm so happy you changed your mind and came back.' I try to hold back the tears of relief.

'Me too. I would have chosen to live in a world without you if I had got on that plane, and I would never have forgiven myself.'

'What did Dominic say?'

'Nothing. I'm sure some part of him is relieved that he didn't have to aid and abet a fugitive tonight.'

'When all this is over, we should do something nice for him to say thank you.'

Caleb grunts.

I leave it because I'm just happy that he's back home with me. That night, I hold him close, because there is no way I'm going to let him go.

News travelled fast that Caleb was being questioned and, when clients started to distance themselves from Ivory Bow, Bree, along with Park and Jin, the new sales guys, kicked into gear, covering Caleb's clients.

As a company, the official line was that he hadn't been charged with anything and was merely helping with the investigation. He was pulled from representing Ivory Bow and attending public events and encouraged to work from home until it blew over.

I expected it to have a devastating effect on him, but Caleb simply adjusted by supporting the team from home. He helped with their diaries, client information and targets. He upped his training with Honey to twice a day, and started working on a plan for the gyms with Jasper.

When my request to work from home twice a week was declined by Samir, Lara offered to spend the day at mine on Tuesdays and Thursdays to help break up his week as she waited for the paperwork for her DMVI job to come through.

Caleb was in and out of the police station a lot for those three weeks, but we made up for his stressful days with quiet evenings, early nights, weekend road trips exploring the country and lazy Sundays in whatever hotel we had managed to end up in the night before.

Then, six weeks to the day Melissa was declared missing, an email appears in my inbox. I open it and click on the white play icon.

It is a video of Melissa in a soft, oversized bathrobe, cocktail in hand, looking as fresh as a daisy. I pause immediately and let the relief that this exonerates Caleb wash over me. It's quickly followed by a wave of nausea.

'Lydia!' I whisper urgently and she whips round and, when she sees my screen, her eyes bulge.

'I'm pinging Bryce now,' she says.

Bryce is with us in a flash, so I grab my ear buds, share one with Lydia and give the other to Bryce.

'Closed captions,' Bryce suggests.

'Wait,' Lydia says. 'Screen record just in case we only get one view. Bryce, record it with your phone too just in case the screen capture is disabled.'

Her fingers fly across my keyboard and then, when we have taken every preservation precaution, I hit play.

'Hey, everyone! I'm still on my honeymoon and it's been an absolute blast so far. Gustaf has been looking after me and let's just say I'm having the time of my life.' She smiles coyly at someone off camera in a way that makes me think Gustaf might be having the time of his life too. 'Now that I'm a little more relaxed, I've decided to do a three-part storytime. There'll be business, pleasure and jail time. It starts tomorrow, link below. Put them all in your diaries.'

Melissa takes a sip of her cocktail and then speaks off camera.

'Oh, before I forget, obviously I'm not dead.' She holds up a copy of the UK's *Financial Times* with today's date.

'Okay, that was exhausting. I haven't lifted anything in weeks!' She laughs at the camera. 'See you tomorrow. Expect arrests.'

The video cuts off. Caleb is calling me.

'Mason, Melissa just sent me a video.'

'I got it too. I just watched it with Bryce and Lydia.'

'I haven't dared to open it.'

'The general message was that she's alive and will be spilling secrets for the next three days.'

'What secrets?'

'We're going to have to wait to find out. Are you okay?'

'Not really. She's a nutcase. She could say anything.'

'Do you want me to come home?'

'No, I'm fine. I'll see you tonight.'

'Shall I share it with Samir and start the process of you coming back to work, or leave it until these storytimes are over?'

'Samir has already called twice since I've been on the phone to you. I guess he's seen it too.'

Dominic's name pops up on my phone. 'Dominic is calling.'

'I'll see you when you get home then. I love you.'

'I love you.'

I accept Dominic's call.

'Have you seen it?'

'Yes.'

'Can I pick you up for lunch? We need to talk.'

I look at my diary. 'I can meet later, around four?'

'Sounds good. I'll be on the bike.'

I know what that means. As I am making a note to change my hair from the bun into two pigtails for the helmet, an alert pops up on my screen.

shusssein:

Ariella, a word when you get a moment?

I go straight to his office. Samir does not believe in a open-door policy, so I have to knock.

'Come in. I take it you, Lydia and Bryce were huddled around watching the video?'

'Yes.' I sit opposite him. The video has left me feeling tired.

'How would you handle it?'

'I'd get everyone at Ivory Bow into the meeting room, show them the video, talk through it, very clearly state what this means for Ivory Bow and specifically for Caleb, then reinstate him. I'd also send him a huge apology gift for not quite believing him when he said he had nothing to do with it.'

'Would I be sending that apology gift to his or yours? Or isn't that the same thing these days?'

'Samir.' I look him dead in the eyes. 'What can I help you with that is directly related to my employment here?'

'Your relationship with Caleb is directly related to your employment here.'

'How so? He's delivering everything asked of him and more. Whatever you may think of me, the operations team is doing an incredible job. There are no gaps in service, execution ratings have gone up, your time sheets are accurate – and, if they are anything to go by, you really should be offering immense over-time bonuses. In addition to that, the girls still find time to be out, in their own time, promoting this company, regardless of how undervalued their efforts are, by you. So, Samir. What can I help you with that is directly related to my employment here?'

Is that a smile?

'What do you know about Melissa's investment in Ivory Bow?'

'Ivory Bow UK was doing well in Singapore. She saw potential and secured a franchise. She met me when she came to finalise the deal and Caleb was selected for his local success.

She entered into investment talks with DMVI, as our largest client in the region, and eventually decided to sell because DMVI made her an offer she couldn't refuse.'

'Have you had any contact with her since?'

'We went to her wedding because she was our chairwoman and steered us up to the point DMVI took over. I haven't seen her since.'

'Are you aware of her past relationship with Caleb?'

'Samir, any questions about the nature of Caleb's relationship with Melissa should be posed to him, not me. I'm an inaccurate source.'

'I'd like to hear your opinion.'

'I refuse to engage in hearsay. Can I help you with anything else?'

'Is there anything I should know that I don't already, Ariella?'

'Yes. Everyone here loves this company and wants it to succeed. What you have the privilege of shaping today was created by everyone out there. It'd be nice if you could show them some respect. If you also can find it in you to extend some thanks, it would mean the world to them.'

'That's it?'

'That's it.'

Samir studies me for a few seconds before he lets me go.

Surprisingly, he does exactly as I suggested and calls us all into our meeting room, plays the video and explains our position. In a shocking plot twist, he actually thanks the team before he dismisses us to go back to our desks. All everyone can seem to talk about for the rest of the day is the video. With that and so much work to get through, the day speeds past. I'm unaware of the time until I get Dominic's text at four on the dot.

Ready?

Ready.

We whiz through the streets of Singapore and I realise how much I miss being on the back of Dominic's bike. I tune out everything in my head and just watch the city whiz by until we stop in front of a tiny nondescript restaurant sandwiched between some Peranakan houses. As soon as we sit down in the empty restaurant, the server produces two menus.

'Just water please,' I request.

'Are you sure? It could be an adventure.'

'I'm not in the mood to eat. Today's news has made me a little queasy.'

Dominic orders a coffee and waits until the server leaves us.

'Aside, obviously, from the agreement that will pretty much destroy us all if she spills, do we have anything else to worry about?' I ask.

'Nope. Since her departure, which can be explained away, Ivory Bow is good.'

'I'm not sure, Dominic.'

'I am. Kevin and I have been talking to Devin since you fired him.'

'Devin?'

He nods.

'What does Devin know?'

'Everything, but I promise you Ivory Bow is fine. Bryce caught it before it was something. Devin is also prepared to sing like a canary if need be.'

'Can Ivory Bow in the UK be affected?'

'No, Harrison's departure with those accounts helps a bit and Preston, your old CFO, is pretty much in the same position as Devin.'

'When did all this happen?' I ask, astounded.

'It's kind of still happening – I like to keep my investments clean.'

'You prepping two people to squeal, should something terrible happen, doesn't sound very clean, Dominic. Is any of what you're doing legal?'

'I never claimed to be a saint, Ariella. I'd relax if I were you. You have sealed documents along with the minutes of a meeting that don't exactly radiate moral or legal purity.'

He's right, and the shame makes me avert my gaze.

'Hey,' he says, reaching for my hand across the table. 'That wasn't an attack. You did something morally and legally grey for people you care about. I'm just doing the same.'

I can't argue with him on that. 'Why do you think Melissa is doing this?' I ask.

'In a word, Kevin. I think the wedding was a step too far. I don't know much about the ins and outs of their relationship, but I don't think that I can recall a time when Kevin has been faithful to Melissa. Even before she started seeing Caleb.'

It hurts to be reminded.

'Kevin could have put a stop to it but I think he let it happen.'

'What do you mean?'

'I'll tell you this. Kevin and Melissa are intentional people. Very little in their world happens unless they make or let it happen. I suspect they had plans for Caleb before he sat down at our table that night. No one accidentally ends up on a table that powerful, especially not at the Tech Awards. What I can't tell you is who had those plans – Kevin, or Melissa.'

'How have you survived this?'

'I tend to keep my nose out of other people's lives. I have my own problems to deal with.'

'Dom, I don't know if I can take two years of this.' I well up and he moves to put his arm round me.

'I know. It will blow over. I promise.'

I nod and move away carefully. His natural scent, that I kind of liked at one point, is a little hard for me to bear today.

'So what do you think we should do?'

'Sit tight. Caleb is fine now. Let's hear what these story-times are all about, and we'll handle what comes up. We're fine. It's Kevin that's losing his shit. Nothing is going to happen to you on my watch, Aari.'

I believe him.

'Do you mind if I share all this with Caleb, Lydia and Bryce?'

'Sure, but please keep it to just them. Samir has no idea what is going on.'

'I will.' I move my chair back to stand.

'Wait. I have a favour to ask you. In a couple of weeks, I'm entertaining some local and international friends in my home. There will be about sixteen, maximum twenty of us. My caterers are great for local cuisine but are terrible at American classics. I need you to work with the caterers to do what you did during film night.'

'The caterers don't mind? I suspect they might have a problem with that.'

'If they want to keep their contract, they won't.'

'Are you asking me as my friend or my boss?'

'A bit of both? It's an important dinner, Aari, but it needs to feel homely.'

'All I'd have to do is cook the movie night menu for twenty?'

'Yes.'

I've never cooked for that many people before, but it's a challenge and a welcome opportunity that might help to take my mind off things. All I'd have to do is cook at the caterer's facilities and they will be responsible for taking it to Dominic's and serving his guests. It will be an education to meet the cater-ers, have a behind-the-scenes peek at their operations, use their industrial kitchens and learn how they execute the fast-turn-around dishes.

'Sure.'

'That's wonderful. Please send me your bill.'

'You're my friend, Dom. I'm not doing this because you're my boss. There is no bill.'

'I really want to believe that we are still friends, Aari. You seem so much farther away than you used to be.'

He's right. I am. I've needed to create distance to discourage any 'more than friendly feelings' evolving. Right now, he looks so sad, I just feel like I've abandoned him after all the times he was there for me. I reach out for his hand and cover it with mine.

'Maybe we can work on closing the gap?' I suggest.

'I'd like that very much.'

When he embraces me this time, he does so carefully and respectfully, putting me at ease.

TWENTY

CALEB

Aari looks tired when she walks in. These few weeks have taken a toll on us, but especially her. She has lost her appetite, is struggling to get up to do her yoga flows in the morning and seems to be surviving on toast and tea.

With that in mind, I plan a little celebration tonight to break the worry and stress we have been under the last couple of weeks.

With Ms Pat's help, I manage to pull off the good old Sunday roast. So what if it's a Monday evening?

She walks straight into my arms when she gets home and the feeling as she presses her head against my chest, knowing that we are safe for now, is overwhelming.

'I cooked,' I say into her hair as I hold her tight.

'Mmmm, cheese on toast. Yes please.'

'No, I cooked properly. I'm no Dahlia but I had a bash at a Sunday roast. Ms Pat is responsible for the house still standing. And making sure the beef was sealed. And the potatoes staying crisp. And rescuing the veg. I made the gravy though. Actually, come to think of it—'

Ariella is on her tiptoes kissing me before I can finish.

'Thank you, Caleb.'

We eat, holding hands, as she fills me in on the day and what Dominic has been up to. I can't help picturing both CFOs strapped to a chair somewhere dark, wet and underground, having their testicles zapped every six hours to remind them to throw Melissa under the bus. I wouldn't put it past him.

Dominic Miller may be making super-shady moves but he actually hasn't done anything incriminating that I know about – yet. I didn't tell Ariella what went down at the airfield because she still trusts him and, while I plan on eviscerating him from her life, I'm going to wait until I've gathered indisputable evidence before I burn him to a crisp.

Right now, he's respecting my boundaries and—

'Dom asked me for a favour today,' she says cautiously.

'Oh yeah?' I check my tone and volume because I'm still trying to behave like a grown-up.

'He has a dinner party in a couple of weeks and wondered if I could produce some authentic American dishes for it.'

'What would you like to do?'

'It's for twenty people and it could be a fun challenge. I haven't spoken to the caterers yet, but I imagine I'll be cooking in their kitchens and they'll take it, finish it off there and serve it.'

Good. She's not going to his home.

'It sounds like an opportunity to learn something new.'

'It is, and I'm a little flattered that he asked me.' She smiles that sweet smile.

'My money is on Lydia, Lara or Akiko having told him you're good with food. They must have been very convincing for him to ask without trying it first.'

She bites the corner of her lip. Shit. What now?

'Caleb, when I first moved in, Dominic came over – I made us some dinner and we watched a couple of films together.'

She looks down at her hands in her lap. Oh shit. I know any answer she gives will destroy me, because intimate TV and movie nights are our thing, but I have to ask.

'Did anything happen?' I shut my eyes and wait for it.

'We kissed by the door at the end of the night, but when he tried to take it past that I stopped it and told him that I was still in love with you.'

'Have you done anything more than kiss him?'

'No.'

'Are there any more kisses that I should know about?'

'No. We kissed twice. That first time in front of the building, and then at the end of the movie night.'

'I want you to know that I love you and I know we weren't together at the time, but I need a second.'

I know it's arrogant, selfish and childish, but I want to smash Dominic's face in for trying and getting a second kiss. I walk out into Ariella's garden, take deep breaths and exhale the anger I'm feeling. This guy isn't going to stop poking for weak spots.

'I'm sorry. I won't cook for his guests.' I feel Ariella's hands slide across my chest as she hugs me from behind. I feel every negative feeling fall away. Her understanding how agonising this was going to be was all I needed.

'No. You should. You'll enjoy it and, like you said, it's an opportunity to learn something new.'

'Not if it hurts you, Caleb.' She sighs, resting her head against my back.

'I love you and trust you, Mason.' I hold her arms in place and we stand close to each other under the night sky for a few minutes until I feel her yawn.

'When this is over, I am going to take us very far away from here and we're going to spend a month doing nothing but eating, sleeping, drinking and swimming. Just the two of us,' I promise her.

'That sounds heavenly.'

. . .

I don't want to be away from Ariella during Melissa's storytimes, so I go into the Ivory Bow office to watch the first one. An invitation has been extended to all the staff and they all show. We hit the link and a countdown pops up on the meeting room's screen. While new members of the team look excited, there is trepidation on the faces of everyone who knows exactly what damage Melissa is capable of doing. My blood runs cold with fear as I watch the numbers count down to zero.

The stream starts, revealing a fresh-faced and relaxed Melissa wrapped in a different-coloured bathrobe, with a towel round her hair. This video looks more like a spa advert than a three-part blackmail plot.

'Thank you, Gustaf,' she says, bringing what looks like a cocktail into shot.

She takes a sip, holds up a newspaper with today's date, and flips through the headlines.

'I'm not in it.' She frowns to someone we can't see, before turning to us all and winking directly into the camera.

'Bet I'll be in tomorrow's – and, just in case anyone is wondering if this is a deepfake or AI-generated, here's proof, which you can confirm with any one of the women Kevin Wong has had an affair with.'

She leans in as we all wait with bated breath.

'Kevin has a tiny wee-wee.' She raises both eyebrows and nods enthusiastically at the camera before she crumples into laughter.

'Fine. His password to everything is money, hustle and power. All you need to do is substitute all the 'e's for the number three, all the 'o's for zeros. Capitalise the first letter and stick an exclamation mark after each word. No spaces. He's not as clever as he'd have you all believe; in fact he is a bastion of incompetence. Just ask his father.'

Melissa pauses to take a slow sip of her cocktail, then sighs.

'My name is Melissa Chang, and, after my father died, Kevin Wong and his father – who previously worked with mine – took over my autonomy and my finances and thrust me into a life of crime. This is me, claiming my life back.'

Melissa takes her time detailing her heartbreak at the news of her father's death, how her father's business partner – who was clearly a gangster of some description – promised to look after her just before she signed papers for betrothal to Kevin, and how she refused to consummate the relationship. By the end of the hour, she looks exhausted. We all sit there riveted, unable to take our eyes off the screen.

'Time for my massage now.' She smiles into the camera. 'Tomorrow, money-laundering. Expect frozen accounts and assets. See you at the same time.'

With that, she ends the broadcast.

'I feel sick...' Aari whispers, then looks at me and stops. 'Are you okay? You've gone as white as a sheet.'

There's only one word for it.

'Fuck.'

The nerves we had about the first storytime were minuscule compared to the ones we are all feeling next day. A large part of me walks into Ivory Bow ready to be arrested.

We all glare at the screen when Melissa appears in a new bathrobe, holding a cocktail and today's paper.

'I made it. Finally,' she says. 'About time. Right. Money-laundering.'

She sits there detailing the elaborate operation, name-dropping bankers, countries and huge global conglomerates like she was reading a class attendance roster.

Aari and I hold hands under the table, waiting for Ivory Bow and the United Kingdom to be included, but it isn't.

The only organisation that is untainted in the group of companies that Melissa was involved in is the hospital group.

'If your name or company has been mentioned, I suggest you start running now. The authorities in all seventeen countries I have mentioned have received all the evidence. I hear Mongolia is nice this time of year.' She laughs so hard at the camera, she has to wipe a tear away.

'Finally, just before I came on my little sojourn, I cleared out all our legitimate accounts. The ones with all the juicy suspicious activities are still active. Kevin would have found this out almost immediately after I disappeared, so if he's running around fake crying and pretending to be worried that I'm dead, don't believe him.'

She shakes her empty glass at someone off camera and puts it down.

'No more cocktails for me today, apparently.' She frowns.

'Tomorrow, the final instalment. Sex and lack thereof, lots of lies and the battle of the videotapes. Expect divorces.'

The broadcast ends.

The relief in the meeting room is palpable. Ivory Bow wasn't one of the businesses mentioned.

'Aari, can we get popcorn and ice cream tomorrow for the last storytime, to celebrate the fact that we're off the hook?' Sian asks as Jess and Akiko nod along.

'What do you mean by off the hook?' Samir immediately bites.

'Melissa, as you know, was our chairwoman. Thankfully, no criminality infiltrated Ivory Bow since we set up here in Singapore,' Ariella explains, choosing her words carefully.

'What about—'

'Samir. Lay off her, mate. This is beginning to look like bullying and it's making us all a bit uncomfortable. You've been on her for weeks. Give it a rest, mate,' Bryce says, annoyed.

'Ariella, my office, please,' Samir says, standing to button his jacket.

'Yes please to popcorn and ice cream, Sian. Let's toss in a cake to welcome Caleb back.' Aari stands, pats Bryce on the shoulder and follows Samir out of the meeting room.

TWENTY-ONE

ARIELLA

'I want to know what happened to your CFO,' Samir demands, sitting down in his chair.

I stand where I am.

'He refused to put in systems that ensured our due diligence requirements were met. There were gaps in the clients' contract that needed to be closed and demands for more transparency.'

'As my COO, why didn't—'

'I'm not your COO, Samir. You are yet to recruit your COO and I would appreciate an indication of when that will happen. The team really could use someone in that role.'

'What aren't you telling me, Ariella?'

'Samir, I have answered— Excuse me.'

I walk quickly to our bathroom, where I vomit the contents of my stomach into the open toilet. The cool floor is welcome and, just when I'm thinking about standing, I throw up again.

'Aari?' I hear Lydia call.

'In here.' I unlock my stall for Lydia to push the door open.

'Are you okay?'

'Yes. Food poisoning, I think. I cooked some chicken last night and it tasted strange.'

'Do you know—'

'Lydia?' I hear Caleb call from outside the bathroom.

'She's fine!' Lydia responds.

'Can I come in?'

'Yes.'

I retch as he makes his way to the stall.

'Aari,' Caleb says as he strokes my back to soothe me.

'I think it must have been last night's chicken.'

'I'm going to get you a car. I think you need to go home. I'll let Ms Pat know what has happened and tell Samir that I'm sending you home,' Lydia offers before she leaves Caleb and me in the bathroom stall.

Caleb sits on the floor with me, rubbing my back gently as the waves of nausea arrive and depart, until the car comes. Lydia grabs my things and a sick bag from the medical box then sends me home with Caleb.

When we get there, Caleb holds me under a cool shower and, when I am feeling better, he makes a little bed on the living room sofa for us.

'Mr Caleb. I need ginger and fresh mint please,' Ms Pat says, emerging from the kitchen and handing him a strip of paper. 'You go, I look after Miss Ariella.'

I really don't want Caleb to leave and, by the look on his face, neither does he.

'Ms Pat, can we pick it up tomorrow?' Caleb asks.

'No, Mr Caleb. Please go. Now.'

Ms Pat has never asked for anything, and looks after us so lovingly, the forcefulness of her request takes us both by surprise.

'I guess I'd better go then,' Caleb says and kisses my head. 'I'll be quick.'

'Hmmm,' Ms Pat says as she frowns at him. I must be imagining it. She loves him.

As soon as Caleb has left, Ms Pat returns to the kitchen quickly, then joins me on the sofa, holding a cup of fresh ginger tea.

'Drink,' she says as she sits.

'Ms Pat, I really don't feel like—'

'Drink.'

I sit up and take a sip of her tea. She motions for me to have more with a couple of flicks of her wrist, and I do. Only then does she take the tea from me, place it on the coffee table, reach for my hand and clasp it in hers.

'Good. Miss Ariella,' she starts, looking at me with love and warmth in her eyes. 'You not sick. You have a baby.'

'Well, I guess Caleb's pull-out game sucks,' Lara says from where she is sitting on the side of the bath, flicking the pregnancy test around like a mercury thermometer.

'Lara, you have to leave it alone on the side or I'm going to have to do another one.'

I'm sitting on the loo with my knickers round my ankles, still reeling from the shock.

'Do another one now just in case. I don't think I'll be able to wait for another three minutes.'

'We'll have to wait for another three hours. That's how long the urine needs to be in my system for an accurate test.'

Lara drops it immediately.

'So, I'm thinking Elsie if it's a girl. To be fair, I'm also thinking Elsie if it's a boy. What do you think?'

It's times like this that I love Lara and I'll be forever grateful that she's my best friend. If she wasn't here distracting me by making ridiculous suggestions, I'd be unable to cope with the anxiety that is currently threatening to take over.

When Ms Pat told me her theory, I went completely numb with the shock. It was her who called Lara from my phone and asked her to discreetly bring two pregnancy tests so we could know for sure before I told Caleb. Lara arrived with Honey, just after Caleb returned with Ms Pat's fresh ginger and mint.

Lara picks up the test and her eyes widen.

'What?'

'Yup. Ms Pat was on the money. You're knocked up.'

The chaos and confusion in my mind explodes and the tears start to fall. How can I have a baby now? I'm thousands of miles away from home, tied to a two-year contract, in love with someone who I have a short, intense but tumultuous history with, and I'm not ready. I'm only just discovering who I am, how can I possibly look after another human being?

'Lara, I don't know if I can have this baby,' I admit, bursting into tears.

'Oh babe, you don't have to know right now.' Lara comes over and kneels by the loo to hold me, underwear round my ankles and all. We stay like that until I feel I need to stand under the shower for a while.

Lara carefully wraps the test for disposal and promises to confirm Ms Pat's suspicions quietly to her. By the time I return to the couch downstairs she, Honey and Ms Pat are gone.

'Lara told me you wanted me to give you some time to become less disgusting from all the puke, or I'd have come up to check on you. She said it was like the *Exorcist* pea soup scene up there. She did the sound effects and everything.' Caleb smiles sympathetically. 'Come here.'

He arranges himself at one end of the couch and stretches out his arms so that I can cuddle him as I lie down. I go straight into him and curl up, pulling our couch blanket over us.

'Seeing you sick is awful, Aari.' He pulls me closer. I can't not tell him.

'I'm not sick, Caleb.' I exhale softly to rid myself of the nerves as I sit up to face him. 'I'm pregnant.'

I have never seen Caleb so shocked or silent. I curl back into him and wait. After a while he holds me tighter.

'What do you want to do, Aari?'

'I don't know.'

'Whatever you want, I'll support you. All the way.' He kisses my head.

'What do you think?' I ask him.

'I think I'm in denial because I really want to take the piss. It hasn't sunk in yet – but it explains why Ms Pat had a go at me earlier.'

'She had a go at you?'

'Yeah. She gave me a dirty look, said I play too much and that I was a grown man now. All I did was juggle the ginger before I gave it to her. She looked sad and I was trying to cheer her up.'

It starts as a little laugh and ends up building to a point where I can't stop. Caleb joins in and we hold on to each other, laughing.

'I love you, Caleb.' And I do. I really, really do.

'I love you too. And let this be a warning to naughty girls who do what they want. They don't get to escape the consequences of their actions.' He hugs me tightly. He has pinpointed when it could have happened.

'You were a willing participant!'

'For sure, but let's not forget that I was also the voice of reason. I told you what good girls would do.'

'I haven't been a good girl since that first night on the kitchen counter, Caleb.'

'I doubt you were a good girl before that!'

My shocked look makes him laugh.

'Thank you for making this feel lighter, Caleb.'

'Don't thank me just yet. I don't trust my judgement when it comes to you, Ariella Mason. I'd literally commit to raising a colony of rabies-infested vampire bats in the middle of any war-torn country of your choice, as long as I was doing it with you.'

I believe him. I close my eyes and he hugs me to sleep.

TWENTY-TWO

CALEB

I spend the entire evening fighting the urge to tell Tim, Jack, Jasper or Dahlia. The only person I can really talk to is Lara. I want to text her, but the silence surrounding us as Ariella snoozes the evening away on my chest feels like something I need to hold on to. So after I check my calendar for her last shark week's dates, and establish that it was six weeks ago, I do the most destructive thing I could possibly do. I go on the internet and search the word 'baby'.

Truthfully, I don't know how I feel about it. There have been many times when I have looked at Ariella and imagined what our kids would be like, and concluded that as long as they were like her, they'd be bloody brilliant. They'd be loved and cared for, and we'd dedicate our lives to making sure they were fine. They'd be immersed in Dahlia, Hugh, Zachary, Isszy, Jasper and Gigi's love from the start. All that would counter the family horror I'd bring to the table as baggage. While I may not know how to be a good parent, I certainly know how to avoid being a bad one. When I follow this thread of thought, my hope is that she keeps it.

But right now, our lives are a shit show. I'm not ready. We're stuck in Singapore. I own two gyms that I highly suspect are money pits, and have an embarrassingly weak plan for them. Ariella doesn't know what she wants to do once these two years are up. We have the flat but I've never really wanted to raise a child in London. Then again, I've never actually wanted to raise a child full stop. I love Alfie, but he has always belonged to someone else and the reason why I can give everything I am to him while we are together is because I know that, eventually, he has to return to Tim and Em.

The internet search doesn't help. Instead, it scares me absolutely shitless. On the one hand, some experiences of parenthood sound profound and sublime. On the other hand, people are losing their minds out there. I look hard for a simple, balanced 'meh, it was all right' experience and there isn't one. Whatever we do, we're fucked – which means whatever we do, we're going to be okay.

It pains me to stroke her arm awake because she seems so tired, but she hasn't eaten since breakfast and even that ended up down the loo.

'Mason,' I whisper. 'Would you like something to eat?'

She stirs and shakes her head.

'Cheese on toast?'

She opens an eye before she sits up slowly.

'Maybe just toast?'

I can definitely do that. I plant a kiss on her head. There is so much more than I can fathom going on in there. I wish I could reach in, grab a load of the thoughts that torment her and throw them out. She hides it well, but I know that sometimes they can get the better of her. When I get to the kitchen, I make three slices of the most careful cheese on toast that I have ever made. I know how she likes it, so it has to be perfect. When that's under the grill, I make the toast she requested and boil the kettle for some ginger tea. This way, she has a choice and Ms Pat will be pleased that I listened.

Whatever happens, I'm determined not to be a passenger. I want to be involved, helpful and supportive for her.

She eats her toast slowly and gratefully moves on to a piece of the cheese on toast that I made, then I give her my second slice.

The more I watch her slowly eat and drink her tea, the more I think I might want this pregnancy. We've created a little miracle, currently the size of a sesame seed, that contains something from both of us.

'Come on, let's go to bed.'

She nods and I let her lead the way up the stairs. I lock and check our doors twice before I turn the lights off behind us. Nothing ever happens in Singapore, but I am hyperaware tonight.

I put her in bed, hop in and out of the shower quickly, then lie down beside her. I pull her in close and hold her hand as she places it on my heart. I start the belly tickles she adores and she's asleep in minutes.

I may not be able to share what's going on, but there is no way I am letting today go unnoticed.

I flick on my bedside lamp, grab my phone and take a picture of Ariella sleeping peacefully on my shoulder. She looks absolutely beautiful.

Then I open my social media app, upload the image and add a simple caption below.

Perfection.

I put my phone back on its charging disc and return my hand to Ariella's tummy, hoping that the sesame seed can feel me silently telling it how much I love it already.

'Caleb?' Ariella whispers to me in the middle of the night.

'Mason?'

'I think I want to keep it. What do you think?' she says, placing her hand over mine, still resting on her tummy.

'I think I want to keep it too.'

'I'm a little scared.'

'I've been on the internet. I think we might need to be a lot scared. They're cute but it turns out they are all frightful little monsters and no one is ever really prepared for their arrival anyway. Also, the general consensus is we sleep now because, the second it's born, we're never going to sleep again. Ever.'

'But I'm not sleepy,' Ariella says, climbing on top of me.

'You do realise it was exactly this sort of behaviour that got you into your little spot of trouble, Mason?'

'It's not like it's going to get any worse,' she says, smiling, before she brings her lips down to meet mine.

'Nope. In fact I suspect it's only going to get better.'

I pull my girlfriend in, make love to her and hold her in my arms, softly chatting like we used to do in London, until the sun comes up.

'Granny Pat!' I call as I happily come down the stairs in the morning, ready for Honey to turn up. Ms Pat is exceptionally early today. She usually doesn't surface until about six fifteen, well into my beatings. Sometimes she stops for a few minutes to watch for fun.

She whips round. She has the biggest smile on her face.

'You keep the baby?' she asks excitedly.

'Yes, we're keeping the baby.' The force with which she hugs me almost knocks me over. 'Can I juggle the ginger now?'

'No!' She smacks my arm and laughs loudly. 'Miss Ariella must take to work in a flask and drink all day so she is not so sick. When she get tired of ginger, we try mint.'

I have an overwhelming urge to hug Ms Pat, and I do. I cover her tiny five-foot-two frame with my entire body.

The doorbell goes suddenly. Honey is early too. I open the door to her and an excited Lara.

'Well?' Lara says.

'We're keeping it, Aunty Lara.'

Lara squeals, shoves me to the side and dashes up the stairs.

'In honour of your news, I'll go easy on you today. Come on,' Honey says as she gives me a quick hug. Then she walks into the garden and onto our training mat. We are soon interrupted by Ariella.

'Caleb, did you post a photo of us in bed together to your social media?'

'Yes,' I say as I finally manage to grab one of Honey's legs.

'Why?'

'Because I'm sick of hiding.'

'Lydia's phone has been going off since midnight. Honey's fans are going crazy online and people are accusing me of cheating on Dominic.'

I'm not going to lie, the second bit of the news tickles me. People think I've nicked Dominic's girlfriend, whereas in actuality he's trying to steal mine. Social media is such a scam.

Honey swats me aside, like she has been playing with me this entire time by letting me think that I was getting the upper hand.

'I can fix part of that,' she says. She walks off the mat to her phone and taps quickly, then reads her comment aloud.

'Sometimes, friends become best friends and love finds its true path. I couldn't be happier for this beautiful couple. Wishing my best friend Caleb nothing but happiness with his soulmate Ariella. Please be kind.'

She looks at Ariella.

'You love each other. Stop hiding it. The stakes might be a little higher for me, but I'm thinking of doing the same.'

Honey walks past Ariella, grabs Lara's face and kisses her in front of us. Honey is a legend. Not only did she fulfil one of Ariella and my deepest wishes – for those two to get together – she managed to get Ariella to temporarily forget that she was angry at me.

When I meet Ariella at work later for the final part of Melissa's storytime, the first person who comes up to me as soon as I step out of the lift is Lydia. She'd been waiting for me to arrive before she entered the meeting room. I don't want to give the news away and I won't, but I know I'm going to struggle. Ms Pat warned us earlier that morning to make our medical appointments as discreetly as possible and not to tell anyone until after the three-month mark.

'I'm glad you told everyone, Caleb. Samir has lost his mind and Ariella's profile is an impossible firefighting nightmare, but well done. I'm happy for you both.' If she's this excited about the post, our other news is going to blow her mind.

When we walk into the meeting room, everyone apart from Samir and Aari bursts into a round of laughter-filled applause.

'You're still alive,' Bree announces, setting everyone off again.

'Only just.' I shake my head and take the seat next to Bryce.

'Well done, mate,' he whispers, then asks if I want sweet or salty popcorn from the machine in the corner of the room. I opt for ice cream, and grab it from one of the mini ice coolers sitting in the middle of the boardroom table.

Soon enough the countdown hits zero and Melissa appears in her bathrobe, waving today's paper at us for what we hope is the final time.

'I was hoping my last storytime was going to go out with a bang, but I don't feel like it today.'

She lifts her cocktail to her lips, downs it and uses her hand to call another one forth before she continues. Gustaf's hand is quick with a replacement.

'So, I don't want to be mean but... oh, who am I kidding? I'm always mean. Let's just get into it and start with the sex. Who was having it with whom and Kevin almost losing his tiny wee-wee when he tried to come on to me for the first and last time.'

She details all the people Kevin has had affairs with. It includes some pretty high-profile names and people who had no business having affairs with anyone. She detailed the lies that were told to make meetings happen, conferences that were made up and secret congregations on Indonesian islands that perhaps had a different kind of agenda.

'Video tapes was going to be my grand finale, but I've changed my mind. Kevin may be a disease-ridden, weak-spined, disgusting waste of space, but I had an affair too. It started off as a bit of fun, but I fell in love. I now realise that's what it was. At the time, I responded the only way I knew and did some pretty atrocious things. I now have to live with that and settle for Gustaf.'

Melissa looks off camera, shrugs and smiles. I get the feeling Gustaf knows what this is and he's not complaining. Poor Gustaf. Vultures will always find roadkill.

'So this is my final gift to him. Anyone so much as leaks, touches or tries to find and interfere with him, I'm releasing the tapes. All of them. And if yesterday is anything to go by, you know I can do it in multiple locations all at once. Gotta hand it to blockchain. So you're all now in charge of his safety. Any one of you so much as touches a hair on his head, everyone is getting it. He wandered blindly and stupidly into a carefully laid trap. He had no idea what he was getting himself into and I was completely unprepared for the effect he was going to have on me. I truly hope that he holds on to his perfection.'

Lydia, Ariella and Samir glance at me.

'Shit, mate,' Bryce whispers.

I daren't look at Ariella.

'I'll resurface eventually, when all of this has died down and the appropriate arrests have been made, investigations completed and the law has done the best it can. In the meantime, I'll be making bigger, meaner and scarier friends. I've always been resourceful like that. Here's a toast to not seeing or hearing from each other for a very long time – unless, of course, I absolutely have to.'

She raises her glass in the air and the stream cuts out. My phone vibrates. It's an unrecognised number.

> I may have been a monster but I was your
> monster. I'm sorry. Be happy. Goodbye.

'Wow,' Sian says. 'And life goes back to normal.'

'Ariella,' Samir starts, much more softly this time. 'Can we finish the conversation in my office please?'

'I'd like to join that conversation,' I say. Fuck Samir. I'm tired of his shit. He's not going to treat my girlfriend how he likes.

'Lydia?' Bryce says, standing.

'Yup.' Lydia stands too.

And the four of us follow Samir into his office.

'I want to know everything, right now,' he demands.

'What would you like to—' Ariella doesn't get to finish.

'You can stop with the innocent—'

'Hey!' I interrupt. 'Don't you dare talk to her like that. I don't know who you think you are, Samir, but before you rocked up with your fancy suit, watch and shoes, we were here. We built this. From nothing. Every client we currently have is less than a year old. She led that. Bryce stood at the gates and protected us. Lydia made sure we were all functioning. Was it perfect? No. Are we here today? Yes. So you can show some respect and let her finish her thought.' I turn to Ariella. 'Mason?'

'Samir,' she starts, finally taking a seat. 'You need to recruit your new COO. There is an irreparable disconnect between you and me. You deserve to have someone who you can trust to make the changes that you wish to make. I'm not that person. I've delivered as much as I can of your vision, but morally, strategically and philosophically we are not aligned, and I'm tired of fighting and making excuses for you.'

'And you're a horrible person,' Lydia adds.

'Leave my office now. All of you,' Samir demands, clearly at the end of his tether.

TWENTY-THREE

ARIELLA

'Samir called. He has absolutely no idea what to do with you.' Dominic laughs down the phone. 'That's a first.'

It's nice to hear Dominic laugh, especially after our last conversation. It has been a long day and I'm looking forward to getting home as I hop in a taxi.

'He needs to hire a COO, Dom. I don't understand what's taking him so long.'

'Maybe the people he had in mind have been swept up in the wave of arrests Melissa set off.' He chuckles.

'That was wild. How is Kevin doing?'

'Not well. His father is doing everything in his power to find Melissa.'

'I'd start by querying the internet for five-star-plus-hotel bartenders named Gustaf.' Dominic and I erupt with laughter. 'Did you know all those things about him?'

'Of course not. No one is ever really completely clean in business, but I wasn't expecting that.'

'I was so happy that DMVI didn't come up.'

'So was I,' he says, sounding relieved. 'Some of our clients weren't so lucky. I was scared that next week's dinner party guest list was going to be three people, including me. Thankfully I haven't lost anyone yet. Well, apart from you.'

I knew Caleb's post was bound to come up.

'Dom, you haven't lost me. We're still friends.'

'He's kissing your head while you're sleeping peacefully and posting it online for the world to see. I've lost you.'

He sounds deeply hurt.

'Dom—'

'You told me. Repeatedly. Life happens. Are you happy?'

'Yes, I am.'

'I think maybe we needed a different time, different place and different circumstances. And for Caleb not to have been born. I get the feeling that I'd lose out to that guy every time when it comes to you.'

'Maybe.'

'I wouldn't change anything though. Anyway, Samir.'

'Yes, Samir.'

'Can you be more cooperative? He said he finds you challenging.'

'All I am doing is my job, Dom. He needs to hire his COO, then he won't have to deal with me.'

The car pulls up outside my home.

'I'm home. I have to go, Dom. See you next week.'

I open the front door, excited about seeing Caleb. Today was the last storytime and we have finally managed to get rid of Melissa. I am in the mood to celebrate.

'Surprise!'

Lara, Honey, Caleb, Ms Pat, Bryce and Lydia stand in front of me, holding a large cake iced with the words, 'Congratulations Mama!'

'I told Bryce and Lydia. Sorry. I couldn't help it.' Caleb

laughs, not looking sorry at all, as he steps forward to give me a kiss.

'Can they be it though?' I laugh into his kiss. 'No more people until three months?'

'Can I tell Tim, Em and Jack? After that, I promise that's it.'

'Caleb! We're supposed to be keeping this quiet.'

'Let's promise each other not to say anything after Tim, Em and Jack.'

'Let's? Caleb, you're solely responsible for every single person who currently knows that we're having this baby.'

'Just think about it. Please?'

'I will murder you and happily have this baby in prison if this ends up on social media.'

'Is that a yes?' I have never seen him this excited.

'I'll think about it.'

I'm happy he told Bryce and Lydia. They deserved to know. Lydia has already spent the day making sure that I won't have to go to hospital. She has also arranged for a private medical team to do my first tests at home. Even Bryce showed up with a cute stuffed kangaroo for the baby.

It's a lovely evening with the seven of us. Lara is fully committed to the campaign for the name Elsie.

I'm exhausted by the time I get into bed.

Caleb is already there, smelling of shower gel and tooth-paste. He lies on his side, propping his head up with his palm.

'Well?'

'Well, what?' I ask, smiling at his happy face.

'Can I at least call Em? She'll be home now.'

'That's the same as telling the three of them.'

'I know. Can I?'

'You can tell her tomorrow,' I concede.

'Thank you! I promise that'll be the last person.'

'Only because you will have run out of people to tell,' I tease him.

Caleb lies back and opens his arms and I find my space in them.

'Aari?' he says quietly after a while, as he slips his hand over my tummy.

'Yes, Black?' I yawn.

'Thank you for putting up with me. I know it's not going to be easy to endure; but carrying, nurturing and growing my love inside of you means everything to me. I never imagined that I'd want to have kids, but there is nothing I want more than this child, because I'm having it with you. I wouldn't want to do this with anyone else.'

I can't help the tears that fall. I am in love with this man.

'Also, I've been on the internet,' he continues after a long pause. 'Your libido is about to skyrocket. Just so you know, I'm here to serve.'

I sit up, turn and climb on my boyfriend and he fulfils his promise.

TWENTY-FOUR

CALEB

I can't concentrate. Normally I'd be following the blood in the water and going for the kill at this event, but all I can think about is Ariella. I took her home early from work today and had to leave her throwing up in Ms Pat's care just before I left the house. I almost didn't come, but babies aren't cheap. As confirmed by the internet. And Tim.

When I call and tell them, Em simply gasps loudly. Tim takes over the conversation.

'You know her father is going to kill you, right?' he says happily.

'Cheers for that, mate. It may not be that bad.'

'Didn't he refuse to give you his blessing to marry her?'

'Only because he thought I wasn't ready.'

'Think he'll change his mind now you've done this?'

'Why do you sound like you're enjoying this?'

'Because I am. You're going to be a dad. It's great news and is going to be so enjoyable on so many levels. I can't wait for the day you're going to try to give useful advice,' he teases.

'I can give useful advice!'

'Really? Okay. Quick test. You're down to your last twenty quid. Are you going to spend it on hair wax or nappies?' He roars down the phone. 'Oh! Can I be the one to tell Jack?'

'Yes, you can tell Jack.' I let him have his fun.

'Mate, start saving now. You're going to be so poor.'

'I know!' We both crack up.

I got a single message from Jack shortly afterwards.

> Goodness knows why the universe has let this happen, but congratulations mate. Poor Ariella. She's in for a treat. Cigars and whisky when you're next about.

I am aware that I need to be able to support whatever Ariella decides she wants to do. I'm making really good money in Singapore and the bonuses I'm pulling in are fantastic, but I need to start focusing on what I'm going to do when we get out of here. I have no doubt that Ariella will be an exceptional mother and will fill our home with nothing but love, so I am committed to being a good man – providing for and protecting our family.

I'm not doing much 'providing' here, so I call it a night. By the time I get home, Ariella is sleeping. She has been busy in the kitchen tonight, playing with the recipes she's going to make for Dominic's dinner party. I am not happy about this whole dinner party malarkey, but I'm trying to be an adult about it. She seems genuinely excited, so I let it go. I found out the other morning that Ms Pat shares my Dominic concerns. She stopped short of demanding that she assist when Ariella goes off to cook with the caterers.

Ariella has been chasing the caterers down for her preparation slot at their industrial kitchens, but no one has managed to get back to her. I know exactly what is going on here. There isn't going to be a slot. At this point I'm not even sure there are caterers or a party, but I keep my mouth shut. Ms Pat may be tiny, but she is formidable and, as long as she is there with Ariella, everything will be fine. Besides, I've got other things on my mind.

I spend the whole of the next day looking at secluded islands for two nearby. Ariella and I haven't taken a proper holiday since we got here, and now would be the perfect time to do so. I'm deciding whether I should opt for something in the middle of an ocean, a river or bay when Lydia walks past. I solicit her for help.

'You're going to propose, aren't you?' She grins.

'Shhhhh!' I say, looking around.

'How far do you want to go?'

'Pluto is too close.'

'Just you or do you mind having other properties nearby?' Lydia snickers.

'Just us.'

'Have a look at this one,' she says before taking over my keyboard.

A house in the middle of the ocean appears, surrounded by white sand and crystal-clear blue water. As Lydia zooms in on the details of the four-bedroom villa, I see that it has a plunge and swimming pool, hammocks, beach cabanas, kayaks and an open beach grill. We read more. It comes with the option to have staff present or just daily check-ins for housekeeping and deliveries. It's exactly what I am looking for.

'Lydia, you're a legend,' I say, squeezing her hand.

'Don't thank me yet!' She scrolls to the bottom of the page.

'How much?!' I gasp loudly when I see the figure.

'And that's per night, plus service and taxes.' Lydia tries to keep her voice down.

'I could buy a house in the north of England for that!'

'You probably could.'

'It's fine.' I close my laptop. I thought I was doing well until I saw that.

'It's not where you are, Caleb, it's who you're with.' Lydia pats me on my shoulder and goes back to what she was doing.

Two hours later, I reopen the tab for the house and fire off an enquiry, praying that they'll come back and admit the price was in fact a mistake and they added that additional zero accidentally.

When I get home that night after yet another event, Ariella is nowhere to be found. Just as I pull out my phone to send her a text, she comes bustling through the door with Ms Pat, both laden with groceries. I help them with their bags before I pull her to me and plant a long, loving kiss on her lips. I've missed her today.

'Hello, Mason. What's all this?'

'Dominic's caterers got caught up in Melissa's crime sweep and he no longer has any catering on Thursday.'

I feel the anger rise, and push it down.

'So he's asking you to do it all?'

'He asked if I didn't mind stepping in. I think I can do it. We'll need to expand the menu to have some local dishes, but, as long as we present on platters for people to help themselves, I should be all right.'

'That's a lot, Ariella, especially in your... state.'

The giggle-filled kiss she rewards me with takes every negative feeling out of my body.

'I'm pregnant, Black, not dying, but I am going to need your help. I have a day and a half to get this right and my tastebuds have gone all weird. So I need yours.'

She's so excited, I can't take this away from her. Dominic is up to something; but I don't have any proof, so I keep my opinions to myself and pull up a stool.

'Okay. How can I help?'

We actually have a lot of fun that night. Ms Pat is sent home by Ariella at ten to get some sleep, but I stay up until almost four in the morning with my girlfriend testing, trying, giving my opinion and helping her pull her menu together. She is radiant and excited all night, laughing through her mistakes with food in her hair, and happily jumping and clapping at her successes.

By the time she decides to call it a night, my love for her feels like it's going to burst through my chest, and I can't keep my hands off her in the shower. With precautions no longer required, I hold her up as we make love and squeeze her tightly as we climax together. When we curl up to sleep, I start my little belly tickles, hoping that our baby feels the presence of my love through them.

TWENTY-FIVE

ARIELLA

'Thank you for stepping in. Who knew caterers could be criminals too?' Dominic says as Ms Pat and I arrive at his front door. He kisses my cheek. 'You smell so good tonight.'

'I don't like this, Miss Ariella,' Ms Pat whispers, giving Dominic a dirty look as we unload all the food we could pre-prep in advance onto the kitchen counter.

'We're fine, Ms Pat. All the equipment is already here, and Lydia made sure that the replacement catering team will arrive in thirty minutes. We won't be alone for much longer.'

'What can I do to help?' Dominic asks.

'Your guests don't arrive until seven. Pretend we are not here and do whatever you'd normally do on a Thursday afternoon.'

He nods obediently. 'I'll head to work then.'

Once he has left, we get to work. The decor team arrive to make his patio beautiful; service teams get to work polishing all the crockery ready to serve. The beverage team prepare ice, drinks and decant for the evening ahead, while Ms Pat and I focus on the food. We are ready when Dominic arrives back at five fifty for a shower and a change.

Ms Pat relaxes when the guests start to arrive. They are a lively crowd and rip through the champagne like it's water. It's a good mix of local businesses and international investors looking for partnership opportunities. The evening is a lot more casual than I expected for a meeting like this, which is probably down to Dominic's demeanour.

He's cheerful when he checks on me, and helps to move drinks around his guests and tastes little bits that I have set on the side to try.

I'm truly enjoying myself. It's been nice being in his kitchen, focusing on the business of cooking with waiting staff and the sommelier keeping the guests occupied. I've missed this. Me and simple, delicious ingredients ready to become something greater than they started out.

Going for the large platters of the contemporary chilli crab and the crispy baked chicken wings on blue cheese Caesar for the guests to dive into, family style, was a big risk but, when the pleas for more came through from the waiting staff, I feel like that's one course down.

The same anxiety takes hold as I send out the main courses of truffle macaroni cheese, shredded duck salad, garlic and ginger steamed fish and vegetable fried rice on their platters. There is absolute silence until one of the waitresses enters the kitchen, stands opposite me and excitedly delivers the line that relaxes me.

'They love it!'

It's smooth sailing after that. Dessert, of course, is a fruit salad Ms Pat made and a selection of ice creams and sorbet – I may be ambitious but I'm not trying to orchestrate my destruction.

'Aari! Come join us,' Dominic calls into the kitchen from the garden.

'Yes,' his guests from the USA rowdily agree, beckoning me to join them.

'No, Dom,' I reprimand him jokingly. 'Stop distracting your caterer.'

'I don't believe I have ever seen anyone I've outsourced toil to this happy.'

'That's because I volunteered for the aforementioned toil.'

By the time I join them for a glass of water at the end of the night after I've cleaned and wiped down the kitchen surfaces, everyone is full and buzzing.

'You're incredible,' Dominic whispers to me as I take a seat next to him.

'You know, Ms Pat and I just might be.' I smile shyly. I'm proud of myself. I've never fed this many people before and it's the first time I've cooked for strangers. Looking at all the empty platters that have returned to the kitchen, I'm not sure I made enough. I make a mental note to increase the portion sizes next time. If there is a next time.

'Here.' Dominic slips me an envelope.

'No. I told you I'd happily do it for free...'

'It's not money.'

Inside it is an image of my favourite wine, Ridge's Monte Bello, bearing my birth year.

'I bought you a couple of cases to say thank you.' He clears his throat nervously.

'Dom, this is just—'

'What's the nightlife like out here?' one of the guys asks tipsily.

'Not bad,' Dominic responds loudly, before he turns to me. 'Wanna come? Actually, don't answer that. Of course you don't want to come,' he teases with an understanding smile.

'I'll stay and supervise clear-up with Ms Pat. The guys are going to be here for a while.' I nod, smiling at the table full of wine, beer, cocktails, champagne and spirits.

'The crew usually leave now. We've asked them to return tomorrow morning.' He points at the chattering catering crew, who are putting on their coats to leave.

'In which case, I'll have an earlier date with my shower and my bed.'

'Let's find you guys some nightlife.' Dominic stands, prompting the entire table to do the same. Ms Pat and I follow behind the loud group and Dom puts them into cars, instructing his PA to arrange for them all to get into his members' club. Ms Pat follows his PA and, just as I step forward to exit after her, Dominic pulls me back against the wall and shuts his front door, sealing us both in his house.

'Miss Ariella!' Ms Pat calls from the other side of the door.

'She'll be out in a minute,' Dominic responds before he steps closer to me. 'You know what I'm going to say.'

I know what he's going to say because he has said it many times before. He has been saying it all night with his eyes, his smiles, his hand on my waist each time he came to check on me in the kitchen. He said it with the procurement of my favourite wine. He's saying it now with his finger slowly tracing up my arm.

The only problem is that he knows what I am going to say too. That I can't. That I'm in love with Caleb. But it's time to add that we can't keep doing this, and the sad reality is that we can't keep trying to be friends any more because, no matter what he says, these scenarios keep popping up.

'Tell me you don't feel it.'

'Dom—'

'You're different tonight. You look different. You smell different.' Dominic leans his forehead against mine.

'Dominic, please—'

'I know he's at home. Waiting. But I don't care. This is where you should be. We're good together. Leave him,' he whispers in my ear, pushing against me. 'I've been fighting the urge to kiss you all night.'

'Dominic, stop,' I plead. He has me pinned against the wall and I can't move from under him.

'I really want to trace my tongue down your stomach, wrap your legs round my neck and taste you.'

'Miss Ariella!' Ms Pat shouts from the other side of the door, distressed.

'I'm done playing your games of possibility with you. Am I going to have to fuck you until you call me Six, Ariella?'

'I'm pregnant, Dom!' I shout over him, then burst into tears. I didn't want to tell him like this because of what Mackenzie did to him, but it was the only way to make him stop.

Dominic takes a slow step back and I find the courage to look at his face. All I see is pain.

'You said maybe.'

'What?'

'I said I only stood a chance if Caleb hadn't been born and you said maybe.'

'I didn't mean—'

'Are you keeping it?'

'Yes.'

'Does he know?'

'Yes.'

Dominic takes a couple of more steps back, then sighs.

'I'm sorry, Dominic, this is partly my fault. I couldn't let go of you even though I knew we couldn't really be friends. Now, we've pushed each other to a place where I don't think we can salvage any kind of relationship from this any more. I think it's time to leave Singapore and go home. Please.'

'You want to go home with him?'

I nod.

Dominic immediately retrieves his phone from his pocket, scrolls, finds what he is looking for and taps it to dial.

'Samir! Tomorrow morning, I want Ariella Mason fired effective immediately. Give her the full two-year pay that she is due. If she tries to negotiate for more, give her whatever she wants. I just want her gone. And cancel her work visa. I want her out of the country within two weeks.' Dominic pauses. 'And Caleb Black too.'

He is silent for a while, in a way that suggests Samir is asking questions to try to understand what is going on.

'I don't give a fuck if they all walk out with her. I want both of them dismissed by the end of the day tomorrow, and out of the country as soon as possible.'

Dominic hangs up.

'Goodbye, Ariella,' he says sadly, then steps forward. I know he's going to try to kiss me. I put my hand on his chest gently to stop him.

'Dom—'

I am cut off by loud banging and the doorbell ringing chaotically from fast, repeated depression.

'Dominic! Open the FUCK up. NOW!' Caleb shouts as he bangs.

As Dominic does so, the door is pushed forward and knocks him back. Caleb rushes in, grabs Dominic by the front of his shirt and punches his face with such force, I think I hear something crack. I run over to try to pull Caleb off him. Caleb's fist continues to smash into Dominic's face with every word.

'Leave. My. Girlfriend. Alone!'

Dominic is on the floor by the time Caleb is done.

'Caleb!'

'What the fuck, Aari.' Caleb is fuming. 'We are going home. Now!'

I hear Dominic laugh through his bloodied face.

'She is. You're not. You're going to pay for this, and do every single second of your time here. And I'm going to make it hurt.'

'Dominic, please, no!' I cry.

'Fuck him. Let's get out of here,' Caleb says, grabbing me by my arm. He quickly guides me from Dominic's house with Ms Pat following.

My emotions are all over the place when we get back home, while Caleb is still dialled into pure fury.

'What did he do to you?'

'Nothing.'

'He kicked Ms Pat out and locked you in his house for nothing? When are you going to stop making excuses for him?'

'He misunderstood a conversation we had, that was all.'

'What conversation?'

'He said he'd lost me and I told him he hadn't – but I meant as a friend.'

'What is your obsession with being everyone's friend? I've repeatedly told you that this man doesn't want to be your friend!'

'Lower your voice please, Caleb.'

He doesn't. 'No. This guy has been hovering for months!'

'Are you going to beat up everyone that hovers, Caleb? Your fists will never rest.'

'He locked you in his house, Ariella! He has got at least thirty kilos of pure muscle more than you and is a full head taller. Your brand of goody-goody diplomacy wasn't going to do a damn thing if he wanted to hurt you!'

'My brand of goody-goody diplomacy *did* work. He was going to—'

'Oh my God. What if it didn't? Am I going to have to kill someone for you to stop putting yourself in risky situations?'

'I didn't put myself in a risky situation. He's our boss and he was my friend.'

'Friend my arse! You know he wanted more and you let him think he had a chance.'

'Well, at one point he did!' I shout back. Caleb looks like I've just slapped him, and gears up to counter-attack.

'Is this child even—'

'NO! Mr Caleb! Do not say!' Ms Pat shouts over him.

'Say it,' I seethe. 'I dare you.'

Caleb suddenly looks unsure.

'No! Please, Mr Caleb! You will lose everything. Please! Do not say!'

'I need some air,' Caleb says, and goes back out of the front door.

The sigh of relief from Ms Pat as she falls to her knees infiltrates the silence. I feel deep shame and embarrassment settle.

'Thank you for being there tonight, Ms Pat.'

'No problem, Miss Ariella. I happy I came,' she says sadly.

'I'll be moving back to London in the next couple of weeks. Tomorrow, can we talk about how I can help you secure a job before I move?'

TWENTY-SIX
CALEB

I don't return home that night. I'm furious, and I don't want to be around her. She knew he liked her and, instead of putting him firmly in the 'not going to happen, ever' zone, she kept trying to stay friends with him. It's such bullshit. Obviously, having witnessed Jasper's car crash, the last thing I wanted to do was control her or try to tell her what to do, but tonight was inevitable.

Ariella has a way of being evasive enough to drive anyone mad. I know. I've been at the other end of it. Repeatedly. Whether she is aware of it is irrelevant, and I have never been more sick and tired of her shit.

I knew he was circling, but he could be forgiven when he didn't know about Ariella and me and we were on hold. When we finally got back together, though, he still kept coming, and Ariella let him. That bastard tried to put me on a border-hopping plane to Vietnam with enough cash to disappear, for fuck's sake. Even the stupid meetings they had to have. I don't care if they were talking about helping Christopher. Why did it have to be after work or on his ostentatious boat? What's wrong with a well-lit conference room in the middle of the day? So what if time zones aren't on our side and Christopher's day was starting just as ours was finishing? Christopher would have gladly made an 8 a.m. video call at the healthy time of 4 p.m. in Singapore. She has been leading him on, and finally, tonight, he reached the end of his tether and I reached mine.

I'd been at home reading up online on what to expect from our first scan and how Ariella's body was going to change, because she was already two months down. Apparently, things were about to get much more exciting in month three. The last thing I expected was Ms Pat's frantic call telling me that Dominic had locked Ariella in his home. I'd never been more relieved that we lived in the same community.

I ran the two miles, on the twisty, hilly roads, through golf-course-sized parks and gardens, to Dominic's house in ten minutes flat; but seeing Ms Pat shaking with fear was what tipped me over the edge. My girlfriend and my baby were trapped in there by this man. We were both lucky I didn't kill him with my bare hands.

For Ariella to then have the audacity to tell me, mid-argument, that he stood a chance was the gut punch from her that I wasn't expecting. I was so blinded by rage that, if Ms Pat hadn't been there, I would have crossed a huge line; and she was right – there would have been no coming back from it.

When I knocked on Honey's door at two in the morning, I was a mess, and she did what I needed. She let me in, didn't ask any questions, led me to her spare room and placed a bottle of water beside me before promising that whatever it was would be all right in the morning.

It wasn't. I woke up, still fuming. I was so ferocious in training that Honey had to stop us every few minutes to remind me to use my head, because I was leaving myself open and vulnerable to attack. Sounds about right.

I went home to shower and change for the day when I knew

Ariella had definitely left for work and, when I got in, she was in Samir's office. We were all called into a staff meeting at noon.

For once, Samir isn't standing at the top of the table, Ariella is.

'I will be leaving my position at Ivory Bow today and I will not be rejoining Ivory Bow in the UK,' she announces quietly. The gasps around the table drown her next sentence out.

'It's fine. It's time.' It's her next sentence that delivers the blow for me. 'I love Singapore, but it doesn't feel like home any more and it's time that I returned to my real home.'

Clearly I'm not her 'home' any more.

'Lydia, you're going to take on a more strategic executive role with Samir. You're ready. It's time you started working towards the role we both know you can do with your eyes closed. Sian, Jess, Akiko. We're splitting projects into three different departments. One of you will head each one. You will have the opportunity to build your own teams – congratulations. The last year has been extremely challenging, but it has been the most rewarding year of my life and I am so grateful for you all.'

With that, Ariella walks out of the meeting room and straight off the Ivory Bow floor, leaving her bag, laptop, notebook and work mobile on her desk.

Samir takes her place.

'I know this will be shock—'

Lydia is the first to walk out. Bryce follows. Then Akiko, before Jess and Sian. Bree mouths a quick 'sorry' to me and follows the girls.

'We expected that, and Ariella is going to help to ensure their return. Caleb, can I have a word with you?'

We head straight into his office.

'I imagine you, more than everyone else, want to go and

check on Ariella, so I appreciate you fighting the urge to do so and staying.'

I immediately feel like shit.

'Your performance has prompted a review of your contract,' Samir says uncomfortably.

My performance is stellar. Dominic has prompted a review of my contract.

'You've been doing well and hitting your targets and this might be a good time to remind you that, whatever happens with Ariella, you're still expected to perform for the remaining duration of your two-year contract. There are perks attached to your employment, such as your living allowances and expenses, and, should your performance significantly drop, you fail to hit your targets or seem to be engaging in any kind of sabotage, it is well within the company's rights to respond accordingly; and with legal action if deemed necessary or appropriate.'

I feel the metaphorical chains going on. 'Sure. Anything else?'

'Please remember that all travel and all holidays must be approved.'

'Fine. Is that all?'

'I've been asked to reclaim Ariella's home in two weeks. Do you have somewhere else to stay?'

'No, but I'll find somewhere. There's time.'

'That's all for now.'

He catches up to me just as I am about to leave his office, and puts his hand on my shoulder.

'I'm not sure what happened last night but I'm not comfortable with the way things have played out today. It wasn't my decision to let Ariella go, and it certainly wasn't my decision to pull your contract and enforce every single point on it. I'm going to do everything I can to make things as easy as possible for you, but please be aware that sometimes my hands may be tied.'

'Thanks, Samir,' I say, understanding that he's not exactly happy with what Dominic has done either.

At the end of the work day, for the first time, I dread going home. I'm still pissed off at everything that went down yesterday, but Ariella just got sacked in front of the whole company.

I hear everyone before I see them. A large part of me is happy that we won't be alone.

Everyone who walked out after Ariella is sitting in our living room, surrounded by bottles of wine and platters of food as they chatter loudly.

'Caleb! Did you quit?' Jess shouts in the direction of the door.

'Eeeeeyyyy!' everyone choruses as I walk towards them.

'This is where you've all been, on a work day? We really need a proper HR department,' I joke.

When my eyes meet Ariella's, she turns away. Oh, don't worry, love, I'm still pissed off too.

I stay in the living room and join in as we share fun memories and challenges we have had together. Ariella spends most of the evening trying to persuade everyone to go back to work the next day. She falls asleep in the armchair just as the sun begins to set and, after she has encouraged everyone to stay, takes herself up for a nap. We stay chatting and laughing until well past ten. Once the team leave, I take myself off to sleep in the guest bedroom.

TWENTY-SEVEN

ARIELLA

'That bastard.' Lara barges into the house around lunchtime the next day, waving her phone around.

'That could be any number of people, Lara, help me out.' I'm full of nothing but the sorrow that has accumulated over the last few days as I make myself some toast. I can't wait to get away from Singapore and, after the other night, Caleb.

'Dominic Miller. DMVI withdrew the job offer and cancelled my work visa application. I'm back to square one.'

'Did they give a reason?'

'Simply that the role no longer exists and I'll get six months' pay and they'll cover any associated expenses. I didn't even get to start.'

I retrieve my personal phone and send a text message to Dominic.

> Please don't punish Lara because of what I did.

> You didn't do anything and I'm not punishing her.

> I'm really sorry Dominic. For everything.

Me too. I heard you turned down your
severance package. I've asked them to send it
to you anyway.

'What did he say?'

'A lot has happened in the last seventy-two hours, Lara.'

'Oh no. He let me go because of you, didn't he?'

'Have you eaten? I'll make some more toast.'

'I will help, Miss Ariella.' Ms Pat descends from upstairs. 'Sit.'

I fill Lara in and she sits quietly, listening.

'Caleb is a total wretch for even thinking about dragging Elsie into this, but you behaved terribly too.'

'I genuinely just wanted to stay friends.'

'I know, but you knew that man was into you and, every time he called, you went running. That's enough to drive Caleb round the bend. And that's before you add the fact that you admitted you were attracted to him.'

'I know I messed up, Lara. And now I can't do anything about it. I don't even recognise myself. Who have I become?'

'Ariella, calm—'

'No! Everything is too much at the moment. I can't cope, Lara! I'm pregnant, I haven't told anyone, Caleb and I are fighting, Dominic is going to make things hard for him and I'm not sure I want to raise this child with Caleb anyway because I don't think he can control his temper. I've got two weeks to get out of Singapore, there is no way I am moving back in with my parents and I'm not living with Jack at Caleb's. I really need Jasper's help but Sophia will be rightfully furious if I reach out. I can't tell Zachary because he'll spill before I get home, and I'm leaving everyone at Ivory Bow in the hands of someone I don't trust. Ms Pat won't have a job in two weeks. Even you... I convinced you to come back to Singapore and look at what has happened. What have I done? What am I doing?' I feel my breathing start to go shallow as I cry, and I know what's coming.

'Okay. I'm going to help you slow your breathing,' Lara says. She slowly takes my hand and helps lead my counts. When we've managed to slow it down, she hugs me and holds me there. It's exactly what I need. I release all the fear, anxiety and uncertainty through my tears.

'We're going to fix what we can. I'm going to call Jasper,' Lara finally says.

'No, I promised Sophia that I wouldn't contact him.'

'She didn't say I couldn't.' Lara is dialling before I can respond. 'Jasper,' she starts, and waits for a response. 'Good. No love lost then. Listen. I'm keeping this short and sharp. Ariella has been booted from Ivory Bow, she'll be back home within two weeks and she needs your help, but Barbie won't let her call you.'

Lara looks bored as she lets Jasper speak.

'Yeah, okay, whatever. She needs a home. Somewhere between you and her parents. Preferably a cottage. She'll need do-gooding, friendly and slightly nosy neighbours. Maybe one of those streets with a bunting and Christmas lights kitty. Three bedrooms. Garden. Somewhere with a swanky postcode with maybe parks, lakes, rivers, swans, rabbits and ducks and shit – but on a tube line.'

Lara mouths, 'It'll be fine' at me before she continues the conversation.

'Bloody hell, Jasper, let her live in it for five minutes first. A rental is fine, and you're going to have to ask Caleb that.'

After a couple more short exchanges that end in Lara swearing Jasper to secrecy, she hangs up.

'House will be sorted. He'll arrange for you to be picked up at the airport, not by him, of course, and he won't tell a soul. Expect him to call Caleb for details though,' she warns.

'Thank you, Lara.' I just feel so helpless, I don't know what else to say.

'You need to learn how to ask for help, babe. I've been running around Singapore necking cocktails and terrorising the locals completely unaware that you needed me. You just bottle it all up, letting it go haywire in your head until it explodes. Now look at you.'

I nod and stay in my best friend's arms until I fall asleep.

I wake up alone on the couch to Lara's frustrated whispering.

'Maybe if you stopped thumping innocent fucking civilians, you'd be in better shape.'

'He's not innocent.'

'Who died and made you a vigilante? This isn't Gotham. Stop your reckless nonsense and stop beating up random people because they breathed in her direction! You're scaring the shit out of her.'

I feel uncomfortable listening in, so I sit up noisily.

'You were out for a while,' Lara says as she approaches me from the kitchen. Caleb walks in the opposite direction and out into the garden.

'I can't wait until I get my energy back.'

'So a few things happened while you were sleeping. Honey, unsurprisingly, is taking Ms Pat on when you leave, I've reached out to my wedding thirst club to let them know I am still looking, and Jasper has already found you somewhere. Wait till you see the kitchen.'

Lara pulls up the house on her phone and takes me through the floor plans and images. She leaves the large light-filled kitchen till last.

'It's perfect, thank you for everything, Lara.'

'I just can't believe you've conned me this whole time that

you had your shit together. You're still as bloody useless as you were in London.' Lara laughs and I laugh along too.

'How are things with Honey?'

'Good. Really good.' She looks really happy. 'We're obviously lying low and definitely no strip clubs, but I don't mind. I like it. It's different. It feels special.'

'Do you think you'll move in with her while you're looking for something else?'

'No. I'm not sure what I'm going to do, but I like that we live apart. It feels like I'm choosing to spend time with her, rather than having to be together because we live in the same house. I might crash with Caleb instead. I'll get to see her every day and we can both still have space.'

'I am so happy for you, Lara.'

'I'm happy for me, too and I think taking it slowly helps.'

'Do you think she might be it for you?'

Lara takes her time and looks into the distance to give my question some thought before she answers.

'Yes, I think she might be, but we'll see. I think we need to make some progress first before I know for sure.'

'What progress?'

'None of your business. Are you going to be okay? I'm supposed to be meeting her tonight.'

'Yes. Thank you for today, Lara.'

'I love you, my secretive little nutter.'

I get one last hug from my best friend before she calls her taxi and makes her way out of my front door, leaving Caleb and me alone in the house.

I'm not in the mood for a confrontation so, while he is still out in the garden and we can't see each other, I escape into the bedroom for a shower and an early night and commit to turning things round tomorrow. I really need to start planning for this baby, packing up my things and winding down life in Singapore.

I walk as quietly as I can up the stairs to avoid Caleb, only to find him sitting on our bed with his head in his hands. I stand there considering taking a step back to leave.

'Please don't leave.'

'I don't want to fight Caleb, please.'

'I don't want to fight either.' He reaches both his arms out towards me from where he is sitting and I step into them. Caleb pulls me in and presses his cheek against my belly with such longing, I feel the intensity with which he loves this baby.

'I hate that I drove you away to the point that you could only speak to Lara. I understand why, but you asking Jasper for help rather than me is particularly devastating.'

'I'm sorry.'

'You don't have to apologise, it was my fault.'

'No, it was mine. I knew Dominic wanted to be more than friends. He told me every time I saw him but I chose to ignore it and I didn't really, fully shut it down. Instead, I wanted to keep him in my life so much, I tried to force a friendship that I knew deep down had turned into something else.'

'Why did you want him around so much? What gap was he filling, for you?'

'None. I'm not like you, Caleb. I don't make friends easily. Inconveniently, he's the only friend I have made in Singapore. I was lost and lonely for a very long time when I got out here. He saw that and changed it exactly when I needed it. He wasn't a colleague I had to see daily or someone paid to be nice to me. He easily could have been an uninvolved client but he chose to be a friend. We were kind to each other. Inspired each other, made each other laugh. Hanging out with Dominic was my equivalent of you going for casual beers with Tim and Jack or your pub quiz. Not seeing him any more when we got back together felt like I was abandoning him and I knew that, if I let go of him, I'd miss my friend. Before you showed up, I told him that we couldn't be friends any more. Caleb, no matter how much being friends with Dominic was important to me, it was threatening our relationship, and I want this more.'

I put my hand through his hair and hold him close.

'Lara told me he instructed Samir to fire you because you asked him to let you go home.'

'Yes.'

'And you have to be out of Singapore in two weeks?'

'Yes.'

'Okay.'

I intentionally didn't tell Lara that Dominic had agreed to let both of us go back to London because I knew there was every chance she would mention it. If Caleb ever found out that he had jeopardised his chance to come back with me and the baby, he'd never forgive himself. So, I lock it away and stand there for a while, holding on to my boyfriend as we figure out what the next best steps for us would be.

TWENTY-EIGHT

CALEB

When Jasper called earlier that day, I was still fuming at Ariella, so I was expecting him to give me a hard time.

'Caleb, what's going on?'

I really didn't want to be the one to tell Jasper but at this point it looks like I'm going to need all the help I can get.

'Dominic locked Ariella in his house against her will, so I went over there and beat the shit out of him.'

'Nice,' Jasper says encouragingly.

'Finally! Thank you! Everyone out here is running around behaving like I'm some kind of beast that needs to be locked up.'

'I'd have done the same thing. She's your girlfriend. That's completely out of line.'

A sympathetic ear feels so good.

'Then, he told Samir to get rid of her.'

'Lara told me. He's not even hiding the fact that he's spitefully making her leave the country within two weeks.'

'Wait, what?'

'He's given her two weeks to leave the country. How come you don't know this?'

'Things aren't exactly rosy at the moment.'

'What did you do, Caleb?'

'Why does *everyone* always assume it's me?'

'You do have a self-destructive track record...'

'It wasn't me, mate! I love her, but dealing with Ariella is fucking painful. She knew that guy fancied her and still kept running to him every time he called, insisting that they were just friends. Goodness knows all the filthy things he has done to her in his mind, and would have probably done to her if I hadn't showed up.'

'Goodness.'

'She'd been happily wandering into the lion's cage for months, taking fucking private jets with it, letting it lick her face twice and calling it a big kitten. And then she stood there, proudly telling me she could have run off with him at some point. I was sick of her shit.'

'Uh-oh. What happened?'

'I started to say something I shouldn't have, but Ms Pat stopped me. So I didn't.'

'Could she have filled in the blanks? What did you not say?'

'I was going to ask her if the baby was even a consideration. She put both of them at risk.'

'What baby?'

'Ours. She's pregnant. You can't tell anyone. We're going to figure out how to tell Dahlia and Hugh together.'

'Ah. Hugh.'

'Yes, Hugh. I leave all five whole pounds in my name to Ariella even though she's the most annoying person in the world. You can be the executor. She can choose between a single note or five shiny pound coins.'

'Congratulations, mate. You know this means we'll be new dads around the same time? I'll be about three months ahead.'

'Do you know what you're having?'

'Twin boys.'

'Bloody hell. If we have a girl, there will be absolutely no play dates at yours.'

Jasper laughs. 'You sound like Hugh.'

'Ugh, Hugh.' I mirror his earlier comment.

'Yes, Hugh,' he says on cue and we both erupt with laughter.

'So, the reason I called. This house Ariella wants.'

'What house?'

'Caleb. If she's not telling you that she's leaving in two weeks, not going back to her parents and is quietly looking for a home, she's building a new life without you. Things are really bad. If you remember, that's how my story ended. All you're missing is a sticky note.'

'Shit.'

'Yes, shit. I've had a quick look. There's a house in Richmond that fits her criteria perfectly but it's not for rent, it's for sale. Shall I buy it?'

'Can I afford it? Without having to sell a major organ?'

'It'll mean a chunky mortgage, but yes.'

'Buy it. Tell her she can stay for free. If she does that "I want to pay my own way" nonsense that she does, rent it to her. I've been returning all her rent since Jack moved in anyway so she won't be squeezed in two places.'

'Got you. On it. Ariella can be challenging, but please try to fix things with her if you can or you'll regret it.'

I hang up, once again thankful that Jasper and I have somehow managed to forge a solid friendship from a relationship that saw us start as adversaries. Regardless of how I'm feeling, I hold on to his advice and commit to try. Then I hear her feet coming up the stairs. As soon as our eyes meet, I know she's planning to turn round.

'Please don't leave,' I beg as I open my arms. As soon as she steps in between them, I know we are going to be okay.

.   .   .

It takes a while to accept that I'm not going to be as present as I want to be for Ariella and the baby, so I spend the next few days plotting to be as involved as possible.

Ariella, since our chat, has been unusually subdued.

When the official line that she has decided to leave her role in the company to start a new chapter of her life was released, the farewell dinner, drinks and party proposals from her clients, business networks and industry associations came in thick and fast.

Lydia declined every single one at her request, but invited them all to one large drinks and casual dinner reception to say goodbye. Not only did Samir approve the budget immediately, he sent personal invitations out to everyone himself.

Trolls online didn't disappoint. The predominant rumour was that Dominic was getting rid of her because she wouldn't sleep with him. For once, they weren't too far off the mark.

The team could not have planned a more fitting departure for her. The evening was short, from seven to nine. The food and drink was from the best Singapore had to offer, and she wasn't required to speak. Samir gave a surprisingly hilarious and unexpectedly moving tribute, labelling her the quietest but most formidable battle he'd ever had to fight. Dominic said a few words, admitting that her leaving was a greater loss than any of us could imagine.

Ariella spent the entire evening having quiet conversations with everyone who wanted one, before slipping away without fanfare at half past eight. If she thought she was going to have a quiet night after that, she was mistaken. The guys turned up at our home after the party and we had our own celebration until the wee hours.

.   .   .

The next day, thinking things may have thawed, I request holiday days to fly out with her, but they are declined. Samir couldn't look me in the eye when I challenged him on it. He knows it's bullshit. So I do the next best thing.

'Christopher,' I say into my laptop screen.

'Caleb. How can I help?' He's curt.

'I'm about to ask you for some favours and I need you not to say no.'

'I'm not sure you deserve any favours, Caleb. Dominic told me what you did. I'd have put up a fight for you if this wasn't your second known incident.'

'Did Dominic tell you he kicked out Aari's housekeeper and held her hostage in his house?'

'Well, not in those terms – he said he wanted to have a private conversation and there was a huge misunderstanding.'

'There was no misunderstanding.'

'Did he open the door when you pressed his bell?'

'Yes, but—'

'It doesn't sound like he was holding her hostage, Caleb.'

'Chris, I need you to hear me out.'

'I think I've heard—'

'Ariella is pregnant.'

His eyes widen. 'That bastard got her pregnant and now he's tossing her aside?'

'No. The baby is mine.'

'Caleb, I'm going to need you to start from the beginning and tell me everything.'

So I do.

'What do you need?' Christopher asks when I am done.

'If I give you a couple of specific weeks every month, can you request my presence in London to help with a range of different challenges?'

'Caleb, I'm not Harrison. I can't manufacture enough issues for you to be in London every other week.'

'That's not what I meant. I've submitted two holiday requests already that have both been rejected. I'd like to be there at least a week a month, and for a couple of weeks minimum when the baby is due.'

'Don't they have paternity leave out there?'

'I have to be a Singaporean citizen and I have to be married to Ariella by the time the baby is born for it to be enforced at a governmental level. And that's only a shitty two weeks. I've looked through my employment contract too. I don't get paternity unless we are married.'

'Are you not thinking of marrying her then?'

'Of course I am, but not like this. She's not a legal get-out-of-Singapore-free card.'

'I don't think I have enough for once a month. Maybe once every two months? Once we know her due date, I can work towards getting you out here for a couple of weeks and find a huge problem that might require you to stay out for an extra week or two?'

'Thanks, Chris.' I hear my voice shake.

'A word of advice, Caleb. Seek help. Your anger has robbed you twice. Don't let it happen a third time, and especially not with someone who really matters.'

I know what he is saying. 'I understand.'

'Good. Because if you hadn't laid into him, you'd both be coming home.'

'No. I may have been able to come back and forth as much as I wanted, but it would have been just Aari.'

'No. She requested both your returns. He'd agreed. Then you did what you did.'

The full impact of regret for what I did hits me. Dominic is absolutely evil for retaliating with this. I am going to make him pay.

'Don't, Caleb.'

'Don't what?'

'Whatever you're thinking, just don't. Let me know when Ariella's flight back is. I may not be able to get you out together, but I can arrange for you to follow the week after. Piers is acting up anyway and I could use your help straightening him out.'

TWENTY-NINE

ARIELLA

The house doesn't feel or look any different to when I moved in, after I've packed my belongings ready to go to the airport. It only reinforces what I already know. This was never my home.

It has been a calm day. Caleb and I moved around each other quietly. He packed the final bits to move into his new place later tonight. He spent the rest of the day checking the house and ensuring we haven't left anything. Things haven't been the same since that night at Dominic's and, while we are still together and talking, there remains a distance between us that neither of us can reach across. What used to be intimacy-filled nights with intermittent spells of sleepy chatter are now silent as Caleb holds on to me with a hand on my belly.

I don't have much to say either. All I can feel is the fog around me getting thicker, pushing me deeper into myself. I'm returning home in a state that I never could have imagined. Single, unemployable thanks to the pregnancy, with no idea what the future holds. Everything is destroyed and it's only a matter of time before my relationship with Caleb deteriorates too.

The only shining light is that we are creating something

beautiful, but the devastating truth that I dare not tell anyone is that I feel nothing for it. From everything you see, watch, read and hear, I'm meant to be beyond awe and over the moon, but I'm not. I feel nothing. Caleb was the socket of love, power, excitement and joy that I plugged into, and now it's gone. The most frightening thought that is currently lurking, is that there might be a future where I won't love this baby, and it makes me feel guilty, anxious, overwhelmed and vulnerable. At the same time, to admit that out loud would be almost blasphemous; so I have no choice but to carry these feelings silently.

My thoughts are interrupted by the doorbell as I sit on the couch alone.

'I'll get it,' Caleb calls from upstairs as he dashes down.

'Is she still here?' I hear Lara ask and I turn to see her push Caleb aside.

'Hello to you too. Hey, Honey.'

'Oh phew. Good.' Lara sounds out of breath.

'Hey. What's going on?' I ask her.

'Honey and I talked about it. I'm coming with you.'

'What? No, I'll be fine,' I protest. Lara and Honey just got together and she's still looking for a job.

'Shut up, Aari. I'm coming. Just to help you and Elsie settle in, and then I'll be back.'

'Honey?' I stand to find her.

'She'll be back soon, don't worry. I'll keep an eye on Caleb.' Honey shrugs in that sweet nonchalant way she does.

'Hear that, Caleb? I'll be back soon! I will kill you if you give my room to someone else.' Lara points at him.

'What room?' Caleb looks confused.

'I'm moving in with you when I get back and you can't say no because I'm unemployed and about to assume responsibility for the most important things in your life. You owe me. You can pay me back in rent-free accommodation. And no bills. I'm poor.'

The speed with which Caleb grabs Lara and pulls her into a tight grateful hug makes my heart melt.

'Yuck. Ew. Ew. Ew!' Lara tries to detach herself but he holds on. 'Still a lesbian, you idiot. My girlfriend is literally right there! Honey, beat him up for hitting on me.'

Honey laughs and approaches me for a hug.

'You're going to be okay, Ariella Mason.' The way she says it is so reassuring, I believe her, and a tear escapes.

'Please look after Ms Pat,' I beg.

'I will. She's already thrown out half of my kitchen cabinet and is replacing it with healthy fruits and vegetables. And she's demanding a day a week off to sort Caleb's life out.'

All of us laugh.

'When do we head out?' Lara asks, pointing at a suitcase I didn't notice initially. I look at my watch.

'About an hour?'

'Okay, great. Come on, Honey.' Lara grabs Honey by the hand and leads her out to the patio for some privacy, leaving Caleb and me in an awkward silence.

I pretend I need to go to the bathroom to get away from him, and ascend the stairs to avoid the route that allows me to see through to the patio. I sit in stillness on the cold toilet lid, wishing the time away. After a little while there is a soft knock on the door.

'Aari?'

I flush and wash my hands before I open the door to Caleb. I let him lead me into our bedroom and shut the door.

'I'll be over in about a week.'

'I know. I'll be fine.'

'Is there anything you need?'

'No, I'm okay.'

'I've been putting the rent for the flat back into your account. Jack's covering the bills and is contributing enough.'

'Thank you, Caleb.'

'Are you still happy for me to arrive before you tell your parents? I'd like us to do it together.'

'Yes. Of course. They'd definitely appreciate it more coming from both of us.'

'I'm sorry I fucked up, Aari.'

'I'm sorry I fucked up too.' Me swearing puts a tiny smile on Caleb's face before he sighs deeply.

'Come here.'

He pulls my face towards his and plants a slow kiss on me. It's tentative and unsure at first, but soon I surrender to my boyfriend. I love this boy, I really do – but how can we love each other so intensely, but hurt each other so painfully?

I stay, standing, comforted by Caleb's hug, until we hear the taxi beeping outside.

'Yes! Jasper did well.' Lara walks into the hall of the beautiful home. She's collected our keys from the next-door neighbour.

'He did.' As I step into the house, I feel a release of responsibility that I've carried since I arrived in Singapore fall off my shoulders. I don't have to fight any more. I don't have to prove myself. I don't have to hold it together for anyone. And I most certainly don't have to pretend to be the imposter I've been for the last year and a bit. In fact, I don't have to do anything any more; and I don't want to. I leave my suitcase in the hall and make my way up the stairs.

'Where are you going? I was planning to nick the biggest en suite! Don't you dare beat me to it!' Lara laughs.

'You can have whatever you want, Lara,' I say quietly, then I find the tiniest bedroom, get under the duvet and cry myself to sleep.

It's dark when Lara softly taps me awake.

'Babe, you've been asleep all day. I brought you some water. Do you want something to eat?'

'No thank you. I'd just like to stay here please.'

'Do you want to take a shower? I finally figured out how to work the boiler.'

I shake my head, too exhausted to move.

'Okay. Is there anything I can get you?'

'No thank you. I'd just like to go back to sleep please.'

Thankfully, Lara lets me do just that. I don't want to talk, think or move. I just want to sleep.

The next time I hear from Lara is the following afternoon.

'Aari. Would you like something to eat? I went to the shops this morning.'

'No, thank you.'

'Please have something, if not for you, for Elsie.'

'Don't do that, Lara!' I snap. 'And stop calling it that. I don't want to eat. I don't want to do anything. I just want to lie here. Please leave me alone.'

I pull the duvet over my head and lie awake, feeling nothing, until I fall asleep.

It feels like I've been asleep for only a few minutes when Lara returns to poke the duvet.

'Caleb is on the phone.' I uncover my head and see her stretching the phone towards me. I reach my index finger out and hit the red phone icon to terminate the call, then bury my head again.

'Fucking hell, Aari. You're scaring the shit out of me. You've been in bed for three straight days,' Lara shouts.

I wish I could make Lara feel better, but the darkness has won and I've never felt more lost.

. . .

I wake up when it's dark, and feel my way through the unfamiliar path to the loo in the en suite. For the first time, I reach for the shower taps and turn them on. The comforting noise of water beating down on the shower tray calms me and I strip slowly. I relish the sharp, relentless stings of the high-pressure shower and take my time washing myself carefully from head to toe. When the water runs ice cold, I get out and wrap my body and hair in two towels. Lara at some point brought my suitcase up the stairs, so I fish around for my toothbrush, toothpaste and mouthwash. Once I've done my teeth, I descend the stairs and, guided by moonlight, find my way to the kitchen and help myself to the bread on the kitchen top. Deciding that I don't have the energy to put any butter on it, I bite into a slice. It feels dry and unappetising, but I force myself to chew and swallow before I grab a bottle of water and drink the whole litre.

I'm too tired to climb the stairs, so I settle on a comfortable-looking couch in the living room and pull the throw over my towel and go to sleep.

'Babe, can I make you some tea?' I open my eyes to see Lara sitting by my feet on the couch.

'No, but thank you, Lara.'

'Aari...' she pleads.

'I just don't want to do anything for a little while, that's all.'

'I understand that, but this is just frightening.'

'I'm okay, Lara.'

'You're not. I'm this close to calling Jasper.' She pinches her thumb and index finger. 'But I've already voluntarily called him once and that's enough for this decade.' She chortles softly. 'Caleb is on his way,' she goes on. 'He went straight to the airport after our last call. He should be landing soon.'

Dread fills me. Caleb comes with too much pressure. He'll want to know what's wrong. He'll bring everything I left behind in Singapore with him in the form of fun breaking news, only I don't want to hear it. He'll want to know about the baby and I'll have nothing to tell him. Then, he'll start doing everything he can to try to fix it, when I just want to be left alone.

'Lara, please can you find a way for him not to stay here?'

I see Lara's expression change to one of annoyance.

'What did that dolt do now?'

'Nothing. I could just use some space. I don't want him breathing down my neck about the baby.'

'Ariella,' Lara says slowly. 'You do want this baby, right?'

'I do.'

'So, what are you finding difficult?'

'Everything.'

THIRTY

CALEB

All I have been able to think about since I walked out of the office to catch the next available flight is everything I have put Ariella through since Melissa showed up in London over a year ago. I replay every moment I made things worse in my head, which coincided with Ariella doing her best to extinguish the fires I started. The last incident with Dominic was the worst. I was home free until I destroyed my own chances of being with my girlfriend and our child.

Thankfully, Ariella's new home is in south-west London, a mere twenty-minute taxi ride away from Heathrow, and in no time I am pressing the doorbell.

Lara opens the door, pushes me back and steps outside, shutting it behind her.

'Listen. I think she's having some weird breakdown, but you have a role to play.'

'I'm listening.'

'No Singapore talk, no baby talk. For once I'm going to need you to channel vacuous, shallow Caleb and just be fun to be around – but not too much fun.'

'Okay.'

'You know that thing you do that makes the worst idea in the world sound like a Nobel prize-winning opportunity?'

'No, not really but—'

'Do that. Just that. And you can't stay. You can spend as much time as you want here, but you can't stay.'

'Why can't—'

'You can't stay. That's it.'

'Fine.'

Only then does Lara let me in. Aari's lying on the couch in her towel, staring up at the ceiling.

'Mason. Come on.'

I lift her in my arms, carry her upstairs and lay her on the bed of a room that hasn't been slept in. Then I quickly strip, have a shower and wrap a towel round myself, and get into bed with her.

I arrange us into our favourite co-sleeping position and hold her until she falls asleep. For the first time in a long time, I don't touch her belly.

The sun is setting when I open my eyes. She's awake, just lying there with her head on my chest.

'Mason, what can I do to help?'

'Nothing. Please just lie here with me.'

'I want nothing more, but can I get us some water and maybe I can make you some cheese on toast?'

I give her a little kiss on the lips before I extract myself and make my way downstairs.

'You have got to be fucking kidding me.' Lara attacks as she sees me appear.

'What?'

'You animal. You slept with her in that state?'

'Of course not! I had a shower because I boarded the flight

straight from work and only stopped at home to get my passport. See any bags?'

'Oh. If you give me your clothes, I'll put them in the machine for— Ugh. No, actually. Yuck. Do your own laundry. How is she?'

'Awake. I'm going to make us something simple to eat.'

Lara is upstairs before I get to the kitchen. She isn't quite as thorough a grocery shopper as Ariella but she has the essentials. Bread and cheese. I layer the cheese carefully and pop it in the oven. While I wait, I text the only person who I know can help.

> Ariella might be depressed. I don't know what to do.

Em replies immediately:

> What do you mean?

> She's been in bed since she got back. Not really eating or saying much. She doesn't want to talk about the baby.

> Oh no. I'm so sorry Caleb.

> What should I do?

> Be with her. Find tiny things that don't require a lot of effort and suggest them. When she talks, just listen. Try to understand, not fix. Meet her where she is and gently guide her out of it. Baby steps though. Most importantly, ask her what she needs.

> Thank you Em. I was also thinking of calling her mother.

> Maybe run that past her first. She won't want to see everyone.

I don't tell Em I'm already home because we need the quiet. I take the tray with six pieces of cheese on toast upstairs with three bottles of water. Lara is Ariella's happy place and I have no doubt that she will eventually reach her. Lara is mid-flow when I arrive.

'...and we couldn't figure out why Nicole hadn't set him on fire!' She laughs softly.

'Did I ever get my bra back?' Ariella asks weakly, also laughing a little.

'No, Bamidele found it. She was so furious, she ripped it apart with her bare hands and put it in the outside bin.'

'Why are we talking about Nicole? And who is Bamidele?' I join in as I place the food and water on the bed.

'Entertainment. Bamidele was CrimeSpree's girlfriend at the time.' Lara grabs and bites into a piece of cheese on toast. She moans with exaggerated pleasure, then hands Ariella one.

'You slept with CrimeSpree's girlfriend?' I ask, shocked.

'Repeatedly,' Ariella contributes quietly as she gives her best friend a loving side-eye glance.

'It was more of an entanglement. Then Harrison found out while we were at a strip club. It all blew up and I got promoted.' Lara shrugs.

'You didn't really get promoted though, did you?' Ariella giggles.

'Wait. Is this the reason you were taken off the floor so quickly?'

'Yup!'

Ariella reaches for a second piece of toast and I subtly nudge the plate closer to her.

'Okay, you're going to have to spill. Tell me everything.'

'No, I was saving it for a drunken night.'

The expression on Ariella's face suggests that, even though she was there, she wants to hear the story too.

'Fine. There I was, minding my own business—'

'You weren't minding your business, you were meant to be working,' Ariella interrupts.

'Hey!' Lara complains.

'Sorry.' Ariella laughs.

'Thank you. Anyway, there I was, thinking purely, "I'm not going to sleep with my client's girlfriend" thoughts...'

That was our way back in. Lara Scott is a fucking genius. She laughs, complains, takes the piss out of and adores the versions of Ariella, Caleb and Lara that existed before Singapore. I play my part and fill Lara in on the details of Ariella's dates that she hadn't shared, while Ariella pitches in with the story about the boyfriend who turned up with the metal pipe.

We talk until the small hours of the morning. Before Ariella falls asleep, I manage to convince her to jump into the shower, and I have a fluffy bathrobe waiting. I shower after her. By the time I get into bed to cuddle her to sleep, my dirty clothes that I arrived from Singapore in are gone.

I let her snuggle in closely and wait until I hear her cute little snores before I let myself fall asleep.

'Caleb?' I hear her whisper in the dark.

'Mason?' I answer softly as I wake up and kiss whatever body part of hers is closest to my lips.

'I'm scared.'

Hearing that breaks my heart and I pull her so close, there is no space between us.

'Aari. Please don't be. I'm here. You've spent the last few months fighting everyone, including yourself, for us. Now it's my turn. I will die before I let anything harm you. In here,' I touch her head. 'In here,' I touch her heart. 'Or out there. If you can find a way to tell me whatever you need, I will make it happen. It doesn't matter what it is, even if it's for me to leave you alone. I will.'

'I don't want you to leave me alone.' She shakes her head sadly.

'Then I won't. You don't have to tell me now, but whatever it is, and whenever you're ready, I will be too.'

'Thank you for coming. I'm so happy you're here.'

'There is nowhere else on this planet I'd rather be, Aari.' I decide to go for the little push Em suggested. 'Fancy a tiny walk tomorrow whenever we get up? There are swans nearby. Let's take Lara. She's bound to piss one off and get attacked.' I chuckle. Her body shakes in a way that tells me she's laughing too.

'A tiny walk will be nice.'

I jump for joy inside. It will be slow and it will be gentle, but we are on our way.

She has kept her promise and we take a thirty-minute walk along the nearby river that leads to a small park. Jasper has picked the perfect place. She comes back hungry and tired, so I microwave a potato soup and we have a light lunch before she returns to bed for a nap. I grab Lara before she disappears.

'We need to talk about the baby.'

'What is wrong with you? We discussed this.'

'I know, but she's three months. She needs to register with a doctor, get assigned a midwife, do tests, get her scan, get signed up to some new mum classes. We can't just pretend the baby isn't happening.'

'Lower your voice. You're obsessed.'

'I'm just saying that there are a load of factors that are contributing to this. For the average excited mum-to-be, it's still a lot. Maybe she doesn't know where to start. Maybe she needs help there. I'm getting very heavy vibes that everything is too much at the moment – so why don't we break it down into bite-sized chunks?'

'How do you know so much about this?'

'Internet. I've been tracking every week.'

'No. She's not ready.'

'We should casually toss it into conversation and see if she is.'

'No, Caleb.'

'Whatever she is going through, I know that she is freaking out about the baby. Why don't we help her get it out of her head and help?'

'Because she doesn't want to talk about it.'

'But what if her hormones are completely messed up and it's contributing to this?'

Lara is silent.

'We need to get her checked out. Besides, don't you want to see a scan of little Elsie?'

Lara's face tells me that I've got her.

'Okay, fine. Let me do it.'

'Thank you, Lara.'

'Go away. I need to think.'

'By the way, thanks for putting my clothes in the wash.'

'Fuck off. I don't know what you're talking about.' She gives me an irritated look before disappearing into her room.

I hope Lara succeeds, but if she doesn't I have a backup plan. Ariella may hate me for ever but, if Lara and I can't get through to her, I'm calling Dahlia. It will be a rough ride because her parents don't even know we're in the country, but we are past the point of keeping Ariella's little secrets. They are hurting her.

THIRTY-ONE

ARIELLA

'You need to go back, Caleb. Samir says you've been dodging his calls.'

'I have, and I'm not going back.'

'They will easily make the case that you're causing financial and logistical problems and take legal action against you.'

'Let them.'

'We had a plan. It was approved. You can't just walk out and cancel all your appointments for the foreseeable future.'

'Christopher, I'm not going back.'

'He will destroy you, Caleb.'

I intentionally make a noise on the stairs so that Caleb knows I'm there.

'I'll call you back.' Caleb cuts the call. 'Aari?'

'Hi. I just wanted some water.'

'Go back upstairs, I'll bring it up.'

'Can we talk?' I ask as I clear the last step.

'Of course. Take a seat, I'll get your water.'

He grabs two waters and when he sits on the couch, I move into his open arms.

'I heard you. You have to go back.'

'Aari, I'm not leaving you like this.'

'I'm beginning to feel a little better.'

'You're not, Mason.' He kisses my head and holds on to me a little tighter. He's about to say something that he thinks I'm not going to like.

'Mason, you need to see a doctor and a midwife. We need to get you properly checked out to make sure you're okay. There are tablets you should be taking. You've survived the last couple of months on variations of toast, cheese and ginger tea. Before I can even think about going anywhere, I need to make sure that you're okay. You don't have to do anything apart from show up and have the occasional phone conversation. I will do it all, I just need you to let me.'

Everything inside me is rejecting the idea. It's too big, it's too daunting, too many new people. Then there will be the prodding, the poking, the pressure to be the happy, bubbly mum. I don't feel like that at all.

'Please let me help, Aari,' Caleb pleads.

'Okay. Please can we stick to the absolutely essential stuff?'

Caleb hugs me so tightly, I absorb some of his courage.

By the end of the week, I have a new GP, I've had an appointment with a midwife and, because I've left it a little late, a scan has been confirmed for the following week – by the midwife's calculation, I'm already at fourteen weeks. Caleb has picked up a load of vitamins that I've started taking. To stop me from stressing out, he called Samir and agreed to return after all my tests were done. He's still going to face some form of disciplinary action, but at least he's not going to be dragged through court.

On Friday shortly after noon, for the first time, Lara and Caleb left the house together, having asked me to relax on the couch in order to receive a delivery. They've been a bit too close and it's wonderful to have the house to myself. The ground floor is open, with isolated structure pillars giving away where demarcating walls used to be. The walls are a comforting Scandinavian blue, with white trims surrounding a yellow accent wall. The wool couches are neutral and pristine, with inviting rugs and throws. Everything feels and smells new. The windows flood the living room and kitchen with light and, for the first time, I feel like this could be my home. The huge, gleaming kitchen calls to me. I've stayed away, aside from one late night when I came looking for bread. I run my finger along the countertop and it makes me smile. I pull out my first drawer. The doorbell rings, startling me, and I slowly go to answer it.

'Ariella Mason?' the smiley woman asks.

'Yes?'

'Right. Please can I come in?'

I open the door and only then do I see what's on her delivery trolley. She places the boxes from my butcher, grocer and fishmonger on the kitchen counter before she asks me to sign. It's a lot. It's too much. I can't. I feel my breathing quicken.

'Are you all right, love?' the kind lady says.

I close my eyes, take a few deep breaths and step towards her to take the clipboard. I sign quickly and escort her out before I can ask her to take it all back.

I leave everything where it is, return to the solace of the living room, climb on the couch, pull the throw over me, close my eyes and try to breathe through the anxiety of having to deal with the puzzle on my kitchen counter.

'Hi.' Caleb kisses me awake. 'I'm sorry we were out so long. Lara wanted ice cream after I picked up some clothes from the flat and made me go all the way to Covent Garden.'

'I have second-hand cravings.' Lara smiles. 'I picked up a couple of tubs of gelato for us.'

'The best gelato place is literally here in Richmond.'

'Not the same. My tastebuds are changing. It's for sure Aari's hormones.' Lara smacks her lips a couple of times.

'I'm sorry we missed the delivery. I called your guys and just asked them to repeat the last order. They were delighted you were back. The grocer gave you a free order and the butcher threw in a rib of beef on the bone, but your fishmonger was stingy—'

'Caleb, I can't. It's a little overwhelming and—'

'Aari, this food isn't for us. You're still struggling with most things that aren't toast. I thought we could maybe cook something for the shelter together. If you don't feel up to it, we can just take all the ingredients over tomorrow morning. No pressure, but I thought either way, we could go and say hello?'

The fact that he still cares about the shelter warms my heart.

'Can I think about it?'

'Of course. I'll put it all away so it's not staring at you.' Caleb gives me a quick kiss on the forehead and walks to the kitchen. Watching him do his best, which is shoving things recklessly in the fridge, from the couch becomes too much to bear.

'Wait.'

'Huh? I've almost finished.' Caleb turns round, looking proud of himself. Bless him.

'Can I help?' I leave the couch. Now that most things have been unpacked, it doesn't seem so scary.

I spend the rest of the afternoon cleaning, cutting, packing, repackaging and labelling the items. Caleb sits attentively opposite me on the kitchen island with a pencil and paper, making a note of the combinations and potential recipe ideas I throw at him. We also make a list of staples we need, hit the supermarket app and place a delivery.

I manage to cook a few simple dishes with Caleb's help, while Lara spends most of the afternoon trying to learn and record a social media dance to send to Honey. She doesn't get good until she has had two big glasses of wine. I'm not ready to face the shelter yet, so Caleb runs the food over for me.

'You know, just to be clear, I'm not saying that I was wrong about Caleb...' Lara trails off.

'But?'

'I may have misjudged him the teeniest, tiniest bit. I swear, if you tell him, I will deny it and never speak to you again.'

'Okay.' I smile to myself. The revelation that Lara cares deeply about Caleb isn't the news she thinks it is.

'Basically, he can stay. I could tolerate him if he sticks around.'

'Sure. Good to know.'

Just then, my phone vibrates.

It's a text from Caleb.

> Delivery done. Can I pick anything up for you
> on my way back?

'Oooh! Tell him nothing. And then when he actually turns up with nothing, we can accuse him of neglect. Today has been too wholesome. I'm feeling toxic.'

> Lara says 'nothing'.

> Right. I'll pick up some wine and chocolate
> then. See you in a few. I love you.

I don't hesitate.

> I love you so much Caleb.

On the day of the scan, Lara is the first to be ready, and she sticks by me so closely that they have to let the three of us into the room for the ultrasound.

'It'll be a little cold.'

I'm holding tightly onto Lara's hand as the cool gel goes on my tummy.

'Ready?'

I nod.

'Wait,' Lara says, letting go of my hand. 'Caleb?'

She quietly swaps places with Caleb and he interlocks our fingers.

All three of us stare at the small screen. The hard roller presses down on my stomach until the baby comes into view.

'It's got Caleb's head!' Lara laughs.

For the first time, it hits me. This baby is real. It's clearly unhappy that it has been disturbed and is wriggling around. The little heartbeat is what undoes me. The rush of love I have been praying, hoping, waiting to feel hits me all so once. It's so forceful, I gasp.

'Strong,' the technician says, as she takes some measurements. 'Would you like to know the gender?'

For the first time, I take my eyes off the screen and look at Caleb. He is in absolute pieces and can't wipe the silent tears he is shedding, fast enough. The technician has to hand him a box of tissues with her spare hand.

'Caleb, what do you think?'

It's the first time I've ever seen Caleb unable to speak. His voice is inaudible as it quavers, but I manage to decipher that he doesn't mind.

'Lara?'

'Yes please, but only if you want to. I can live with the suspense.'

'I think so,' I say to the technician.

'Are you sure?'

'Yes. I see Caleb nodding along too.'

'Mum and Dad, you're going to have a little girl.'

Caleb, Lara and I burst into tears that won't stop as our

daughter continues to entertain herself on the screen and the technician takes a few pictures for us.

'From what I can see, everything looks good. Mum and Dad, we should get all the other test results soon. Congratulations.'

The three of us hold on to each other tightly, sobbing, until the technician leaves the room for us to compose ourselves.

Seeing our little baby switched something on in me. I would do absolutely everything to nurture, protect and keep her. I left that room feeling a renewed sense of purpose. In that one afternoon, I went from the sharp, anxious chaos that was going on in my mind to absolute focus, to create the best environment I could for her.

When Caleb and I get into bed that night, I lift his hand and place it on my belly, where it has always belonged.

THIRTY-TWO

CALEB

'Hey, Mommy.'

'Baby.' Dahlia Mason throws her arms round Ariella, and immediately steps back, wide-eyed. She stops to look at me, confused, before she turns to Ariella.

'Ariella, are you pregnant?'

A bright smile breaks across her face and confirms Dahlia's intuition.

'Oh!' she says quietly, pulling her daughter back in and squeezing her.

'As for you,' she goes on, turning to me with a smile playing on her lips, 'I think you know you're in for a rough ride.'

I nod.

Zachary and Isszy are already in the kitchen with Hugh, chatting as they nibble some crisps, wine in hand.

'Daddy!' Ariella approaches him with open arms and I feel a deep longing for a relationship like that with mine. After initial hugs and kisses with Zachary and Isszy, I reach out my hand to shake Hugh Mason's, who pulls me into a hug instead.

Shit. The hugs are going to be over soon.

'Mr Mason, please can I have a word?'

'Of course.'

Hugh Mason opens their sliding door and we walk into the garden.

'Ariella is pregnant. Fifteenth week.'

His face doesn't change.

'Congratulations. What's your plan?'

'I'm working on moving back from Singapore—'

'So, my daughter is going to be pregnant and alone.'

'No, I'm tied into a contract that lasts for another eighteen months but I'm planning to visit and—'

'Ah. It gets better. She's going to be a single mother for only *some* of the time.'

'It's not that simple.'

'Seemed simple enough to get her pregnant.'

'Daddy, stop it,' Ariella interrupts as she joins us. 'You don't know what's going on here. Or maybe you do, and you've just forgotten.'

'Ariella—'

'No, Daddy. I love you so much but your expectations are impossible and we're pregnant because of me, not him. I made a beautiful mistake.'

Ariella rubs her belly.

'Aari, he's not ready.'

'You don't know that. You have no idea how much we have put on the line for each other. Daddy, please embrace it. Embrace him. It may not be a shotgun and a porch, but you're about to make the same mistake Grandpa Spence made. I'd never run off, I'm not Mommy—'

'Hey!' I hear Dahlia interrupt to complain.

'—but I'm not going to stand by and watch you embarrass and demean the father of my child either.'

'Dad has had this coming for a while,' Zachary says a little too loudly, drawing attention to him, Dahlia and Isszy, who are all listening as they huddle by the sliding door. They're not even trying to hide that they are eavesdropping.

'Dahlia?' Hugh Mason calls for reinforcements.

'I like Caleb. It's not how I'd want it to happen either, but I remember being eight months pregnant when I walked down the aisle. We didn't have a plan either. Is it risky? Sure. Can it work? We've got a beautiful family with two appropriately stubborn children to show for it.'

'Is this why you showed up that night?' Hugh rounds on me.

'What night?' Ariella asks.

'He—'

'Hugh Mason!' Dahlia interrupts. 'I invited Caleb to dinner the last time he was in the UK just to catch up. If you're fifteen weeks now, you won't have been pregnant then. He wasn't hiding anything, Hugh.'

'Why am I the villain here?'

'You're not, baby,' Dahlia says, stepping into the garden to hold her husband's hand. 'You're just realising that Ariella is human too and, no matter how much you love her, her choices won't always align with yours. If we really think about it, you chose Jasper for her. They both just didn't realise it. Maybe it's time to truly support her choosing Caleb rather than just tolerating him as long as he doesn't put a foot wrong.'

'This isn't just Sunday lunch, Dahlia. This is for ever.'

'Mr Mason, I have no plans to leave,' I inform him.

'Only, your plans to leave are already in motion, Caleb.'

'Daddy! That's really unfair,' Ariella objects.

'Ariella, you didn't honestly think he'd stick around, did you?'

'Hugh, stop it,' Dahlia whispers to her husband.

'Are you trying to tell me that no one else is wondering why he won't just quit his job and move back with her?'

'Then he'd be the loser who quit his job and can't provide

for his family, because according to you love doesn't pay the bills. He can't win with you, Dad,' Zachary adds in my defence.

Dahlia holds her hand up. She has had enough.

'That's it.' Dahlia Mason shuts the conversation down. 'We're supposed to be a family. If everyone can't sit at the table and be fully accepted into this family, then no one is sitting at the table.'

'Mum! No, please. I'm hungry,' Zachary pleads.

We all watch Dahlia return inside the house and head up the stairs. Hugh Mason shoots me a look that would give anyone not used to his antics a heart attack, and follows his wife.

'Well, I'm eating,' Zachary says sitting at the dining table.

'I'll join you,' Isszy says happily. 'Caleb, Aari. Come on,' she encourages us as we join them. I'm happy to sit but I'm definitely not eating. I've pissed Hugh Mason off enough already today. I risk pouring myself a glass of water.

'Zach, I was thinking...' Isszy starts, stroking his head affectionately.

'Oh no,' Zachary says, dropping his fork. 'We had a plan, Isz.'

'I know but,' Isszy says with her eyes shining, 'let's move the plan up.'

'What plan?' Ariella asks.

'This is your fault,' Zachary complains. 'It was bad enough Sophia getting pregnant. And now you too? Nightmare.'

'Oh shush. I want our kids to play together,' Isszy explains, 'There are no guarantees you guys are going to have more kids so, if everyone is pregnant now, I might as well join in the fun. That way, they can grow up together.'

'I'm going to be so poor,' Zachary says. I laugh because that's exactly what I thought.

'Zach, you have to admit it is a great idea going through it together,' Ariella adds, supporting Isszy.

'You're only supporting this because Sophia has branded you her nemesis and you need someone else.'

'Maybe, but Isszy would be an amazing pregnancy buddy.' She chuckles.

'Hurry up and finish eating. Let's start tonight!' Isszy says, clapping.

We don't see Dahlia and Hugh for the rest of the afternoon. While we all know that they are up there fighting, there is a certain respect that I have for them, starting a challenging conversation in front of us and making it private when it seems neither of them is willing to budge. We wait until Zachary finishes eating – slower than I have seen anyone eat in my life to delay the trip home. When he eventually finishes, Isszy drags him out of the house as he continues to complain. We leave with them, after sticking a copy of the scan to the front of the fridge. It makes me laugh. Ariella Mason is the only person I know who seems to gravitate towards using the sticky note to deliver life-changing news.

'How did it go?' Lara calls from the couch as soon as we walk in. There are upsides to having Lara living with us, but the disadvantages require a workaround.

'It's all a bit up in the air,' Ariella responds, walking toward her friend.

'Aari, can I have a word upstairs please?' I ask before she reaches her destination.

Lara drops her phone and looks at both of us suspiciously. 'You have a child in there. Do anything to jeopardise that and I will end you both.'

I reach out my hand and lead my girlfriend upstairs. Once we are behind the closed bedroom door, I step close enough to her to hold her face in my hands and look directly into her eyes.

'Thank you for today,' I whisper, just in case Lara is eaves-dropping.

'Thank you for every single loving, frustrating, heartbreak-ing, consuming, freeing, infuriating and supportive thing you have ever done, Caleb.' She means it.

I kiss my girlfriend from the depths of my soul and, when she returns it, I know this is it. Our kiss tips over slowly into desire.

'So, I've been on the internet...' I raise an eyebrow.

'I asked the midwife,' Ariella giggles, beating me to my thoughts.

'Ariella Mason, what am I going to do with you?' The fact that, through all of this, the idea crossed her mind is astounding. What is going on in that mind of hers?

'I don't know, but we only have two days left and, thanks to me, we're behind. Make them count, Black.'

'Ariella, with you, we are always right on time.'

We slip too easily into that bubble of nothing but each other and stay there well into the next afternoon on our familiar sleep, chat, shower rotation. I only come down to get some water, snacks and Ariella's vitamins. All I get from Lara is, 'Disgust-ing,' but, as much as she tries, she can't hide the smile that is making its way across her face.

The hardest thing I have ever done in my life is get on that plane to Singapore. Aside from personal and financial ruin, I don't believe there is anything I won't do to return to Ariella and my daughter. As soon as I get back to my new flat, I cast the video of the scan to my TV. She's perfect. And feisty. She wiggles around, tossing and turning on the screen throughout the ninety-second video. She was a sesame seed at one point.

I place a quick call to Ariella to let her know that I have

arrived safely, before I find a way to separate the life I want from the life that I currently have.

Thankfully the work that has piled up over the last three weeks will need some careful handling but, before I get going, I have a 7 a.m. meeting with Samir. He obviously wants to release his wrath before everyone gets in.

He's sitting in his office when I turn up. 'Caleb. The way you disappeared was completely unacceptable.'

'Samir, I'm not a child. What are the consequences?' There really is nothing Samir can do or say to make me regret what I did for a second.

'You're grounded in Singapore.'

'I was expecting that. What else?'

'You need to catch up and repair the relationships you almost destroyed while you were gone.'

'Catch up, fine, but the relationships are good. Lydia told them I had a personal emergency, which I actually did. The clients have been much more understanding than you have. Dominic, I get. You, on the other hand, know what's happening here. It's much harder to understand.'

'I don't make the rules, Caleb, I just play the game.'

'Then play it better, Samir.'

He's not going to do or say anything else, so I walk out of his office. I have other issues to take care of.

My diary when I open it is packed. Samir has me going to every envelope-opening and opportunity. I'm not going to sleep at this rate; but I've been in worse situations. The team was great those first three weeks. The sales team offered to take on some smaller opportunities to give me space to breathe, because Samir's strategy was to take everything and anything that came across our desks. Ariella had been much more discerning. We dived into huge projects that came in but for the smaller projects we identified how we could help for free, did that and returned ownership to the client to deliver. It was a win-win. Samir was dropping in dinner for ten internal staff projects with the same might as week-long, thousand-delegate conferences.

Akiko was the first to quit. The Ivory Bow entry and new job title on her CV landed her a huge role, working for one of our current clients. The same client hired two of her direct reports and that's how delivery started to crumble. We're only a month in and, with Samir not responding to what we needed as a business quickly enough, projects are beginning to fall behind. When Lydia starts to get freelancers in to help, projects do get pushed through, but at varying service levels.

Part of me is gutted to see something Ariella built so lovingly begin to crumble, but the glee of watching Dominic's investment fail dominates that feeling.

The only thing that keeps my soul alive are the daily updates from Ariella. The little conversations we catch, the texts, the voice notes, the images; they all contribute to the lifeline that keeps me going. She's cooking every week for the shelter now and volunteering on some days too. She's still a little anxious about our future, but that's okay. I'm happy holding us up, even though she still doesn't know that I'm the landlord she's paying rent to. Jasper Goldsmith saved this one. She's working on her dad and he's taking a little while to come round.

I manage to finally get a Saturday night free and I decide to spend it with Honey. We spend the first hour on a video call with Lara and Ariella. Ms Pat has stayed too, to catch up on our news. Aari is in the background, cooking for the shelter, and Lara is filling us in on the neighbourhood gossip. The best bit is when Lara carries us to the kitchen and makes Ariella show us her little bump. It's so cute, I wish I could touch it. The urge to return home seizes me with such force that I have to walk away for a second.

'Caleb. It's okay. We're okay. I'm okay,' Ariella says lovingly to the camera.

'She is, and so am I, not that you bothered to ask about me, you twerp.' Lara grins, showing us all her teeth. They do seem to be having a lot of fun together.

'You look lovely, Lara,' Honey says.

'I've gained eleven pounds. Aari is cooking daily and this place is wall-to-wall bread. It's all baby weight though.'

'But you don't have baby, Miss Lara,' Ms Pat teases, reminding us of their love–hate relationship. 'It's okay to be a little bit fat. It suits you.'

Lara's mouth springs open in shock.

'Stooooooop,' Honey warns. Lara's eyebrows meet in a v in the middle of her face, then she aggressively tilts the camera towards Ariella. Ms Pat, having established a victory, walks away from the conversation.

'Have you felt the baby move yet?' I'm careful because we've decided to keep the gender to ourselves.

'No, but I'm only nineteen weeks. It's still a little early, I think.'

Honey and I spend as much time as we can with our girls before they have to go to a farmers' market in the middle of town. When the call ends, I am completely crestfallen.

'I can't do this, Honey. I need to find a way to get back home.'

'They've got you trapped. The only way you had was Christopher requesting your support, but you've blown that.'

'I can't be away from my daughter until she's fourteen months old. That's insane.'

'It's a girl?' Honey says delighted.

'It's a girl, and Jasper is having twin boys. I'm going to have to watch her like a hawk.'

'It's girl!' Ms Pat emerges from nowhere, clapping until it ends with a warm embrace.

Ms Pat has this uncanny ability to make everything okay, and I feel the warmth of becoming a father settle over me.

'Yes.' It's nice to say it out loud.

'You know, Mr Caleb, maybe Mr Dominic is not so clean.'

'I know, Ms Pat, but unless I can prove it I'm stuck here.'

'You know the person to prove.'

'I wish I did, but I don't, Ms Pat.'

'Think, Mr Caleb. Who can prove? That you know?'

Ms Pat is trying to tell me and I'm not getting it.

'Samir?'

'Oh God. Ms Ariella is so much smarter than you.' She gives me a disappointed look, then moves close to whisper.

'Ms Melissa can prove.'

'Yeah, well, Ms Melissa has disappeared and, if she wasn't impossible to find, I wouldn't want to find her anyway. Aari will kill me.'

'Okay. No problem.' Ms Pat suddenly stops our conversation and starts tidying.

'Wait. Ms Pat, you don't know where Ms Melissa is?'

'Will you ask?' Ms Pat is not budging.

'I will consider asking if we know where she is.'

'Ms Melissa is in Brunei.' Ms Pat whips out her phone and sends a message. 'Now we wait. You must ask. For Little Miss Elsie.'

'Hold on! Ms Pat. How long have you known?'

'Not Brunei all the time. First Vanuatu, then Maldives, then Russia, then China, then Brunei. She move again soon.'

'You've known where she was this entire time?'

'Yes. Housekeeper network. We know everything but we say nothing.'

'So when I was accused...'

'Mr Caleb, like I said, we know everything but we say nothing. Sometimes we help, but you never know.'

Ms Pat taps her nose twice and smiles lovingly at me before walking away.

Shit. Ms Pat should be an international fucking spy. All housekeepers should. Forget the CIA and MI5. They're the ones we should be scared of. I start to think of a load of weird unexplainable things that have happened and start to find ways to pin them on Ms Pat.

It doesn't even take an hour until I am given a number with a country code I'd never seen before to text.

> Mel?

> Why are you so bad at this? Buy a burner and text me from there. You're such a liability. Pay cash and delete this. Honestly!

Ms Pat immediately dispatches a member of Honey's assistants with careful details of where to purchase a burner and send it to the house. It feels like for ever waiting, but it eventually turns up. I don't want to know exactly how Ms Pat knows so much about buying a burner at almost midnight in Singapore.

> Sorry.

> Previous stupidity aside, I'm shocked, impressed and disappointed that it took you this long to reach out – all at the same time.

> I need your help.

You want dirt on Dominic that will force him release you from your ridiculous contract so that you can join Ariella. How am I doing?

Is there any? Is he clean?

He's about as clean as Gustaf's gym clothes post-workout. You should see what that man can do with a skipping rope. Heaven help me. Anyway, I heard you rearranged Dom's face. Thanks for that. I've wanted someone to do that for a while. He's so smug.

Can you send me some information?

Nope.

Can you at least tell me where to look?

No.

So this is just a game. There's nothing.

There's plenty but I don't trust you. You're going to fuck it up.

If there is something, why did you leave him off your finger-pointing spree?

We have other collaborations in play. Kevin's little problems aren't necessarily bad news for him. He did help orchestrate my disappearance.

He knew?

It was actually his idea. Where did you think you were going when he tried to put you on a plane? Mars? You were supposed to be coming to me, moron. Not that you can prove any of this, of course. Even these messages are two burners just talking to each other. You could have written them to yourself.

'Dominic!' Honey exclaims.

'I told you, Mr Dominic is pretty but not so clean.' Ms Pat raises an eyebrow.

'Is that why you insisted on going with her that night, Ms Pat?'

Ms Pat shrugs and says nothing.

'That bastard actually made me consider the probability that I was being paranoid and maybe he did just want to talk to Ariella.'

'I'm really pleased you beat his face in, Caleb,' Honey says angrily.

If Melissa is in cahoots with Dominic, there is no way she is going to give him up. I tried. Contacting Melissa was pointless.

> Thanks for nothing Melissa. Goodbye.

Hold on. I didn't say I couldn't help.

> Are you going to help?

Come and see me. I'm not as far as you think. Gustaf will be pissed because he's insanely jealous of you but there's nothing an apology, the way he likes his apologies, can't fix.

> I'm not coming to see you Mel. There's nothing we can't share over a secure line or text and I can't leave the country.

I can take care of your travel ban. Besides, I have absolutely no intention of talking. Gustaf has his limitations. I've missed you.

'Don't do it, Caleb. There will be another way, especially now that we know there is something to find,' Honey says, pulling back to exhale deeply. 'However, if you do, I won't judge you, but I don't want to know because I can't lie to Lara.'

'This is Melissa. There may be nothing,' I say.

'Mr Caleb, do not do. Say bye-bye. She love you but crazy.

You don't want half-Singaporean baby in eighteen years to say hello sister to Elsie.'

> Thanks but no thanks Mel.

> I'll leave the offer open for a couple of weeks, then I have to move. I won't be so easy to reach then. Think about it.

'What if—'

'NO!' Honey and Ms Pat shout in unison.

'Miss Melissa ask too much, Mr Caleb. Dick pic, maybe.' Ms Pat says it so seriously, Honey and I burst out laughing.

'Yeah! One lady boss with my friend, dick pic get you anything. And Mr Caleb, you know her.' Ms Pat winks happily.

'Ms Pat! Who?!' I really want to know.

'We see everything, but say nothing. Do not go to Brunei, Mr Caleb. Throw burner away,' she warns sternly, pointing her finger at me.

'Okay,' I promise Ms Pat, as I slip it into my pocket.

THIRTY-THREE

ARIELLA

'So, don't get angry.' Lara climbs into bed with me on Monday morning.

'What?'

'I've been thinking.'

'Uh-oh... ow!'

Lara pinches me. 'You're back to normal now, so no more passes. Honestly, you're so rude.' She frowns.

'Okay, I'm sorry. What have you been thinking, Lara?' I smile as I reach out to stroke my best friend's arm.

'Thank you. So, I've been thinking. We're both here all day, doing nothing, and we aren't earning any money.'

'Continue...'

'I've also been wandering around, getting the lay of the land. We are surrounded by lots of women, specifically mums.'

'Right?'

'And you, you're doing all this cooking. For free. You love it and to be honest the only time I've seen you happier than in the kitchen is when you're looking at El— the baby's scan or Caleb is giving you pervy looks with his lechy eyes.'

'I know you still call her Elsie behind my back by the way, keep going.'

'Anyway, all these mums can't be on top of everything all the time. Some hate laundry, some don't want to cook, et cetera, but, because they are technically stay-at-home mothers, most of their stupid husbands think that they are live-in slaves that have to do everything. They are often reluctant to offer support because they think that going to work and playing with your colleagues for eight hours a day is the hard part.'

'Your logic is a little flawed, but I'm getting the general gist of what you're saying.'

'So how about we help ourselves cheat a little. Someone who loves to fold their laundry offers that service. Or maybe someone who loves to cook makes dinner and sneaks it over there ready to go in the oven so it looks like they've been slaving away while they're really catching up on that tiny basic human right, sleep.'

'It sounds like a nice idea, Lara, you should pursue it.'

'I did. I'm in pretty much every secret mothers' WhatsApp group within a two-mile radius, for now. Funny what people will add you to if you go in there and cry. The support network is real.'

Oh no.

'And we have a little company. It's called The Housewife's Secret. I'll show you the website. You can exchange favours, pay for favours, and you can set up a profile to let people find you and what skills you offer. Obviously, there's a personal interview with me before you join because it is a closed community, and no sex stuff, no matter how much you don't want to sleep with your husband.' Lara guffaws.

She shows me her phone. She has built a sweet little soft pink, grey and white site offering six services, with more coming soon.

'This looks amazing, Lara!'

'I know, I built it. Anyway, we have our first order.'

'Already! That's nice. What service is it for?'

'Six people, any kind of vegetarian pasta bake, no allergies but they've signed the "if we kill you, you can't sue us" waiver.'

'Lara, tell me you're joking.'

'You cook for the shelter all the time. No one has died yet. You also did Dominic the ick's party in Singapore for like a zillion people.'

'Twenty, and look what happened there.'

'That was different. He fancied the pants off you. There you were a COO, all over heavily curated social media, swanning around in designer gear, being all not pregnant and evasive. Here you're a single unemployed mother whose partner is AWOL. No one is checking for you like that.'

'Your unwavering commitment to making me feel good is astonishing, Lara.'

'You're welcome. So, are you going to do it?'

'No. Lara, meeting personal standards is a massive challenge.'

'It's for our gobby neighbour three doors down. I've seen her husband. She doesn't have standards. She was hostile at first until she found out I was a lesbian. Sweet as pie now. She may think you're a lesbian too, by the way. If it's amazing she'll tell everyone. She likes being the one in the know while diving into everyone's business. Plus, it's a freebie.'

'How is this thing meant to make money anyway?'

'Subscription. Two pounds a month. But then we can sneak in staff for hire later and ramp up to celebrity chefs, designers, declutter experts and charge a mint when we have everything in place. Right now it's a start – and, good news, I can work from anywhere in the world, so Honey and I can be anywhere.'

'Thank you, Lara, for coming and staying with me when I know you really want to be with Honey,' I slip in. She has been my rock.

'You've thanked me loads already and I'm liking this big house, rent-free situation; but if you feel like thanking me again, let's do this together and make the bloody veggie pasta bake.'

There is no way she is going to let me say no.

'Only to the gobby neighbour with no standards as a freebie?'

'Yes. For now. Let's just feel our way through.'

Lara is right. After she carefully delivered that first bake, orders came pouring in for the same dish and, by the end of the week, I'd made twenty-two creamy three-mushroom and truffle rigatoni bakes that Lara delivered all over the borough, charging thirty pounds a pop plus delivery for each eight-person serving.

'Babe, we made over five hundred pounds after costs, in four days! I'm thinking we should scrap the site and just do food orders!'

'I never want to see another pasta bake again! You closed us down for orders, right?'

'Yes, but I opened a waiting list. There are four people.'

'I don't want to make pasta bakes any more, Lara. If we get caught we are going to be in big trouble. There is so much training I need to do. We need to register, I need certification – this is so risky!'

'No one is going to say anything. They're pretending they cooked it themselves. Besides, we'll get all that. For now, let's operate under the radar and only to the THS members and swear them to secrecy. Shall we find something else to do if you're sick of pasta bakes? We can push a new angle and announce a new dish every week. It has to be vegetarian though, because we can reach more people.'

'Can I have a few days to think about it? I still need to cook for the shelter this week and Mommy has asked me to come home for Sunday lunch. You're invited.'

I've been speaking to Daddy all week, but our conversations have been careful. I think this is Mommy's attempt to mend things, and, if she is inviting Lara, it means things have been sorted.

'Sure, I'll come – but don't keep our customers waiting!' she sings as she dances up the stairs to her room.

This week may have been exhausting, but I feel proud. I look at the time. It's too late to call Caleb, so I send him a voice note.

'Hello, sleepy. I think I might give the food thing a shot after all. Lara is at the helm, she has been delivering prohibition-style pasta bakes. There's every chance I might get arrested while we are operating under the radar but I'm going to get my paperwork together as soon as possible and, once I've done that, I think I might like to give it a shot. We love you and we miss you. Talk in the morning.'

I sit back and rub my belly.

'Think we can do it?' I ask my baby. 'Yeah, I think we can,' I tell her as I kiss the fingertip of my index finger and transfer it to my belly, before making my way up the stairs and into the shower.

When we get home on Sunday, Lara gently pushes ahead of me.

'I've missed Dahlia. I want to be her when I grow up, but not just yet,' she admits before pressing the doorbell.

Mommy opens the door with a blinding smile and lets Lara in, before wrapping me in her arms in a way that makes me tear up. It feels so good to be home. As I step into the warmth, I walk into Daddy's arms for a hug.

'I'm sorry, love,' he says quietly.

'I'm sorry I disappointed you, Daddy. I love you so much.'

'You could never disappoint me, Ariella.'

'Will you embrace him? Please?'

Daddy nods and pulls me in tightly.

And that's all we need. Things are going to be fine.

It isn't until I walk past Daddy that I see Isszy, Lara, Sophia and Em at a table full of food and drink. Lara is already wrestling with the red wine. They all stand as I walk in and come over to give me a group hug. I'm so overwhelmed, I freeze on the spot.

'Right, young lady. Sit,' Mummy instructs softly when the ladies have returned to their seats. I put my bum in the chair at the head of the table that Mommy points to as she stands behind the empty one next to me.

'And that's me gone,' Daddy says, kissing my head, then grabbing the car keys and coat.

'Thank you so much, everyone. I can't—'

'Don't thank us yet, baby. This is less of a party and more of an intervention. Lara says you've been good at taking your vitamins and attending your necessary appointments but you rarely leave the house and you're not going to any classes. We're not here to force you to do anything, but you need women around you while you're going through this; so here we are. Today, you're going to share what's going on with you, we're going to listen and then we're going to help. Ask us anything. We have either been through this, are going through it right now or are excited to be where you are in the future.'

'Eeee!' Isszy squeals as she wiggles excitedly in her chair. 'We're officially trying!' Seeing how excited Isszy is makes me instinctively stroke my bump.

'Before you leave, you need to make a promise. No more hiding. If you're worried, unsure, have a question, you call and you ask for help.'

I nod.

'Ariella. What do you need to know?' Mommy asks as she sits and pours me a sparkling juice.

'I don't know. I haven't dared to look. What can I expect?'

'The big one!' Em laughs. I'm delighted that she's here. I really like Em and I've missed her. 'Do you have morning sickness?'

'Not any more.'

'What? You're lucky!' Sophia jumps in. Her belly is humongous. 'And Jasper has this cologne that makes me want to vomit. We've thrown it out but it still lingers. Do your boobs hurt?'

'Yes! It's not too bad though.'

'That'll change!' Mommy laughs. 'And if you're not peeing a lot, you're not drinking enough!'

'Get a pillow. One of the big long ones. They help my back,' Sophia says as she grabs a nacho from the middle of the table.

'This all sounds a little horrible,' I say.

'Wait until your first kick!' Em says. 'It's magical.'

Mummy and Sophia nod enthusiastically.

'In my case kicks. These ones are going to be rugby players.' Sophia lovingly rubs her much larger bump. 'Oh, and my hair, skin and nails have never looked this good!'

'And just in case you were worried, your baby will be fine, you will cope financially and you will be a good mother,' Mommy adds.

'And you will develop excellent multitasking skills,' Em pitches in. 'But write everything down. You're about to become a little forgetful.'

We spend the rest of the afternoon snacking, chatting, laughing and scaring Isszy. It's dark when the intervention winds down, and I feel loved and supported – but also ready to love and support Isszy.

'Jassie is outside,' Sophia announces as she grabs her coat. It hurts a little but I sit where I am. She may have been lovely today, but I made her a promise.

'Ariella, can we have a quick conversation?' she asks softly.

'Of course.' I lead her outside to the cool garden.

'I'm sorry I was so cruel to you,' she says regretfully. 'I'm deeply ashamed of the way I behaved.'

'I understand, Sophia. I was around an awful lot.'

'You were, but that wasn't it. I knew you didn't want Jasper, and that was what infuriated me the most, because I did,' she admits quietly. 'You were besotted with Caleb. Jasper was besotted with you. I was besotted with Jasper, but no one was besotted with me. I just wanted to be chosen by him and I took it out on you. I'm sorry.'

'Jasper wasn't besotted with me, Sophia. We'd just loved each other for a very long time and it's crushing to walk away from that. He was truly my best friend, but that's all he was.'

'Is. He is your best friend, and he has been insufferably miserable without you. Do you want to go out to the car and say hello?'

'Really?' Tears spring to my eyes.

'Yes.' She nods, tearing up too.

I run through the house and out of the front door. Jasper is out of the car in the blink of an eye and we're wrapped round each other in a matter of seconds. We just stand there, holding on to each other, over the moon to be back in each other's lives.

THIRTY-FOUR

CALEB

I'm jittery when I take my first-class seat on the plane. I can't believe I am here, doing this. I neck two double rums to try to knock myself out even before we take off. When the hostess comes to check on me, I ask her to let the team know that I'd like to be left alone for the entire flight. I just want it to be over. I'd rushed through the airport with no luggage to check, and only just made it.

Melissa had been persistent for the entire time she gave me to make my mind up. She spent most of it texting daily with Gustaf titbits and teasing me with information that might incriminate Dominic. I should have listened to Ms Pat and thrown the burner away, but I'm a weak idiot and have no idea what good advice is when I hear it.

I've spent the last two weeks, with Jasper's help, looking for anything on Dominic. Now that he's reignited his friendship with Ariella, I've made him swear repeatedly not to breathe a word. No matter how hard we tried, we couldn't find anything.

Today is the fourteenth day of the tortuous two weeks that

Melissa set. Time is up. I woke up to a voice note from a tired Ariella telling me that she'd had a lovely day trying 'Mums with bumps' yoga and met Em afterwards for cake and a hot chocolate by the river. She then ended what started as a wholesome voice note with a filthy memory and a naughty giggle. Arrrgghhh. I need to get home.

Melissa's first text came through before I woke up.

> Well?

>> If I do this, it will haunt me for the rest of my life.

> Haha. I wasn't that terrible in bed was I?

>> No, and if you were, I wouldn't have cared, because for a very long time you were everything I wanted.

> Why didn't you say anything?

>> I did. You threatened to turn me into your house husband and said my work was boring.

> I'm sending you a first-class ticket. Let's talk.
> Really talk.

Within ten minutes, the ticket to Brunei is in my inbox and Melissa has texted me.

> Come.

I stare at the ticket and decide to bite the bullet.

> Melissa, I'm sorry for all the things that
> happened to you. You didn't deserve them. If
> Gustaf makes you happy, hold on to him. We all
> have our limitations, and believe it or not,
> Ms Melissa Chang, you have fewer than most.
> Use your freedom. Stay safe. I can't come to
> Brunei. I will find another way.

I take the sim out of the burner phone, snap it and toss the phone in the bin. I then open my email, delete the ticket and empty my mailbox's bin.

When Honey arrives for training, I can barely stand. Just like that, the cage is shut. We don't train that morning. We just sit together on the floor as she holds me. Just as training time is about to be over, my phone buzzes. It's a message from an unrecognised number with another ticket attached. It's Melissa.

> Don't ask me for anything, ever again, Caleb
> Black. You may have been the first man I slept
> with but I won't be in love with you for ever.
> Your flight leaves in four hours. Be on it before I
> land at my next destination and change my
> mind. I will deal with Dominic. You win.

'Caleb?' Honey pokes me awake. 'We're about to land.'

'Thanks for coming, Honey.'

'I didn't come for you. I miss my girl.' She smiles shyly.

Both the girls are home when we show up unannounced. Lara seems to fly through the air to land on Honey. Ariella is so shocked, I just pick her up carefully, put her over my shoulder and head straight upstairs.

'Hey!' Lara calls, still attached to Honey. 'Whatever disgusting things you're about to get up to, just remember you've got fourteen heirloom tomato, fresh basil and caramelised onion quiches to make before tomorrow at noon!'

'Okay!' Ariella calls from over my shoulder. I wouldn't be so sure. First we're going to shower, then I'm going to make her pay for that filthy voice note. Repeatedly.

'You made it back!' Jasper laughs happily as he comes round from behind his desk to give me a rough hug and two pats on the back.

'I did. Just. I needed a week to get over the trauma.'

'You going to tell me how you did that?'

'Over lunch at the pub if you have time?'

'As long as Sophia doesn't go into labour, I've got the time, but we need to talk first.'

Jasper returns to his seat and points to the one in front of him, so I take it.

'If we don't do something about your finances, you're going to have problems.'

'Tell me.'

'You can't sustain four properties, especially now that you're not working. You've got the flat, the house and the gyms. I assume you're going to tell Ariella that the house is yours at some point?'

'Of course.'

'Then I assume you'll stop collecting her rental payments for the house. When you do, you're going to have to lose something.'

'I'd like to keep the gyms. Let's sell the flat. Jack's in it at the moment but it's too big for him anyway.'

'He doesn't need to move out until we find a buyer, but I suggest he start looking. It will go quickly.'

'No worries.'

'That was easy. I'll have it put on the market. Second problem. You need an income. The gyms are sustaining themselves but they won't be able to provide for you too.'

'I have a plan.'

I unlock my phone and email Jasper the business plan for the fight studio. He takes a couple of minutes to skim through.

'Looks good, but it relies heavily on word of mouth, Honey and rotating fighting legends.'

'I'm going to start with the gym closest to us. We'll run seasonal training with Honey and the other fighters. She and Lara are talking about splitting their time between locations, so I know that I can get her here for at least three months in a year. Also, Lara has managed to infiltrate every secret and public parents' WhatsApp group within a five-mile radius and is setting herself up as some kind of mum and dad whisperer.'

'How?'

'No idea, but they all think that she's a gay mum-to-be, expecting with her faceless partner. She's been taking pictures with Ariella's bump and cooing in the groups.'

'She's going to get found out.'

'Of course she is, but she is giving incredible recommendations, vetting suppliers like MI5, protecting them from scammers, and has got all of them doing favours for each other. The good news is, she owes me a favour or two. So basically, murky beginnings, but honourable intentions, sort of.'

'That's Lara in a nutshell. Let me know if you need an investor. I think you might have a hit on your hands.'

After we have lunch in a nearby pub, I go straight to the gym and get to work. Time gets away from me and I stay there until late. By the time I get home, Aari is in bed, and I commit to not making a habit of working so late – I miss our evenings together. After I've showered I get in, curl over her and drape my hand over her belly. Just as my eyes begin to close, I feel the slightest bit of pressure against my wrist. My eyes fly open and I hold as still as I can. A short while later, the pressure disappears.

THIRTY-FIVE

ARIELLA

'Urrrrggh, Caleb! You're sweaty and horrible,' I complain.

He has settled into a good work routine that ensures that we spend evenings together, and the fight studio is coming along nicely. He has just come back from working all day, dropped his bag by the door and grabbed me from behind as I am finishing the last dishes for the shelter.

'I can't help it. You're so round and juicy...' he says, putting his lips on my neck as he unzips my dress.

'Stop undressing me, Black, this risotto is hot.' Too late. My dress falls, only for the straps to catch at my elbows. He gently runs his hand over my tender breasts.

'They are so full.'

I want to shoo him away, but he feels good too. Even sweaty. I drop the risotto and turn to face him. The look in his eyes tells me that we're doing this. My bra pings open and, as Caleb introduces his tongue to mine, he teases the straps to meet those of my dress at my elbows before he brushes my breast with the palm of his hand and I surrender.

With one quick movement, Caleb lifts me in to him and

carries me to the end of the kitchen island, then plops me on the counter. He takes the clip out of my hair and lets it fall.

'Fuck, Aari, you're beautiful,' he says, before covering his mouth with mine. I'm pretty certain I look a mess with my clothes half on, hiked up and my hair absolutely everywhere. Caleb moves on to my body as he runs his tongue down my neck, chest and breasts, circling a nipple before taking it into his mouth. It feels so good, I let out a small whimper, making him stop.

'Are you okay?' he asks, deeply concerned.

'More than okay,' I gasp.

'You have to tell me if you're not, Mason.'

He looks unsure until I lean forward and slide my hand under his soft navy track bottoms. The moan he produces as he closes his eyes and tips his head up to the ceiling only fuels my fire. I move my hand, slowly stroking him, his hips responding to my touch. When his movements get urgent, I snake my other hand up his shirt and dig my nails into his back.

'Shit. Okay. That's enough fun and games.'

Caleb slides me off the counter before turning me to face it.

'Put your hands where I can see them, bend over and spread your legs, Aari.'

I do as I am told, and bend over the counter. Caleb slowly lifts the bottom part of my dress up before pulling my underwear down to my ankles and instructing me to step out of them. I comply, keen to feel him inside me. My anticipation builds as Caleb traces his fingers up my leg and past my knee. He touches me between my legs so lightly, I push against his hand.

'Don't move, Mason.'

He touches me, again so lightly that I push against him, and he removes his hand.

'So how was your day?' he asks softly.

'Caleb, right now, I can't think of a single thing I did today,'

I pant. He reintroduces his hand and gives me the gift of a little stroke.

'Want to know what I did?'

'No.'

Caleb chuckles.

'That's not nice.' He barely touches me again and I want to scream.

'You're dripping, Aari.'

More pressure this time as he slides a single finger over me. He holds my hips steady and away from the counter edge, then enters me slowly.

'Oh, Caleb,' I exhale.

And that's when I hear his first grunt. Nothing beats Caleb's moans when we're like this. They're deep, soft sounds of pleasure, frustration and urgency. If he was doing nothing else, that alone would undo me. As his long, slow strokes start to build, I am ahead of him. He pushes inside me hard and I know.

'Caleb...'

'Fuck, Aari.'

He pushes harder and faster as I explode. He's not far behind, holding my hips safely away from the edge of the kitchen island as he pours himself into me.

'I've been thinking about doing that all day, Mason. You almost had me here at lunchtime. Twice. You're just so mmmmmmm!'

'After this morning?'

'Especially after this morning.'

He helps me up, turns me round and kisses me deeply.

'So I was thinking, Jack's out tonight with his mystery woman. Another loaded one, I think. Want to spend the night in the flat one last time before the sale completes?'

I'm excited to go back to the flat.

'Maybe the three of us could sleep over?' he says, gently stroking our bump.

'I'd love that.'

'Okay, but I'm not taking you out in this state, Mason. You're covered in sweat. What have you been doing?' Caleb smiles into our kiss and leads me upstairs into the shower with him.

Returning to the flat where all this started makes me a little nostalgic. We have a new home with new beginnings, but the last time we were here we were broken. Saying goodbye together before we move on feels right.

When Caleb unlocks the door there is a beautiful yellow glow and, as I walk in, I see that all the surfaces have been covered with candles and my favourite flowers. I spot an ice bucket with a bottle of Bollinger chilling next to two glasses as Caleb leads me into the centre of the flat.

'It's so beautiful.'

'I wanted tonight to be special. I thought we could have dinner, watch *The Sopranos* and fall asleep on the couch.'

'I think that's a great idea.'

'But before we do...'

I watch Caleb descend to one knee in the middle of the flat.

'Ariella Mason, before you walked into my office, I couldn't have dreamed or wished for you if I tried; because everything that made sense to me back then needed to be dismantled. And you did that. You saved me from the suffocating choke of fear, loneliness, insecurity and shame. My suffering was so familiar, I'd forgotten it was there. It's taken a lot for us to get here, Aari. You've had to forgive the unforgivable in me. Love the unlovable in me. Believe the unbelievable in me. Trust me, being with you was no picnic, but that was mostly because I had a lot of growing up to do.'

'Mostly?' I laugh softly.

'Yes, mostly. You know all the shit you put me through.'

Caleb chuckles. 'But I'd go through it all again to be here, right now, exactly as we are. I love you, Aari. I had no idea life could be this good. I will lay down everything I have and all that I am to be the man you and our baby need me to be. I promise that I will die before anything disrupts us again. What I feel for you is beyond love. I adore you in a way that is incomprehensible to me. It is what makes me know, without a doubt, that I will provide, protect and be devoted to you and our family for the rest of my life. Ariella Mason, please will you marry me?'

I drop to my knees, move the ring out of his hand to the floor, and hold my boyfriend's hands for the last time.

'You saved me from the fear, loneliness, insecurity and shame too, Caleb. And when the darkness, cold and confusion of the world threatens to swallow me whole, you always reach for me and fight with all you have to set me free. There is no version of the future that I want other than one with you – because your love and dedication to our baby tells me everything about what is to come. Caleb Black, I cannot wait to be your wife.'

Caleb puts the heels of his palms to his eyes and, when I manage to gently move them away, his tear-filled eyes make mine fill too. We spend the night eating and talking about our future together as I make my half glass of champagne last for as long as possible.

We decide that sleeping on the couch might be too ambitious, so we go into my old room and sleep in my bed together for the last time.

'I'm going to miss this place.' Caleb sighs.

'Maybe we can visit. What's the new owner like?'

'No idea. Jasper's agent has been tight-lipped.'

'That's disappointing. You did propose to her last night.'

The shock on Caleb's face is hilarious.

'Jasper has been my friend much longer than he has been yours, Caleb. That's why I know that we're running on financial fumes. I also know providing for us is extremely important to you.' I stroke my belly. 'But I have access to an uncomfortably large amount because Jasper has been playing with my salary for years. Let's use it to build the life we want.'

'What do you mean by uncomfortably large?'

'We can keep the flat. Jack will have to find a flatmate or pay enough to cover the mortgage and other bits to stay, though. In addition to that, if you say yes, tomorrow we can be completely debt free. We'll have a little bit left to invest in your business if we're careful.'

Caleb is already shaking his head.

'You can rebuild the studio and do what you need to provide for us, while I go on Lara's ethically dicey adventure with her. Let me clear these debts. We're going to have so many things to stress about in the future, I'd really like for this not to be one of them. Please.'

'I really don't deserve you.'

When Caleb crushes me against him for a kiss and our daughter kicks in protest, he feels it. The look on his face confirms what I already know. The rest of my life is going to revolve around this man and our family.

EPILOGUE

'And where are you sneaking off to?'

'We're going to get ice cream,' Elsie says, looking suspiciously innocent. I know my daughter. At sixteen, she looks like Ariella, fights like Honey and has absorbed just enough of Lara's personality.

'It's Christmas Day. Nothing is open.' I narrow my eyes at my child.

'The corner shop is. It's only a few minutes away.'

'Why is he going?' I point accusingly at Raife, Jasper's son, who is standing next to her with his coat on. His twin brother, Axel, disappeared with his girlfriend back to Jasper's home across the street straight after eating the feast Ariella and Lara's catering company had delivered. This year, a two-Michelin-star chef had created, run the food lab and trained the kitchen team to prepare the Christmas Day menu for their deliveries. Just over seven hundred households ordered exactly what we have just eaten, automatically sponsoring just over two thousand free meals for shelters across London.

'Caleb, let them go.' Ariella smiles sympathetically at her daughter as she gets up from the couch.

'Actually, no, Caleb, continue. This is good.' Hugh chuckles, biting into a mince pie as he watches from the armchair.

'That's your fourth, baby. No more for you,' Dahlia says, wiping the grin from his face. 'Oh! Did you two see that Dominic is leading the polls to be the next POTUS?'

Ariella and I smile at each other. Of course we knew. He'd called Ariella to beg her not to speak to any journalists. Before she could respond, I took the phone from my wife, told him he was lucky she was taking his phone call and hung up. We never would, but he can wrestle with the uncertainty. Melissa hasn't been so lucky. She's still on the run, or so we think. No one has heard from her since she sent us matching Hermès luggage for our wedding. We dropped it off at the shelter's charity shop.

'Daddy, can I go and get ice cream with them too?' our youngest daughter asks from my lap. Her little seven-year-old arms are round my neck, with her head on my chest.

'Yes, good idea, Gracie.'

'I have ice cream in the freezer for you, Gracie.' Ariella extends her arm out and Gracie bounces her cute curly-haired head over to her mother.

'What's wrong with the ice cream in the freezer?' I ask Elsie.

'I don't want Milky Pops, Dad.'

'Caleb, if anything was going on, all one of them would have to do is cross the road to the other when we go out to dinner or we're working late,' Jasper says from the dining table.

'Yeah, Dad.' Elsie smirks.

'They do that anyway,' our son Spence adds as his hologram lowers his arm to pull his younger brother up the side of a building on the gaming wall.

'Uh-huh,' Josh confirms as his hologram makes it to the top. 'Grandpa!' he calls.

'I see them,' Hugh Mason says, picking off the enemy holograms one by one with disturbing precision.

'Thanks, Grandpa!' they both say as they carry on infiltrating the building.

'Aunty Lara?' Elsie pleads, returning my attention to her.

'Leave her alone, Caleb. Raife doesn't have half of the female population traumatised just because they bumped into you in a nightclub once and made the wrong choices.'

Honey laughs as she pats Lara's leg.

'Exactly,' Elsie says. She looks just like Ariella at that moment, with her eyebrows meeting in a little v in the middle of her forehead.

'What do you mean by that?'

'Nothing.' She backs down.

'Lara?'

'We've had sixteen years of bedtime stories. A couple of historical facts may have tumbled out.' Lara shifts her seven-month-pregnant body around on the sofa to get comfortable.

'Raife, remember, Elsie can kill you with her bare hands.'

'Caleb, we've been training at the fight studio all our lives. I know Elsie is impressive.' He smiles at her and she blushes.

What the?!

'At least you know where we live,' Sophia says, and laughs, then yawns and snuggles into Jasper.

'Come back before Uncle Zachary, Aunty Isszy, Lola, Deola and Bola call from their holiday in Lagos.'

'Okay!' They are out before I change my mind.

'Black, you really shouldn't give Raife a hard time. He is such a good boy,' Ariella says as she follows me out of the shower to get ready for bed. I have both her towels waiting.

'No way. At that age they are all hormones.'

'He's asked her to go skiing with them. I think it would be nice to let her go. Just because we're missing it this year doesn't mean that she should. Jas and Fi will be there with her family.'

'So will Axel and Summer – and they are practically living together in that house, doing goodness knows what.'

'Caleb, breathe. She was going to get a boyfriend eventually and Raife is sweet. It was either him or some other boy named Viggo.'

'Viggo from her fight class? He's going to uni this year and is built like a forty-year-old wrestler! I'm going to kill him.'

'Come to bed. Elsie can kill him herself. She has a cabinet full of gold medals to prove it.' She pats my side.

'Are you still okay for Tim, Em, Jack and Ophelia to come over tomorrow?'

'Of course – are they coming with the kids?'

'Just Jack and Ophelia's girls. Alfie is working tomorrow. He's trying to convince me to open a sixth studio in Manchester. I've asked him to find me the roughest area in dire need of a community class and I'll think about it while we are in Bali with Ms Pat.'

'I can't wait to see her new renovations.'

'She *still* hasn't told me how she retired so quickly after we left Singapore, then managed to buy and move into a three-bedroom beach villa in Seminyak within a year.'

'You might need to get used to it being a mystery Caleb,' Ariella says, laughing.

I get into bed and arrange us in our usual positions, with her head on my shoulder and her hand on my heart. I indulge in my admiration and adoration of this woman. She, over the years, has given me everything I could ever wish for, including the family I always wanted, the love I deeply craved and the safety I so desperately needed. Everything about her makes me feel complete and my only motivation is to make her feel the same.

'So I was thinking, Mrs Black...' I start as she lets my finger trace up her ribs suggestively. Her back arches.

'It's very late and I'm very tired, but continue?' She smirks.

I relieve her of her vest and keep her in my boxers for now.

There is something very sexy about the way her beautifully curvy body looks in them. I sit up in bed, then pull her over to straddle me and hold her close as she kisses me. I will never tire of this girl's kisses, even after all this time together. I slide my hand behind her underwear and do that thing she likes that makes her gasp. She doesn't disappoint.

'You know, good girls would go to sleep right now,' she says softly.

'I know, but naughty girls tend to do whatever they want,' I respond, and then I place my mouth on her neck and make love to my wife; grateful for everything that was, is, and is yet to come.

A LETTER FROM THE AUTHOR

It's an absolute privilege to complete *Endgame* for you and I hope you have enjoyed Ariella and Caleb's less-than-conventional journey.

I have no idea what the future holds, but, if you would like to join my reader community to receive bonus content and other surprises, please sign up for my newsletter here

www.stormpublishing.co/ola-tundun

My social media use is generally appalling, but if you would like to get in touch with me please do so via my website www.olatundunx.com or use my Instagram page.

For an author, a short review can make all the difference in encouraging a reader to discover my books for the first time. If you enjoyed my series and can spare a few moments to leave a review, I'd be immensely grateful.

I enjoy writing about beauty in the messiness of life, encouraging the reader to reconsider where they stand on a series of modern issues while enjoying a fast and fun read. I'm drawn to exploring characters who the reader recognises and finds hard to judge, and who are rarely truly guilty or innocent of their less-than-honourable acts.

To quote Ariella, 'We are imperfect, but we try.'

Thank you once again for being part of this unbelievable journey with me and I hope that we can stay in touch. I am excited about what may come next!

KEEP IN TOUCH WITH THE AUTHOR

www.olatundunx.com

facebook.com/olatundunx

x.com/olatundunx

instagram.com/olatundunx

tiktok.com/@olatundun_x

ACKNOWLEDGEMENTS

'It always seems impossible until it's done.'

The Roommates series is over. The sweat, the tears, the fire, the sleepless nights, the prayers and anxiety for this series are done. I have no idea what the future holds, but I am excited for it. For now, as someone who tries to live every day and embrace every opportunity as if it is her last, this is going to be a long one. Apologies in advance.

Emily Glenister at DHH Literary Agency, my love and admiration for you does nothing but continue to grow. Thank you for keeping my dreams safe, holding my hand warmly, setting my trajectory carefully and guiding my steps lovingly. Your radiant joy, deep humanity and protective pointy finger have made this journey a dream come true, for me. You're also one of my favourite people to have dinner with. Thank you for continuing to shape me into the author that I'd love to be.

Emily Gowers at Storm Publishing, collaborating with your passion, our giggles, your questioning eyebrow when I've written something dodgy and your guidance throughout this series has made this one of the most rewarding experiences of the last two years. You have been responsible for a lot of my writing knowledge and growth. I will forever be grateful.

To the Storm Publishing and DHH Literary Agency teams and author families. Thank you for being so loving and supportive. I feel extremely honoured and privileged to be a member of our community.

For all the people that started with me at 'impossible':

Debola, my ride-or-die for LYFE, Ashley, Myriam, Diana and Oriton; who knew? Well, you knew, I just argued and maintained that it was impossible.

Lola, Natalie, Mon, Saskia, Sara, Seun, Huma, Mr J, Ayomi, Jeannette, Nicky, Jane, Angela, Rosa, Neema, Yael, Beejal, Zainab, Bisola, Damola, Sam, Cenkay, Daphne, Daniel, Meg, Sarah, Natalia, Matthew, Sarveen, Esther, Dave and Segun. Your love, check-ins, extremely welcome piss-taking and support have been so much more than I expected. There are no words to express how humbled I feel. Thank you for always showing up and always being up.

Hannah, Lindsey, Maritess – you know what we did. LOL. I love you ladies so much!

Courtney, Lorna, Kelsi, Christine, Lauren, Jas, Nadine, Cait, Tara, Amy, Holly, Diandra, Jeanine, Laurie, Elizabeth, Ramona, Latoya, Kat, Marietere, Fawziya, Janine, Eva, Mish, Kristen, Cinzia, Dolapo, Julie, Sophie & Pearl, Silje, Antigone, Nikkie, Emma, Kondra, Aileen, Susan, Alix, Becky, Ruth – your messages pulled me through darkness, doubt and fear. Thank you.

Dominic, we made it. I am beyond grateful for you. I really am. We've come a long way from 180,000 words.

Jacqui, Liz and Alex, thank you for everything you have done for this series. Thank you for saving the readers from my raw manuscripts. Elke and Anna, thank you for your marketing magic. You performed miracles with this series that I did not expect and I am extremely grateful.

Savannah Davies, thank you for the almost impossible task of voicing and humanising these characters over this three-book series. I have laughed at, cried with and experienced these characters in a way that leaves me with nothing but absolute awe for your talent. Thank you. Thank you. Thank you.

To my husband and daughter, thank you for your indescribable love, patience, kindness, support, snacks, kisses, hugs and for making my life worth living. Everything that I have and all that I am, belongs to you.

Most importantly to God. I remain faithful, continue to seek your grace, stay at your mercy and bow to your will. Thank you for carrying and blessing me through every step of this journey.

Printed in Great Britain
by Amazon

46625392R00199